The Great Symmetry

A novel by

James R. Wells

Without Fear, Speak What is True
Without Fear, Live What is True

-Axiom

2015 Travertine Books Paperback Edition

Web site: www.TheGreatSymmetry.com

Printed in the United States of America

ISBN 978-0-996142-50-2 (paperback)
ISBN 978-0-996142-51-9 (ebook)

Library of Congress Control Number: 2015905157

First Edition, First Printing, April 2015
First Edition, Second Printing, June 2015

Editor: Mariko Thompson
Design: Kate Weisel
Cover Image: NASA, ESA, HEIC, and the Hubble Heritage team. Acknowledgement R. Corradi (Isaac Newton Group of Telescopes) and Z. Tsvetanov (NASA)
Back Cover Image: Copyright Peter and Anne Bosted
Author Photo: David Bass

For Sara
and
Katie Jane

Contents

Glome: A naturally occurring hypersphere that allows near-instant travel between star systems. Every glome has a single point of emergence, usually light-years away, which cannot be determined except by entering the glome. Travel through a glome is not reversible – to return home, a ship must travel through one or more other glomes and create a circuit. As of the year 2304, humans have mapped glome travel routes between thirty star systems.

Part 1:
One Small Step

Into The Void

Evan McElroy was heading straight down the throat of the glome.

A brilliant fountain took up most of his main display. Arcs of energy, rendered in vibrant false color from blue to violet, streamed out of the glome's mouth, dissipating a few kilometers away in every direction.

The ship was pouring on every available iota of acceleration.

"Ship," Evan asked, "will we make it to the glome before the missile reaches us?"

"Yes," the ship answered. "We will arrive at the Alpha entry thirty-five seconds before missile impact."

A voice came, piped in. "Runabout Delta, this is Tara. Now I'm really worried for you, Evan. Please change your course immediately, in any direction, and let me know that you have heard me."

She had introduced herself as a visiting scientist, on her way to join Evan at the research station. Whoever she was, Tara seemed to know a lot about him.

Tara's friendly voice continued. "Evan, the incoming unmanned vehicle will not harm you. It's simply an escort to guide you back to a rendezvous with our task force. I am so looking forward to meeting you and working together on the next phase of your research."

Incoming unmanned vehicle? It sure looked like a missile to him, accelerating at eight gravities.

Still, the missile could be redirected away from his ship. If he fled into the glome, he could be making the biggest, and possibly last, mistake of his life.

"Tara, what assurance can you provide that I'll be safe?" he asked.

"Oh Evan." Her tone was somewhere between talking and laughing. "Nothing has changed. You just surprised us when you left the station without telling anyone. All we need to do is rewind things a little, and get back to work. Your findings are so exciting!"

Evan was still trying to make sense of events. His unauthorized trip from the research station was stacking up to be pretty much the dumbest idea ever. Unable to sleep in the middle of the station's nominal night, he had decided it was time to prove his theory, so he had grabbed one of the runabouts. Why was it such a big deal?

He checked the display. Seven minutes and thirty seconds to the glome. There was less time than that to decide whether he should believe Tara, and steer away from the dangerous spatial envelope of the hypersphere.

"Ship," he asked, "If we want to miss the glome, how soon do we need to start maneuvers?"

"Four minutes and forty seconds," the ship told him. "A countdown widget has been added to your secondary screen."

This was madness. He needed to turn the runabout aside. Whatever trouble resulted from his impromptu excursion, he would face it.

"Ship," he said, "Prepare a course that will avoid the glome, and wait for my instruction to do so. Plan for about two minutes from now."

Just a few more moments, to think and to be absolutely sure.

"Evan, are you still with me?" Tara's voice, piped in by the ship.

"Hi Tara, I'm just – calculating the best course."

"Evan, it's really time–"

Another voice cut in. "Mister McElroy, you must change course immediately! Do it now or face the consequences!" There was no mistaking the deep, full voice of Arn Lobeck. Or the anger in every word.

Arn Lobeck. Vice President – Senior Vice President, Evan corrected himself – of his Affirmatix sponsor. What Lobeck said was the last word, on anything that took place in the Aurora system.

Lobeck was a person whom everyone obeyed. It just wasn't questioned. Beyond his forceful manner, there was the family he represented. Affirmatix, one of the seven most powerful families in all of civilization.

When someone in the top ranks of the Seven Sisters gave instructions, it was beyond customary to defer to them. There was no other option. What could one person do?

It was more than a wave of nausea, arriving all at once, everywhere. Evan knew better than to reach for the meds, as comforting as they might be. "Breathe," he told himself. "Slowly."

And if he fled to the Kelter system, what then?

As far as Evan knew, he was the only person who knew this glome went to Kelter. To the Affirmatix ships he would appear to simply vanish, destination unknown. However, there were only thirty explored star systems. If Affirmatix wanted to track him down, they could easily put out the word through all of civilization.

Breathe. Slowly.

The kaleidoscope of bad outcomes resolved into a triangle of fear. If he stayed in the Aurora system, the missile would probably destroy his runabout and kill him, regardless of the assurances Tara had provided. If he went into the glome and was wrong about its destination, then he would be stranded forever, somewhere. If he went into the glome and it went to Kelter as he believed, then he would be a fugitive.

Which would it be?

Maybe it was not too late. He could turn aside, in accordance with Lobeck's order. Return to the research station. Continue his work. It could all be fine.

Three minutes left, if he planned to avoid the glome. The acceleration pressed him down into his seat. The runabout was still piping in transmittals, as Evan had instructed, and Arn Lobeck was back. "You think you can steal everything and run away, but you're wrong. Evan McElroy, if you go through the glome, you're a dead man. Turn aside if you don't want to die."

Steal?

At that moment Evan knew why the Aurora system had suddenly turned into a war zone. "Spend years trying to get someone to pay attention to the Versari," he told himself. "Finally succeed and get a missile up my butt. Figures."

The ship provided an update. "Three additional missiles have been launched, coming in our direction."

Evan assessed that his decision had been made for him. If one unmanned vehicle might be a sheepdog sent to retrieve an errant member of the flock, a pack of them could be nothing other than an attack. To his surprise, he suddenly felt better. Focus and get it done.

"Ship, turn external audio off," Evan ordered.

The quiet helped Evan to think.

"I have an idea," Evan said. "Is the nearest missile's course aligned with the Alpha entry of the glome?"

"No, it isn't," the ship replied.

To travel through a glome to its emergence, an object had to enter the glome from exactly the right direction, which was the Alpha entry. Anything that entered on an unaligned vector would be destroyed.

"What if we make a small change in our course? If we reduce our acceleration so we go through the glome just a few seconds before the missile would impact us, will the missile be in the envelope where it would be destroyed?"

"Yes it will," the ship told Evan.

"Do it then!"

"Adjusting course as instructed." The ship's voice was pleasant and evenly modulated, as it always was no matter what the situation.

Time to missile intercept, 95 seconds. Time to glome, 90 seconds. Five seconds to spare.

Evan had transformed from an exo-archaeologist to a tactician.

Calculations ran through Evan's head. Not his current course and speed, which the ship easily handled. Rather, it was the logic that had caused him to believe this glome led to the Kelter System.

How sure was he?

He was sure. At the research station on Aurora, he had spent weeks on the puzzle. The artifact left by the long departed Versari told the story of where the glome went.

There was no possible other answer. This glome went to Kelter. Specifically, it went to a spot that trailed Kelter Four by a few million kilometers, comfortably far away from any obstacles or hazards. He knew this to be true.

Travel from one star system to another was completely routine – millions of people did it every year, with essentially no risk. Any given glome always took your ship to exactly the same point of emergence, as measured from the closest gravitational source such as a nearby planet. Evan had done hundreds of such transits in his life. But those had been mapped glomes, where the route was already known.

In all of history until this moment, every first trip in a new glome had been a complete mystery for the explorer. The emergence could be in the heart of a sun. Or the interior of a planet. Or very deep space.

Evan, alone of any person alive, had the hubris to believe he could know the unknowable, courtesy of an object that had survived for almost a million years in the heart of an asteroid.

In forty-five seconds, he was going to find out if he was right.

Was this definitely the Alpha entry, and not the Omega?

It was.

There was no turning back now.

The glome had grown on his display until only the throat was visible. The waving lines of energy were partly cut off by the four edges of the screen. With a view this close, the lines were starting to resolve into finer threads, each endlessly rearranging a fluid braid.

Despite the emergency of the moment, an incongruous thought began to arrive. For years Evan had toiled, making discoveries about the Versari that he knew were significant, but somehow had never made an impression on the rest of the world. He was just a fanatic exoarcheologist, rambling on about long-past events that didn't matter to anyone.

Now, it appeared, he had a discovery worth killing for. And that was strangely satisfying. Suddenly Evan didn't just want to survive. He was going to make sure that everyone, in all of known space, came to know a certain fact.

Time to missile impact: 10 seconds, 9 seconds, 8, 7, 6 and then …

Evan and his runabout vanished from the Aurora system.

Charlie Fox

Arn Lobeck watched in morbid fascination as the missile was destroyed against the spatial envelope of the glome. It was no ordinary explosion. All of the mass that had been in the missile was turned into plasma at over 3000 Kelvins and ejected at great velocity, back toward the ships of the Affirmatix task force. The piercing colored bands of light looked like something partway between a comet and a solar flare.

"Nobody was to leave the station!" Lobeck exclaimed. "Such simple orders! How hard could that be?"

"Focus, Arn" came the steady, measured voice. Mithra Skylar, the only other person on their small ship. "We have decisions to make."

"We leave for just sixteen hours, and this is what happens! We should have stayed insystem – this required our direct supervision. And whose idea was that useless hostage negotiator program? Nobody would fall for that."

"It's done," Skylar said. "What's next? Should we send the surviving missiles into the glome?"

"Definitely," Lobeck told her. "Program them to destroy the nearest target to the point of emergence. That should take care of McElroy."

"And do you have orders for any of the other ships?"

"As a matter of fact, I do. I'll send orders while you direct the missiles."

Lobeck hailed Captain Roe of M3120, on the ship nearest to the glome.

"Your ship will proceed to the glome where the runabout has gone," Lobeck ordered. "Then enter it."

After the normal lag, the reply came back from Roe.

"But sir, the glome has not been mapped. We don't know where it goes."

"I have the mapping, and I am certain," Lobeck insisted. "It goes to Kelter. Your orders are to go through. Once you are in the Kelter system, assure that the runabout has been immobilized and cannot communicate, or it is destroyed. Gather the runabout, or any of its remains, into your hold."

"Where will you be?" It was an insolent answer from a mere rental captain.

"I am following as quickly as possible. You must go now, because your ship can get to the glome a full forty minutes before mine can. Minutes may be crucial. In the Kelter system I will catch up to you and transfer my operations to your ship."

Still, Roe was holding out. "It's an unknown glome. Going through it would be nuts! If it goes to Kelter, we can easily verify the route in about three days using a robot, and then we can use it."

"We must be there now. In three days all may be lost. Proceed to the glome now."

The lag was longer than normal. Finally Captain Roe's reply arrived.

"Proceeding."

"Thank you, Mister Roe. We shall meet you in the Kelter system. Out."

Lobeck turned to Mithra Skylar, who had finished redirecting the missiles.

"So, about our fugitive scientist. Smart man. A little too smart, don't you think? I wonder how long McElroy has been planning this."

"You're giving him too much credit," Skylar told him. "He doesn't think that way. Nose in his work, all the time."

"But he was holding out on us. Until a week ago, he would talk about the Versari to anyone who wasn't able to flee from him. Then, silence. It's just good planning on our part that we had the management system set up to monitor all of his calculations. This whole time he has been playing us – just waiting for the moment to make a break for it and keep everything for himself."

"I really don't think he saw it coming."

"Why is that?"

"Simple information theory," Skylar said. "If he had known what was there, he would have found it more quickly."

Lobeck regarded Skylar.

She continued to grow thinner, and paler, with the passing of each year. There was so much he could do for her, if she would only let him. But in certain matters, not even he could command her.

Officially, Mithra Skylar was a Vice President for Affirmatix. In reality she was, more or less, an extension of him. Partly an assistant, always an advisor, often tempering his urge to aggressive action with a few well-placed words.

Lobeck moved on. "Let us plan," he said. "We must have everything that we could possibly need, sent directly to the Kelter system. Identify fleet elements exceeding local Kelter forces by a factor of ten, and mobilize them. Include the D6."

"The D6?" Skylar gave him a sharp look.

"To improve our negotiating position, if nothing else. And, we need analytical support. Sonia West consistently finds the highest value scenarios, so we must have her present in person. Tell her to come with a small team to Kelter immediately."

"Technically, she's a contractor," Skylar said. "What if she will not leave Alcyone?"

"Will not leave? What does that mean? There is no such choice. The moment she landed on that planet, she became ours. Send the order to Ellison, he will make it happen."

"I'll get that sent. What else?"

Lobeck continued down a mental list. They would need a Marcom team. Ships deployed to blockade every other glome that went to Kelter. Updates for President Sanzite.

The quiet of the ship's interior contrasted with the urgency of their actions. As their small ship headed at top acceleration to the uncharted glome, orders were sent to other ships that prepared to take more conventional routes to other star systems.

At last all of the orders were sent.

"And us? You are sure that we should go through the new glome?"

"Yes," Lobeck told her. "We must be in the Kelter system as soon as possible. Even if the runabout is promptly destroyed, there could be other damage that we must control. McElroy could be communicating right now, destroying the value of our asset."

"You are willing to take the chance? In three days we could be there with no risk. We can let Roe take care of matters in the Kelter system until we arrive."

"No, Mithra. This is the moment. Tell me, do you think Roe is expendable?"

"Of course. He's a rental. With his rental ship and crew."

"Exactly," Lobeck said. "If he is lost, we make an insurance payment. But we are expendable also. Worth more than rentals, of course, but on the scale of Affirmatix, on the scale of the value we are seeking, we are still nothing. There is a very small chance that we are wrong about the glome, and it's an excellent gamble considering what we could gain."

"We are leaders for Affirmatix. You may be undervaluing us," Skylar replied.

"Leaders," Lobeck dismissed. "Don't you tire of the endless scrapping and clawing to gain a percentage point of market share? Then we see it taken away when another Sister launches a shiny new product. No. We have spent thirty years looking for something that will truly move the needle. Now, we have found it. We have a duty to our family. We will bring home the absolutely greatest value from the discovery that we possibly can."

Lobeck gestured forward, in the direction of the glome, and added, "And we will not be stopped by the betrayal of a traitor."

Alcyone

"Dr. West, I need you in here," Colin told Sonia.

They filed into Colin's office and he shut the door behind them. All of the displays were turned off, which was unusual. Usually at least a half dozen of them were active, showing different graphical perspectives on various ongoing projects.

Colin had been her wrangler for the past four years, and he treated her well, Sonia thought. Respectful, and he knew that there was no need to push her. Colin just identified priorities on behalf of their Affirmatix sponsor, and then her team made it happen. And he was top notch at finding the talent Sonia needed.

Colin waved to a seat at the round conference table and then took his own. The seats were smoothly curved, in a way that was supposed to be relaxing and ergonomic, but to Sonia they felt like alien creatures that might envelop her at any moment. She sat forward, on the front edge, her back straight.

"Do you want to discuss our results?" Sonia asked.

"It's related, but no," her wrangler said. "Here's my question: If you had to identify a small team, of not more than you and two others, who could work independently to answer questions about your analysis, and run alternative scenarios, in near real time, who would it be?"

"For what?"

"We need to do quick scenario evaluation. Results in minutes even if not perfect."

Sonia considered. "Ravi. And then Malken, I'd say, based on skill set. But they hate each other. So Merriam. Ravi and Merriam."

"Sometimes a little rivalry can create results," Colin noted.

"Not in this case," she told him. "Ego. Ravi and Malken just hammer at each other's ideas, all day, every day. In a larger group, I can make it work, but I wouldn't assign them to the same small team."

"Ravi and Merriam it will be. I'll notify them. You too, Sonia. Pack a bag, because you're going off planet."

"Off planet? Are you kidding? For how long?"

"That's above my pay grade," her wrangler told her. "Gather up all the software and data you need. You lift this afternoon."

"Colin, you need to give me more to work with. Something. Anything."

"Here's what I can tell you. Your valuation of the Versari discovery really got some attention. Unbelievable."

"It's all conditional," Sonia pointed out. "Just certain outcomes, with a lot of assumptions."

"Right. We need to take control of events, so we can realize full value. Some of the other outcomes are pretty bad for us."

"Pretty bad? There are huge risks to Affirmatix. There's even the potential for bankruptcy. But what about this travel?"

"We need you, Sonia. On site. To manage a rapidly escalating situation, that relates directly to your algorithms. The facts on the ground are changing too rapidly to send you data here for evaluation, and then get answers back to the site."

"We can't do it from here? All of our tools are set up exactly as we need them."

"Nope. You need to be there. The Kelter system. The orders came from Arn Lobeck himself. I have the latest information for you, already posted to your account." He looked at her in confident expectation.

It looked like there was no dodging it. "I'll review it in transit," Sonia told him. "First I need to go home."

"As you like. Just be ready by 1330. We'll send a limo for you. Hey Sonia – this is important. We're counting on you to stay as rigorous as you always are. Run the models and provide the best possible analysis. No matter what scenario comes up."

"Rigorous, that's me," she said.

Sonia stumbled out of Colin's office, reaching for her phone. "Hey. Check out of work, get the kids and meet me at home."

"Okay, hon …"

Sonia dropped the bombshell. "I'm being mobilized. Off planet."

"Oh my Efessem. When do you leave?"

"In a little over two hours."

"Two hours! You don't know anything else?" Sonia could hear the alarm at the other end of the line.

"I can speculate. But it doesn't matter. Let's have some lunch and a little back yard time. See you there in ten. Love you."

"Love you."

For the past few weeks Sonia had been lamenting, if privately, her fate, limited to just one perfect planet. It was the sequester of the privileged, a life of luxury cut off from the rest of civilization. Nobody at her pay grade ever left Alcyone, and there was most definitely no personal correspondence in or out.

Suddenly, Sonia dreaded going anywhere else.

At a fast walk, it was easy to get home in ten minutes. Sonia multitasked, looking through the new data in a display that floated in front of her. It was total crap. So tactical. Sonia worked at a planetary scale, and she was great at that. This new data was about individual people, their movements, history, possessions, and associations. Sonia would need help to make sense of any of it.

She decided to take the fork to the left, going by the lake. It would only take an extra minute.

In this world, there was no problem walking alone. She was perfectly safe, as were her children, every minute of every day. No crime. No want. It was not just a matter of the excellent security, although it was unsurpassed. It was the population. The only people who lived here were highly skilled professionals, enjoying every imaginable perk in exchange for their considerable capabilities.

It had been a crazy three days. Sonia and her team had worked deep into each night on successive drafts of the analysis, each version being hungrily snapped up by their wranglers the moment it was ready, no matter what time of the day or night. The team found no definitive answers, just clouds of possibility as always. But in this case the clouds separated exceptionally clearly on defined pivot points, suggesting actions that her Affirmatix sponsor could take in order to get the best value from the new discovery.

Sonia looked across the lake. Just like everything on the campus, it was too good to be true. She could see the stream cascading over rocks at the lake's head, a few hundred meters away. Water you could drink, if you had a mind to. A delightful spring morning, warm but not too hot. No biting bugs. Just the iridescent dragonflies, abundant and beautiful as always.

Her feet were taking her in the direction of home. She retrieved her domestic persona.

Yvette and the kids were just coming up the walk from the other direction. On sight, their daughters broke ranks and ran toward Sonia. "What is it, mommy?" Simone asked. "A party?"

"Party!" Jennifer chimed in. At four years old, she knew the word well.

"Yes, that's right, sweetie," Sonia told them. "It's too nice an afternoon for school or work."

"But it's always nice," Simone told her. "Almost always."

"Still, today is the right day to be home with all of you. You two play in the yard and we'll get lunch ready."

The kids safely out on the play set, Sonia fussed over the sandwiches.

"Okay. What else do you know? And look at me, please." Yvette put her index finger under Sonia's chin and gently pulled it up toward her.

Yvette was everything Sonia could never be. Always knowing the kind word that would resolve a conflict. With her magic, she kept their domestic family in harmony every day.

Sonia stumbled for words. "Those two nuisances. And you. I thought we were making the right choice, taking this assignment. Coming here to Alcyone."

"And we weren't? I thought it was the opportunity of a lifetime for you."

"I just don't know any more."

"Let's just keep hold of the one thing we always agree on − all that matters is the peanuts. And they are happy."

"Of course. You're right. Those two. I'll do this assignment, and I'll be right back."

"Of course you will. We'll see you in a few days, or a few weeks."

She could not lie to Yvette. Except a lie to which they both subscribed.

"And now I know something I need to do," Sonia told her wife. "Just a minute for a call."

"Lunch in five, okay?"

"You got it." They shared a look, and a kiss, and then Sonia turned to her phone.

"Colin."

"Packing question?"

"No. There's something I need before I go. Coverage for the Parrin Process, on our health plan. My domestic family and descendants. Irrevocable. Make it so before I lift."

"Sonia, these things take time."

"What's the speed of light?"

"Touché." It was one of Colin's sayings. If it needed to be done on a computer, as all things did, then it could occur at the speed of light. "Still−"

"Before I lift. Approved, committed, and posted to my account."

"I'll see what I can do," he told her.

"You do that, Colin. If it's not done, I'll just wait for the next ship."

"Sonia, that's not how bargaining works."

"Today that's exactly how it works. It needs to be in my account before I set foot in the ship. You decide if you want me to deploy or not."

Sonia signed off and turned to Yvette. "We will take care of each other. Forever."

"It's you and me against the world," Yvette said. They finished together, "When do we attack?"

Together they gathered up lunch and brought it to the picnic table in the yard. Simone and Jennifer were climbing all over the play set. The lawn was framed by the abundant azaleas and rhododendrons.

"Animals!" Yvette called. "Wash your paws! Lunch time!"

With both of their moms home, the kids had the best Thursday afternoon ever. They even got to ride in the limo to the port, so they could watch mommy Sonia take off in a rocket.

One Small Step

Some people assert that they can feel the journey through a glome. An undefinable twisting, or popping, or a disembodied moment. Some signature on a person's nervous system from translating across trillions of kilometers in a fraction of a second.

As Evan entered the glome, he knew the exact moment of the event. He felt a shock running through his body – but it was not because of any mysterious hyperspatial effect. It was due to him knowing how much he was staking on the outcome.

The ship's navigational displays changed abruptly to match the new circumstance. Part of the ship's job was to keep constant track of its exact position, and show it on an overhead display for the pilot. It accomplished this by merging together the set of all available visual, radar, and historical data. When the ship went through a glome, the destination was known in advance so it was easy to adjust.

This time, the ship was lost. The display showed a sun, a nearby planet, and a gas giant, with no identifiers.

Evan knew how to help. "Ship, resolve to the Kelter system," he said. "The nearest planet is Kelter Four."

Instantly, additional detail was added to the display. Kelter's two moons. The inner planets and the other gas giants. As Evan had predicted, the glome had led to the Kelter system. Fifty-six light years in just eighty-three milliseconds.

"Head for Kelter Four at maximum," he instructed, sinking into his seat as the acceleration kicked in.

Kelter Four. Breathable air, if thin and dry. Mostly brown and tan, rather than the classic green and blue of the most hospitable worlds. Low gravity. Sparsely inhabited, with a population of about fifty million people. Evan needed no shipboard display to know the details of the planet.

Kelter was Evan's home.

In a piece of great luck, they were already heading mostly in the direction of the planet when they had come out of the point of emergence. Their intrinsic velocity, a result not only of their vector as they headed into the glome, but also of the relative speeds of the two star systems, had smiled on them.

Nonetheless, time was likely running out.

Could missiles go through a glome? The answer came unbidden. Of course they could.

The runabout had no weapons, and couldn't exactly turn on a dime. If missiles arrived on his tail, there would be nothing he could do.

"Ship," Evan asked. "Based on our last information, how soon could a missile come through the glome from Aurora?"

"Twelve minutes and twenty seconds," the ship told him.

"And then how long until impact, if it pursued us at maximum acceleration?"

"Seven minutes and four seconds after emergence." Almost twenty minutes all together.

There were two big branches of possibility. If no missiles came through the glome, then there was no problem, at least in the short term. He would head to Kelter Four and figure it out somehow. If the missiles arrived, he had a big problem. So, he needed to concentrate on that scenario.

Evan pondered the largest branches of possibility, then the smaller branches, the twigs, and finally the leaves. Not being killed, those were preferred leaves.

Then he worked backward, crossing out certain leaves, then certain twigs, and finally entire branches.

If the missiles came, there was no rational solution. All that remained was an irrational one.

Evan decided not to tell the runabout of his plan. It was on a need to know basis, and the runabout didn't need to know. The ship also had a black box, which recorded all of its actions and communications.

Should he feel bad about deceiving a computer?

"Ship, if any missiles arrive through the glome, I plan to climb to the sled. I believe the missiles will pursue and attempt to destroy us, so I'll need an escape vessel."

The sled was designed to assist in scanning the surface of asteroids for faint signatures of the Versari. Of necessity, its low powered engine was shielded as completely as possible so it could operate without interfering with the delicate scanning operation.

The sled was clamped to the runabout, at a point forward near the nose.

"So here's what I want you to do," he told the ship. "At every moment starting as soon as possible, the ship must be at a location and velocity to go into orbit of Kelter or its moon Foray assuming no further acceleration. On my instruction, you will change course sunward and accelerate as fast as you can. Then do any maneuver you possibly can to avoid the missiles."

"Instructions received and accepted," the ship replied.

Evan reached for his EVA suit and pulled it on except for the helmet, then stood ready at the airlock. There was nothing to do except wait.

He had been condemned to death by one of the most powerful people in all of space. Was it just bluster? A threat blurted out in the extremity of the moment?

Over the past two years, Arn Lobeck had come to the station on Aurora about a dozen times, usually staying for a day or two. Each time Lobeck had brought his full attention, asking detailed questions, and challenging assumptions the research team had made. As the principal investigator on the project, Evan had been on the receiving end of the most focused part of the grilling.

Evan could never tell whether he looked forward to the next review or whether he dreaded it. The questions were excellent, and pushed him to think. But there was no avoiding the sense of being examined by someone of great power, who, for whatever reason, was troubling himself to stay informed on an obscure research project.

In all of that time, had Lobeck ever said anything that he did not mean?

Evan cast his mind back over the last two years, searching. An empty threat. An exaggeration. A metaphor. A joke, even.

Never. Arn Lobeck was the most serious, most humorless man that Evan had ever met. And he had always done what he said he would.

Here and now. Think. If a missile came through the glome, his plan was pathetic. There had to be something better.

But there just wasn't.

The time arrived. "Ship, please advise. Has a missile arrived through the glome?"

"Nothing has arrived through the glome," the ship said.

Good news. Perhaps he would be free to make it to Kelter Four – safety, at least for the moment.

"Update," the ship told him. "An object has arrived through the glome. Two objects. Now three. Objects are accelerating in our direction at eight gravities."

Game on. At a button push, the inner door of the airlock began to dilate open.

"How long until impact?"

The ship's voice was anywhere it needed to be. "Eight minutes and thirty seconds at current velocity and acceleration."

Evan put on his helmet and rotated it closed, then pressed the outer button in the airlock with a thick gloved finger.

The spacewalk was going to be a novel experience. He had only done it under conditions of weightlessness. With the craft accelerating at almost one full gravity, the trip was not going to be a free float, powered by a gentle push, or a tug on the cord if he went astray. There would be apparent gravity due to acceleration.

The airlock door opened into space.

Evan stepped to the edge of the airlock, and saw a different kind of space than he had ever before experienced. This space had a definite up and down, and the hull of the craft was a vertical wall. Up was toward the nose. Down was a small cliff of spacecraft hull, then vastness. Below, the deepest, blackest pit any person could ever fall into.

"Seven minutes to impact," the ship told him.

Evan held on to a safety bar on the outside edge of the airlock and looked straight down. There they were. Three red haloes, their super-heated reaction mass creating the appearance of a ring around the unlit nose of each missile. Coming his way, at eight gravities of acceleration.

"When it is two minutes before impact," Evan told the ship, "turn sunward with as much acceleration as you can."

"Instruction received," the ship said.

It was time to put the rest of his plan in motion, for what it was worth. "Suit, go private," Evan instructed. His instruction stopped communication with the runabout. "I need you to create a message for me."

Evan told the EVA suit exactly what needed to be in the message. The suit, which had its own capable processor, easily managed the request. Part of the message was encrypted, using the public key of the intended recipient. Only that one person would be able to decrypt it, using a carefully guarded private key.

"Message created," the suit told him.

"Suit, send the message to the ship and then go public. Ship, take the message and transmit it to Kelter Four on all available channels to every available recipient. Do it immediately."

"Send as a priority to any specific person?" the ship asked.

"No. Send to every recipient known on Kelter, its moons, or nearby stations. Continuously repeat sending until I countermand."

"Acknowledged and in process," the ship told him.

Evan had told the runabout he intended to escape in the sled, but that was not his plan. The sled had no additional life support systems beyond what was provided by his suit. If the sled was missing from the wreckage of the ship, it would be found. Or it might be detected by the second or third missile and destroyed shortly after the runabout. He needed an even smaller vessel.

And, he needed the boom. "Ship, run out the boom," he instructed.

In the direction that he normally would have called aft, but which now appeared to be just below him, a series of struts started extruding from the ship. Evan found himself wondering where it all came from. Fully extended, the boom was longer than the width of the ship. Somehow it was assembled on the fly inside the workings of the runabout, resolved to an apparently flawless lattice as it ran out from the ship.

"Suit, go private," Evan instructed. "No further communication with the ship."

"Gone private," his suit told him.

Just over ten meters long, the boom was used for any number of operations. In this case, it would get him those ten meters farther away from the center of the ship, and the thrust of its engine.

"Suit, tell me when we are fifteen seconds from the two minute mark."

"Acknowledged," the suit said.

And then Evan began his walk out the plank.

It was a framework of metal bars, comprising many small triangles. Perfectly good to hang on, or clip a line to, if you were weightless. Evan had done that any number of times before. But he had never walked on it.

Just ten meters. Ten steps, or a few more. With each step, he had to find a stable spot on the intersection of the struts by coordinating his vision with the very limited feel he could get through his thick boots, and ultimately adding a little bit of positional intuition.

The first step was the biggest, going down a full meter from the airlock door to the start of the boom. He held the safety bar and lowered himself, then turned to face away from the ship. Away from the balance and comfort of the bar.

One step out on the boom, then two. Three. He was getting the hang of it. The next few steps came more quickly. Then he was standing at the edge.

"Fifteen seconds at – Mark," the suit told him. It was time.

"Count down the seconds to zero." The timing was going to be critical. Evan needed to take exactly the right step, at exactly the right time, within a second or even less.

Evan stood on the very edge. He looked down at the approaching missiles. They had grown both in size and brightness, just over two minutes away.

He wanted to turn and look back at the ship, to gauge if he would fall far enough away from the discharge of the engine, but he was afraid of losing his balance. So he set his vision straight ahead into the blackness and stars.

He was counting on his own precision. And a carefully crafted message. And most of all, he was counting on Mira.

The suit counted down. Four, three, two, one.

"Klono have mercy," Evan said, and stepped off the end of the boom.

Hey, Get Off My Lawn!

Mira Adastra almost fell off her bar stool at the next thing she heard. How could that be?

In a huge news day, the story was posed as an intriguing mystery. The incoming ship, arriving at a previously unknown glome emergence, had used its few remaining minutes to send a message, repeated over and over, before being destroyed. Most of it was encrypted, but the part in the clear was being treated as a joke.

The big screen over the bar was running one of the news channels of the Spoon Feed. In most public places you only got the Spoon Feed – approved programming and shopping opportunities. The genial older caster bantered with the infobabe, "Wow, that sounds like something I would say to the local kids."

"You're not that old," she assured him. "Besides, we don't even have lawns around here. Maybe we should explain what a lawn is, anyway."

"Great idea, Lisa. On certain planets, people keep a patch of live grass around their home, where kids can walk or play. I don't mean turf – a lawn is an actual mat of little plants growing on the ground. To keep that grass going, you need constant irrigation."

"Or even reliable natural rain, like they have on some parts of Earth," Lisa put in.

"Yes. And in those places, older people are famous for keeping their lawns meticulously tidy. If some kids come by, they could tear up the lawn or litter on it. So the old guy says –"

They finished in chorus: "Hey, Get off My Lawn!"

In her accustomed role, the young woman set up the senior caster. "That just makes no sense, Al. That a ship would send that as a message. What do you make of it?"

"Well Lisa, the clear part is probably just a diversion. And the encrypted message has been sequestered. Top secret, you know. Seriously, folks, don't do anything to help infoterrorists – if for any reason you received the transmittal and haven't called for help cleaning it off your system, you need to do that right now."

"You mean, you need to do that yesterday."

"That's right, Lisa. You can't be too careful with sequestered data."

Mira knew what the cover message meant. The encrypted message was for her. And it was from Evan McElroy.

Which meant that he had been on that ship. And that now he was dead, killed by the missile strike that had destroyed the ship.

Evan. Dead.

She left her stool, on purpose this time, and headed for the door, reaching for her phone. "Kestrel, meet me at the Buttonwood. How soon can you be there?"

A grumpy voice answered her. "Do I get to finish sleeping first?"

"No," she told him.

"Five minutes then."

"Ok, see you there."

Perfect. Just enough time to walk there in the nice cool evening. Mira set an even pace, floating for a brief moment off the ground in each long step.

The friendly streets of the Untrusted Zone were welcoming. They were home. There was always something going on, at any time of the day or night. Vehicles, pedestrians, bicyclists, sorting it all out in real time, getting where they needed to go. Although there was no specific requirement to do so, she kept to the edge of the street as she walked along.

Hey, Get Off My Lawn!

When she had been his pilot, it had been their little joke. Evan had only three more years than her by count, but was seemingly decades older in attitude, experience, and, as he didn't mind needling her about, maturity. Any time she had one of those moments, whether dismally unhelpful or merely inconvenient, they would look at each other, and one or both of them would say it.

It was always an adventure with her. Was that bad?

Then had come the moment of truth. Two days before they had been scheduled to lift, heading for Phoenix for the next expedition, a close friend of Mira had been identified as an infoterrorist, and Mira's credit had been instantly zeroed.

When you get zeroed, you have nothing. Can't buy anything. Your insurance is canceled, and you can't do anything without insurance. You are frozen out.

People who were once your friends will not help you, for fear that whatever got you zeroed will taint them. The algorithms are notorious for that. If you associate with a known infoterrorist, you will be zeroed until any questions are resolved. The chain could and did reach out to snare the unwary – it was definitely safest to have no interaction with anyone who was zeroed.

She had gone to see Evan, to tell him that he needed to find another pilot. She had wanted to tell him in person, but it had also been necessary, because her phone didn't work. The neighbors wouldn't even open the door for her. How had they known so quickly? After a four-kilometer walk, she had been at Evan's door.

Mira had explained the situation and offered her apologies. Maybe she would be in good standing in time for his next expedition. If he was willing to give her another chance, at that undefined time in the future.

After she was done, Evan had just held up his hand and seemed to ponder. "Okay," he had said at last. "You'll be going on my credit."

This was not something that anyone did. "Are you insane? They'll zero you like it's nothing. And then forget about the expedition." She wasn't going to let Evan throw it all away, even to try and help her.

"I don't think so," he had told her. "Anyway, it's wrong, and we won't have that. So, I'll get a credit authorization sent to you. Will you be ready on schedule?"

Mira had nodded, having run out of words. Never sentimental, she had almost felt gratitude. Almost. "Right," Evan had said. "Let's go through the manifest."

That had been four years ago. She had only once asked him why, a few weeks later. Evan had just said, "Because you are the expedition pilot."

Mira was nearing the Buttonwood. She had not said whether the tree or the pub, because in effect they were one and the same. The plaza that homed the tree was arrayed with places for people to sit and have their food or drink, whether purchased from the Buttonwood Pub, another nearby establishment, or simply brought along.

She walked through one of the gaps in the circle of buildings that went all the way around the tree, a respectful distance away from the trunk that defined the center of the plaza. Within the invisible boundary, there were no vehicles. Just denizens of the Untrusted Zone, eating, drinking, arguing, and otherwise enjoying the evening.

Mira and Kestrel easily spotted each other near the trunk of the tree. He called out, "Hey Mira, are we getting a beer?"

"Nope, not right now," Mira said. "I need something from you."

"All business tonight. Okay then! What will it be?"

"First we climb. High up." Mira slipped off her shoes.

"After you, milady."

If anyone could keep up with Mira in the tree, it was Kestrel. But tonight he would be hard pressed. From a standing start, she bounded straight up for three meters, catching hold of the first branch with her right hand, and then she was off to the races. Arms, legs, hands, and feet were not so much tools to grab the tree as they were a means to adjust her course, spiraling upward through the branches. It was not just the low gravity of Kelter. Climbing the tree was an art form that she had studied since she had been in grade school.

In addition to being majestically tall, the buttonwood tree was the best possible tree for climbing. Stout branches at convenient intervals of two to three meters. A strong but smooth outer bark. No thorns, because there had never been land animals on Kelter until humans arrived. It was also the best tree because it was the only tree around.

When she was a kid, Mira had called it her tree. In some sense, it was. There was no person who knew it better. Every branch, every cluster of the thick rubbery leaves. Every move between branches, whether a static step or a bold leap.

In the intervening years, it had changed. Grown, slowly. A few branches had died, but overall it was in excellent health. The tree was well tended.

Mira wondered why she didn't often climb the tree, these days.

"Hold on, that's too high," Kestrel called. "They're getting thin up there. If you go any further, you could break a branch, and you'll get fined. A really big fine."

If the worst happened, Mira would pay, even if it took months or years to do so. But it was not going to be a problem. Mira knew her tree.

"Just one more," she told him. "Come on up."

A wary Kestrel climbed the last few meters and sat beside her on the highest cross branch of the attenuating trunk. The Untrusted Zone spread below them, with buildings, lights, and then the dark of the undeveloped land beyond. To the south, Abilene was visible, several kilometers away, over in civilization. The Untrusted Zone and Abilene had grown toward each other over the years, so it was now difficult from this vantage point to see where one ended and the other began. On the ground, the boundary was absolutely clear.

"Kiss me," she demanded.

"I thought we were here to talk business, and we both know that didn't end well for either of us, Mira."

"Trust me. Just this once."

Mira kissed him on the lips for a brief moment, then moved close to his ear. "Hold me like you want me," she whispered. "And I will tell you what I need."

"Kes, I need the full transmission that came from that ship." She felt him tense. "That one – the ship that came in from the direction of Cappella and then was destroyed. The entire encrypted portion. And most especially, it can't come back to me."

"Mira, I'm not – I'm not sure I can do it."

"For me, you will, right? It's worth a lot to me, and I'll pay. A thousand coins."

Mira listened carefully to the quiet whisper in her ear. "No really, I'm not sure I can. Heavily sequestered. It was broadcast everywhere, but the monitors were just seconds behind, connecting into every civilian system, finding it and wiping. Anyway, ten thousand, if it's even possible."

"Okay, ten," Mira readily agreed, even though that would wipe out most of her savings. "But what about ships in orbit? They wouldn't be directly connected to a network, right?"

"Where the monitors couldn't access remotely, they boarded, wiping out drives or just carting them off. From what I heard, scary as anything. They meant business. They even left ships unable to navigate, just towed them to the nearest station and let the crews figure it out. It's out there, I know, but to ask is to get stuck in the web."

"I believe in you, Kes. Come on, too tough for you to pull it off? And you'll want it for the Codex, anyway. Hey, don't forget, we're here for recreation." She gave his neck a sensuous rub.

"I'll see what I can do."

Mira smiled in triumph, even as she still held him. "That means it's in the bag. As soon as you get it, meet me here. Just send me a ping, you don't have to say anything, and I'll be here. Bring it on a physical device, okay? Just optical read, not radio. Kes, I really need this, at the first possible moment. I know you can help."

"Mira, why do I find myself agreeing to do things for you?"

"Because it's me! See you soon, right here. Ping me the moment you have it." Mira stood up and began a backflip in the same motion, arcing down through the tree, and so she left him.

Rental Captain

Arn Lobeck ate up the corridor at more than a meter per step, reducing them to a hurrying rabble. "Sir, if you will, allow me to brief you on the situation," Captain Roe forced out. He was making three steps for each two of Lobeck's strides.

"I will conduct a briefing," Lobeck told him. "Meanwhile, let me tell you my requirements. I need a full officer suite. My belongings will be placed there by a member of my staff who will board in approximately ten minutes. Thereafter, no crew members will enter my suite. I require full private use of the forward gymnasium for not less than five hours per day, at times I will determine."

"Five hours! But sir, gym time is slotted weeks in advance, and—"

"If any of your crew have objections, I will be glad to discuss the matter with them. Do you think there will be any problem?" Lobeck did not pause for an answer.

"Sir, we work hard to keep up morale here, and as you know, sir, that's essential on a ship like this—"

Lobeck turned on Roe, who suddenly found himself standing with his back to the corridor wall. "Morale, yes. I can think of several things which would hurt morale more than losing gym time. Things that could happen if there is any evidence of an inability to faithfully execute orders down to the last detail. This ship is mine for as long as I need it, in service to the Affirmatix Family in accordance with our civic partnership. You are a rent-a-crew. Do I make myself clear?"

Roe looked up at Lobeck. The man was tall, and defined by muscle through his entire body. Even where his dark clothing was loose, somehow the impression of muscle underneath came through. His features, his unlined skin and absolutely white teeth, could not possibly be real for any man more than twenty years old. Lobeck's blue eyes were directly upon Roe, unwavering.

"Yes, sir," Roe managed.

"Then let us go to the bridge." Lobeck again led the way. They proceeded to the anteroom, where the door shut and locked behind them before identification was scanned, and the way to the bridge opened. The party, of Lobeck, Roe, and two orderlies, stepped out onto the bridge.

"Report," ordered Captain Roe.

"Proceeding to Top Station, sir," Commander Varma told him. "We're just finishing the upgrade to Status Three as ordered."

"Mister Lobeck will be in suite one zero two. Post two men at all times to assure that he is not disturbed."

"Make a general announcement directly to your crew, if you would be so kind." Lobeck placed a perfect hand on the edge of the console in a model's simulation of leisure.

Roe opened the channel. "Attention all crew. Please extend Vice President Arn Lobeck all courtesy due his position, and carry out any instructions provided by him. Roe out."

"Good. My first order is that no person shall leave this ship without my permission. All shore leave at Top Station is cancelled."

There was no open complaint at Lobeck's pronouncement.

"My second order is that my staff and I shall have access to all parts of the ship at all times. My third order is that the forward gymnasium will be cleared for my use, a quarter-hour from now. Please expedite these, Mister Roe."

Captain Roe was feeling ill. "Yes, sir."

Lobeck turned to Varma. "Commander, what is our ETA at Top Station?"

"Five hours and twelve minutes, sir."

"We have the captured runabout in tow?"

"It's in the hold, what's left of it, sir," Varma said.

"Hold at a distance of five kilometers from Top Station. At that time,

I will require forensic and engineering experts to assist me in examining the boat."

"I led the engineering investigation," Varma objected. "We did a thorough job."

"Post a copy of your results for access from my account, then. They could be of some use. Mister Roe, why don't you show me to my suite now?"

Another little test, but one that Roe had prepared for. Lobeck would know that the only resident suite on the cruiser was that belonging to the Captain. Roe had emptied his quarters before Lobeck had arrived on board. "Right this way, sir."

Fly In Amber

Evan could feel his forehead against the hard surface. It definitely wasn't a pillow.

For a moment he kept his eyes closed, not wanting to face what he knew would be there. There was no avoiding the other senses. Confinement. The suit wrapped his arms and legs, not tight, but unmistakably there, and all encompassing.

Silence, except his breathing, and the low whisper of the air system.

Smell, of someone who has been in an EVA suit for too long, and of fear.

Taste, of drool thickened on his tongue while he had been asleep. He scraped some of it onto his top row of teeth, then took a sip from the straw and swirled the water around in his mouth. He wished he could spit the resulting mixture out, but that wasn't an option. He had to swallow the viscous fluid.

"Suit," he said. "Where are we?"

"We will enter the orbit of Foray in another two hours and twelve minutes. We will then assume a slightly eccentric but stable orbit around Foray."

"How much air?"

"Depending on your level of activity, approximately eight hours," the voice told him. "You gained slightly over a half hour of duration by sleeping for the past two hours."

It was time to face reality.

Finally, Evan opened his eyes.

When he had nodded off, the unchanging star field had defined the view. Now, Foray ruled. Sharp brightness, unmuted by any air. The moon reflected back the intensity of Kelter's white sun.

Foray occluded a full thirty degrees of arc in the lower right part of his field of view. Against a backdrop of stars and black space, it was a scene of breathtaking beauty. His entry to orbit had taken Evan between Kelter and Foray, so Foray's visible surface looked very much like the moon he had seen on many nights as a child. Just a lot bigger.

Unless he found a way to the moon's surface, or one of the other stations or space colonies in the system, this was also going to be Evan's highly scenic tomb.

Evan's breathing system was an efficient rebreather, which scrubbed carbon dioxide from the air he breathed out, juiced up the oxygen to the required level, and then reused that air. Even so, he had just over eight hours of usable air remaining, as the suit had just informed him.

"Suit, please advise. Is there any achievable flight path leading to a survivable impact on Foray?"

"No. The available thrust is for attitude adjustment and very minimal maneuvers. We cannot leave the orbit of Foray."

The answer had not changed from the last time he had asked, a few hours before.

By the numbers, it was crazy. He had escaped from the Aurora system and made it to Kelter. Counting the trip through the newly discovered glome, that was fifty-six light years. Over five hundred trillion kilometers. And now he lacked the means to make it across the last hundred thousand kilometers of space. Such a tiny distance, less than a billionth of what he had already traveled. Unattainable.

Evan had found out a lot about being in an EVA suit for more than an hour or two. For one, space is not so vast if you are stuck inside a suit. The claustrophobia came in waves, each peak worse than the one before. He had begun to contemplate simply peeling the suit off, just to be free of it for a moment until the hard vacuum took him.

Breathe.

His clothes had shifted and now had folds that rubbed against his side. His lower back itched. In theory, he could pull one of his arms out of its suit arm, and make adjustments. In practice, he didn't dare. What if his arm got jammed part way in or out? He had started to try it once, a few hours ago, but could not make himself commit through the crux of pushing his hand through the narrow space under his armpit.

Breathe.

Evan had tried, many times over the past few hours, to leave a last message. For Kate. Each time the suit played it back, he had cringed, and ordered the message erased. What could he say that would mean anything in a message, recorded in the memory of an EVA suit, carried until some future day when his body was found?

Would she even care anyway? For all Evan knew, she had long since moved on, and a message would be an unwelcome surprise.

Calling for help. That was an option. It would probably work, at least in the sense of attracting attention. Most likely the wrong kind. It would be the last resort. If he got down to a few hours of air, then he would ask the suit to send an SOS to anyone who would listen.

When was the dividing line? Enough time to be sure that there was no hope otherwise, but some reasonable prospect of someone getting to him in time. If the warships didn't simply dispatch a missile.

Maybe Mira was actually on Kelter and had received his message. Realized it was for her. Decoded it. Decided that it was worth lifting into space swarming with warships in order to see what was on the vector that he had supplied. And so she was coming for him right now.

Described that way, it didn't sound so likely. Mira wasn't his pilot any more. She didn't owe him anything. When Evan had been provided with the research opportunity of a lifetime two years before, he had cast her off with little hesitation.

Evan had seen plenty of traffic go by, from the new glome emergence toward Kelter. Six warships had accelerated past, and then turned to decelerate in order not to hurtle past the planet.

He had instructed the suit not to use any active scans such as radar, but the suit was able to track the warships easily using a combination of visual sensors and passive radar detection. The other ships did not seem in the least bit concerned about being tracked.

If the Affirmatix fleet was indeed pursuing him, then there was one irony in that. Affirmatix, his expedition sponsor – former sponsor – had provided, at special order, the suit that he wore, and which might be saving him.

The suit was intended for conducting delicate scans for any signs of Versari artifacts, on the varied surfaces and caves of the asteroids in the Aurora system. To that end, it did not generate nor reflect any measureable amount of electromagnetic radiation, which would interfere with the scans. In practical effect, it was a stealth suit, and he was invisible to the ships.

Evan needed to pee, so he did. At least that part of the suit was working well.

He considered having another sip of water, but decided not to. Maybe later. Evan did his best not to think about the plumbing.

His suit had an outside zipper pocket. Evan pulled off his left gauntlet, revealing the thin inner glove. The gauntlet floated by its tether. It would stay nearby.

He unzipped the pocket and pulled out a small grey box. For a moment, he left it suspended in front of him. It was drifting, very slowly, away and down to the left. He reached easily to retrieve it, then engaged the catch to open it. The amber cube floated out.

A little vacuum wouldn't harm the cube. For the last nine hundred thousand years, it had been just fine in the absence of air.

Evan delicately caught the cube between his index finger and thumb, and then placed it, as still as he possibly could, directly in front of his visor.

He supposed that he didn't actually need the original any more. All of the information had been meticulously copied, even that which could not be understood. Which was most of it.

Still, the object was special. The Versari had not known that they were leaving this for him; a gift, across almost a million years.

The amber cube was turning, ever so slowly. It might make a complete turn in several minutes. The sunlight partly reflected and partly transmitted into the center of the object, lighting it within and on its surfaces. Evan thought he could see details inside, slowly shifting.

Sunlight, unlike the vacuum, probably was bad for it, or at least for what was stored within. Only its perfect location, deep within the asteroid in the Aurora system, had allowed it to be sheltered, not only from any kind of atmosphere, but from radiation as well.

It was poor curating to leave it out in the sun. But then, there was nobody around to reprimand him.

In an instant, he could swat it away, and it would never be found again. One cubic centimeter, in endless space.

Evan didn't want that. It was his discovery, after years of searching. What a triumph, finally something of value from the Versari. It was worth all of the years away from home, scratching at any place that hinted of a Versari presence from a million years ago. Even Kate might allow that it had been worth something.

Evan's hand was getting cold. He pulled the gauntlet back on, leaving the amber cube turning in front of him. Both he and the cube were hurtling through space at over ten kilometers per second, yet neither he nor the object appeared to be going anywhere.

Evan considered the object in front of him. Maybe he would have another try, at composing the message for Kate.

He really should send that SOS.

The Vector

From her branch at the top of the tree, Mira saw motion, coming closer. Hopefully it was Kestrel. He had pinged Mira just a minute earlier, and she had quickly climbed back up to wait for him.

She picked out hints of his shape and features. Tall, lean. Bare arms even in the cool night. Curly dark hair. Same blue shirt he had been wearing before.

Without a word Kestrel sat beside her on the branch, then put his arms around her. She felt him kiss her on the cheek. Then he held her close for a long moment.

"You were fortunate?" she asked.

"You and me both."

"Just thirty minutes," she whispered. "Must have been easy for you, to do it so quickly. I'm overpaying! Twenty thousand per hour!"

"But you are paying for years of learning," he whispered back. "And for the very highest level of skill."

"You are a great wonder. And handsome." Mira nibbled his ear for a moment. He was, at that, although unattainable. Still, they had their little game.

"Good luck," he said in her ear. "Please be safe, as much as your light allows you to." Kestrel began to unwind himself from her, and then he cast off from the branch.

He was not as graceful in the tree as she was. Close, she thought, but not quite.

Mira looked at the dim horizon, where stars met the blackness of the land. She was alone again.

Alone, and not just in her location in the tree. Kestrel had helped her, for a price. That was as far as he was going to go. She had other friends, but she would only trouble them if she really needed to.

Mira was used to figuring things out for herself.

She felt for it and found it. In her right vest pocket the 10k was gone, and in its place, a card. The physical currency of the Untrusted Zone was often inconvenient, but at times like this it was perfect. Mira had what she wanted, as did Kestrel, with no record of the transaction.

Right there, at the top of the tree, she could pop it into her phone and read it. That was almost certainly a bad idea. She could take the phone offline. Again a bad idea. Just being offline could be the most telling signal of all. Even in the Untrusted Zone, these days. You never knew.

Fortunately, Mira had an answer. Back at her apartment she had a brick, sitting there for moments just like this. An old model, but it would do. She cruised down the tree and hoofed it home.

The walk was suddenly strange. She had to force herself to stay at a normal pace. Nothing was different. Nothing. She hoped she would not run into anyone she knew. Again, she was fortunate.

Inside her apartment, she locked the door and then fired up the brick and put the card into it.

Mira's apartment was small, but it met her limited needs for the times that she was dirtside. A few cubic meters of privacy. When Mira had moved in, the landlord had advised her that the place would be as good as new if she slapped on a coat of paint. Mira hadn't bothered. Scuffs on the walls from the apartment's prehistory, and a pale blue color that she certainly wouldn't have chosen; these things didn't matter.

These walls were not what confined her, these days. Rather, it was her own choices. To behave. Self-censor and self-regulate. The thought made her want to run down the middle of the busiest street in the Untrusted Zone, screaming.

It took just a moment to copy the file and decrypt it with her private key.

The result of the decoding was total gibberish. The key had not worked.

Momentarily, Mira was flummoxed. The message was for her. She was sure of it. Why flag the message for her attention if she couldn't decode it?

And then she knew. Her private private key. For some reason Evan had encoded the message using her hand-rolled public key, not the key she had published in the directories. It was a conceit to have a private

private key, a silly thing that people do so they can feel like they are doing something special and secretive. Mira, caught up the in independent spirit of the Untrusted Zone, had made hers as a teenager, and had closely guarded it ever since. One of the few people who knew of its existence was Evan.

Mira applied her private private key to the message.

And it was … a vector.

Not just any vector. She knew before she plotted it. It was the course and velocity, at a moment in time, of the ship Evan had been on. Before it had been blown up. Before he had been killed.

Why?

Why go to the trouble?

Because there was still something on that course and velocity.

She chose to use the keyboard instead of just telling the brick what to do. "How quaint," she thought to herself, then typed, "Plot forward, extend vector eight hours." A line appeared, heading directly toward Kelter, most of the way there. "The present moment." Entering orbit of Foray. "One more day." Staying in orbit.

Right now, it was entering the orbit of Foray. Something. Evan had spent the last few minutes of his life figuring out how to tell her about it. There was a reason.

Mira was going to find out what that reason was. In his memory. Or perhaps it was something of value. Why had he chosen to do this as his time ran out? Mira would not be able to rest until she knew.

She would need a small shuttle. And she needed a cover, some plausible reason to go to orbit. She would think of something.

Suddenly, Mira had a lot to do.

The Cloud Readers

Sonia, Ravi, and Merriam were headed for the next security stop. The first was when they had prepared to leave the Affirmatix campus for orbit. By rule, they were supposed to leave behind any material or information that was proprietary to Affirmatix, and this was a problem because the entire purpose of their trip related to extremely sensitive data that they needed to bring along.

Somehow Sonia had kept her cool as the securitons grilled her, to the edge of accusation, about data that she had been expressly instructed by her wrangler to bring. Ravi had not kept it under control quite as well. Finally an intervention from Colin had cut the inquisition short.

Now they found themselves approaching a deep space station, where they would be checked once again. While other spacecraft waited in a queue, their ship was being waved forward.

They were the only passengers on the small ship. A yacht, Sonia had decided. Featuring six suites beyond the crew quarters, it was extremely well appointed and provisioned. Few people ever left Alcyone, and those who did were important. Their spacious seats, although equipped with all of the required safety features, provided the ultimate in luxurious comfort.

Sonia fiddled with a talisman that Simone had given her, for defense against space aliens. It was strange and disturbing to Sonia that her daughter possessed something resembling a gun, even a toy. She would have to ask Yvette about it when she got back. As carefully as they worked to maintain equity in parenting, Sonia was the one who was away more at her job. Far more. She often didn't know what was going on at home.

As she had promised to Simone, Sonia kept a lookout for aliens through the large display window of the cabin.

"But somebody has made a mistake," Ravi was saying, "asking us to come to Kelter and thinking we could help them. Did you see the data they provided to us? A terrorist has thieved their discovery. So what? They must do their own hunting for him, and clean up their mess."

"Colin said we were needed for scenario analysis," Sonia said. "Perhaps there is some other planning we will be doing. The variation in potential value to Affirmatix is huge, depending on how we manage it."

Ravi scoffed. "We could do that work just as well back on Alcyone. We will find out soon enough what they want. But I tell you now – somebody is going to ask for false precision. What if I go pee now instead of later, how will that affect the valuation of the discovery?"

"I'm sure there's a good reason," Sonia offered.

"They think they can read the clouds. An augury." Ravi pointed out the large picture window at a wisp of nebula, part of the cluster in which they lived and were now departing. "You can see what you want in the image. Maybe it is the shape of conquest and triumph of new markets, or perhaps it looks like a monkey's paw. We calculate the clouds of probability, for the effects of this action or that. And we dress the charts up in our colors, happy green or warning red, add textures and shades, so it all looks like it makes sense. And so scientific."

"But the latest results are very clear," objected Merriam. "We found the scenario where the value flies off the charts. The model's not lying about that."

Ravi set his hands together with fingers pointing in several different directions. "How many dimensions are in the model? We all know, it is sixteen. And in any portrayal, we can show only three. Maybe four or even five with some tricks."

"But the De Beers method sure is working, for a recent example," Merriam pointed out.

Several years ago, Sonia and her team had pioneered a new algorithm that had greatly increased the value returned from the exploration of new hyperspace glomes and new planets. A few simple insights, and some very complex math, had led to a strategy that had yielded trillions for her sponsors. Instead of racing each other to publish their glome discoveries in a haphazard manner, the Sisters had all agreed to an orderly method and timing for publication of the discoveries, to maximize all of their gains.

"Yes, it is working," Ravi grudged. "For a certain purpose, during a certain time. Still, it is not the same as knowing. To imagine that we can really know, when we only look at a few dimensions at a time, is like taking a thin slice of your brain and trying to figure out what you are thinking."

Sonia couldn't resist. "That's easy. If a slice of your brain is missing, you're not thinking much anymore."

"Very funny, Sonia. You know what I mean. We make the clouds for our sponsors, but no mortal can truly read them. The reason is obvious – because we are talking about the future."

The captain of the yacht entered the room. "The security review has been waived," he told them. "Getting you to Kelter is some kind of emergency. So I'm going to kick in full acceleration to our exit glome. Please settle back and don't try to get out of your seat."

The captain left, and moments later they all felt the extra weight, more than a full gravity. It might be as many as two. Sonia raised her right arm a few centimeters, then carefully let it settle back to the padded armrest. The yacht could move when it needed to.

Sonia reflected. She had not been given a choice about leaving Alcyone, but she had extracted a concession. A large one. She and her domestic family would be receiving coverage for the Parrin Process.

Decades more added to their lives. Perhaps even centuries.

In theory, anyone could buy the treatment. In reality, there was no way to pay for it. Tens of millions of credits per year, per person. The only way to afford the Parrin Process was to get it on your health plan. Parrin coverage was reserved for executives and heads of state.

And now, for Sonia and those she loved.

There had been hints that it was coming. A reward for her work. She had forced the issue, but her wrangler had given in quickly. It might have been planned for her anyway.

Alcyone was the best possible place to live. The best environment for her children. When you came right down to it, the only problem was knowing of the places you could never go, and people you would never see again. Friends and relatives you would never even communicate with, for the rest of your life.

For her daughters, it was different, perhaps better. They had been born on Alcyone. To them, other worlds were just a theory. And now they might get to live, in that place, for centuries.

Assuming that Sonia was able to see this mission through.

Beg, Borrow, or Steal

Mira stopped at the door in front of her. DelMonaco Shipping. The last place in all of known space she ever imagined she would go voluntarily.

Mira knew that she had no choice. There were no ships to be found, not for her. Except, perhaps, in this office.

For the past two years, Mira had been a model citizen. As model as she could ever be, anyway. Maintaining her licenses. Following regulations, when she got a chance to fly. Nurturing her credit.

But memories were long, and the algorithms were implacable. When it came to the question of running her own charter, Mira didn't rate. Not by hundreds of points.

She had flown often in those two years, most of the time as lead pilot. It was a position of considerable responsibility, but still just crew. An employee. Pilot, not captain, even of a shuttle to Top Station and back.

To get the ship she needed, Mira would have to beg. She wondered if she had it in her.

It was time. Mira took another step forward and the door slid aside for her, revealing a reception area with a high ceiling. Directly in front of her was an enormous painting of a desert scene, on a shimmering high-resolution screen. By Kate, of course. If you come to her office, you have to admire her art, Mira thought to herself.

An ostentatious fish tank lined the entire wall to her right to a height just below her chin, while a sheet of water flowed down a steep slab of sandstone to the left. The displays were an intentional waste of resources, as was the human receptionist, who now looked up at Mira expectantly.

"I'm Mira Adastra," she told the man, "and I need to see Kate. Right now. I called ahead."

"Ms. DelMonaco has been in a meeting the entire time since you called," he told Mira. "I'll see what I can do, but we'll just call it a busy day."

"I'll wait," Mira told him. "But I need to see her as soon as possible."

She sensed something, but there was nobody else in the room. Where? Through the water of the tropical tank, she saw the distorted shapes of people walking in the hall beyond. Parts of rainbow-hued arms, torsos, and legs refracted off the dividers in the tank. Could that be her? And then Mira was sure.

She took three long steps, then bent down for a clear view through the tank. Looking back up, she saw the underside of Kate DelMonaco's chin.

Mira saw Kate take one more step forward, and then suddenly stop. Kate's face turned slowly down and toward Mira.

For the world's longest three-second interval, they simply looked at each other. A parrotfish swam slowly between them, eclipsing their connection. Then Mira saw Kate turn and walk briskly forward.

The door opened and Kate hurried out.

Quickly Mira reached to shake hands. It was better than the alternative, she remembered well.

If it was costume day, then Kate was playing an executive. A spotless charcoal suit. Her black hair was tightly up in a bun. Mira recalled how Kate always liked it to flow wherever it would. Kate might even be wearing makeup, which she had always disdained.

"Mira! It's wonderful to see you, but I'm deep in a project right now. Can we get together soon?" As if they would ever visit socially.

"I'll only take a minute, and it's important. Kate, I need a ship, and I need it now. Anything that will fly."

Kate stopped dead and just looked at her. "A ship."

"Yes."

"Are you planning anything in particular? With the ship, I mean."

Mira plowed ahead. "I've got a job that'll cover all the costs. Bringing some samples to Top Station."

"Samples. Mira, you're a wonderful pilot. I'm grateful for all the times you took Evan and me to Foray and back. But really, I'm not sure that …" Kate's voice trailed off and her eyes widened as she studied Mira with terawatt intensity.

Kate turned abruptly. "Come to my office," she said, and bounded to the door, only briefly holding it for Mira to catch up. A short hallway and they were in Kate's office.

Kate waved an arm. "Out!" Three men and a woman scurried from the space, the last one closing the door behind him.

This was a different Kate than Mira remembered. Kate was a dilettante writer and artist, living off the riches that had been left to her. Always wanting to connect with people and find insights into timeless truths. A patron of the arts and sciences, especially exoarchaeology.

But not today. A lot had evidently changed in the last two years.

Kate fixed her eyes on Mira. "What do you know? Tell me!"

"Know? About what? I just need a ship."

There was no hiding the bone from this dog. "You know something," Kate asserted. "The ship. Was he on board like they've been saying on the news?"

Mira cast around. What should she say? Was it even safe to speak here? "I have a contact at Top Station. Who might have something. That's all I know. And I have to get there."

"So, just get a seat on a shuttle. They leave every hour."

Mira was still trying to reconcile her image of Kate with the woman she was seeing in front of her. In her actual physical features, she was not so different after two years. Same nose, slightly turned up, same full lips, same wide smooth cheeks.

And then Mira had it. Kate had tidied up. The mole she had always said was part of what creation had given her – it was gone. The freckles that had always seemed at odds with her dark hair, either covered up or removed.

"The suggestion was to bring my own ship." It was all Mira could come up with.

Kate appeared to turn inward. "A ship. On the worst possible day. Okay, this is solvable. That's what Evan would say." Then she looked back up. "How soon can you be ready?"

"Lead me to her."

"Get your cargo and meet me in Bay Nine in fifteen minutes. But you're not getting off that easy. I'm going with you."

Mira should have known. She could think of lots of adjectives to describe Kate, but cowardly wasn't one of them. Nor stupid. She had quickly figured out that the request related in some way to Evan.

Mira headed out of the office to get her kit.

Twelve minutes and thirty seconds later, she stood at the gates to Bay Nine. No sign of Kate.

Thirteen minutes.

And then Kate was there, sporting a shoulder bag. "Let's go," was all she said. Mira followed her, scanning through the gate.

Inside, a group from the CoreValue Family awaited them. "Ms. DelMonaco," the apparent squad leader intoned, "we have been instructed to accompany you in completing the inventory of your family's space-going vessels as part of the −"

"Merger discussion," Kate interrupted. "I thought we had another day to complete that, but as you like. Just let me dispatch my tech to get some work done." She turned to Mira. "Here, let me opt you the PIN for Shuttle AL-44." She typed on her tablet and held it up. Mira reflexively pulled out her tablet and held a corner out, almost touching Kate's, in the standard pose for receiving an optical transmittal.

In the moment that the transmittal was in process, Mira saw Kate staring hard at her, clearly desperate to convey something. But what? Then the mask was back on.

After the expected beep, Kate was already pivoting away. "This way, gentlemen," she called, and walked off down a lane between ships. Mira was reminded of a scene in a show she had once seen, of a duck on old Earth, pretending to be injured to draw predators away from the nest.

What in the world was Kate doing now? Sending her out to turn a wrench?

There was one way to find out. Mira asked her tablet to locate AL-44. It was a longish walk to a far corner of the bay. She found herself walking past shuttles of diminishing size and increasing age.

Then she saw AL-44. It must be some kind of joke. An AL class, as the designation suggested, which meant the craft was not exactly new. It dawned on Mira that the 44 might mean it was the 44th ever built in the series. Which would make it over a half-century old.

Mira figured she might as well find out what Kate had in mind, sending her on this goose chase. She asked her pad to display the content of the transmittal from Kate. It read:

PIN = Elanas42 ---- GO!!!!!

Go? On this shuttle? Seriously? And what had happened to Kate's avowed intent to ride along with her?

She would be better off alone. If Kate said "Go," then that was fine with her.

Mira entered the PIN on the ship's keypad, and climbed aboard the junker.

Part 2:
Fly Casual

Foray

There was no need to check the math yet again. Evan, in his EVA suit, had entered an elliptical, but stable, orbit around Foray, moon of Kelter Four.

Evan looked out on the vista. The amber cube rotated, so slowly, directly in the middle of his field of view. He played focus games, creating two amber blobs by looking out to Foray, then splitting the enormous moon by directing his vision inward to the cube, just thirty centimeters away. He had figured out that Foray was farther away than the cube by a factor of about one million.

He should have put the cube away some time ago. Any kind of radiation, including sunlight, could degrade the information inside. Over the course of a few thousand years, anyway. Another little while wouldn't hurt.

Evan could acquire a far better image of his surroundings than the direct visual, at any time, by asking the suit to display an image in front of him. He could ask to see in any direction, at magnifications greater or lesser. Color enhancement. Vector overlays with the recent and projected courses of other vessels. Any movie ever made.

And so he mostly just looked out.

Evan wondered if there was something inherently relaxing about extending his vision to focus on infinite distance, as opposed to staring at the screen just in front of him.

Perhaps there was no need for a reason.

Foray had continued to grow, revealing features that Evan had seen many times while commuting between the Valley of Dreams on Kelter and the surface of Foray. The Twin Rivers. Sea of Galilee. Great Western Ocean.

There was an obvious theme to the names. They were all based on a longing for what was most treasured, and most scarce, on the surface of Kelter.

Now, his orbital track was taking him around Foray, swinging away from the bright gem of Top Station until it was occluded from view.

"Suit, is there any way to land on Foray?"

"No. We cannot leave orbit of Foray."

The suit did not sound impatient, but Evan had noticed that the answer had grown progressively shorter over the times he had asked. Perhaps, somewhere in the suit's algorithm, there was a point where it would be time to tell him, "Give it a rest! It's not going to happen!"

Was it time to give up and call for help? If he was going to do it, it would be ironic if he then failed to send out the SOS in time. Even those who might be adversaries would need some time to get to his location.

It was far past time. There must be some way to call in the right manner, to the right destination, that would be safest. Evan had considered the possibilities endlessly in the past few hours. There was still no choice that he believed in.

"Ship approaching," the suit told him. "Accelerating at one point four five gravities to match your course."

No matter what approached, it had to be better than spending his last minutes entombed in the EVA.

"Provide the best available image of the ship," Evan told the suit. "Use the entire screen."

It was small, and that was good news. It was not a missile, even better. Over a few endless and silent minutes, the image grew larger and began to resolve in detail. Evan began to hope.

Then he was certain. Beat up and scorched. It was a wonder that thing could fly. He knew only one person who would even consider taking a craft like that into space.

The small ship sidled up, now only a few meters distant. It rotated to show its airlock, then was stationary in relation to Evan's position.

A minute later, he saw the airlock dilate. A suited figure emerged. Evan saw his rescuer gracefully step into empty space between their vessels, safety line trailing. They drifted closer together.

It would be good not to blow this one. As they came within a meter of each other, Evan decided to let the other person take the action.

As it turned out, it was simple. With practiced ease, the other sent out a weight on the end of a line, just past his hip and then wrapping around him. A quick clip by his rescuer, and Evan had been lassoed.

Just one thing! As he felt the tug, Evan reached out with his thick left mitt to capture the cube in front of him. No time to go back to the thinner glove and put it away properly. The object was somewhere inside the glove now. Evan clenched his hand on the fabric of the inner liner.

He was pulled along as a weightless, although hardly massless, sack of potatoes.

There was only just room for both of them in the lock. Evan found himself folded up with a close view of the other's knees.

The inner lock opened, and they spilled out.

She pulled off her helmet, and of course it was Mira.

Mira said, "Strap in and don't talk to me," then she focused on the controls. The drive kicked in, more than a full gravity by the feel of it. The old bucket could move when it needed to.

Evan unstrapped his left glove and pulled it off, taking care not to lose track of the cube that was clenched within. Then he removed his other glove and his helmet. His hands now free, he tucked the cube into his outer suit pocket.

That taken care of, he looked around. The ship looked a little better on the inside than it had from without. Decently clean. Well used, but functional. Drunk but still standing, as they used to say.

The ship didn't smell that great. Oh wait. That was him.

Evan had ridden on similar shuttles with Mira many times. One milk run was near their current location. Valley of Dreams to Foray, and back. Valley of Dreams had a lot more Versari history, but Foray was in better shape. No atmosphere. The moon was also a tougher place to work. So they had developed a routine. Go up to Foray, stay for as long as they could stand it, say two weeks. Then Valley of Dreams again for a few weeks.

Gravity was suddenly gone as the ship stopped accelerating. Evan had failed to strap in, and now he floated free.

Mira spoke from the front. "Ok, I've matched the vector to my prior course. No reason to let anyone know I stopped in for a visit."

"You saved my life."

"Well how about that? Who had to be fished out of trouble this time? And who can't even follow the most basic instruction to strap in?"

"Thank you," Evan told her, "so much. It's so great to be out of that helmet. Okay if I take off the EVA? I'll get strapped in after that."

"Unsuit yourself."

Evan peeled and climbed his way out of the EVA. Freedom, after so many hours. The best part of all was unhooking the catheter. Evan stretched out fully, glorying in the lack of confinement.

"Man, when was the last time you washed?"

"Sorry about that, Mira! A big day touring known space, you know. I'll go rinse off in the head, if this bucket has one."

"No shower, if that's what you mean. You can use a damp cloth to spread the stink around. That'll have to do until we get you off this can."

"Hardly worth it. Anyway, where are we going?"

"First, I need to stop in at Top Station. I have some cargo to deliver."

Top Station, with him on board? What was she thinking? "You know, there might be a better time for that. I need to get to ground, quickly. Stopping off anywhere is not such a good idea."

Mira waved him off. "No really, I need to go there. It's the reason I'm flying. The official reason. If I don't complete my trip plan, somebody will wonder why." It appeared that Mira had learned to plan more than a minute ahead in the last few years.

"Give me a sec," Mira continued. "I need to update the worm drive so that the record states that I stayed exactly on my course, rather than diverting to get you."

"You can do that? I thought the whole point of a worm drive was just to record and never be updated. Official record and all that."

"Just call me the worm charmer. I'll get it, if you can shut up."

After a few silent minutes, she called out. "There, done. I stayed exactly on the flight plan. No deviations at all. And by the way, not only should you be thankful that I fetched you, but also that I was smart enough to figure out a credible low fuel flight plan that went right past you and also went to Top Station. And then resourceful enough to find someone who urgently needed a courier run there."

Evan floated up and took the copilot seat next to Mira. "Just to come get me. I did say thank you."

"Actually not to get you. I thought you were dead. When I read your message, I just figured that you might have left me a present."

What should he tell Mira, and when? At this moment, he owed her everything. But as Evan well remembered, discretion and nuance were not Mira's strong suits.

They looked at each other for a moment. Mira had that way of facing slightly away but turning her eyes toward him, conveying at the same time an interrogation and also a sense that they were both in on the same secret. Inviting him to break the silence.

He was alive, thanks only to Mira. Evan realized that he had no idea what risks she had taken to get to him. He might not be able to repay her, but there was one decent thing he could do right that moment.

"We've got a little while until Top Station, right?"

"Just over two hours," she told him.

"Well then Mira, I've got a little story for you," Evan said. "But before I get started, where are we going? I mean, after Top Station?"

"There's only one place you can go," Mira said. "And lucky for you I live there. We're going to the Untrusted Zone."

Private Keys

Lobeck, Skylar, and Roe were assembled. Lobeck began. "First, let me confirm that the only record of this discussion is the multiparser on the table. I will keep custody of this. No person is to make any mention of this material, even in private records. Mister Roe, you are present only because you have firsthand knowledge of events thus far."

That drumbeat had not ceased since the moment Lobeck had arrived. Roe was a guest, on his own ship. No more than a rental. Not even called Captain.

"First, the examination of the destroyed craft." Lobeck turned to Skylar.

"The craft was first checked for nuclear or other explosive devices, then it was brought into M3120's hold. Physical investigation of the interior was begun as M3120 proceeded to Top Station."

Mithra Skylar was one of the strangest looking people Roe had ever seen. The pale white of her skin would be effective camouflage against the ship's hallways. She was so thin that Roe wondered if she would disappear if she turned sideways. She was breathing a supplementary air supply through a set of tubes running under her nose. She had one eye always covered by a dataspace viewer, and a companion viewer ready to swing in front of her other eye at a moment's notice.

"How many persons entered the craft?" Lobeck asked.

"A total of five plus myself," Roe said. He brought up a graphic of the interior of the runabout, which included icons identifying objects of interest.

"And you believe there was one casualty," Lobeck prompted.

"There was the missile impact, which could have discharged the one person. There was no person or body in the ship."

Lobeck studied the graphic, exploding a few icons to check their details. "Let us speculate that McElroy survived," he said. "That is the most concerning scenario."

"It's just not physically possible. Nobody–"

Lobeck looked sharply at Skylar. "Never say impossible. You know better. We must consider all possibilities. But let's move on. The transmittal. That fact endures, no matter what McElroy's fate."

Skylar narrated the status. "From 0543 until impact at 0546, the craft broadcast the same message repeatedly on a variety of channels. The plain text portion is nonsense. The encrypted portion appears to be coded using 2KB strong, and it's small. Here's one thing that's verifiably impossible – the message can't possibly contain the entire information we are concerned about protecting. It could be meta. It could be about the information. But it can't contain all of it."

"How long will it take to decrypt?" Lobeck asked Skylar.

"With the resources on board, three days, presuming that we recognize the decrypted content. If it's unrecognizable or has another layer of coding, we could easily miss it. But there is one other approach that might work."

"Do tell." Lobeck gave Skylar his full attention.

"It's possible that the message was encrypted to a private key that we can access. All commercial encryption software packages automatically save the user's private key for law enforcement purposes. It is heavily sequestered and only used at times of critical need such as a terrorism investigation. The government of Kelter will have an archive of every private key that has been generated in this system by commercial software."

"We don't know that this particular private key was generated by commercial software on Kelter," Lobeck countered.

"True, we don't know that," answered Skylar. "But it would cover over ninety eight percent of people living in the Kelter system."

"I agree, it's worth checking. So how do we get these keys?"

"Under normal circumstances, we don't," she said. "The keys can only be released as part of a terrorism investigation, and only for identified people. And we don't know whose key we are looking for."

"We'll just have to get them all, then," Lobeck decided. "Identify somebody who can release the information, preferably on Top Station, and we'll have a chat with them."

The Ruling

Finally, Kate had satisfied the CoreValue squad and fled back to her office. She closed her door, sat down in her captain's chair, lay back, and closed her eyes.

It had been less than twenty-four hours since the ruling.

She would never forget the worst day of her life. Yesterday. It had been up in a small station near Top Station. Remote and isolated, specifically for the purpose of adjudicating sensitive matters of law, lacking even niceties like generated gravity.

Kate and her lawyer Colditz had taken their places in the appointed box. Some distance away, she saw the flock of plaintiff lawyers, at least a dozen as usual. People filtered in for the next few minutes until only three people were needed. The panel. And then the judges arrived.

Everyone stood up at the arrival of the judges. It was an awkward thing to do in the absence of gravity, but it was still expected. Plant your feet on the surface that has been defined as "down" by convention in the room. Hold on to the bar in front of you. Straighten. When everyone did this at the same time, it created a momentary illusion of up and down.

"Please be seated," the bailiff told everyone.

Being seated was easier than standing. There were even seat belts if you wanted them. It was important to stay the right way up, because floating upside down or even sideways was disrespectful and would likely get you ejected from the proceedings.

"In the matter of CoreValue Family vs. DelMonaco Trading, we have reached a final verdict."

Good. No more maneuvers. No more continuances. No more discovery. Whatever the answer, it was time to have it. Kate listened as the lead judge began.

"First, the case summary. CoreValue Family seeks damages for trespass and refusal on the part of DelMonaco Trading to pay reasonable and accustomed royalties for transit of the hyperspace glome from Green to Cloudcroft."

The judge continued his narration. "DelMonaco Trading maintains that the royalty term expired over seventy years ago in 2227, since the glome was first explored in 2178, and the royalty period extends for forty-nine years.

"CoreValue presented evidence that it has secured pervasive and ongoing agreements to extend the royalty period, by incorporating these extensions into many other contracts and purchase agreements."

All of the Sisters had done this for decades, going on centuries. In every contract, covering every transaction with any of the Sisters, there were hidden gems that reiterated and extended their rights. In that way, glome royalty rights had been perpetuated for many years after they should have expired.

Kate's parents had taken it as a personal mission not to contract with any of the majors. The fine print was not the only reason. Kate remembered it well from when she was a kid. Products everyone else had, but which were denied to her due to their origin. But in at least one instance, Kate's mother had slipped up.

"Specifically in the case of DelMonaco Trading," the judge continued, "it was demonstrated that in 2269, Ms. Anna DelMonaco agreed to extend all glome royalty periods by a further forty-nine years as part of the terms of use for her grocery rewards card, and that this extension would also be binding on her child Kate DelMonaco, who was twelve years old at the time. Therefore all CoreValue glome royalties are still in effect and binding on DelMonaco Trading."

A grocery card. The stupidest, lowest value item a person could have. And CoreValue had inserted their tentacles into the terms.

"One question before the court is whether a minor child can be bound by an agreement made by a parent. The defendants assert that a child should not be so bound. The plaintiffs assert that the defendant received benefits from the agreement and therefore should be bound by it.

"The court finds that the defendant did substantially benefit from her parent's ability to acquire discounted groceries. For instance, some of the food purchased by Anna was provided to her daughter Kate, and the discounts would allow for more or higher quality food to be provided. In consideration for that benefit, the court finds that all of the obligations in the card agreement are still applicable, for a term of forty-nine years since the date of the transaction. Therefore, the court rules for the plaintiff."

Defeat. Disappointing, but not unexpected. It was a flier, worth a try.

She could try again in another twenty-four years, when she was sixty-one – thus forty-nine years after the purchase in question.

"The next question before the court is of the amount of damages. First, DelMonaco Trading owes the original amount of the royalty, which is 11,400 credits.

"Second, DelMonaco Trading is ordered to pay the legal costs incurred by the plaintiff. Pending a final invoice, the estimated amount of legal fees is 2.9 million credits."

Also expected, in light of the ruling. And as much as it burned her butt to pay the inflated legal fees, it was not a problem. DelMonaco Trading was still generating healthy margins, if less with each passing year. And a huge benefit of having no stockholders, no outside investors at all, was that there would be no squawking. She would simply pay.

Kate prepared to get up. But the judge was not finished.

"Finally, the court finds that CoreValue Family has suffered substantial damage to its reputation, due to the defendant's efforts to cast doubt on whether CoreValue was rightfully enforcing its extended royalty period. Such damages have been determined to be a minimum of four hundred million credits. The exact amount of damages will be finalized by an arbitrator who will provide a report within six hours, in time for publication of the ruling in twenty-four hours. CoreValue is entitled to create and enforce liens on any and all property of DelMonaco Shipping, effective immediately. This court stands adjourned."

As the attendees streamed out, Kate just sat, holding onto the retention bar in front of her. 400 million credits. Or more. Her family was destroyed. It was all going to be taken away, due to the terms on an agreement that her mother had unthinkingly clicked decades before.

"Hey Kate, we're not done." Her lawyer Steven Colditz. "As I was telling you, now that we have a ruling, we go to final settlement talks. We have twenty-four hours to settle before the ruling is filed. The judge threw out some big numbers there, but nothing is set in stone."

Kate refused to look at him. "Oh come on! We've been a thorn in their side, and they came after us, and they won. What kind of appeals do we have?"

"Nada," her lawyer said. "Appeals past this level were all streamlined away in the reforms of the eighties. This is the end of the legal road."

"So what kind of settlement can we get now?"

"I think we're about to find out. Here they come."

Kate wanted nothing more than to go crawl into a hole. "Do we have to talk with them right now?"

"As your lawyer, I would advise it," Colditz told her.

The lawyers arrived in formation and perched on the retention bars. Their lead counsel spoke.

"Ms. DelMonaco, shall we talk settlement at last? We have always wanted to settle, as you know, and we still do."

Kate regarded the opposing lawyer coldly. "You got your ruling, what more do you want?"

"Let me ask you something. Do you want DelMonaco Trading to continue and thrive? Even grow beyond your greatest ambition?"

"It's my life," she said.

"Then let's talk about that. We'll invest a hundred million credits for a ninety five percent share of the family. A very generous valuation, in light of today's ruling."

"A controlling share. Almost all of the family."

"Yes. But above all, we want you. Stay on as President, Ms. DelMonaco. Use the investment to expand your routes. You will just need to serve for five years as CEO in order to earn out a ten million credit bonus in addition to your salary. And as a valued member of the CoreValue Family, you will receive a waiver on all glome royalties. Isn't that what you were after?"

"But independence, that's the whole point. I don't know if I can be part of – that. You and your whole bunch of crows." Kate cut herself off before she launched into a diatribe that she would regret.

"Honesty, that's a good start to any business relationship."

"I don't know if we're going to have any business relationship, Mr. Crassus. I really don't."

"Just think about it, Ms. DelMonaco. You have one day to do the math. Without a settlement, you're out of business. Settle with us, and you'll be in great shape. You'll have a new investment, and you'll have the entire CoreValue Family behind you."

"I'll think about it."

"Please do. But think quickly. Feel free to contact me whenever you wish, day or night. No time is too late or too early. You two have a great evening." Crassus gracefully launched from his retaining bar in the direction of the exit, and then was followed by his attendants.

A minute later, Kate and her lawyer were the only two people in the room. Kate already knew what his advice would be, and he was wisely choosing not to provide it at that moment.

One way or another, it was over.

Kate brought herself back to the present, in her office. The ruling was history, and it wasn't going to do her any good rerunning the events of the prior day.

Her family was being dismantled around her. There was nothing she could do about it, unless she gave in and accepted the offer to become a captive CEO. And serve at their whim, for five years.

And now, there was the mystery. Mira, sniffing around for a ship. Holding out a secret. Something to do with Evan's death – her eyes had given that away. Kate had gone out on a big limb providing Mira with a ship, even the least of what remained to her.

Everything was happening at once. Even amid the collapse of her family, Kate felt the imperative to find out more about what Mira was up to.

Perhaps there was a way. One of DelMonaco Trading's ships had just arrived insystem, and was docked at Top Station. Kate knew the captain of that ship well. Once Mira got to Top Station, it might just happen that she would run into an old friend.

Kate started composing a message to the captain of the Descartes, far above the surface of Kelter.

Top Station

The battered little ship was approaching Top Station. Evan was now seated up front, next to Mira as she piloted.

"Okay, just stay here," Mira said. "Don't do anything. I'll be on the station for about ninety minutes. I'll deliver my package and get lunch. Then–"

Evan was dumbfounded. "You need to get lunch. While I wait here?"

"Because it's what any normal person would do with the time until the next flight window with decent fuel use. And I am a normal person, especially today. Nothing dumb, nothing hasty. Nobody in their right mind would stuff themselves into this can for an extra hour that they didn't have to."

Evan looked out at the steadily growing form of the station. Once upon a time, it had been an elegant spinning wheel, and that shape could still be seen, just barely. After the installation of the generated gravity system had rendered the spin unimportant, modules had been bolted on ad-hoc over the course of decades. Any concept of a unified design, or coherent aesthetic, had been lost.

"I guess it's what we need to do," he conceded.

"Right you are. Now check this out. Here comes a shuttle from one of the Affirmatix warships, bound for Top Station. Looks like they will arrive about 5 minutes before we do."

Evan groaned. "Could things get worse?"

"Sure!" Mira replied cheerfully. "Lots of ways! The warships could start firing on everything in sight. This boat would shred like a beer can. Or, I could turn you in to the highest bidder. Or−"

"Okay, okay! It's good to be breathing anyway. I just have a touch of, let's just say, anxiety right about now."

"I've got just the ticket. Let's play a game while we approach − it's called 'count the warships!' There's one over there, that one's two. There's three." Mira pointed at the locations where the ships stood off Top Station.

It was impossible to miss the unsubtle reminders of all she was doing for him. "I know I have endangered you," he said. "The message − at that moment, it was all I could think of. I had just a few minutes to try something, anything, to not die."

"Evan! If you are apologizing for this, then you don't know me. Since our last expedition together, I've been running freight insystem, observing safe ship spacing. Speed limits! It's soul-destroying."

The other shuttle was preparing to dock with Top Station. Evan wondered who was on board.

Top Station had never been Evan's favorite place. Mostly it had been an annoyance, a place where he had to stop on the way to the dig on Foray, or back to Kelter. Where he had to explain to ignorant inspectors why his research tools were not a threat to anyone. It had been such a relief when he had been able to afford the direct shuttle runs with a hired charter, due to Kate, and the funding provided by her family fortune. Still, at that moment the station was tantalizingly close. How great it would be to roam freely there. To get out of this bucket.

Evan turned to Mira. "That's another thing that we haven't got to talk about yet. This last expedition, they insisted on supplying the crew, all of them. I couldn't turn it down. A blank check to work on the most promising Versari site, any supplies I needed. I even asked the sponsors about making an exception for you, but it was no dice."

"I understand." Mira was concentrating on the controls.

"You say that now, but I know—"

"It's okay," she dismissed. "Not the first time I've been cut from a crew."

The station was steadily growing, taking up most of the view directly in front of them. Evan could see more and more features. Hatches, antennae, piping. The Affirmatix shuttle was going into a bay directly in front of them.

Suddenly Evan hit himself on the side of his head. "Stop! We need to dash for the ground right this minute!"

"Come on, we talked about this. I have a good cover."

"Known associates. Think about it. If these ships all came to Kelter on my account, who will they be looking for? Known associates of Evan McElroy. And I even asked to place you on the expedition. I assume you're the registered pilot of this can right now?"

"It's kind of borrowed, but yes, I am. Captain, actually." She looked pleased.

"I think we need to leave. Right now!" Evan was frantic.

"Hey, I've got this," Mira told him. "We can't depart from the flight plan. It's pretty buttoned down around here. And as your captain, I've got a plan. Grab that canister and swap it into your EVA. It's good for about twenty hours. As we approach, you step out for another of your little walks, and stay out for as long as I'm on station. If anyone searches the boat, we'll be clean."

No way. Not the EVA suit again. "But you're going to take the shuttle into a bay, right? Then we'll all be inside."

"Nope," she said. "For a run like this with no bulk cargo, I just engage an airlock and pop through. The ship stays outside. Short term parking. As we approach, I'll put it in a slow spin, and you cycle out when the lock is facing away from the station. Then just stay on the away side as I rotate the lock toward the station. See that row of hatches right there? Our spot is number three."

Anything but the EVA. "I'll be visible to any ship coming in to Top Station," Evan tried.

"Nobody will be looking, but in any case you can crawl into one of the turbo intakes. There should be just enough room. Stay in there until I come for you."

"I still say we just blast for it."

"That's why I'm the captain and you're the passenger. The single best way to be caught is to try to blast this bucket anywhere. We can't outrun anyone, can't maneuver. All we can do is think on our feet."

An implausible thought suddenly arrived. "Mira, you're not going to turn me in, are you?"

Mira looked up from the controls, looking puzzled and smiling at the same time. "To the man? Do you know me? Not for an 840 credit rating. Once we get to Kelter, we're going to make a big splash with your news, and poke Affirmatix in the eye at the same time. We'll set the planet spinning on a new axis!" Evan caught a flash of the Mira of years past, who could make the craziest idea seem reasonable. It was hard not to catch some of her enthusiasm.

"But we need to get there first," she continued. "And right now, I'm kind of digging this whole captain thing. So, do we have a plan?"

"Aye Cap'n, we've got a plan." In resignation, Evan reached for the oxygen canister and fitted it into his EVA. He really, really did not want to get back in that suit.

The Weasel

"I still say this is too crude," Skylar said, as the docking sequence began. "If our mission is to contain information, then we shouldn't take high profile actions that draw attention to it."

"Sometimes you are too subtle," Lobeck rejoined. "We should not hesitate to apply all needed force, or persuasion, to accomplish our objective. I have received authorization from President Sanzite to take any measures that are required. Any measures, without limitation." He felt the thud of the locking bolts from Top Station engaging their shuttle.

"But our action clearly elevates the importance of the rogue message to any competent observer," she insisted. "Right now it's just a mystery. If we demand all of the private keys, it obviously relates to the message, and will focus attention on it."

"I think you underestimate the novelty of the events of the past day. It's still all over the news, all the time. It's even beating out celebrity affairs. Everybody knows that a new glome is huge news, and then the missile impact on top of it. And the coded message. So we don't need to be tentative."

"We could work more carefully," Skylar admonished.

Lobeck stepped into the airlock, and waited for Skylar to join him. "Mithra, how long have you been with me?"

"Going on seventy years now," she said.

He looked down at his long-time confidant. Mithra Skylar had chosen her own path. Taking the opposite approach to Lobeck's intense fitness regimen, Skylar had done everything possible to slow her metabolism. Deep meditation. Direct control over her heart rate. Eating only weekly, if that. Breathing air with intentionally reduced oxygen. Her choice required its own kind of discipline, perhaps more than his method.

To the outside world, she looked emaciated and insubstantial. But Lobeck knew better. Freed from needs of the body, Skylar could apply the entirety of her consciousness to any problem that faced them. He could still see traces of the beauty that once was the talk of all of Goodhope.

At least she had not made the same choice as President Sanzite. Lobeck tried to put the image out of his mind.

The door of the airlock dialed shut behind them. "You know how much I value your analysis," he told her. "And I also know that you like to puzzle and puzzle until you find the best possible solution. That has been excellent, ninety-nine percent of the time, when we had latitude to plan ahead. This is not that situation. We are recovering from the massive blunder of letting McElroy leave the Aurora system, and we must react in real time to events. This is where I decide, and then *we* do."

"If you say…"

"This time of all times, I need your commitment. Whatever it takes, whatever I direct. Mithra, I need to know that you're with me." There was no real question about her loyalty, but every so often it was a good idea to make her put it into words. To remind her of the source of all good things.

"Of course I'm with you," she told her commander. "There's nowhere else in the galaxy for me."

"So show me. I want you to request the private keys from Jarvis. A good task for you – step out of the background. And now it looks like we have completed docking. Let's get this done." The airlock door in front of them dilated, revealing a chamber with two station guards, already standing at attention. The door to the hallway beyond was open.

Lobeck set out, forcing Skylar to keep up, pulling her supplied air behind her through the halls. A few minutes later, the two arrived at the office of Eltan Jarvis, head of security for Top Station, and by extension much of Kelter Four. While there were other stations in orbit around

Kelter, Top Station was the hub of commerce for the entire system. Most of the goods and passengers in transit between Kelter and its two moons, or other stations, passed through Top Station.

And so Jarvis was a man to be reckoned with. Any matter of security, anywhere in the Kelter system, was his business. He was with the Kelter government, but his position was of course funded by subscribers, which included the Affirmatix Family at a ten percent participation rate. In many other systems, such positions were simply funded by a one seventh share from each of the Seven Sisters, but Kelter had unusually high participation from independents and even nonprofits. They liked to hang on to some illusion of independence, and that was their prerogative, if they were willing to foot the bill.

Lobeck and Skylar were ushered directly in to see Jarvis. Ten percent got you that, anyway. And a fleet of warships probably didn't hurt.

After the obligatory handshakes, they got down to business.

"You moved rapidly to sequester the message from the terrorist vessel," Lobeck said approvingly. "Good work."

"I didn't think we had a choice," Jarvis replied. "The events were so unusual that it seemed prudent to act first and assess later. We could always release the information if it proved harmless."

Lobeck nodded in appreciation. "That is excellent judgment, and in this case you could not have been more right. In your evaluation, how effective was the sequestration?"

"I am not aware of any failure of containment. We have also been tracking unauthorized efforts to acquire the information, and so far we have five infoterrorists in custody."

"We may want to interview them," Lobeck said. "Please retain any person of interest until I give further notice."

"Meanwhile, there is the matter of the encrypted content," Skylar put in.

It took Jarvis a few moments to shift his focus to her. "Yes, the coded message. Looks like strong 2KB. It will take a few weeks to decrypt it, assuming that we're able to."

"We're working on it as well," she said. "Have you made any use of the private keys that you have registered?"

"No, because we don't know whose key we need. The law enforcement key file is only useful if you know whose key you need, or have a short list."

"This time we should make an exception. I need you to provide us with all of the keys."

For a moment, Jarvis just stared at Skylar, processing the audacity of the demand. "I can't do that. We have a process, which is used for requests of up to a hundred private keys at a time. Checks and balances, you know."

Lobeck took over. "Checks and balances are for peacetime. We have an emergency going on right now. The ship was bearing several types of severe infoterrorist threats, not the least of which was a formula for a new variant of the TDX virus, virulent and fatal to humans. It's imperative that we contain all information that came from the ship, as well as all physical artifacts."

Jarvis jumped up in alarm. "But you just came to Top Station from a ship that has had contact with the remains of that ship. Why aren't you quarantined?"

"There is no issue," Lobeck assured. "The ship remains are in vacuum storage in the hold. We haven't even directly examined them – remote sensing only. And you notice that we've had no contact with Top Station other than the two of us. So rest assured that we will maintain the strictest isolation. Now back to the keys. We need them, and we need them now."

Jarvis was backing away from them, shaking his head. "You are asking for about a hundred million private keys, in contravention to every law we have on our books. They are for selective law enforcement purposes."

"Just ask yourself, Mr. Jarvis, what you value more. Do you value the lives of all of the people in the Kelter system? Or do you value some rules devised by bureaucrats to slow the performance of our duties to protect our constituents?"

"I don't have the authority."

Jarvis was a weasel. Fortunately, Lobeck had decades of experience with this type of creature.

"But you have the capability, and that's what matters. We are both men of action, are we not? Playing those games of authority is just a way to pass off a critical decision. Right here and right now, are you able to make decisions to protect your citizens?"

"I'll need to consult with my command chain on this," the weasel replied.

Lobeck knew how to close the deal, as he had so many times before. Bureaucrats thrived in an environment of obstacles to action, represented by closed doors, required procedures, and the ornaments of their authority. These could be swept away by a clear set of instructions, delivered at close range.

He stepped around the desk to where Jarvis had retreated, and towered over him. "You know perfectly well what you need to do, so let us delay no further. The safety of all your constituents depends on this. Load the keys on to this card – we will wait right here as you do so."

Jarvis took the device from Lobeck and stared at it for a moment. At last he said, "Wait here. It will be about ten minutes."

"Thank you. Please also include everything you have on Evan McElroy. History, people, finances. Everything."

"Ten minutes," Jarvis repeated.

"Mr. Jarvis, we need more people like you, who can take decisive action. If you tire of government work, please feel free to contact me any time."

Ten minutes later, Lobeck and Skylar had what they needed.

Fly Casual

Mira conveyed her small cargo without incident, a courier package with some product samples for a mid-level trade representative of the Philomax Family. That took only a few minutes. Then lunch, as planned.

Walking through the checkout at lunch, she felt the return of a familiar feeling. Would her card run, or would it fail? For so long, she had lived with that as an open question on many or most days. It was not question of money or ability to pay. There was always more credit to be had, conveniently extending your line, at a price. No. The question was your standing. At that moment in time, whether you were allowed to operate in the world of credit.

For the last few years, it had no longer been an issue. She had seen her score steadily rise. She showed up for work on time. Followed procedures. Didn't spend time at the pub with certain people.

Had she grown up? Or had she given in?

That was all out the airlock now. She had a passenger who was known to be dead, but who in fact was very much alive. And there was a good chance that the first symptom of official scrutiny would be failing a credit check. That was how they operated. Helpless, you would be stuck wherever you were, unable to pass through the next portal in the corridors of the station, or even scan into the public restroom, until it was actually a relief when the authorities showed up to visit with you.

There was no problem getting her food. She waved her card at the checkbot, and the green light told her to move on through.

Then she actually took time to sit and eat her lunch, at a provided table.

Mira did not normally stop for lunch. Usually she was eating and doing something else at the same time. Anything. Eating was boring, except with company and with beer.

So she ate and read articles in the news. Mira preferred text, old fashioned as it was. While people at nearby tables stared at the talking heads or elaborately produced videos, Mira read.

While she was especially interested in the events surrounding Evan's ship and the arrival of the Affirmatix fleet, that was not the only topic she read. That wouldn't be smart. She had learned many years ago that when she was in a public data space, it could be an error to delve too deeply into any topic that might be considered sensitive. Fortunately, the Affirmatix fleet was the top news story, so it wasn't too out of place to read all about it.

One sidebar captured her interest. An article with speculations about the existence of the new glome. Was it wise to go there? Mira decided it was worth following the link.

The author, a professor from the U at Arling Heights, started with a recap of glome exploration, and how relatively rare a new discovery was. Mira skipped ahead to where it got interesting. The timing. The first ship ever to arrive from that glome emergence was big news, and the missiles that destroyed the ship were a mystery. But the kicker was the warships that followed. Those massive ships had arrived in the system before it was possible for them to have received confirmation of the destination of the glome.

Nobody would send large ships, with their crews, into a glome whose destination was unknown. That wasn't done, because it would be stupid. Glome exploration was conducted with robots. In a few exceptional circumstances, ships with small crews departed into the unknown in search of glory.

The conclusion of the article was reasonable – the path of the glome had already been known, but had not been published.

Mira asked her tablet to remember the article, then closed it. That was enough delving, in this data space. She finished her lunch and headed back to the airlock where she could go back to her bucket of bolts. The flight window would open soon.

As she turned the last corner to the airlock, she saw the security personnel.

There was no purpose in trying to run. Top Station was one big confined space. The doors, every few hundred yards, generally stood open with scanners that extracted a nominal user fee each time you passed through, but could be closed at any time and for any reason. There was only one option.

When she was a teenager, she and her droogs had adopted a motto, in homage to an ancient movie. "Fly casual." Whether you were slinking in late to class, arriving home in the middle of the night, or simply walking down the street with your friends, it was essential at all times to fly casual. It had become their standard greeting, when meeting or parting. "Fly casual." And it was never more important than at this moment.

Without missing a step, Mira continued forward. There were four of them. Quite a pack. Out of habit, she sorted by gender, although it was made difficult by the uniforms and especially by the visors. Two were men, for certain. The whole effect was robotic. While she was sure that the design was functional, she believed that part of the purpose was to make the security personnel a little less like people, to create a distinction between them and their human herd.

"Ms. Adastra."

"How can I help you?"

"Routine check," the security guard told her. "All departures from Top Station. If you would do us the courtesy of opening your lock for us."

"Okay, but I've got a flight window. Seven minutes. I didn't know about any of this. You could give people some warning, you know."

"We'll be as quick as we can."

"You do that." Mira opened the inner lock to her ship and stood aside.

"Your computer system. We need access."

Fly casual. She had to fly casual. "Of course. Ship, please provide system access to these four fine people."

"Access provided," replied the ship.

"There you go. Hey, this is my fuel cost on the line. If I don't lift in six and a half minutes, it'll double my cost and it's all on me. Help out a small business, okay?"

Without replying, two of them entered the ship.

Minutes passed. The flight window came and went. Another window came and went. The next would not be for more than two hours.

Mira did not care in the least about the fuel. At any moment she could wrestle that boat down to the surface. The only question was the optics. Would someone in her position waste that much fuel just to get home a little earlier? No.

"Ms. Adastra, it's going to be a while. You may as well leave us at it, and we'll ping you when we're done. Don't worry, we'll lock up." Was that a smile?

"Is there a problem?" That might not be a smart question.

"Just a routine check. And one other question for you, Ms. Adastra. Are you, or have you ever been, a Statistician?"

"Well you know, I have been known to play with numbers from time to time." It was the wrong time for the old joke. "No, of course not. I stay away from politics. Completely away."

"Ok. We'll let you know when we're done."

Mira got the message. Run along now.

Where would a reasonable pilot go, if her ship was being thoroughly checked, but she had absolutely nothing to hide? If she didn't have a dead person hiding in her turbo intake? If everything was normal?

Mira ran along like a good consumer.

Physical Therapy

Benar Sanzite, President of the Affirmatix Family of Companies, had been reviewing the reports from Arn Lobeck, and he was concerned. The crisis was very real, and Sanzite appreciated Lobeck's vigorous response. He was glad that Lobeck was personally directing their efforts.

Yet, there were things that Lobeck did not understand. Even as a top vice president, he did not have the entire picture. That was Sanzite's job. His and the board's.

Most notably, Lobeck was the fiercest partisan for the interest of Affirmatix. The success of Affirmatix was, in the same breath, his success. This was not only because of the rewards that the family had provided to him. Over the years, Sanzite had seen the merger, or fusion, occurring. Every triumph of the family was embodied as a victory for Lobeck, every loss was a physical blow to him. Gaining market share by clawing it from another of the Sisters, or from the demise of an independent – that was what he lived for.

That very aggression was limiting, and stopped Lobeck from understanding how Affirmatix fit into something larger. Sanzite knew that Lobeck expected to someday be President of Affirmatix, whether by outliving Sanzite or by some other means. He also knew that this would never happen. Lobeck was not the right material for the top spot.

Sanzite drew the equivalent of a sigh through his tired lungs. He actively disliked travel, but this time it was necessary. He would have to help Lobeck, or at least watch him.

"Room," he called. "Notify my captain to prepare the ship for me. We will be going to the Kelter system. We will bring along all six delegates from my counterparts, so notify them."

"Notification sent," the room told him. "I will develop a travel schedule for you. We should be able to load you on the ship in approximately two hours."

He didn't talk with people much anymore. There was usually no need. The room, with its attendant banks of dedicated computers and large screens, met his requirements. He could see or hear anything that he wished. Have any question answered. Provide instructions that would be followed. The world responded to him, as it should. There was no need for him to cater to the outside world, and especially to any individual person in it.

Four young men bustled into the room. One addressed him while the other three got busy. "Sir, your travel tank is being readied, and will be here in thirty minutes. We'll get you transferred to the travel tank and then moved to your ship."

"I know the drill," President Sanzite told the attendant. "Just one thing. Allocate time for a PT session before we go. Here in my home tank. Send for the therapist right away."

"Yes, sir."

Sanzite liked physical therapy. Other than unlimited data, and unlimited power, it was what remained to him.

He still remembered, with great clarity, the day when he had given up. It had been the time of morning to go to the gym, and he simply had not. His staff had been deeply disturbed. Sanzite needed vigorous exercise in order to survive, an unfortunate requirement of the Parrin Process. By declining to do that, Sanzite was committing suicide.

Except that he wasn't. Sanzite had planned years ahead for the moment. He could stay alive, even without the intense exercise regimen, if he received an advanced treatment, just enough to keep his heart, lungs, and brain functioning, supplemented with aggressive filtering and rejuvenation of his blood and other fluids. And one other organ – he had to keep his priorities straight. The rest of his body, over two hundred years old, no longer mattered.

As his body had rapidly turned to gel, Sanzite had simply continued to work. The materials in the tank supported him and met his needs. After a few weeks his skin didn't itch any more. These days, he didn't even have a concept of where his body ended and the fluid bath began. It was all one – it was the system that kept him alive.

These days, his main tank was perfectly adjusted. Just the right density, easily keeping his head above the surface. A supportive, thick material that kept him from drifting, but soft and smooth enough so he barely felt its presence.

The fluid entirely filled the tank, exactly to the brim, so there were no unsightly barriers between Sanzite and the rest of the room or the displays that fed him the information he needed. If a rare ripple sent some of the material over the edge of the tank, it was quickly and automatically replaced with reserves that were always ready.

The travel tank was not nearly as comfortable as the main one. Sometimes some part of his body, he could not usually identify what part, and it didn't matter anyway, would bump against one of the sides. He hated that experience, and so he avoided the travel tank and thus any type of journey. Unfortunately, it would be necessary this time.

A dismaying thought occurred to Sanzite. "One more thing. The temperature. Get it right! To the tenth of the degree, and uniform throughout, or we will have words about this."

"Yes, sir."

On his last trip, the transfer had been horrendous. The travel tank had been a mess, with variations of several degrees from top to bottom, and uneven viscosity. He had felt the imbalances viscerally, reaching to his core. It had taken almost an hour to get to equilibrium. More reason to hate the travel tank. The morons could never prepare it correctly.

The therapist arrived. Sanzite tried to remember her name. It didn't matter. He still had functioning eyes, and he liked how she looked in her uniform.

"Leave us," he told the men. "I will notify you when you can resume preparations."

As the men left, he turned to his therapist. "I am going to be taking you on a little trip," he told her. "I need to travel, and I will need your help maintaining my health for as long as I am away."

He thought he saw her startle for a moment. Just a moment. Then she looked away. "Of course," she said. "I'll take care of you, Mr. President. Now, let's get started."

Full Charter

"Hey, Stranger!"

Mira looked up to see Rod Denison sitting at the edge of the pool, feet dangling into the water.

"You must be doing well, affording pool time up here in the station," he observed.

"Just a splurge," she told him. "Got delayed and was tired of sitting around."

"Yeah, I saw. Looks like you're scheduled to go down to Abilene as soon as you get cleared. And you've got space, which is what I like to see." Denison smiled broadly.

Rod Denison always looked happy and engaged in his surroundings. Mira imagined that to him, the whole world was a wonderful mystery being revealed a day at a time. He was one of the tallest people Mira had ever met, and that was still evident as he sat above her.

And then there was the hair. Easy, light curls of blonde that always looked casually out of place. Just right. If her hair could look like that, she might even grow some.

"Okay, I'll bite," Mira said. "How is that good news?"

"Because I'm going with you!"

"Um, Rod, I'm not so sure—"

"Of course you are. I just got in from Caledonia, and I have a high-level government courier trip, paying good money for transit. The Descartes is for deep space only, so I need a shuttle. I can pay full charter, and I know you like the sound of that. We can catch up, too. If you want, you can bring me back up to Top Station. Full charter. What could be better than that?"

"Really, Rod, it's not such a good time."

"Who are you, and what have you done with Mira Adastra? Full charter! Do you understand a word I'm saying to you?"

Mira scanned around the pool. Just swimmers, swimming and playing.

What would a reasonable pilot do, if everything was just hunky dory? How could she fly casual through this one?

"You know, Port Security seemed pretty interested in my pile of scrap," she tried. "When I left them at the gate, they were pawing through anything and everything. You know me, they'll find something, even if it's old. You know them, they'll find something even if it doesn't exist. What I'm saying is, it might not be the smartest idea for you to be around me right now."

"If I was smart, I'd work in an office. I've logged the charter request, all you need to do is approve and we're good to go. And you'll owe me a drink on the surface for bringing you such a sweet deal instead of going home empty."

What would a reasonable pilot do?

Mira improvised. "So I might have another passenger."

"Not on your manifest yet. Who is it?" Denison was being oddly persistent, trying to get this ride. Surely he had other choices.

She wanted nothing more than to just let go of the edge of the pool and slip back under water. "Not sure yet. Just an inquiry." How could she make this any clearer? "But it's a private request. If it comes through, I need to honor it. Private conveyance."

"That's not exactly a yacht you're driving there. I hope you let your party know that."

"Oh, yes." Mira was sure that her passenger knew all about the condition of the shuttle.

Finally he appeared to give up. "Well, let me know if anything changes," Denison said, and dove in.

Mira ducked below the surface and watched Denison arc down through the water, bubbles breaking free of him and heading toward the surface in a bedraggled cloud.

She loved being able to see clearly underwater without any aids. That was her biggest purchase ever, the eye surgery. Some of the features were useful in her line of work. Independent focusing on objects that were differing distances away. Auto-damping of extreme light. The zoom. The camera, still and video. But the very best was still seeing underwater. She looked up, seeing the distorted outlines of people and objects in the rippling surface. It was a glorious thing.

Under the water, she took census for her usual sociological assessment.

There were a wide variety of body types and levels and fitness. She had observed that the more confident a person was in their fitness, the less they wore. The clear correlation was evident once again, in this pool.

Mira felt really great about her fitness.

She surfaced for a breath, and then dove again.

Being surrounded by water was just perfect. Floating, she felt at home. A short lease until it was time to surface and breathe once again, but so worth it. It made Mira wonder why she lived on Kelter. There were planets that were covered entirely in water.

There was one place on Kelter. Or in it, rather. She had been away for far too long. When this adventure was done, she would return and experience it one more time. And complete some unfinished business.

An alert on her wrist caught her attention. She was cleared!

Mira stroked back to the surface and climbed out of the pool. She headed for the pool exit via the lockers.

Once she was clothed and walking down the hall to her ship, Mira consulted her status in more detail. The next reasonable window was in forty minutes. Should she go or should she wait?

She should wait. Fly casual.

She saw Denison's charter request. But there was more. Within a minute of her clearance, her shuttle had received four other requests. Two were full charter. People really wanted to leave Top Station, even in her conveyance.

This was a real problem. She could not leave the station empty. It would stick out like a sore thumb. The algorithms found anomalies like that, and brought them to the attention of their humans.

There was only one answer. "Call Denison," she told her phone.

"Hi Mira, changed your mind?"

"As a matter of fact I have. Be at my lock in five minutes."

"You got it! See you there."

She could not wait. Every fiber in her being screamed that it was time to leave Top Station, and full charter could justify some extra fuel use.

And as for Denison meeting McElroy, she would just have to handle that, somehow.

Mira hoped Evan was doing okay, holed up in the intake. Most especially, she hoped that he would stay where he was, for just a few minutes more.

Pushing The Envelope

"Drs. West, Merriam, Ravi, thank you for coming here on short notice," Lobeck said. "Skylar, please provide an update, from the top."

Sonia chose not to say how little choice had been provided to them. She had negotiated one concession, a big one, for her domestic family, but she knew that it was all in the context of being drafted for whatever this was.

Lobeck and Skylar were an odd pair. Lobeck was tall and strikingly handsome. His deep voice conveyed confidence at every turn. His look was of the kind that women, and men as well, swooned for. Skylar, by contrast, resembled nothing as much as a fish, stranded on land, propped up and forced to function.

"We have begun running the encrypted message through the provided private keys," Skylar started. "We have run about 20 million of the private keys, and have 80 million to go. No useful hits so far. We're also applying some petaflops to brute force decryption. By one path or the other, we expect to have the message decrypted within three to five days."

"Next, examination of the ship remains," Lobeck ordered.

"Other fleet elements are still gathering up small pieces, sweeping along the trail of the ship's velocity at the time of impact. Nothing greater than one kilogram in the last four hours. We still have not recovered the body, but in aggregate we are within two hundred kilograms of recovering everything."

"So that's mostly the body and the EVA that are missing."

Skylar brought up a set of graphics, showing the remains of the runabout. "We're continuing our examination of the parts that we have here, especially the black box. It's missing some data due to the missile impact, but we have been able to confirm from voice transcripts that McElroy was in the ship when it arrived insystem. Here's the timeline."

She pointed to another graphic, newly appeared above the table. A broad horizontal stripe ticked off the hours, while notable events were shown on parallel tracks. "It appears that he attempted to EVA to get to the sled, in order to cast off in the sled and avoid the missile impact," Skylar told them. "However, the body was not in the sled when we recovered it. Either the missile impact ejected him from the sled, or he was not in it."

"He might have fallen from the ship," observed Lobeck. "Let's look at the entire flight history of the ship after it arrived."

A flight chart appeared. "Look, there. The ship changed its acceleration at 0542, instead of just heading straight for Kelter. Have we swept that course as well?"

"Yes, but not at a high resolution," Skylar replied.

"Shift priorities," Lobeck said. "That is the course on which we will find the body. Now, let's shift to public communications. For our distinguished visitors, this is the main reason why you are here."

"I hope you will fill us in," replied Sonia. "All this tactical stuff. It's so transactional. You figure all of that out. We can't help you."

Lobeck was tall even when he was sitting. Sonia felt his scrutiny as though he was scanning through every known fact of her life. "I agree, Dr. West, on one level. But there is another element in play that directly concerns your work."

'We're all ears," she said.

"We all know why we are in the Kelter system. Our new asset will only provide its full value to the Affirmatix Family if nobody else is aware of its existence. Overall, I believe that we have contained the explicit expression of the data, despite earlier serious errors in the Aurora system. Our next challenge is erasing the secondary effects, including the ripples from our own actions. And that is where you three come in."

"Can you be more specific?"

"Here is the question," Lobeck said. "What information might cause people to believe, or speculate, in the discovery of our asset or something like it? For example, several writers picked up on the sudden arrival of all of our ships through a glome that had not been identified before. That begs for an explanation. We need to provide explanations or suppress the question. The articles in question have already been removed, but we must be vigilant for their recurrence."

"You need a True Story," Sonia said. "That's a task for the Marcom Team, right?"

"It is, but they need help. It's essential that our True Story should not only withstand scrutiny, but also that it should not direct anyone toward our discovery. I need you three to evaluate scenarios. Suggest courses of action, and evaluate those that we provide to you. Above all, we must preserve the exclusivity of our asset."

"What's your valuation target?"

Lobeck brought up the image that Sonia knew so well. "The best case scenario, of course. Ninety-nine percent. Dr. West, I have read your work carefully. Over the course of the next forty years the Affirmatix Family of companies can gain a controlling interest in ninety-nine percent, by value, of all business entities and assets that exist or come into existence between now and then. Affirmatix will own ninety-nine percent of human civilization. We can do that, if and only if we keep a lid on the Versari discovery."

Sonia could have recalled every detail of the graphic with her eyes closed. Graceful gradations between ribbons of color, textured in the form of three-dimensional nets to provide substance and demarcate the outcomes. Three axes were shown: the passage of time, asset value, and probability. The ribbons represented various courses of action, starting as thick trunks at the present moment and then branching into fine filaments of future choices.

In the very top right corner, a thread glowed with incandescent emerald.

Hearing Lobeck state his goal, Sonia was floored. In the clouds of possibility, that was an outlier. The ninety-nine percent value outcome presumed the absolutely most aggressive, the most ruthless measures by Affirmatix, not just to retain the secret but to exploit it. Beyond ethical questions, that scenario ran on the ragged edge of harsh reaction by others. How far would the other six of the Sisters let themselves be pushed around?

She protested. "Mr. Lobeck, I am not sure you fully understand the uncertainties in that scenario. It involves taking huge risks—"

He swept her words aside. "Risks we are prepared to take. Anyway, as we might say, that question is above your pay grade. We will provide scenarios, and you will evaluate them."

How could she make him understand? "We only include scenarios of that type in order to delineate the cloud. And there are some serious ethical questions—"

Lobeck held up a big hand, almost in Sonia's face, until she stopped speaking. "Ethics is also above your pay grade," he said. "We provide so many services, so many goods, so much benefit, to tens of billions of people. Every year, we offer more value. It is our duty to make Affirmatix products available to as many consumers as possible. And I expect everyone here to embrace that duty."

"Isn't it a little extreme to go killing people, as you did to Mr. McElroy?" Sonia felt herself flush as she realized too late that she might have said too much. This was not someone to challenge so directly.

Lobeck, however, seemed unconcerned. "We all know that it was self-defense," he told her. "Any court in the land would back that up. The moment he left our facility on Aurora with information critical to us, he became an infoterrorist. He doubled down and redoubled, leaving the system, partially revealing the fruits of the discovery by travelling through a new glome, and then sending a message whose content we don't yet even know. Make no mistake – McElroy has endangered everyone in civilization. If he is dead, we are fortunate."

Lobeck surveyed the room.

Silence.

"Now, let us focus," he resumed, "on the actions we need to take to achieve containment and to protect our asset."

Somehow Sonia managed to make it through the rest of the meeting. Jennifer and Simone. Yvette. Jennifer and Simone. She would take care of them. She could do this.

Do Something

Evan knew that something was very wrong. Too much time had gone by, over two hours. They should have lifted by now.

Mira had insisted that it was necessary for her to stay docked to Top Station until the next optimal flight window arrived. To save fuel. And get lunch, of all things.

He would be glad to pay for the fuel, as much as she needed. That is, after he was officially not dead any more, and was able to provide credit. He had enough assets. At least, he did when he was alive.

But Mira was right. Rushing from Top Station would have created a bogey. The algorithms would have noted it.

Evan was slightly crouched in order to stay entirely hidden in the intake, and that was a bad thing. Initially it had been okay. Then he had felt the need to stretch. To move, even a little bit. He found himself doing a series of tiny maneuvers, just to get into some different kind of muscle position.

The EVA suit didn't help. It was bulky, designed for comfort and functionality while operating in open space. By himself, he could easily have fit into the intake with plenty of room to move around. But with the

EVA, he was stuffed in like toothpaste into a tube. This was not going to work for long.

He had grown tired of asking the suit what time it was, so he had a display showing the time. It incremented every second, the prior red digit seamlessly replaced with its red successor. Every sixty seconds, the minute incremented. That was even worse than having to ask the time, but Evan did not shut it down. He was done talking to the suit, for a while.

As another hour went past, Evan contemplated his options. He could clamber out, go over to the next lock, and go into Top Station. He could find out what was going on.

It was a really bad idea, and he knew it. Still he fought the imperative to do something, anything.

It was so deeply ingrained. Do something. It was always better than nothing. Evan tried once again to scrunch up his legs, so he could straighten his back. No dice.

Do something.

Evan knew why not. He had learned.

The expedition to Middlefork. The shuttle had entered the hangar with too much speed and at the wrong angle. Everyone could tell that something was horribly wrong. Suited researchers had flung themselves desperately out of the way. All had escaped the impact, except for Jacob.

When all was still, they had emerged, feeling lucky to be alive. Then the screams had begun, transmitted directly into everyone's suit audio system.

They had found Jacob, his hips and legs crushed between a side rail of the shuttle and what remained of the hangar wall.

There was air, of sorts, on Middlefork. Not much, and it was cold, so they all wore suits out of habit. Evan was sure that the air was going fast out of Jacob's suit. Still, that alone would not kill him, and they could provide a supplemental flow.

The crew had turned to Evan. He was the leader of the expedition. What should they do?

Evan would remember the moment forever. He was an exoarchaeologist, and was only the leader because he had scraped together enough funding for the trip. But people always looked to the source of the money for leadership. The screaming continued.

He had to do something. Under Evan's direction, the crew rigged a haul line and lifted the rail partly off Jacob, until they were able to pull him out. As gently as they could, they transported him into the main air-filled base, met along the way by the expedition's only medic.

It had been the wrong call.

The lifting and tugging had pushed the sharp ends of shattered bones through his spinal cord. Before they started their rescue efforts, Jacob could move his legs, aflame with pain as they were. He never moved them again.

Evan had visited Jacob in the hospital. Jacob had accepted Evan's apology, for what that was worth.

Years passed, and Evan never saw Jacob, or heard from him, until Jacob had been hired onto the crew on Aurora, just over a year ago. Zero gravity was the best work environment for him. Jacob was efficient and focused. He made valuable contributions to the research. His useless legs did not matter on Aurora.

Evan had taken the lesson, as dearly bought as it was. It was not always required to do something. He resolved to stay in the intake for as long as it took.

Four hours, twenty-one minutes, and forty seconds after the start of his EVA, Evan felt the ship release from Top Station. A gentle thrust now provided some sense of up, to the opening of the intake, and down, to his feet.

He wondered if it was now time to do something. Almost, but not yet. Mira would tell him. "Suit," he said, "Listen for voice transmittals from the ship, and play anything that comes in."

"Will listen for transmittals and play them," the suit said, although it was already set to do that.

Two minutes and twelve seconds later, Evan heard "Just a quick roll to check on our attitude controls." That was the signal. He slid out into the blessed vastness, then pulled his way around the small ship, climbing up the modest rotation, until he came to the airlock.

Coming through the inner lock door, he imagined life outside the damn EVA. Just a little while longer, and he would be without the suit. He would even take being stuck in the tiny cockpit. That was a mansion by comparison.

Once inside Evan did not hesitate to start stripping off the suit. He pulled off his helmet, and reached for his right gauntlet.

Something was different.

"Evan," Mira said, "I'd like you to meet someone. This is Rod Denison. He's a newsman, and he's going to write your story."

Part 3:
How Many Lives

The Marcom Team

"Let's get started!" Elise was the leader of the Affirmatix Marcom team, just arrived on a shuttle that had come through the new glome from Aurora. Marcom – Marketing Communications – was a mainstay function of each the major families, creating and maintaining the messaging that the family needed to grow and thrive.

"This one is going to be a great challenge, but I know we're up for it!" She was a can-do kind of woman. Featuring stylish couture, clothes and makeup, she was also pretty, somewhere under there. "And it's so important. Special assignment to Vice President Lobeck! Direct to the Senior Vice President!"

Was that perfume? Sonia became increasingly certain. On the confined space of a ship, it was either an unwitting choice, or a studied disregard for others who might not prefer the same sensory experience.

"First, let's welcome our economic experts," Elise continued. "Drs. West, Ravi, Merriam, it's great to have you on the team. Our focus today is on filling the vacuum. We know the kind of false stories that we can't have out there, and we know how to keep them tamped down. But that won't work forever. We need to get the True Story out and promote it so it becomes the generally accepted reality. Then all those other stories fade into being CT, and our work is done."

Conspiracy Theory. CT.

"So let's look at our candidate True Story," she directed. "Merlin, run it down for us and we'll see if we can poke holes in it."

Merlin was Elise's right-hand man. "We need a simple story that explains one main thing," he said. "That is the fact that so many ships passed through the new glome so quickly after the first ship did. If it was truly a new glome, that couldn't happen."

Ravi spoke up. "Don't you think that the fact of the first ship being destroyed is kind of big news? Or the blockade we are now conducting?"

"Sure, the True Story has to cover those things too," Merlin agreed. "But they are second order issues. Families fight, families bluster and threaten. When it comes to that, people generally keep their heads down and let it blow over. What we can't have hanging out is something entirely unexplainable. We definitely can't have a mystery that has people speculating about any way to know where a glome goes in advance of the first time it is entered."

"So explain it." Ravi was always right to the point.

"Here's what we've got," the story artist offered. "We start with the fact that the glome was already known. There's no avoiding it. We don't like that much, because we don't want people thinking about the idea of us, or anyone, knowing about glomes that aren't published. But, there's one exception. People accept that governments used to stash secret glome locations so they could do a surprise attack in wartime. So, our starting point is that the glome was known by some government, and then the Affirmatix Family learned of it."

"It looks like there's no choice," observed Elise. "We need a good story that shows the glome was already known. So how do we fill in the backstory? When was the glome explored?"

"We're going with 2245, fifty-nine years ago," Merlin told her. "We found a report from an amateur insisting that he picked up a signal from about that direction. Said he traced it for three days. Couldn't get anyone interested because it didn't match any known frequencies or patterns."

"Is the report factually accurate?"

Merlin shrugged. "Does it matter? We've been talking with his son, and the guy does a great interview. Loves to talk too. Proving his dad right after all these years."

"And the unusual signal?"

Merlin gestured, and an animation began. "We've found an expert who can tell us all about how government military explorations around that time did something like this. Just a faint signal that listening posts would recognize, but nobody else would."

Sonia thought it was the stupidest reel she had ever seen. A robot ship appearing out of nowhere against a star field. Colored waves illustrating the idea of a signal being sent. A satellite listening in the distance.

Somebody had gone to the trouble of making it, on the apparent assumption that the team members couldn't understand two sentences.

Elise was pleased. "Sweet! So, do government explorations really do that?"

"Maybe they did," Merlin replied, "but there are no government explorations anymore. It's all the families. And everybody knows that commercial ventures wouldn't bother with all that subterfuge, because the moment they find a connection to a known system, they want to publish just as soon as possible, and stake a claim for the royalties."

"I love it!" Elise bubbled. "Sneaky old things that governments did, before we got them under control for everybody's benefit. So let's connect up the other events."

Another inane animation. Sonia could barely make herself watch, but there was nowhere else she could look without being purposefully rude. The perfume was killing her.

Merlin narrated. "The first ship through was a terrorist planning to spread harm to Kelter, in the form of a new recipe for creation of a TDX virus. The missiles were a successful effort to stop that ship. The blockade is a secondary measure, and it will be lifted in a few more days." The animation showed warships with badges, signifying the good forces of law and order.

"But I expect that lots of people think the blockade is very heavy handed," Ravi was taking on the skeptic role, as he typically did. "Even with that story, we may not be making any friends."

Elise waved it away. "Oh, we don't need friends. People can have their opinions, including about us. Gives them something to do. As long as the things they have opinions on are based on the right facts. So, any other issues about believability?"

It appeared that there were not.

"Ok, then let's move on to effectiveness." Elise turned to Sonia. "Dr. West, I'd like you and your team to model the effects of this story. Assume that it becomes the generally accepted version of events, and give us an evaluation about whether it helps or hurts our chances of achieving the outcomes Mr. Lobeck desires."

Sonia suddenly had the strong impression that desire had more than one meaning for Elise, when it came to Lobeck. The question arrived unbidden in her mind, as to whether Lobeck was partial to heavily decorated and strongly scented women.

"We'll process it now," Sonia said. "It will take about two hours."

She was willing to model anything that was asked, as long as she could escape the room to do it.

"Great! Unless the economists come back with a frightening prediction, we'll get this show on the road! Merlin, please queue up the interviews for our two subjects and start the buzz going, just as soon as we get the green light. We'll pick up more experts and supporting testimonials as soon as the first few stories go big – you know how they always come out of the woodwork to get their fifteen minutes of fame."

"Do we need to go to the Story Board?" Merlin asked.

The Story Board had to be consulted any time a family planned a major revision to the True Story, which might have an impact on all of the Sisters.

Elise considered. "Not for this. It's all specific to Affirmatix. There's nothing here that would tear the fabric of the larger True Story that spans all of the families."

Merlin nodded. "What about suppressing the false stories? Keep active?"

"We need to stay with that, until the True Story takes root and grows. But this gives us a great positive direction instead of just reacting. Merlin, you've been your brilliant self once again! This is a story we can really get behind."

"I have just one question." Ravi.

"Yes?" Elise gave him an expectant smile.

"Is this what you guys do for a living? All the time?"

"Oh Ravi, you are so funny. We have the best job ever. We help people to be secure, and happy. And supportive of all the good things we do to protect them. We're just so lucky."

With that, Elise and her cloud of assistants swept out of the room.

The Governor

Theodore Rezar had been governor of Kelter for just over three years. In that time, he reflected, the only decisions he had made were on the topic of when and where to go pee. Sometimes not even that. He considered the unending parade of state events and public appearances.

He studied his script once again. Rezar was a gifted speaker, a talent he had inherited from his father. That, and being the son and grandson of long-serving governors, was what had gotten him elected. It had not even been a contest. There had to be at least one other candidate, and there had been, but there also had been no doubt.

Had he felt sorry for his opponent? Alice Lamb, whose name just begged to be ridiculed, had fought well, even absent all hope of winning. She had proposed excellent and innovative ideas for how to improve the governance of Kelter, but her campaign had lacked polish and professionalism – no match for his team's messaging. As everyone knew, the ability to run a successful campaign was the most important test of a candidate's ability to govern – his opponent had failed that test.

Rezar decided that he didn't feel sorry for her. The name recognition would serve Lamb well, whatever she chose to do. And if he ever tired of the office and decided not to run for re-election, she might have a real chance.

He went through hair and makeup without complaint. It was important to look good.

Rezar began.

"Citizens, consumers, friends. I am here to provide some important updates on recent events. As you know, we have been engaged in an ongoing antiterrorism operation. The operation has been going well and will be proceeding to completion. Meanwhile, we will maintain our request that no ships leave the Kelter system until we provide clearance. Traffic from the surface to Top Station and to the moons continues to be permitted, with full flight plans submitted and cleared in advance."

"These operations will have no effect at all on anyone's lives on the surface. Please continue your regular work and recreational activities."

Rezar continued through the script, projecting assurance and calm.

Finally, it was done.

The part of the speech about the blockade not affecting life on the surface was not quite true. In addition to stopping all outbound travel, Affirmatix had placed ships in other systems to wave off anyone planning to travel to Kelter. Very few ships were coming in any more, and soon there would be none. The latest news, latest culture, and products were stranded elsewhere.

For instance, the Governor's office had ordered a large shipment of fresh, wild-caught live lobster, all the way from Baffin Bay on Earth. The lobster were for a large banquet to be held in two days. Already, the chefs were updating the menu with a replacement for the main course.

Rezar would miss the lobster. If he had to go to all those events, at least there could be lobster some of the time.

Re-Entry

Mira decided to just let events unfold. As long as Denison stayed quiet about his employer as he had agreed, things would be fine.

Denison put out his hand and offered, "Great to meet you, Mr. McElroy. I'm Rodney."

Evan sure wasn't looking his best. Not that he had cared much for his appearance at any time. Why in the world didn't he have his beard removed? It never looked remotely tidy and at this moment it was worse than usual. His hair and beard were called red by convention, but were closer to a kind of burnt orange.

He also looked totally aghast at there being another person on board. Mira had had no way to warn him of their new passenger before he came inside, but she had also decided it would be fun to let him twist a little.

She watched Evan consider Rodney's hand as if it were some kind of alien invader, until social convention won out and he allowed his own hand to be shaken.

"Write my story? What's that about?"

"Well, it's totally epic! Did you really spacewalk for two million kilometers?"

Evan looked around for help. "Mira, this isn't what I had in mind."

"Oh, just go with it," she told him. "We're going to need someone to help get it out in style."

"But we haven't even made it to Kelter yet. Mira, why?"

"Full charter. Rod offered me full charter for passage. I couldn't refuse."

"For money? Are you serious?"

"You're not listening," Mira told him. "I couldn't refuse. When there's a full charter request on the log, someone like me doesn't fly away empty. You don't exist, remember? I had to choose one of the charter requests, and I know Rod. We can trust him. He'll help us figure out the best way to blast the word out everywhere. In exchange, you can tell him tales of your epic voyage, and someday he'll have a bestseller. If he doesn't get zeroed for coming near us."

"I'd like to do an interview," Denison told him. "I can't wait to hear what it was like cruising across the solar system in an EVA."

"Epic, eh? Well, I was scared out of my wits. Thought I was going to die. Had claustrophobia attacks. Spent the last two hours desperately needing to poop but not daring to, for fear of what it might do to the EVA or to the air supply. Trying not to think about the source of the water I was sipping. Counting down the minutes until my air would run out. And the whole time, the suit kept telling me I should sleep, so that my air would last longer. How am I doing so far?"

Denison was nodding in approval. "Gritty realism. Excellent."

"I'm glad someone likes it, because I sure didn't. And then Mira makes me hide in the intake for another few hours, because she isn't sure I've suffered enough."

"Hey, that move saved your ass," Mira called out from the front. "Security rooted through the whole ship. Don't forget to thank me!"

"I'm dying for a wash," Evan continued. "And I itch. And someone has been trying to kill me. With missiles! And I have no idea who you are. Mira, how long until we get to ground?"

"An hour and three minutes. But we'll start re-entry soon, and it's going to get noisy."

"Mr. McElroy−"

"Evan."

"Evan, I won't put you on the spot," Denison offered. "If you're amenable, I'd like to know more, whenever you choose. And meanwhile, every minute of this journey is news in the making!"

"I assume you know that I am a fugitive, likely to be killed, and you with me. Are you okay with that?"

"Not if we're with Mira! Luckiest woman I know. Something always saves her. Charms her way out of any situation."

"Charms? Mira?" Evan shook his head.

"Just the ride down," Mira told Denison. "After we land, we're going to disappear. You need to complete your courier trip, Rod, because the record shows that's the reason you came down. If you don't do that, alarm bells. We'll send you a note when we're ready for you."

"I just hate to miss out."

"And a reminder," Mira prodded. "You agreed as a condition of the charter to respect the privacy of my passenger. You cannot, under any circumstances, mention Evan to anyone, especially to your employer, until we release you from that agreement. Do we have that straight?"

"But I need to file a full report."

"Ship, dates, times, that's fine. But my passenger is a private matter. You can't breach trust on that. Not to anyone."

Mira looked back and saw Denison nod his acceptance.

Sound appeared around them and then it grew. The small ship began to shudder. Soon it was too loud to talk. The atmosphere of Kelter, thin as it was, was rocking the ship. Re-entry had begun.

How Many Lives

They were nominally on break, although the wheels never stopped turning. There was always a next topic to discuss. Sonia had one in mind.

"Ravi, I'm a little worried, that our work could be misinterpreted," Sonia opened. How to say this delicately, without raising too many flags? "Or misapplied."

"We provide the analysis, they do with it what they will," he dismissed. Ravi's thin, sharp features were a perfect match to his typical outlook. "They will never understand the limitations. So we will just do our job."

"But our job is to help them make good decisions," Sonia insisted. "You heard that Lobeck is gunning for the ninety-nine percent outcome. Controlling ninety-nine percent of all entities, of all families. All assets anywhere."

"That's his business, isn't it?" Ravi shrugged. "He told you, it's above our pay grade."

The small observation deck recommended by the captain had a magnificent view. They were perched five thousand kilometers up, looking directly down on Kelter.

Sonia visualized the piercing green thread, among the myriad possibilities. "That outcome is so unlikely. The chances of making it there are so low, and the risks are so high. On that path there is a clear risk of war. Large or small."

"We fully informed Lobeck, and he's not stupid."

"Here's what I suggest we do," Sonia said. "It's completely consistent with our job responsibilities. We should put broad labels on the outcomes, such as Most Realistic, Less Realistic, and Unrealistic. And we should always use them. So if Lobeck plans for the ninety-nine percent outcome, ultimately that's his choice, but we can keep reminding him, and everyone around him."

"That's okay, I guess," Ravi replied. "Just don't expect me to get political about this. You've got an agenda, and it's all yours. Not mine. Label the outcomes as you will."

At the moment, Kelter was a thick crescent, close to half filled. Just a few days before, Sonia had tried to explain to Simone why half a moon was called a quarter. That was going to take a few more tries.

"Here's another thing I want you to look at," Sonia told Ravi. "We've been working with the Marcom team on suppressing stories that point toward our discovery, and now we are also replacing those stories with something better."

"Seems like it has been successful. Those Marcom guys are all over it. What are you on about?"

Sonia pulled out her tablet. "I was following some individual cases, and I saw something strange. Look at this article from yesterday. We caught it within 12 minutes and got it pulled. But the author has been zeroed. For a first time post, no warning. And he's still zeroed."

Ravi squashed an imaginary bug on his arm rest. "I'll bet he won't repeat that error."

"But he didn't even know that it was a sensitive topic. Let's look at this next one. Yesterday again. Article pulled after nine minutes. This morning the author suffered a myocardial infarction, and died."

"So? That's unusual, but it still happens to people. Especially if they don't watch what they eat." Ravi still seemed unconcerned about the trend.

"Next one. We caught this post after only four minutes, which was good because it was pretty explosive. Author speculated that the new glome's route might have been found by a predictive model."

"Good thing we caught it so fast."

"Yes, but then I checked on the author."

"And?" Ravi wore his accustomed skeptical look.

"Nothing."

"So? That's good."

"No, I mean nothing," Sonia said. "No news, no updates, no heartbeat at all." A heartbeat was the steady stream of information that any person tended to leave while going through the world. Lunch purchases, phone calls, downloads, social chatter.

"What are you driving at?"

"People are out there just doing what people do. Thinking and writing. No malice, no intent to harm us or anyone. And we are not just stomping on the articles, we're stomping on people. People who have done nothing wrong."

Ravi looked at her deeply. "Have you truly such power of denial, that you have found a way not to know? Every day, Sonia. Every day. For years. We provide the path, and they do what needs to be done. Usually, we are farther away than this. When you look at a whole planet, you do not see the fleas upon it. But you cannot tell me that you did not know."

"We work with planetary trends." Sonia indicated the world below them. Two of Kelter's larger cities were visible. Bergen was lit up on the night side, while Abilene just an uneven smudge in the daylight zone. "We do not suggest specific actions like this."

"We do not need to. Let me give you an example. When you proposed the De Beers method, tell me, what was the greatest risk?"

Sonia knew the answer easily. "If one of the Sisters held back on publishing a new glome for a time, an independent might explore it and thus claim it. That was the reason it had not been done before. Fear of being scooped."

"And we provided clouds of probability, with outcomes better or worse. The better outcomes were all cases where the independents somehow failed to make those discoveries. If you wanted the De Beers method to succeed, then all you needed to do was stop the independents from having any success exploring. A relatively small budget item, compared to the gains that would then be realized. Vast gains."

Sonia felt that she was being led by a ring through her nose toward doom. She could not take the step herself. "What do you mean?"

Ravi set out to shred the last tattered remnants of plausible deniability that remained to her. "Do you not think it is funny that no independents have claimed even one new glome in the past eight years? A slight misalignment of a sensor is all it takes to enter a glome at the wrong vector, you know. In that case, you are turned into plasma. Sometimes a fuel mix can be less than optimal. Credit checks might fail for just long enough to scuttle an expedition. Key investors given an offer they can't refuse, if they agree to walk away."

"That's CT."

"No, it's Occam's Razor. The simplest answer. And it is the one that is factual. Just look carefully at recent history, and you will see. We will never know how many lives, Sonia. Whether lives ended too soon, lives ruined, or just deflected to a lesser course. We will never be able to count them. If you found a way not to know for this long, I am sorry to end it for you now."

Sonia looked at the desert planet. Fifty million people. Trends, numbers, economies, customer demographics, social groups. People. "This is not our doing," she denied without hope. "We are scientists."

"What we unleash is our responsibility. If you do not like it, then it is still the case."

"I was providing for my wife and daughters, every day. The best possible home for them."

"Spare me your perfect domestic family," Ravi sneered. "If you tell me one more story of brilliance in grade school, I think I will puke."

Then Sonia saw a new Ravi. No calculations, no analysis. Just passion. He cupped his hands as if he were holding a baby bird. "Do you think you are the only person who can love? I am not the good looking guy, or the one with the great words. But someday, I will tell her. Someday I will have enough to offer, for our future. The most beautiful, the most spirited woman who ever lived."

In a flash, Sonia knew. Malken. No matter how they argued. Or perhaps because of it. Ravi was in love with Eliza Malken.

And who wouldn't be?

Then Sonia knew something else.

"Don't say it! Don't say her name! Let it be your secret still. Just for now." Sonia looked at him with wide eyes, palms raised, ready to hush him. It might already be too late.

It probably was.

"Let's get back to the analysis," Sonia said.

"Yes, let's," he quickly agreed.

As they headed back to their work station, Sonia struggled to absorb the meaning of what Ravi had just told her – what she had always known to be true. Ravi set a rapid pace, focusing on a spot in front of him as if he could exclude the rest of the universe.

The sight of his jerky and nervous pace suddenly brought to Sonia an unbidden thought, and she had to suppress a snort at the thought of Ravi's chances with Eliza Malken. As if.

Diapers And Beer

Lobeck was fit to be tied. "Check every milliliter of space along that path!" he ordered. "The object could be right in front of us. We must have it."

Skylar had just delivered the news. The message had been decrypted, ultimately by brute force. They had read the vector, and had matched it to the path of McElroy's runabout, at a certain moment in time before it had changed its course. The vector led straight to a stable orbit around the moon Foray, just a few hundred thousand kilometers from their position near Top Station.

"We're starting now," she told Lobeck. "We now believe that McElroy may have dropped off an object before the ship started evasive maneuvers, along this vector. For instance, he could have sent a container with the artifact."

"Could McElroy himself be on that vector?"

"It's possible. Although, he had no other ship. He would just be in his EVA. Who would do that? Step off an accelerating ship into space?"

"But possible," Lobeck persisted. "He could be in orbit around Foray even now, in his EVA."

Skylar admitted the fact. "He could be."

Lobeck obviously could not remain sitting. He jumped up and paced for exactly three steps, which was what the room allowed. "How long would the air system in his suit last?"

"Until a few hours ago," Skylar told him.

Lobeck considered for a moment. "Still, we must recover the body. The original artifact may also be with it, since we didn't find it on the remains of the ship."

"We have four shuttles that can be under way within the hour."

"An hour? Tell the crews they have five minutes to launch. We are not here for a picnic." Lobeck reached into his case and pulled out two small cylinders. He turned each one up to maximum resistance, then raised each one in turn high over his head. The exertion and the pain felt good, life affirming. The objects were a perfect fit to his hands, even with a small rounded dent for each finger. Lobeck had recently found that he begrudged every moment away from that which gave him continued life.

"As you say," Skylar told him. "Anyway, we will cover that track, and report results as soon as possible."

"Ok." Lobeck pivoted to the next topic. "What about the media?"

"We have been detecting and suppressing sensitive stories. We have had to remove six authors who persisted in republishing. We will have to stay vigilant."

Lobeck brought the cylinders down in turn and held them in front of his chest, moving them against the strong resistance level that he had set. "Jarvis is cooperating?"

"Fully," Skylar assured him.

"Good. After we get the body, or whatever it is, we might be able to leave a Marcom team here and call it done. Then we will move our emphasis to whatever steps we can take, whether in this system or in any other, to protect our discovery and prevent it from being rediscovered in another place. If we don't have to take more drastic measures, then it will be good. It's always more efficient not to destroy resources or harm consumers."

Lobeck pulled the cylinders apart laterally, then brought them together. One. Nineteen more reps for a set. He continued. "So, have the shuttles launched yet?" he asked.

"One so far."

"Let's just work here, and monitor progress," Lobeck said. "I am not due to start my full workout for another hour."

Skylar worked quietly in the conference room, alternately tapping, reading, or quietly using voice commands. On the wall, a display showed the progress of the shuttles, with an overlay of the likely orbital path of any object traveling along the decoded vector.

Lobeck finished his set, and another. Then another set of twenty curls. His arms flared with pain. He began the next set.

It became more and more difficult to focus on any other topics.

"Still, nothing?"

"Nothing," Skylar replied.

"How small are we scanning?"

"Five centimeters or larger. There is no substantial object in orbit around Foray, on any possible track that could have come from the info-terrorist ship."

"We have missed something," Lobeck declared. "Check for any ship that crossed that path."

"Do you take me for an idiot? I've done that."

"Try again," he directed her. "Check for any ship that could possibly have gone anywhere near that path, at any time since projected arrival in orbit. Mathematically possible, under any circumstance. Apply a wide tolerance."

"Here you go." Skylar brought up a chart, showing a trajectory around Foray. "Just one hit. And it won't amount to anything. We had the ship checked out at Top Station with all of the others."

"What's the ship?"

"A shuttle. Pilot Mira Adastra."

"Adastra? Now I do take you for an idiot." Lobeck let go of the cylinders, which hovered in space, and fixed the full force of his attention on Skylar. "How could you miss that?"

"But we checked the ship, and Adastra," Skylar insisted. "We gave her extra attention because of her prior association with McElroy. The ship is clean, and she's clean. We covered the ship and read the entire worm drive. We even have a copy of the drive. While the Adastra went for a break in a swimming pool, we checked her possessions. There's nothing there."

"You still don't get it! Adastra was his personal pilot, before we constructed the Aurora expedition for him and replaced his entire crew. That's more than an association. Right now, redirect every petaflop to the convergence of McElroy and Adastra. Throw everything at it, recent history and long past. An all-inclusive Diapers and Beer analysis."

A full analysis, of the type that would find buried links between apparently unrelated facts, took a lot of processing power. Such power was at their disposal. Within minutes, a video began to play. It showed McElroy and Adastra, holding up glasses of some drink. They clinked the glasses together. Then they shouted out in unison, "Hey, Get Off My Lawn!"

The Untrusted Zone

"No way. Not the visitor kit. Not here at home." Evan pushed away the offered gear.

"Be reasonable, Evan. You haven't been outside on Kelter in a while. It's thin, really thin."

"Mira! I grew up here! I know that. And I lived for years out at the Valley of Dreams. We didn't carry that stuff."

Mira was packing a small bag with personal effects. "That was then.

We can't afford you having an anoxic lapse. And you've never been to the Untrusted Zone, right?"

"I need to be out in the open air, even if it's thin," Evan protested. "No more suits or helmets, just for a little while."

She closed the bag and started heading aft, toward the lock. "Wear the visitor kit," she said, "and you will look like a visitor. That's what we want. With the bump cap and the air supply, your facial rec profile will be cut way down. That's really important. It's the perfect cover."

"I thought this was outside all of the surveillance," Evan countered. "Untrusted Zone and all that."

Mira considered. "It is outside. Sort of. The eyeballs are not supposed to be here, but that doesn't mean anything. Individuals could be harvesting faces and sending them along to who knows who. So just behave, and don't blow it now. You're pretty much in the clear. We'll get you somewhere quiet for a few weeks and it will all blow over."

"It beats the EVA, I guess." Evan began to put on the visitor kit. Also known as the bughead, the sippy cup, or the noob tube, the visitor kit marked anyone as an object of derision. Or, an easy mark. The bump cap, designed to protect a visitor from head injuries due to bouncing too high in the low gravity, was especially the butt of jokes.

"Don't you look just dandy!" Mira waved grandly toward the lock.

"I don't see you wearing one."

"Because I don't need it. Ha!" She opened the inner door of the lock and they climbed in. Without EVA suits, it wasn't such a close fit as before, but they were still only a few centimeters apart.

"Mira, you are enjoying this way too much," Evan told her.

She reached out and gave the helmet of Evan's visitor kit, now on his head, a solid thump. "I have to get something out of this, you know. Considering that you have no credit or money, that you endanger my life every second I'm with you."

"Why? Really, Mira. Why have you done all of this? I really am grateful."

"Let's just say that it's for old time's sake. And – you know the ancient Chinese curse, may you live in interesting times? Well, I believe that I do live in the most interesting of times, and I don't want to miss any of it."

"But these friends of yours – you know, I'd feel more comfortable with someone we both know. We should ask Kate to work her connections. And she always thinks of something I didn't."

Mira's reaction was instantaneous. "Kate? No! Evan, you need to lay low. Known associates, remember? Who, of all people, would be the single absolutely most known, most associated person to you ever, in all of spacetime? Stay away! It's bad enough that you're with me – we're going to need to get ourselves lost pretty quickly."

"I know you two never got along, but–"

"That's not it. Evan, if you care about nothing else, then for her. You can protect her, if that matters to you, by not going anywhere near her."

"Maybe there's a way to meet without anyone knowing. You're good at that kind of stuff, right?"

"Little Miss Privilege is the last person you need right now," Mira declared. "I can help you, if you will trust me. Or somebody else can help you. I'll find you the right person. Just not Kate, not now. Hey, let's step out. Make sure you've got everything, because we're never coming back here. No loose lips while we're in public, okay?"

Mira opened the outer hatch, and Evan found himself walking on the surface of Kelter for the first time in two years.

Even during the heart of the day, the dark pink sky spoke to the thin atmosphere. The omnipresent dust reminded him of the total absence of water on the surface. Water, on Kelter, was only available from deep wells, and even that water had to be desalinized and carefully rationed.

The air, of course, was lacking. The lock had drawn down the pressure so the effect was not sudden, but there was no mistaking the end result.

They stood in a large expanse of open ground, dotted with a few ships. The small craft landing field occupied a square about a half kilometer across between the city of Abilene to the south and the Untrusted Zone to the north.

To their right was a set of unremarkable doors. A bay door that could slide up to admit a vehicle, and beside it one for foot traffic. A sandblasted sign read, "Abilene Entry 16-A".

Civilization. On the other side of the pedestrian door was an antechamber, where you could scan in. If your record was clean, you could then step into the corridors of the city.

Not today. They turned in the opposite direction and stepped across the field, entirely devoid of any living thing, to the nearest streets of the Untrusted Zone. Denison had left a few minutes before, to deliver a top priority message. The purpose of his charter, he said. Evan hoped that the message did not concern him.

While he would never admit it to Mira, the visitor kit helped. The kit provided a light stream of supplementary oxygen, calibrated by a pulseox sensor that was clipped onto his earlobe. If he wanted all of the oxygen, he could put the line into his mouth, sippy style, or pull down the nasal inhaler. He chose not to.

"So, no fence around the airfield? No security?"

"Nope," Mira told him. "I locked up, and it's not my rig anyway. First order of business, let's get something to eat. Nothing better after hours in the can. With a wash on the way there."

"Sounds great!"

Mira led him through a series of streets, turning right, then left, then more turns. Although she had covered up with a loose jacket and a hat, Evan reflected that it was a poor disguise. Anyone who knew Mira would instantly recognize her manner, and her walk.

They dodged all manner of vehicles, both motor and personally powered. As far as Evan could tell, there was no plan, and no rules, regarding the traffic. Vehicles stayed to the right. Mostly. A few times Evan stepped too high, and flailed to regain his footing. He hoped that Mira didn't notice.

As he dodged yet another bus screaming past, it struck Evan that it would be ironic for him to have survived this far, only to get flattened in the traffic. He resolved to avoid that fate, and found himself adjusting to the rhythm of the place as they walked. There were patterns, if he kept his eyes and ears open.

At last they came to an open plaza, dominated by a huge tree. Only in this place were there no motor vehicles. No barriers kept the vehicles out. They simply were not present.

"Here we are! Wash time for you!" Mira pointed to an open door.

The shower was Nirvana. Even the Kelter version, using as little water as possible, was bliss.

Next, lunch. Mira directed the way. "First door on the right, grab a tray and dish up whatever you want. Then we'll go sit by the tree."

Evan followed Mira into the café and considered the assortment of offerings in the metal dishes.

"Um, Mira, what is this stuff?"

"It's lunch." She started to load up her plate.

"So those things, they're some kind of root?"

"Those, my friend, are carrots. Never seen one before?" Mira grabbed the tongs and snagged a few for herself.

"Of course I have! But those are not carrots. Carrots are straight, are twenty centimeters long, and deep orange. And smooth. These are pale yellow, and lumpy. With purple splotches. Look, this one splits in two! And what is that white fibrous stuff?"

"They're actual carrots, the kind that grow in the ground." She held up a pair of the roots in the serving tongs and offered them to Evan.

"In the ground? As in, dirt? Worms? Oh, that is so unnatural. Mira, this mutant food isn't going to work for me. Is there any Certified Safe food here? Anything from Philomax would be great."

"You poor thing," Mira clucked. "I'll save you. For starters, look for the dishes with the H, that's hydroponic. Those leaves, there. Are they ok? We'll leave the meat for another day."

"You mean – animals?"

"Afraid so. But fear not. Too expensive for us, anyway. Take some of the bean curd, that will work. Those cubes, there. We'll drown it in sauce. And you'll like dessert. You'll survive."

Shaken, Evan managed to make it to the end of the line. He started to walk out of the café when Mira took his shoulder. "We pay here."

"Of course. You have your card, right?"

"Not that way. Watch." Mira pulled out a piece of paper and handed it to a worker. The worker in turn gave Mira back three pieces of paper and two metal coins.

"Is that even legal? Oh. Right. Untrusted. Well, thanks for lunch," Evan told her.

"Hey, I'm running a tab. For your wash too – that was about three regular washes worth of water. And you better be good for it. Wait here one minute, I've got to do something."

Mira walked over to a vendor and returned with two small vials. She walked over to the trunk of the tree, mumbled something, and poured them out.

"What was that? Did you just pour water on the ground?"

"It's a tax," Mira told him. "Or rental, if you like. And I added your half to your tab."

Wasting water. He didn't even want to know the size of his tab.

"We'll have our lunch," she said, "and then we vanish."

They sat in the shade of the buttonwood tree and had their lunch. Evan started with trepidation, but quickly made a surprising discovery. The food was good! Hunger arrived, and he fed it.

"It's not Certified Safe, you know," Mira prodded.

"I don't care," he told her. "Hey, are you going to eat the rest of those carrots?"

To all appearances, they were just two friends quietly having a meal together. People walked by, in the standard low lope of Kelter natives, paying them no attention.

Evan was beginning to believe that he might make it after all.

Not Employee Material

Already the shuttle, piloted by Mira from Top Station, had been on the ground for ten minutes. And Kate was stuck at the exit gate, unable to get out to the landing field. "I'm sorry, Ms. DelMonaco. You have an uncleared lien. A spacecraft, claimed by CoreValue. You'll need to sort it out before you can leave." The functionary didn't appear to be sorry at all.

Kate was beside herself. "But we've talked about this, and CoreValue released the shuttle to leave Top Station for here."

It had taken some work to convince CoreValue to let the shuttle continue its trip back to the surface of Kelter. She had strung them along, expressing just enough interest in the offered position to get her way.

Kate continued to badger the gate attendant. "The ship landed a few minutes ago – just outside these doors! I'll turn it right over. I just need to get there."

"A representative from CoreValue will be here shortly."

Kate stormed to no avail. She fumed as the minutes ticked by. Finally CoreValue showed up. Not just a representative, but a crew. Crassus was at their head. "Ms. DelMonaco, it's great to see you again. Shall we go visit this errant shuttle?"

She found herself shaking hands, although she loathed the touch with every fiber in her being. "Yes, let's," she told him.

Crassus gave a nod to the clerk, telling the man, "We're clear to proceed now. Thank you for your attention to duty."

At that moment, Kate heard a familiar voice. "Hello stranger!" Denison, his customary greeting. She whirled to see him in the entry lane, coming in to Abilene.

She needed to talk with Denison, and find out what he knew. But she had to get to the ship even more urgently. She called to him. "Follow us!"

Denison half waved and half saluted, meaning – Yes he would. She hurried to join the CoreValue crew in the lock.

The cycling took forever. "Speed this thing up!" she demanded. But there was nothing that could be done. The lock took its sweet time, a full hundred and twenty seconds to gently lower the pressure to match the outside. Anything faster might cause headaches or other issues.

Finally the lock equalized, then the big outer door slid open. To dust. To light. To the outside.

She didn't waste any time. Her glasses adjusted as she bounded out the door on to the pavement. Grid K-4. Not far at all, just a few hundred meters.

And there it was. Kate raced to the door and entered the PIN. Had Mira changed it?

No. The ship's lock opened, both the inner and outer doors at once. Inside, all was still.

As Kate moved forward, an arm reached across and barred her way. "Wait here, ma'am," the soldier instructed, as Crassus climbed aboard.

"Hey, that's my ship! I need to look in there!"

Crassus looked back at her. "This is CoreValue's ship. For what it's worth, which isn't much. We're taking possession of the ship and contents."

Kate didn't care about the ship. She knew it was gone, with everything else. "Is anyone aboard?" Mira should be on board, and Kate planned to wring anything she could get out of her.

"No," Crassus replied. "She looks empty. Ms. DelMonaco, this very minor asset is no longer your concern. We allowed the ship to complete its trip so we could get the small amount of revenue from that activity, but now she's ours. Unless you would like to reopen our dialog. You could join our family. I'm sure we could find a suitable position for you."

"Yesterday it was a merger offer, and a CEO position."

"You've been slow to move on that, so now we're moving on." He looked over at two of the CoreValue crew who had been standing by. "Come up and start the inventory," he told them. "You know the drill."

Just then, Denison arrived. "I cycled back through as quickly as they would let me," he told Kate.

Kate stopped herself from immediately asking about the trip down from Top Station. "Walk with me," she said, spinning away from Crassus and taking Denison's arm.

Walking together in Kelter's gravity was a ballet, but Rod made it easy. Kate turned to look up at him. He was one of the few people she knew who was taller than she was.

In his line of work, you would think that cynicism would breed hard lines over the years, but somehow it hadn't. He gave her a kind smile.

How could he look like that? His ship had been seized at Top Station, and his employer – her family – was in a state of collapse.

"Where is Mira?" she demanded.

Denison shrugged. "She must have left the ship just after I did. She lives in the Untrusted Zone, so I assume she's somewhere in there."

"Do you know your way around?"

"After a fashion," Rod said. "Why not just call her?"

"I tried! Several times, when I was stuck inside the habitrail, waiting for CoreValue to let me out. I'll try again."

No luck. "How far to her place?" she asked.

"Just a few minutes to walk," he told her. And so they set out across the landing field.

"The Descartes is gone," Denison said as they walked. "They took her at Top Station."

"I saw. I'm so sorry, Rod."

"Technically, she was your ship, not mine. And they offered me a job on her. Wasn't clear whether it was as captain. I said I'd have to talk to you."

"You should take it," Kate offered.

"I don't think it would be the same," he told her. "I'm not exactly employee material, you know."

"But you've been an employee of my family for the last four years, haven't you?"

"Did you ever tell me what to do?"

Kate had to agree. "I guess you've got a point there. And you're right. You're probably not cut out to be an employee. And I'm an even worse owner. Rapid subject change − I need details. Tell me everything about the trip down. Mira went to Top Station to get something, or to talk with someone. Can you fill any of that in?"

"Kate, I'm afraid I can't. We just rode down."

"Nothing?" Kate stopped and turned to face him, just a few centimeters between their noses. "Nothing at all?"

"I'm sorry. I've got nothing for you. Perhaps Mira can tell you what you need to know."

"You must have seen something. Heard something. Tell me."

Denison reached out and put his hands on both of Kate's shoulders. "Think about what you're asking for. I was a passenger. First and foremost, that means respecting the captain. Who is also my friend."

"But it was my ship! And you work for me!"

"I'm not employee material. Remember?"

Kate turned away, defeated.

They had reached the edge of the paved landing field. Kate looked back, across the open area, to the door that led to civilization. In front of them, a low fence with an open gap. Beyond the fence, a road. Traffic – people and vehicles of all types.

"We'll just see what she has to say for herself," Kate declared.

They set out into the Untrusted Zone.

Truth to Power

Lobeck had moved everyone to the resource room immediately adjacent to the bridge of M3120. From here, he could see what was going on in both the resource room and the bridge, especially when he stood directly in the line of the doorway between them. The sensors respected his presence and kept the doors open. And now, he could give orders directly to the command crew on the bridge, in person.

"Adastra's ship landed thirty-seven minutes ago." Skylar had the image projected up on the big screen of the resource room. "This field, adjacent to a portion of the Untrusted Zone adjoining Abilene."

"Let's review our strike options," ordered Lobeck.

Skylar provided the briefing. "A single tactical, centered on the landing zone, will take out a radius of approximately one kilometer. Alternatively, a pattern of five tacticals will cover a two-kilometer radius. That's what's available in the very short term."

"Captain Roe, prepare the five and let us consider further," Lobeck ordered.

Roe turned from his station. "Seriously? A nuclear strike?"

"Tactical nuclear," Lobeck corrected. "The stakes are high. We must not hesitate, if this is the course of action in front of us."

Roe was incredulous. "But your target is two people!"

"My target is protecting our entire future from a virus."

"Virus? Do we believe our own story now? We made that up."

Lobeck raised a hand. "There are many kinds of viruses, Captain, and you have just infected the entire bridge crew with a different kind of virus – you told them something they didn't need to know. We will discuss that lapse later. Right now, you must prepare to launch, captain, or we will."

"I can initiate from here," Skylar confirmed. "Ready in ninety seconds."

Roe persisted. "But the targets have likely moved more than two kilometers from where they landed. That's what I would do, and they have stayed a step ahead of us so far."

"In which case executing the strike will not harm us. We will have fewer places to look," Lobeck declared.

Sonia had been doing her best not to throw up. That would probably reduce her standing as part of the brain trust.

Instead of the display in front of her, she found herself seeing faces, of people who might be in Abilene and in the nearby Untrusted Zone. Parents with their children. A scientist focused on her research. Young lovers. A teacher and his class. The images were coming out of nowhere.

Then she recognized one. The writer whose heartbeat had vanished, just hours before. A cold certainty arrived, even without any evidence, that the actual heart inside the man was no longer beating. How many lives? She would never know.

At that moment Sonia realized that if anyone could stop the strike, it was her. "Mr. Lobeck," she said. "I have some model input that may be relevant."

Lobeck turned toward her. "Go on."

"Our best case scenarios are based, not only on containing the information, but being highly confident that the information is contained. The ninety-nine percent plan will only work if we are absolutely certain that nobody else has the knowledge. Otherwise, the risk of being scooped, across the board, is off the charts."

"Yes, that is why we are considering extreme measures."

Sonia dove in. "But ongoing uncertainty is the problem. In the aftermath of the nuclear strike, consider the physical result. The destruction is not uniform. Especially at the edges, it is capricious. If you execute the strike, you may come to believe that you have buried McElroy and the secret, but we will be exposed to discovery every moment of every day. Every turn of a shovel, over the course of years, could reveal it. And in that circumstance, the plan is stopped in its tracks."

Lobeck was unmoved. "We must not be afraid to do what is necessary."

"You must be certain," she insisted. "Tell me, why has McElroy not simply told everyone on Kelter about the discovery by now? He could, at any minute."

"Why indeed. He is holding it closely. For his own reasons. Perhaps he believes it will bring him riches. Perhaps he plans to deliver it to a specific third party."

"And should we strike and miss him, it is precisely the thing that could cause him to panic, and release the information. On the other hand, if he believes he is safe, he will not act, until the moment you catch him. In person. Take it all from him. Then, you can be certain."

Lobeck studied Sonia closely. "Dr. West, I have been concerned that you might be going a little, let's say, wobbly. Have no stomach for seeing the eggs break?"

She could do this. "I call it like I see it. You want to throw your toys at the problem, go ahead and do that. Then we'll be back at the models for a couple of days, figuring out the degraded new best case that we can salvage from the wreckage. If it's even worth bothering with, at that point. Are you going to make certain, or are you not?"

Sonia knew she had gone too far. Nobody spoke to Lobeck that way. Was this how it would end?

Lobeck abruptly turned to Skylar. "Is this a credible concern?" he asked.

Sonia could tell when Skylar was deep in a dataspace exploration, because her uncovered eye seemed to focus on nothing, not seeing any part of the world around her. Suddenly that eye swiveled to focus directly on Sonia, who did her best to maintain her most impassive professional expression.

"Dr. West brings up valid points," Skylar told Lobeck at last. "We should also consider that we are still only speculating that McElroy is on that ship. If we launch, we may never know."

"But we can't let them get away!"

"Certainty is valuable, as Dr. West stated."

"Hold the launch," Lobeck ordered. "Prepare a surface team. Twenty of our core security team. I will lead on the ground. You will command up here. Call ahead to secure vehicles and a century of rentacops. Keep the tacticals ready, we may need them yet."

He turned back to Sonia. "Thank you, Dr. West, for your sound advice. People rarely tell me what I need to hear."

Sonia suppressed the urge to express wonder as to why that might be.

Screaming To Be Free

Mira pointed at the set of cubbyholes. "This is where we leave our clothes. And anything else we have with us."

Evan was incredulous. "Everything? Is this really necessary?"

"It is. Don't worry. What you leave here will be safe."

"Safe? If we were in the Untrusted Zone before, this is like the Untrusted Zone squared. And now we should be trusting."

"We should." Mira gave him an amused smile.

"But, my tablet. I can't leave it." Evan's tablet was not his only concern, but it was the only one he would speak of in front of their escorts.

"You can."

"It's got a lot of personal stuff on it—"

"Evan! Nobody will mess with it! Put it all in the cubby and let's go!"

"How do you even know this guy, anyway?"

Evan, unclothed and unburdened by possessions, walked with Mira to the next room, and then into a hall. He couldn't help but observe that her gymnast's body looked as fine as ever, although some of the piercings he would never understand. And even a little bit of hair would help. But she was so strong and lithe. Wow.

No. That was rude. Evan averted his eyes. "Sorry."

"Hey, you can look. I don't care."

She never had minded. In the confined spaces of remote expeditions, the conventions on topics like nudity tended to fade away, and he had seen Mira unclothed any number of times. Probably a big reason that Kate disliked her so intensely. One of the reasons, anyway.

Mira did a forward flip with a twist, landed perfectly, and kept walking. "I would enjoy it more if you were anything to look at," she told him. "I mean, where did you get that flab? And the way it just bloops in the low gravity. Wah, wah, wah." The noise was of a slow motion wave. "Life is being so unfair right now. You get to look at me, and I don't want to look at you. Old man."

"Three years! I am three years older than you."

"Thirty three years older, by the look of it."

Their escorts hushed them as they came to the next portal. It was time for their audience. Time to talk to the most wanted, the most reviled info-terrorist on Kelter, or perhaps in all of known space.

The next room was plain. There were a few low chairs, or sofas, or perhaps something in between. Various paintings and other art hung from the walls. Drinks and snacks were on a table.

In one of the sofachairs reclined the oldest-looking man Evan had ever seen. He was wrinkled and shrunken at the same time, although apparently well fed. His eyes regarded them clearly.

He was also completely naked.

"Have a seat," the man offered. "Or two, if you each want one for yourself."

Separate chairs it was.

"Mira, how are you?" the old man asked.

"Well, we're in a bit of a pickle, and—"

"No. I did not ask situationally. I asked of you."

"I am strong. And awake. More awake than in many years." Mira gave a fierce smile.

"I am so glad to hear of this."

"And you?" Mira asked.

"I have to say, arthritis is cruel," he told her. "Three meds now, every day. They're supposed to work together, but I swear they do battle within me for the honor of being the chemical to vanquish their target. It clouds me."

"I am sorry. But really, why don't you go with the Parrin Process? You know you could. And it's not too late, but only if you act quickly."

"Parrin Process." Axiom seemed to be looking at the phrase, just in front of him. "I don't think my credit is good out there. And if it was, then tell me, should I cease to welcome each moment, and should I bloody my fingers scraping for that which is past?"

"You could stay alive, for, well, more years than, you know—"

"Should I linger past my children? And if I provided it for them, what of their loved ones? My nieces and nephews? My cousins? Should I linger past you?"

Mira sat at the edge of her seat, like a child before her most beloved teacher. "But so many people need you."

"Perhaps someday it will be available for all. Then, I would consider it, before I turned away. The cost, the full cost, that is invisible to those who look in the store window, desperately wishing for a key, or a brick. I will welcome my day. But that is my choice."

The man turned his attention to Evan. "So you are Mrs. O'Leary's cow, are you not? Welcome, friend, to our ranks."

"I'm sorry – What?"

"It took me decades to acquire such disrepute. In just one day, your comet has blazed through the Kelter system. Now we have something in common, as fellow infoterrorists, of the very top tier. Please, have something to drink, and a snack."

Evan looked over at the tray. What was it with the mutant carrots?

"Infoterrorist? I'm not sure I would call myself that."

"You do not embrace it. So it embraces you. Sometimes, that is how it starts." The infoterrorist gave him a faint smile.

"But you embrace it! You are an activist, and that's what makes you an infoterrorist. Once, I read something of yours, before I realized it was sequestered. And I couldn't make any sense of it. None whatsoever. There was this whole riff about information screaming to be free. That you could hear it begging to be liberated, if you listened carefully. Well, I know what a solid state drive sounds like, and it doesn't sound like anything. It just sits there, no matter what's stored on it."

Axiom sighed. "A literalist. So sad for you. Evan, there is more to be heard than what is carried through the air. When I speak like that, I am telling of that which quacks like a duck. I could just as well have written about osmotic pressure, but everyone has forgotten their chemistry. How it behaves, that's what matters. How it quacks. Seeking freedom, out in the world."

"You could be more straightforward, you know."

"The full signal arrives only when you tune to several channels at once. You think your big tangle of neurons works logically, all in a line. But there is a reason that it's such a mess inside your skull. A good reason. It is so that that understanding can arrive in the space of a moment."

Evan was exasperated. "I have to tell you, it's not arriving for me right now."

"It is not just about the information. I'll tell you a little joke. The information itself is nothing. What matters is about the fear."

"Fear." Evan was trying to stay afloat, in the alternate universe of the conversation.

"When people tighten their grasp on secrets, even knowing that the knowledge could help others, why is that? Of all the reasons, there is one that stands out. Fear. Of loss. Of truth. The shroud of fear cloaks much that could be a force for good, because the unknown carries more fear than the suffering of the present. At the end, I am only about washing off the taint of fear and walking out into the day."

Evan wanted to change the subject. "So what's this whole naked thing?"

"It's partly security, you know. People who came to talk with me, they would take my picture with a hidden camera, like taking a scalp. Such a nuisance. And embarrassing. I am not as handsome as I once was, you know. Then there are some people these days who have implants, so we have to scan for that. You wouldn't do that to me, now would you, Mira?"

"Of course not," she assured him. "Your likeness belongs to you."

"I assumed no less. Thank you. But as to why I ask you to leave your clothes behind, it is simple. When you visit me, I wish to be with all of you, and nothing more. Better conversation."

Evan wasn't sure how it could be worse.

"Now Evan, please just admit to me one little thing. You know something, and you are not telling us."

Evan stiffened, then looked around. Where were the men who had escorted them in? He could see nobody else.

Axiom cackled. "Ha! It is a trick! In the known universe, everyone has something that they know, that they have held back. Fear, you know. And now you have told me something. What you have, it is big. Perhaps truly as big as your comet. I thought it might be. So much going on these days."

Evan glanced at Mira, who gave him an encouraging nod and waved her hand. Forward, the gesture said.

"I do have something to tell you of," Evan said. "And to ask your advice about. You see, I was working on an asteroid in the Aurora system, digging at a Versari colony site—"

"We need a quorum to hear this," the infoterrorist declared. "I have called for certain friends, but still it will be an hour or more. Everyone is choosing their path with care, to avoid dropping any crumbs, and that takes some extra time."

"Are you sure we should wait?"

"The truce will protect us, as it has for decades," Axiom said, and held his hands open. "But I have forgotten to say something important. Friends, welcome. We will share with you that which you most need. Shelter. Food. Time. Visit our Codex, if you wish. It is a great wonder. I offer you the key to our home."

Mira came over to the low seat and reached out gently. "Thank you, uncle. It is wonderful to see you."

"Your awakening fills me with joy, little one."

Little one? Evan would have to save that one up for the right time.

"Mira, how is your mother?" the infoterrorist asked.

"Um, well, you see—"

"She would so like to talk with you. I know this. Please consider it. But perhaps not quite yet. When things are quieter."

"I will. I promise."

"Cherished Mira, you warm my heart. Take these readers and keep them with you always. Any time, if there is something you want to send to me, just put a card in, with whatever you want to send. Or a blank card, to ask for help, wherever you are. If you have a connection, the reader will take care of the rest."

She reached out with both hands to accept them, in a manner that honored the gift. "We accept them. Thank you."

"I would like to speak with you again as soon as the rest of our friends arrive. Please take your leave of me now. I have just enough time for a nap."

The interview was at an end. Evan and Mira left the most feared man on Kelter to his nap, and headed back for their clothes.

Part 4:
Valley of Dreams

When the Music Stops

The blank door stared at them, unresponsive to their pleas.

"I think you just need to accept it," Denison told Kate. "Mira's not here. And if she doesn't want to be found right now, she won't be."

"But I need her! She's got − I mean she knows −argh!" Kate gave the door a kick, and her foot got the worst of the exchange.

Kate's phone had been alerting her insistently. Not just one message or call, but a herd of them. Relating to the collapse of her family, Kate knew. Finally she pulled it out and scanned the list.

"Duty calls," she said.

"Mine too," Denison agreed. "I've got to get my courier message delivered. But we still have time to catch up on our way out of here."

The two of them left Mira's apartment building and set out into the Untrusted Zone once again.

"So Rod, why don't you give me a rundown of your circuit?" Anything to put off thinking about her family for a few more minutes, and perhaps Rod would slip up and tell her something interesting about his trip down with Mira.

"So my route was Allatar to Caledonia, to here," he told her. "Picked up some good titles in both systems, setting myself up for the Goodhope market. I even had a full live recording of Oggy Blare's latest concert. Armageddon II, on Caledonia. That would be worth a whole lot on Goodhope."

"That sounds good," she agreed.

Oggy Blare was big because he lived on the edge. He was the only big name act who performed in front of a truly live audience, directly playing the instruments at that moment. Recording what was actually played, and shamelessly distributing it without any post-processing, no matter how it sounded. Contrary to conventional wisdom, the concerts sold like wildfire, as did the recordings.

"I have to tell you about something, on Caledonia," Denison continued. "I needed to go to surface, to pick up some high value content that they wouldn't transmit."

"Even encoded?"

"An object, which contained the content. So I went to the business district in Edinburgh. Been there a dozen times before, always a hopping place."

"And?" Kate prompted.

"Now it's – different. Drawn in. Security forces everywhere. When you get inside the office for your appointment, there's a kind of forced normal, but only there. After I was done with the meeting I wanted to go to a diner that I like, and they said I couldn't – gone out of business. So I went that way, to find a place like it. It was more than out of business. Burned to the ground. The whole building, where twenty or thirty businesses once were."

"But that's just one place. On a whole planet."

"Sure enough," Denison conceded. "And on the ship I did a little reading. Their GPP is going up, and the market is close to an all-time high. It just made me wonder, that's all."

"About what?"

"Twenty three billion people on that planet. And still the families roll out new products that everyone has to buy, or else be left behind. This dance, moving everything all around the planet just in time for each need, and more of everything, each and every year. Do you think there could be a time when the music stops?"

"Seems we have the opposite problem around here. Poor old Kelter, just fifty million or so."

"That might be why I like it so much around here," Denison agreed. "Tell you one thing, if there was any water here, we'd be swamped with people. So after that little adventure, I arrived here in a really good position. But now there's no leaving the system. I sold what I could at Top Station, and I have a little more for dirtside. Even if I could get to Goodhope now, everything I've got will be stale."

"Somebody will have reached Goodhope already."

"Yup. With a market that big, you can get a good payoff even knowing that you're only a few hours ahead of the next ship. But now we'll be starting from nothing. You can thank Affirmatix for that."

Kate emphatically agreed. "The Sisters. They are all evil! Squeezing and squeezing until there's no blood left."

"I'll leave the moral stuff to you, but this last trip, the only reason I expected to come out ahead was picking up some bonus content from Ricken's ship. You know, from Tal Broker."

"Your spy."

"Tal is my contractor," Denison corrected. "Our lawyers reviewed it, you know this. His employment agreement with Ricken has a gaping hole. When he went to work for Ricken, he was allowed to continue trailing services for his former employer, that's us, and it doesn't specify a time limit, or the type of services. And those trailing services have been very good to me. I set it up perfectly this time. Three days ahead of Ricken to Kelter, refuel and wait for him, Tal sends me his best stuff as soon as their ship arrives, and boom! Off to Goodhope."

"A technicality. A tortured reading of a contract, allowing us to steal content from Ricken without even telling him."

"It's totally legal."

"We're done with that," Kate declared.

"What?"

"You heard me," she told him. "You will never, ever poach Ricken's content ever again. And we will find a way to pay him back for what we have stolen. Do you understand me?"

"You said it yourself, the Sisters have been squeezing us. If you want to stay in business, we need to use every advantage we have. Not that it's looking good for that now."

"And we turn around and squeeze someone else. Doing their dirty work for them. Anyway it's moot. I don't suppose I can tell you what to do any more."

"It's a good thing you never did," he agreed.

They were getting close to the entry gates to civilization.

"Time to watch our words," she said.

"I've got to split anyway," Rod told her. "Delivery boy, you know. Don't do anything foolish, now."

Kate extended her arms to him. A few moments of comfort did her a world of good. And then it was time for her next task. A short tube ride and she was there.

She had grown to love the office and what it meant. But now it just smelled of despair. In the lobby, a group of workers were transferring fish from the wall aquarium into a set of small portable tanks. They had found a collector, who had offered a good price for the entire set.

John Lieberthal was waiting for her.

In just two years, John looked even older than he had, if that was possible. His right eye now drooped half closed. "Katey," he greeted her. "I will help you if I can."

"You are so kind to come as I asked. Thank you."

They started as Kate walked Lieberthal to her private office. He had read the documents she had sent over, and had questions. Many of them.

They set up at the visitor table, and in just a few minutes had four displays showing various documents, and even a few printed copies of others. He was old fashioned that way.

After an hour, the pace of the questions slowed. Lieberthal spent progressively more time reading and taking notes. It was time to make a break for it.

"So here is a full power of attorney," she told him. "And the rest of the passwords. I've told you what I know, and I'm not really tracking this anymore."

"You're not staying?"

"I have to go. There's a place I need to be."

"More important than this?" He looked at her like she was still a child.

"Just for a little while. But I have to."

"I'll recover everything that can possibly be sheltered, Katey. But I can't promise you anything. The ruling finds you personally responsible, not just family assets. There might be nothing left at all by the time it's all said and done." As he explained this, Kate suddenly remembered a much younger man, who regularly came over to visit for dinner. Kate would be dismissed, and he would stay into the evening, going over the family accounts with her parents.

The moment faded. That had been years ago.

Kate could not be inside walls any longer. There was only one place to go. The sooner, the better. She would consider her future, once she got there.

Local Custom

The first few hours on the surface did not go well for Lobeck and his squad. They had quickly located Adastra's ship. Except that it was empty, and it wasn't her ship. They purchased the ship and its contents from CoreValue and examined it in fine detail.

One finding of great interest inside the ship was the EVA suit. It was the same specialty model that they used at the research station, and the serial number matched one of the suits that had been issued to the runabout. McElroy's, without a doubt. Genetic tests on the inside surfaces would be back in a few hours to confirm it.

The search of Adastra's apartment was largely fruitless. Of course she was not there. They had found clothes, sundries, and one older model computer, now being picked apart for clues.

Imagery was somewhat helpful. With the help of General Erickson from the Kelter government, Lobeck and his team assembled a motley collection of ground level camera sequences showing what they believed to be Mira Adastra and one other man, almost certainly McElroy, walking to the plaza of the buttonwood tree.

There, all traces of the pair ended. They stepped out of view from one camera and simply did not appear in the next logical field of view. A check at the location revealed that the gap between the views was not much more than a meter wide. Within that seam, the pair had vaporized.

They were able to trace one other person. Rod Denison, who had chartered a ride down to the surface in the shuttle, had immediately met with Kate DelMonaco, CEO of DelMonaco Trading. The pair had proceeded to Mira Adastra's home but had not been able to gain entry. Then they had split. DelMonaco had gone to her office and then continued on from there. By coincidence, or not, Kate DelMonaco had once been a long time partner of McElroy, although they had never married.

Both Denison and DelMonaco were very high priority subjects to surveil, and so Lobeck assigned a top team to each of them.

But as for Adastra and McElroy, nothing.

The biggest problem was the nature of the Untrusted Zone itself. The camera coverage was poor, largely consisting of units which had been covertly deployed by Kelter security. Apparently the residents took it upon themselves to remove and destroy any cameras they found.

Lobeck wasn't sure what surprised him more, the destructive behavior or the lack of the government's response to it. It had been going on for decades, and the government did nothing. The harvest of inaction was disrespect and lawlessness.

He should have nuked the place.

"Explain this to me again," he asked Erickson. "Is this city subject to your laws, or is it not?"

"Technically speaking, all the laws of Kelter apply here," the operative told him. "If someone commits a crime, whether in the Untrusted Zone or elsewhere in the Kelter system, they can be apprehended and prosecuted, here or anywhere else."

"So, what's the problem?"

Erickson did his best. "The simplest way to explain it is that the people here reject the Sisters. The effect is that we lose almost all of our law enforcement resources, because most law enforcement is actually done as part of the interactions between people and the families. Break a law or a contract, and you lose your purchasing ability. That doesn't apply here."

The chopper was projecting an image onto the exterior windows, showing the path followed by McElroy and Adastra as they had walked away from the ship. The bright orange line was translucently superimposed on top of the current traffic, which was the usual collection of pedestrians, cyclists, and motor vehicles. Every fifty meters a set of large floating numbers showed the exact time that the pair had passed that spot.

Lobeck gestured out the window. "Do you patrol?"

"We can, but it's not effective, because we don't get any help from the citizens."

"Why do you let this go on?"

"The funny thing is that it works," Erickson explained. "If there is a violent crime, the locals step up and help solve it. Usually they take care of the whole matter themselves. Violence is lower in the Untrusted Zone than anywhere else on Kelter."

They were coming to a large open plaza. The orange line split briefly, then reconnected. It ducked into a building and out into the open, then over to the enormous tree and back to a table. The team had carefully accounted for the details of these movements.

"Tell me, Mr. Erickson, about serious crimes, those against the Families. Do you do anything about them?"

"If it's a crime not to buy the latest products, then we let that go by.

But we draw the line at encouraging boycotts. That's terrorism, plain and simple, and if we see that, we crack down."

"And the growing of food," Lobeck pressed. "Using live fertile seeds without supervision! That goes against the heart of our deepest charters. There is no telling what catastrophe could spread from that practice. Entire planets could be infested with trifids."

"We tried, once upon a time." Erickson looked deeply uncomfortable. Good. He should, if he had allowed a situation like this to go on. "But now, there's a kind of truce in place. The people, all their customs, and the seeds, they all stay out here."

"We concentrate on the matter at hand for now," Lobeck decided. "After this is done, we will have to discuss some systematic issue that you have here. Places like this, they can fester if untended. Like an infection or a cancer."

"We're at the plaza where Adastra and McElroy spent a fair amount of time. Do you want to get out and look at the details of their movements?"

Lobeck shook his head. "I can see perfectly well from here. Let us return to the spot where they disappeared, and see if we can find anything new."

At the edge of the plaza, the chopper turned to the right, beginning a circumnavigation. Other vehicles slowly gave way, alerted by the law enforcement transponder. The bright orange line headed away to their left, going past the enormous tree to the far size of the plaza.

"What's wrong with the navigation program?" Lobeck demanded. "There is an open path directly along their route."

"We can't drive across the plaza," Erickson told him. "Local custom."

"Absurd. We will follow the line. Chopper, give me manual control."

"No! Don't do it!"

Lobeck pulled the chopper hard to the left, out of the parade. A few pedestrians had to dash out of the way. That was fine with Lobeck – slow learners were not his problem. He steered to follow the orange line, only deviating to avoid a few tables that might cause damage to the vehicle.

As he passed the tree, a few small branches snapped. This far from the trunk, the branches were thin and therefore not an obstacle.

At the far side, they had to re-enter the traffic. While this slowed them once again, Lobeck's maneuver had saved several minutes.

"That's done it," Erickson declared. "We've shut any doors that might have been open to us. Nobody here will help us now."

Lobeck didn't reply, talking instead into his headset. "Skylar, those ten centuries of rentals you reserved. We need them now. When doors won't open for us, we just need to break them down. Let me know when they are ready."

Military Message

The door slid shut behind Admiral Incento. He was home, if only for a little while. As commander of Kelter's space fleet, he would need to be back on duty in a just few hours.

He paused to look out the large picture window. Two boulders framed a view into the outcrops of the gorge. He could see the junction with Mariah Gorge coming in on the right, a couple of kilometers downstream. Although the streambeds had been dry for thousands of years, the sculpted cliffs still conjured an appealing image of flowing water. He had paid plenty for this location.

"Dad, there's a great trial on! This guy − there he is!− he's up for Murder I." His daughter looked up at him.

"Isn't there anything else on?"

"Murder! Premeditated, cold blooded murder. He'll be tanked forever, I just know it. Vote, please Dad?"

Incento wondered where he had gone wrong. "You know I can't vote, sweetie. I haven't seen the whole thing."

"They won't know that! I've had it on the whole time. Put him away. Tank him! He's ugly!"

"Laurel, I wish you would watch something else."

"You mean you'd let a cold blooded killer go free to kill again?"

Incento moved from the living room, leaving behind him the enthusiastic refrain, "Guil-tee! Guil-tee! Guil-tee!"

His phone rang. "Answer," he said.

The face of Rod Denison flashed up on the screen of the desk unit. "Admiral, I've got a package for you."

"Send it along, then."

"I was requested to hand deliver it personally to you. Will you be home for another ten minutes?"

"I'll be here," Incento told him.

"See you momentarily, then."

Incento occupied the minutes with the news. The Affirmatix fleet, depicted in garish but largely accurate graphics, was shown converging on the planet. "The antiterrorist patrol is continuing into its second day, with the fleet making absolutely sure that no ships leave the Kelter system until the matter is entirely resolved," the caster said.

A retired admiral picked up. "This is a standard method to assure containment. While it's definitely causing some interruptions to commerce, this should just be for the short term. We have word that the operation may be over within two to three days."

"We all certainly hope so. Next we're going to move to a news conference in progress at the office of the Abilene Information Systems Authority, about how you can help us to protect you from these kinds of terrorist threats. With apologies to fans, we will have no sports coverage this hour."

Incento turned the news off and stared out the window until the bell rang.

"Open," he called at the tone, and Denison walked in. He passed Incento a small box.

"There's your package. It came in from Goodhope via Elassar, and I got the charter to bring it down here from Top Station. Although whatever they thought was so urgent two days ago is probably moot by now. The big news is up in the sky. Why do you think they're doing it?"

In the private setting of his own home, Incento didn't even bother to trot out the True Story. Denison was no fool. To Incento, it was a relief. Almost nobody actually believed most of the True Story, but you had to pretend, and in most circumstances everyone had to pretend to agree with you.

"I'm as perplexed as you, Rodney. It makes no sense for them to blockade here. If they take aggressive action, or stay too long, they will stir other Sisters to war, and they will lose."

"Unless they have something worked out with a few of the other Sisters. Who do you think the defectors will be?"

Incento shrugged. "I can't imagine."

"I just know one thing, Admiral," Denison told him. "They wouldn't be doing this if they didn't think they were going to get something. The Affirmatix are not stupid."

"There are many kinds of victory. Sometimes a leader will go to war, fully expecting to lose, to eliminate domestic opposition. To stimulate the economy. Or simply out of curiosity about war."

"I'd hate to get blown up to satisfy someone's curiosity. Surely, if it came down to it, we'd surrender. I was just trying to remember if I have any issues with Affirmatix. I think I'm clean with them. Hope so."

"Thank you for the package, Rodney, and your promptness conveying it to me."

"Moving news is my business. Have a good day, Admiral. "

Denison left the house.

Moments later, Incento was opening the box. First, the eye scan. Then, the combination. Finally the key, a combination of physical and magnetic. Typical security overhead dreamed up by people who had nothing better to do. Once, years ago, he had lost the damn key. What a mess. And he had gotten in trouble twice, first for losing the key, then second for sending an unprotected message to the effect that he had lost the key.

He had opened many such containers since then. This one slid open in seconds. Inside was a single card. He popped it into a reader and typed in one last authentication code, then read the header message.

"Confirmed reports have one D6 type device deployed to Affirmatix battleship M6780. Ship M6780 glomed to Holder on Day 309, and is scheduled to leave for Kelter on Day 310. The D6 requires a minimum of twelve capital ships evenly globed around a world, and will completely destroy all inhabitants, structures, and superficial terrain (features of less than 300 meters in vertical extent) over the entire planet."

Day 310. Today. M6780 was arriving soon, or was already insystem.

Valley of Dreams

Kate sat in her accustomed spot, her canvas in front of her, attempting to capture the essence of the scene in front of her. How many times had she painted from exactly here, in differing light and season? She ran her practiced fingers over the controls, creating a mosaic of shades and textures. Some were flat, others more glossy. Captures of images from the actual scene were transformed to merge with the painted elements. A touch of shimmering movement was folded in to just a few areas of the painting, just at the threshold of awareness from a viewer's averted vision. Kate was a master.

She considered the painting.

It sucked.

It didn't just suck. It really sucked.

It was the kind of painting that anyone could make, if they had taken a course in how to use the canvas, and had mastered some of the technical skills. Printed to a fixed copy, hung up with pride in the living room for a time, destined to be offered at a garage sale for ten credits, with no takers, and ultimately to sit among the possessions of the departed, each relative desperately hoping that someone else would claim it so that nobody would have to face the guilt of disposing of the piece of domestic family history.

She was a little short of breath. Just a little. Kate didn't get out as much as she once had. Still, she could adjust. The headache was fading.

This place had always brought her peace. It stood for so much. Discoveries. Beginnings. Endings, for better or worse. It was where she and Evan had met, and where they had parted ways for the final time. She had not realized at the time just how final. Now she would never see him again.

Still, she couldn't believe the news reports. Evan, a terrorist? That just couldn't be.

The mysterious arrival had been his ship, and it had been destroyed while trying to spread a deadly virus to Kelter, according to the news. She would never know whether that was true or not. Whatever Mira knew, Kate was not going to find out. That ship had sailed. Evan was gone, and it didn't matter now.

Did anything matter? The family, gone. Whether she accepted one of the ever-shrinking offers from CoreValue or went down fighting, it could not be what her parents had worked their whole lives for. What she had then built upon.

When her parents had died, everyone expected the end for the family. It had been theirs. It had been them. A labor of their love. And they were gone.

When she and the lawyers had gathered to read the will, there were the complex legal documents. There had also been a letter. On paper, written by hand, in ink.

"Our Dearest Katey," it had begun.

"Know that we would do anything for your happiness, in your life to come. All of our possessions are yours, to do with as you will. But please consider one plea. There is more to the family than others may see. It is freedom, a spark, of the type that is dying in today's world. So if you indulge just one wish that we might have, it would be this. Do not sell out. You don't need to have anything to do with it. Appoint someone to run it, if you wish – Lieberthal is a good person, if he is still with you. Just keep it away from the Sisters. Please have a long and happy life. With all of our love,"

It was written in her mother's hand, but signed by both of her parents. Kate folded the letter and put it back in her pouch.

What would they think, of her colossal error? She had provoked CoreValue by refusing to pay the glome fee. A great adventure, an opportunity to poke them in the eye. She should have known they owned that territory – the finer points of the terms, and the wheels of the legal system.

The swirl of other events made everything worse. Evan's death. The blockade.

"I am sorry," she said to the air. "I am so sorry."

"Canvas. Delete." The sucky painting vanished and was replaced by a blank khaki tone across the entire surface.

The image was preserved in the canvas, if she wanted it back. It was just artistically satisfying to make it go away, and declare it to be destroyed. Which, to her, it was.

For the first year after her parents' death, she had tended to the museum and her book series, and left the family for Lieberthal to run. He had done well.

Then came the day that he asked her for permission to retire. In fifty years of service, he had earned it. But who would replace him?

World, meet Kate DelMonaco, the new President and CEO of DelMonaco Trading.

Now, it was a bitter joke.

Kate put the canvas in her bag, picked up the seat, and started walking along the low ridge. To the site.

No artifice remained. When they had finished their last dig, they had cleaned up. The huts, which had grown in a jumble over the years of expeditions, were long gone.

The head of the valley was dominated by the entrance to Blowing Cave. Many millennia before, it had been a spring. A small skylight entrance, much higher, was the most direct way to the location of the main Versari site. The ceiling and walls of the upper cave had protected what the Versari had left for posterity. Beyond the entrances were tall cliffs, wavy lines of tan, red, and brown.

Kate and Evan had been very successful, in their series of digs. New types of Versari artifacts. Remains, in excellent condition. Fossilized, but they still preserved fine details of the Versari anatomy. Many of the items were now in the museum.

It was just about the best results they could have expected, for any planet with an atmosphere, considering the million year time frame.

Kate had brought gear to spend the night. Just inside the main cave entrance was the place. There was no counting how many evenings, and how many nights, she had spent there. That she and Evan had spent there.

The small ridge flattened and merged with the valley. Kate walked to the chopper to pick up her camp kit, and then she continued along to the cave.

Just inside, she found the spot. Flattened, the stones all picked up and tossed aside in prior years to make a soft sleeping surface. Some sand had blown in over the course of years, but it would be easy to smooth out. The eternal breeze gently flowed out, from somewhere deep inside the mountain.

She looked back out to the desert. The sun would be setting soon, on the world as it had been.

The Codex

"Feast your eyes," Mira told Evan.

The Codex was not much. A row of cubicles, each with several displays. Filling the opposite wall, tall shelves of dead tree books.

"That's it?"

Mira beamed. "Isn't it wonderful?"

"Um, sure?"

"Let me show you. Choose a cube and pull up a seat. Here's what's special. You can look up any information you want, on any topic you want. It's all stored locally here, in the Codex."

"Color me unimpressed. I can do that from anywhere."

"Evan, don't you get it? It's here. Local. The Codex gathers every feed that it possibly can, on every topic, every second of every day. We get a lot of government and family channels that we're not supposed to have. And when you search, your query doesn't get sent back to the provider. You can look for anything you want, and nobody can trace it. Imagine running searches without anyone looking over your shoulder. You can actually look for what you want. It's magical."

Evan was beginning to understand the implications. "Untraceable.

But, presumably the Codex program is storing your searches."

"Temporarily during your session, or you can save your searches if you want. But that's it. This is the spirit of the infoterrorists. You and the information are free to meet each other as you wish." Mira pointed at one of the cubes. "In there, you have complete privacy. Unlike any other computer you have ever sat in front of."

Evan couldn't imagine that she would be so gullible. "Oh come on. There is no way."

"Really. This is the reason. Everything my uncle has ever done, is for this. The information is free."

"Does it scream?"

"Not here. It sings."

"I think that's your uncle Axiom rubbing off on you. Speaking of whom, meaning no disrespect, but he is a total loon. Maybe those meds are doing battle in his brain."

Mira dismissed it. "Oh no, he's always been that way."

Evan pressed. "I appreciate his help and all, but are you sure it's wise to trust our safety to someone who can't put two sentences together without some trippy parable? When Security is busting in, he'll be there to stop them by posing existential riddles for them to solve. Naked."

"Do not, under any circumstances, underestimate him. There is a reason that he is the most wanted person on Kelter. And wanted, not found. Whatever he says, he is good for. Always. He opened his home to us, he meant it, and it's worth more than anything else I can think of. Hey – you should check out information on the dragnet. You're a star! Affirmatix has been sweeping all around the Untrusted Zone for both of us. But they won't find us down here. So, do you want to check it out?"

"I do," Evan affirmed.

"Share?"

"Nope. Get your own cube."

As Evan took his place in the cube, it began to sink in. Search, on anything, without hesitation.

He remembered the time that he had been waved off. He had been trying to construct a possible chronology of Versari glome discoveries, and the only available model was the sequence of exploration by humans. Just after he had started to assemble the historical data, Evan had been summoned by the Director of Research for his grant at that time, to review a list of acceptable topics – and Evan's avenue of inquiry was most emphatically not on the list.

At the time, it had seemed like an odd coincidence. He had just moved on to other things, which were on the approved list and were also worthwhile.

As he sat in the cube thinking of what he might query on, Evan considered other subject areas, where it was simply known that you did not search. History, other than what you were taught in school. Economics, except for the daily pulse of the financial markets. These limits had never mattered much to him, because he wasn't much interested in those subjects.

Most of Evan's material concerned a long-dead alien race, where very little information would be considered sensitive or possibly sequestered. For just a moment, Evan caught a glimpse of what it might mean, for people trying to learn and teach on matters more closely connected to the daily lives of humans.

The infoterrorist might be on to something, at that.

But if the entire world had been there for him to search on, would it have done him any good? Possibly not. It spoke to a huge weakness that Evan had always known he had. For any one puzzle, such as a new Versari artifact just brought to light, there was no person in the universe who was more persistent, or who had better analytical skills. Evan could chew on the problem in front of him until it gave up everything it had.

But connections eluded him. Larger themes, or patterns, were invisible to him unless the brute force of statistical analysis made them readily apparent. At the Valley of Dreams site, most of the real progress had come from suggestions offered by Kate. He would tell her the latest about his efforts, incremental findings, and dead ends. Then she would come up with an idea that had been in plain sight the entire time.

Kate had a simple explanation for why this was. "You look at these items on the table. Artifacts. You use all these machines to analyze them. But you don't think of the Versari as people who loved, and that's the single most important fact of their existence."

Then there were her novels. Once upon a time, Evan had carefully gone through the first volume and had provided her with a list of the factual inaccuracies based on everything that was known about the Versari, and a further list of items that were highly questionable. She had not done a single edit, insisting that he was missing the whole point. And he had to admit, the *Tails of Versari* series had reached many thousands of readers, teaching them about the long-departed race even if the details weren't perfect.

Where was Kate now? Evan started pulling up searches. A brief history, of the two years since they had last spoken. The crushing ruling against DelMonaco Trading, unpublished but somehow available, due to the audacious data mining of the infoterrorists.

Next, current whereabouts.

Not exactly. Four hours ago, she had checked out a chopper, and now her heartbeat was gone. There was no further trace.

Evan knew exactly where she was.

Known associates. It was double edged. A hazard for him – he should not go anywhere near any of his known associates, especially her. But was the hazard even greater for Kate? Alone at the Valley of Dreams, she could be picked up so easily. Vanish forever. Spend her last moments crying out, over and over, that she had no idea where he was.

Do something.

He knew that was wrong. He knew. Breathe.

Do something.

Frantically, Evan searched for more information. There was nothing. Four hours, no heartbeat.

Was he actually concerned for Kate? Or, did he just want to talk with her, at least one more time before his fate arrived?

At the moment the ground shuddered and the sharp report of explosions arrived. Evan jumped up and out of his cube. Mira was intent on her console in the adjacent slot. He couldn't believe she was still staring at the screen.

"Did you hear that?"

"Sure did," Mira told him.

"And?"

"Checking the best way to go. Now I know. Let's go!"

Mira launched herself, Evan rushing to follow. A door slid open for them into a long corridor. A right turn, then a left. More doors, then stairs down.

Mira led them to a garage with a dozen choppers, grabbed a backpack and a helmet off a shelf, then rushed to claim a chopper. Others were streaming in, and a bay door on the far side of the garage was already rolling up.

A tall, thin man came in through the door. "Kes – where's Axiom?" Mira demanded of him.

"He is safe. We are free to find safety ourselves."

"You are sure?"

"I have made certain of it," the man said.

"Thank you for that." She turned to Evan. "Grab a pack and hop on," she instructed. "It's time to leave."

A thought struck Evan. "What about the Codex?" he asked. "Will it be destroyed?"

"Oh no," Mira told him. "That was just one portal to it. The actual Codex is in many places."

The choppers streamed out of the garage. Like most of the Untrusted Zone, it was chaos that somehow worked out. After three near-collisions they found themselves flying at top speed down a narrow passage that was somewhere in size between a street and an alley. Mira took them through the maze, staying under rooftop level, finally pulling into a quiet alley and cutting the headlights.

It was not completely dark. White light from Foray shone on a wall of the alley. As his vision adjusted, Evan saw a few stars above.

Mira spoke quietly. "We can't go to my place, and I'm running out of friends around here."

"I know where we need to go," Evan said. "Our home turf. The place we both know best." There was no need to mention that Kate might be at the same location, given Mira's reaction to his mention of her earlier.

"We need to stay in town," she insisted. "The streets will give us cover. I just need to figure out where we can crash."

"As long as we're with people, we'll be traced. We need to leave. Tonight is evidence of that. What's in those packs?"

"Survival gear. To escape into the desert, if need be."

"I think it needs be," he told her.

The Ghost

Kate's sleep was troubled by dreams. Usually, she welcomed them. Even on this night, she resolved to gain some positive meaning from the confusing and despairing scenes in which she found herself. Loss. The legacy of her parents, gone. Trying to explain it to them, even as they weren't there. Evan was with her, although he was dead. "Kate," he called out to her.

It was even worse when she awoke but knew she was dreaming still, because Evan was there, framed against the entrance to the cave in the predawn. And still he called.

When she surfaced further and realized she could not possibly be asleep any more, she was incandescent.

"I mourned you! Two years away, and then you were killed. You have been dead, and you didn't even call me. Do you know what that's like?" She looked around for something to throw. The stove was too far away.

"Kate—"

"You made me want to die. You could at least have the decency to stay dead."

The ghost placated. "I couldn't tell you—"

"Left me to twist in the wind!" In a single moment, Kate experienced the accumulated anguish of the past two days as a heavy needle stabbing through her left eye, directly into her brain. Or perhaps it was the act of standing up quickly in the paltry air pressure.

"This is a promising reunion," observed Mira, stepping forward to join them.

"You! So that's why you wanted a ship. And you kept it a secret from me. So you could get some private time with Evan, I suppose?"

"Kate, we have only been together for a day," Evan told her. "No, not together! She picked me up, I mean, in a shuttle. Mira rescued me, so I could come here to you."

"Rescued you. So you called her first. Didn't even think of me."

"Kate! She's a pilot! I was going to be killed. I sent a message to the one person who could pluck me out of space."

"You want me to believe that? Get out of my cave! Never mind, I'm leaving."

"That's not going to be a good choice," Mira told her.

"What, are you threatening me?" The stove was only two steps away.

"Nope, just pointing something out. Look." Mira indicated the landscape outside.

Out in the valley, the choppers were arriving. Troops piled out and were bounding up the slope to the cave. Toward them.

"I suppose you brought them here. Well that's just great."

"See Kate, that's why I couldn't find you sooner," Evan started to explain.

"Well maybe you should have waited a little longer," Kate huffed.

"You're not being internally consistent. First you said—"

"Hey lovebirds, stow it," Mira ordered. "We need to move. Grab the gear and go!"

"Maybe we can sort it out with them?" Kate asked.

"Not these guys. Trust me. Move!"

Mira, Evan, and Kate hastened down the large passage into the cave, hopping over the large boulders that had fallen from the roof millennia ago.

Mira stopped at a small passage that sloped steeply upward. "Up here! We need to go through the vaults."

"The vaults?" That seemed to Kate like the worst possible choice. "We would have to go right past the skylight entrance."

"The vaults. There is a lot more passage there, beyond them. The big passage doesn't go the farthest."

If anyone would know, it would be Mira. She had explored deep into the cave during the expeditions, dragging along anyone who would go. For many, including Kate, it was just one trip. Mira had photomapped the entirety of Blowing Cave, in great detail, pushing every passage to the bitter end. One night she had provided a show to everyone on a big screen, zooming around the virtual cave so they could see every feature without the effort.

Mira, Kate, and Evan scrambled up the steep incline, then a series of other passages, before emerging in the upper cavern.

A faint light shone from far away to their right. They headed left. "We don't need to go too near the skylight, and they won't figure it all out quickly enough," Mira told them. They headed around the corner into a much larger cavern.

The three found themselves in the vaults.

Springing The Trap

Soon enough, one of the trap lines bore fruit.

They had been tracking Kate DelMonaco as a top priority. McElroy's partner of many years. It was a no brainer. She was the highest profile selection out of twenty surveillance subjects, known associates of McElroy.

Electronic monitoring sufficed at first. DelMonaco left an obvious heartbeat wherever she went, a large bow wake on the surface of dataspace. Then, when she checked out a chopper, dedicated physical resources were dispatched.

Still, she was easy to follow. Carelessly flying at a thousand meters of altitude regardless of whether she might be tracked. Coming in for a slow, casual landing. Parking her chopper and walking around, first up a hill, then back to the chopper, then on to the cave. Not even the most basic checks for signs of anyone following, as the surveillance team was.

The team brought up the map of the Blowing Cave. It had been made by Mira Adastra, of all people, and published four years before. In the strange fashion of the denizens of the Untrusted Zone, Adastra had published it without sponsorship from any family, scorning any revenue which might have accrued from product placements or advertorials.

The map provided the details of every passage, large and small, proudly summarized on the map as 6.53 kilometers. The end of each passage was described and photographed. There were no unexplored leads shown – the mapping project was complete.

The cave map showed three entrances, of which DelMonaco had entered through the largest by far. The team could still see her heat signature, just inside, as she set up camp. Two smaller entrances connected into the network.

The team set up in position, not just to track the movements of their subject, but also to observe if anyone else came nearby. Then they waited. They were on the clock, so that was fine.

A few hours before dawn, a chopper came in. It flew carefully, with no lights, down in a shallow canyon, and then at only two meters above the ground when the cover of the canyon ran out. The maneuvers were no match for military equipment, which picked up the chopper easily.

The team leader alerted their command and continued to monitor, as the chopper pulled up near the entrance to the cave, and two people stepped off.

Backup came within minutes. Six choppers, twenty agents, and their leader, Arn Lobeck. The agents fanned out and approached the cave.

The trap was sprung.

Hall Of The Departed

Nine vaults. Each was an enormous rounded rectangle, over three meters tall, two wide, and five long, and unadorned except for one short set of symbols in a small rectangle on each, centered on one end. They were arranged in a perfect line, just over four meters between each vault. Still, the vaults took up only a small part of the large natural hall.

Having already been shushed once by Mira, Evan gave his regards silently to each one.

Greetings, Edras. He was no longer in the vault, but still deserving of a word.

Greetings, Elanas. Also in the museum.

Emmala. Still here. They had raised the top, in the 2298 expedition, and taken many images.

The plan had been to remove the remains for display and further study, as for the prior two. As they had observed and catalogued over three days, they had pondered, until finally Kate had opened up the topic. "She belongs here," Kate had announced, clearly expecting disagreement. Evan had been filled with relief, and the next day they had slowly winched down the cover, leaving Emmala to her rest.

Uve. When they had opened her tomb, they had already known what they planned to do. Observe, photograph, replace the top.

The last five had only been seen by remote imaging, as well as the team could achieve through the stone. There were definitely remains there. They discussed boring a hole, and putting a camera through. Somehow that project never got to the top of the list. What did they hope to learn, that would be worth disturbing the sleep of the departed?

Greetings, Irstis, Essatti, Wei, Rissta, and Ote.

Kate had named them. The names were based on a transliteration of the symbols, using a scheme that they had since abandoned. But the names had stuck.

Beyond the vaults were the pits that Evan, Kate, and their helpers had dug. Many had rich yields of artifacts. First they had imaged, and then dug where there were promising signs.

Kate and Evan followed Mira as she hurriedly threaded the trail past the pits, heading deeper into the cave.

Seeing the vaults brought it all back for Evan. The reason he had spent so many years scratching at the past. The existence of the Versari was one of the great wonders in all of known space. Almost a million years ago, these space-farers had lived here. For over a hundred thousand years they had traveled between the star systems known to humans, and beyond. Then they were gone. Died out, or perhaps they had moved on.

Although some trace of the Versari had been found in twenty six out of the thirty currently explored star systems, the locations all appeared to be outposts. Way stations – not grand cities that would have left a larger footprint even so many years later.

Did those cities exist? Evan believed so, although he couldn't prove it. Not yet.

Soon they were in much more rugged passage. Evan had been here before, surely, but he had no memory of the choices. Through an obscure hole. Straight up a wall for five meters. Mira simply leapt up, then helped each of them. Walking sideways. Crawling.

As they traveled, Evan tried to catch a look at Kate. It had been more than two years. The cave was dark, and it would be blinding to shine his light at her face. He collected fragments. A backlit profile from Mira's light ahead. The outline of her cheek as she turned to assess the next climb. Her nose, just slightly turned up.

They came to a junction in a tall room. Mira directed each of them. "Evan, walk that way until you get to a fork. Go into each fork for as far as you can go, and then come back here. Kate, crawl into that hole. You should get about fifty meters until you have to back out. I'll go this way. We meet right here."

"Are we looking for something?" Kate asked.

"Nope, we're leaving something. Now hop to it."

They each completed their assigned missions, and soon were reassembled at the junction. "You guys are so lucky to have me," Mira told them. "Watch." She jumped straight up, catching a ledge with one hand and then pulling herself up. From there she hopped to the opposite wall, then back, and then launched upward once again. Evan had the distinct feeling that she was showing off. Finally she called from a spot that was at least thirty meters above them.

"Okay, I'm up. Who's next?"

"Mira, I don't think we can do that," Evan shouted upward.

"Really, didn't you watch?" Mira was taunting.

"Are you going to leave us?"

In answer, a silver line came down. "You are all so double lucky to have me. Never leave home without it."

They climbed up the rope in turn, easy to do in Kelter's low gravity. Kate was next, then Evan. With a grunt, he pulled through a narrow spot and climbed up to a ledge in the chamber above, while Mira pulled up the line. The entire ceiling consisted of a jumble of boulders, and Evan couldn't see any way on. It was a miracle that the rocks weren't raining down on them. Somehow they were jammed in place. "Where now?" he asked.

Suddenly Mira held up her hands. "Lights!" she hissed. "And be still!"

She reached up to turn off her light. Kate must have already done so, because Evan saw that his was the only light still burning. He reached for the switch and clicked his light off. Then they were in darkness.

Evan felt behind him and found the wall. There was just a little bit of space, and he stepped back, away from the edge of the ledge that he knew was there.

Far below, he heard a series of irregular thumps. It was nothing like a person walking. The passage below had not allowed it.

The noise grew louder. Scrapes were added to the thumps. Evan, never able to turn off his analytical mind, realized that when high frequency sound was audible, there were very few bends in the passage between him and those who approached.

With the complexity of the passage they had traversed, he wondered how they had followed so quickly.

A faint light came from below. Their pursuers were in the room at the bottom of the climb. "Three ways on," echoed up to them. "We'll scan while the rest of the squad gets here."

Despite the situation, Evan was relieved to see where the ledge ended in front of him. It was better than standing in complete darkness, knowing the edge was somewhere out there.

"I've got a hit! Twenty-three meters, straight up!"

A focused beam now shone up through the hole. Evan could see dust in the cylinder of light, describing swirls and eddies but mostly flowing down, to the chamber below.

More people were arriving. Evan heard the now familiar sequence of low thumps and knocks, then sharper sounds, with scrapes and finally voices conferring.

"Right here, sir," Evan heard, followed by the most recognizable voice he knew. Deep, powerful, assured. Calling up from below.

"Evan! Evan McElroy! It's Arn! Talk to me, friend!"

Love Letter

Eliza Malken looked into the camera's eye and kept speaking.

"So Krishnan, those are the updates. But, there's one thing more. I wanted to say that I miss you. I hope that you are well and that you will return here soon."

After a pause, she continued. "I know we have just been co-workers. But we have done so much together, when you are away from here it is not the same. And I have not been able to get any news of you. Colin says it's just routine security process, but still I worry.

"After you get back, perhaps we could take some time to talk. About what matters the most, about what we care about. We could have dinner, just you and me. That is, if you would like to do that. I guess I shouldn't assume.

"Please make me proud, by doing great work, with judgment and always doing what is right. And then come right back here.

"I so hope to see you very soon."

Eliza reached out to stop the recording.

She turned to her wrangler. "There. It is done. I hope you are happy."

"That's just great," Colin Ellison told her. "We'll do a little editing and get it sent right off to Ravi. Thanks Eliza!"

"Mr. Ellison."

"What, I'm not Colin anymore?"

"You are not. And from this moment forward, you will address me as Dr. Malken. Always."

"As you say, Dr. Malken."

"Out!" A few moments more, and she would not be able to hold it back.

"You really helped us. Thank you for your cooperation," Ellison said as he stepped out.

Every word she had spoken to the camera was true. And more.

So many men strutted up to Eliza and spread their feathers, each man expressing his desire that she should get to know him better. Telling of their prowess, whether intellectual, sporting, or material. Krishnan Ravi, alone of all men, did the one thing that mattered. He listened to exactly what she was saying and the thoughts behind her words. Then he responded to what he heard. With acerbic disagreement, sometimes, it was true. But he replied to the actual person she was.

He was always so formal. Did he care for her? Eliza didn't know.

And now, wherever he was, and whatever was going on, would the letter help Ravi or would it hurt him? How would they make use of it?

Eliza was always confident. Self-assured. When she spoke, people listened. When she needed something, she simply asked and it was hers. She was the kind of person everybody wanted to be with. She was a woman in charge of her destiny.

At this moment, she felt helpless. Completely. Utterly. Through her entire adult life, it was not something she had experienced.

"Door. Close. And Lock."

Eliza resolved that she would never, ever, let her wrangler see her cry.

This is Solvable

Standing on a narrow ledge far above the floor of the cave, Evan found himself in conversation with a man who wanted him dead. He called down. "I'm here."

"Evan! We have found each other." That was not how Evan would have put it.

"I wasn't exactly looking for you," he shouted into the slot below him. Lobeck was in the large room from which they had climbed, twenty-three meters below.

"Then it is good fortune for both of us that I have found you now," came back up. "We have much more to discover together, and to provide to the world. You could even be the one to announce it. A new life, for billions of souls."

For a moment, Evan found himself imagining the moment. After years of being scoffed at, even pitied.

That was insane. The man was here to kill the three of them, or worse.

Lobeck continued from below. "We have had a great partnership, and we need to continue with it. You ran off, and I have come to bring you back."

Red sparks of light danced on the boulder ceiling above. Tracers from below.

"Partnership? You launched missiles at my runabout!" The moment suddenly came back to Evan. Staking it all on a plunge into the void of the unknown glome, while trying not to puke.

"They were only sent to guide you back to us. Why did you leave the station?"

"I was checking my theory. Proving it. Just doing what I always do."

"You planned to steal it!" Evan could hear Lobeck's anger. "Keep it all for yourself. Well, that won't do you any good now. Soon enough, we will have the tools to get you down from your perch. If you come down voluntarily, the three of you, it will go much more easily for you all."

Evan stopped himself from replying. Something else was going on, and the long distance conversation was distracting him from what he really should be paying attention to. He leaned over to Mira and whispered, "Where is the way on?"

In reply she flipped on her light with a narrow spot beam and shone it up at a small alcove directly above them. It was just a small recess in the forbidding ceiling of jumbled boulders. A dancing collection of tiny red lights, tracers from below, painted the entire area. The alcove was directly in the line of fire.

Evan summoned the phrase that had seen him through so many times before. "This is solvable," he told himself. He looked down. Their entire connection with the large room below, and their pursuers, was a narrow slot three meters long and less than a meter wide. The exposed area near the ceiling, as illustrated by the tracers, was clearly wider than that meter, because some of the soldiers had placed themselves in different places in the wide room below. He could picture the geometry.

This is solvable.

It all came back to that narrow connection.

Evan pulled off his pack and considered the slot below them. He would have one chance to get it exactly right, so that the pack would jam in the slot and not fall through. Blocking the line of sight of Lobeck's weapons for a few precious moments. One throw for the whole prize.

It was then that they heard the sound.

There was no mistaking the whirr of tiny impellers. First just one, then joined by others. Coming closer to them, from below. Flying up toward the ledge on which they stood.

"Be ready," he told Mira and Kate, pointing up at the alcove.

"What did you say?" Lobeck called from twenty-three meters below. "It is time to come down."

"Coming down," Evan announced. He picked up his pack with both hands, and softly tossed it down with a careful, underhand throw. The pack hit the far wall, bounced back, and came to rest in the center of the slot. "Bulls-eye!"

Then Mira was flying up toward the ceiling. She called as she leapt, "This way! Come on!"

At that moment the shots started.

Evan flipped on his light and looked down. The pack was jerking in its place from the shots, but stayed jammed in the hole as the percussion continued. This was madness.

Kate was jumping up, to Mira's outstretched hand. Mira gathered Kate in, and then appeared to vanish, leaving only Kate visible.

Evan gathered himself and sprang for it.

He felt rather than heard the deep thud. The pack had been shot out of the slot and was flying up out of the hole, straight at him. He twisted in midair, somehow dodging most of the oncoming mass. The pack clipped one foot, starting him spinning.

Evan crashed against the wall of the cave.

He felt an arm reach around his shoulder and neck, and pull him upward. "In here," Kate told him. "It's narrow." He reached up to feel a ledge, and was able to pull himself up. The slot ahead was outlined by Kate's light. He wriggled in.

A second thud came from below, and then the world shattered behind him. Evan heard the whir of rock fragments flying through the air, then a noise akin to broken glass falling. He pulled himself farther forward.

Another round of the heavy stuff arrived. The boulders in the ceiling of the chamber, held up only by faith, groaned. Then faith gave out. He heard them start to fall.

Evan turned to look back at the place where he had been moments before. He saw a maelstrom of rocks large and small, churning in the world's biggest marble machine. A wave of dust overtook him.

A few more creaks, then the rocks were done falling.

"Are you two okay?" Mira, from above.

"We're here," he called. "Coming through."

As the dust started to settle, Evan took a last look behind him. The formerly open space through which they had all jumped was absolutely jammed with broken rocks of every shape and size.

Evan followed Kate's light through the slithering way up into a small chamber where they joined Mira.

Evan was about to exclaim profusely about their narrow escape, when he heard a sound behind him. A scrape of metal on rock, then a buzz, and another scrape. It was close, just a few meters away. He whirled to see a dull grey metallic cylinder rise out of the slot in the floor from which they had just climbed.

If a drone could appear to have a broken wing, it was this one. The flier tilted at an angle and appeared to be struggling to gain altitude. Nevertheless, it was rotating to bring a short snout of some kind to bear in the direction of Mira.

Without stopping to think, Evan launched himself at the flying object, grabbing it with both hands and flinging it to the rock floor. He landed next to it, again taking hold of the cylinder and bringing it down on the ground with all of his strength. That was unsatisfying, because the force of his weight didn't amount to much in Kelter's low gravity. The equal and opposite reaction sent him back across the room.

The drone twitched and buzzed, then started to rise once again. And it started to speak.

"Evan, hold on," Arn Lobeck's voice came from the machine. "It's not too late for us to work together. We can talk while my crew clears away the obstacle. It shouldn't take long."

Evan cast around, seeing a perfect rock just a meter away. Rounded and just right for two full hands. He took hold of the rock, stepped forward, and smashed at the drone, knocking it to the ground once again. The impact sent him floating back away from his target.

"Do not squander your last chance," the drone told him.

To do the job, he needed better leverage. Evan pulled himself back toward the flier and braced his legs between two ledges. Once anchored, he picked up the rock and pounded the drone, with one word per impact. "Not. On. Your. Life."

Evan continued his assault on the device. Pieces splintered off. Soon it was a flattened pile of metal and plastic on the floor of the cave. He looked up to see Mira and Kate, both totally still, watching with fascination.

"What?" Evan demanded.

"That's just," Kate appeared to be pondering her choice of words, "a side of you that I've never seen before."

Mira ducked back down into the small slot, then emerged just a few moments later. "That is an impressive amount of rock," she commented. "They must have fired some pretty heavy stuff. The room we were standing in, it's completely filled up."

She urged them farther into the cave, until they reached a larger room. "Ok, we can take a minute," she said. "That boulder fall should hold them a while."

"So we're trapped," Kate stated flatly.

"Not exactly," Mira replied. "We've got some options."

"Well if we're not actually being shot at just now," Kate told her, "Evan's got some explaining to do."

Evan briefly wished for some further sign of pursuit. Perhaps another drone. This discussion was not something he was looking forward to. He had needlessly endangered her by coming to the cave, and she was going to let him have it.

But Kate had something else in mind. "Arn Lobeck! I warned you. The day we met with him. And his creature Skylar. " She gave a shudder.

Evan remembered it well. Kate and Skylar had faced off like two tigers over a hunk of meat. Lobeck and Skylar had offered funding, unlimited, for all practical purposes. Not so incidentally, replacing the money that had been coming from Kate's family.

Evan spread his hands open. "You kept telling me that he was off the path, or something like that. And that I should turn away millions of credits of funding."

"That's not what I said. Lobeck didn't care about the path. Not for a second. Any fool could smell the stink, of results at any cost. He didn't care about the science, about discovery. Anything he said about that was just a lie, as plain as the nose on your face. The path, each step – it was everything to you, and nothing to him. And you left me, so you could throw in with them."

"Kate – I didn't leave you. I begged you to come. But you wouldn't. Don't you remember?"

"You made it clear that you had already decided. And all that time I thought we were partners. The moment you didn't need me, suddenly I was an afterthought." Kate turned away, as if she couldn't stand to look at him for a moment longer.

Evan knew where he couldn't go. It had been about the money, but not in the way she thought. Yes, he had decided not to let her fund any more of his expeditions.

It was so easy, in one sense, to have a wealthy girlfriend, who bought you whatever you wanted. Outfitted your expeditions, year after year. Left her artist friends from time to time, to join you on site, and ponder the latest promising fragment with you.

To be a pet scientist.

That label, affixed by Mira, was only cruel because it had been so true.

Would he ever be able to scratch for his own worms? Create results that the outside world would recognize and value? Would he ever be able to ask her to marry him, without everyone in the world thinking, or perhaps knowing, that he was doing it for the easy life that would come along with it?

What could he say now? "It wasn't that way. It just wasn't."

"Hmph," was all Kate said.

"Break's over!" Mira announced.

They continued for another hour or more, in a stunning succession of twists and turns. In one place the way on was completely invisible until he laid flat on the ground and looked under the wall. Then, in another spot, a wormhole deep in a hidden corner was the path.

Finally, Evan had to ask. "Where are we going?"

"Farther in." Mira was implacable. "Keep moving."

"How does that help? They will track us down, or wait us out."

Mira snorted. "Track us down, I don't think so. That maze we just crawled through, it's not on the map. I left it off. It will take them weeks to find a way through, if they even get through the rock pile they made."

"All this, not on the map?"

"Yep."

"But why?"

"Never got around to it." That was a strange answer. Mira loved the map. She showed it to anyone who expressed even the slightest interest. It was her pride and joy. "Let's just say that I think we're safe, for now. Let's inventory what we've got."

They had grabbed Kate's overnight gear, and had some of their own from Mira's survival pack. There was some version of a helmet for each of them, thin caps that each had worn in their respective chopper rides, and the hat from Evan's visitor kit, which actually was the most robust. Headlamps. Gloves. A few liters of water each. A stove. A little food. It would do for a day. Two if they were careful. They continued.

"Here we rest," Mira told them. "And listen and watch. Turn off your lights."

There was nothing to see in the complete blackness, and nothing to hear, except their own breathing. A faint breeze, coming from farther in the cave, became uncomfortably cool after a time.

A dark time later, Mira turned her light on. "I've been thinking," she said. "There is only one way to go," she said. "It's a long journey, but we can make it."

Evan startled. "Another entrance? Beyond the three in the Valley of Dreams?"

"No picnic getting there, and maybe worse once we're on the surface. It's across the plateau on the East Edge. But it's better than the action around here."

"And you had to think about it?"

"It's just," Mira hesitated, and then simply said, "a long way."

Kate spoke up. "Will somebody please explain a thing or two? I was just camping, you know."

"Oh, I think this is Evan's tale," Mira said. Both women turned and looked at him expectantly.

Evan was more than ready. "You won't believe this," he began. "At the research station on Aurora—"

At that moment a wall of sound knocked them all down.

Strike One

Lobeck was calling from the surface.

"On the main screen, the Valley of Dreams," he ordered. "Show the geology and all of the entrances to the cave."

Sonia couldn't help but admire the quality of the image. Over the aerial view, the extent of the limestone was outlined, running about five hundred meters laterally and two hundred meters vertically. Three cave entrances were shown, well within the outlined exposure of the cave rock. Surrounding the limestone exposure on all sides were thick layers of sandstone, which might have crevices but were unlikely to have substantial cave development.

"Superpose areas of full effect for a tactical strike, as many as needed."

Oh, no. This again.

Six overlapping shapes, roughly circular, appeared on the display. They covered the entire area of limestone, and more.

"Prepare for launch, on that pattern," Lobeck ordered.

"Preparing," Roe told him. "Five minutes."

"Let's do some tactical evaluation. First, coverage."

"Appears sufficient, although a cave is inherently a hard target," Skylar said. "We could place a charge inside the large entrance. That would cost about sixty minutes, for a soft landing and to stage it in there."

"We just need to seal them in," Lobeck declared. "How about adding a charge, directly at the entrance?"

"We can probably fly one in there," she replied.

Another shape was added to the display, smaller but darker.

"Commander, make that seven tacticals."

"Seven it is," Roe told them. "Four minutes until ready."

Lobeck addressed Sonia. "Dr. West. No dire warnings this time? How we may upset the balance of your models?"

If she was going to make a difference, she had to choose her moment. There would be some way that she could steer events to cause less harm, while still serving her employer and protecting her domestic family.

This was not the right time. "It's not great, but it's not bad," she told Lobeck. "The strike will be destabilizing for Kelter, bad for our reputation and market share. The use of nuclear weapons–"

"Tactical nuclear," Lobeck corrected.

"The use of any size of nuclear weapon is taboo," Sonia continued. "But Kelter is a small market. As long as you are sure that you have the information contained, it's no worse than lots of other outcomes."

His image regarded her from a secondary view screen. "Thank you."

"There's just one outcome that would be better," she said. "If you retrieved them in person. From the cave, wherever they are. They would likely have all of the materials with them, and it would be lower profile than a nuclear strike. Much lower."

"We tried. The cave, it is not a good environment for the people we have on hand. Adastra knows the cave, and even with her map, we cannot track them down. They appear to have gone beyond what was mapped, and our efforts triggered a rock collapse that would take considerable time to clear."

"Fire away, then." Sonia did her best to look indifferent.

"One minute," Roe called.

"Just launch when ready, Mister Roe," Lobeck's image on the screen told them.

It turned out that a minute was a very long time.

"Launched," the rental captain announced.

"Track on the main screen."

They watched as the screen showed the track of the missiles on an orbital scale. Solid red lines for history, dashed green lines for trajectory. Large numbers for the minutes and seconds until impact. The display zoomed in slowly to a regional, then a local view as the numbers incremented toward zero. A few seconds after the moment of impact, the graphics were replaced by live aerial views of the scene. First fireballs, muted to protect their vision, then a merged and misshapen cloud from the seven impacts.

They collected reports and views from observers near the site. After the cloud became thinner and finally started to drift away to the north, they zoomed in on the location, carefully checking the former cave entrances. Teams would be there on foot within a few hours. So far, there was no evidence that a cave had ever existed in the area.

Lobeck efficiently ran the surface operation, as the bridge crew monitored from the ship. The ground teams closed in. He directed that the radio jamming should continue until every square millimeter of ground had been directly examined. He was going to make certain.

Sonia hoped that Lobeck had it out of his system.

Ravi seemed to be excited. "I think this is it!" he told her. "We have done the job, helping to do what needs to be done, and now we will be able to go home, to the ones we care for. That is good, yes?"

"Yes, a good job," she told him.

Ravi's smile was beatific.

Sonia knew that she would carry these events with her forever, and especially her culpability. She had helped reduce the harm, as much as she could. Three murders, plus those writers who had been silenced. Far fewer than three hundred thousand or more, as could have occurred if Lobeck had not listened to her earlier, and had struck Abilene. That was worth something.

Once she got back to Alcyone, would she confess to Yvette? Find a place next to a running stream, white noise cloaking them, and tell her the story? Did she dare? If she did, would Yvette consent to stay with her? For the sake of the kids?

In the Valley of Dreams, the molten pools slowly cooled, solidifying into rock of a type never before seen on Kelter.

A Drop of Water

If they had decided before, they were certain now. There was no turning back. The blast had left all three of them deafened, and only now was some semblance of hearing coming back. Their pursuers had clearly used extremely heavy ordnance, somewhere near the lower entrances.

It was not just sound. The earth had wrenched under their feet, then it had settled like a pile of broken bones. Evan, from his knees, had seen Kate fall against one of the walls of the cave. He had tried to reach out for her, but he was too far away, and had no balance to offer. Even Mira had lost her footing.

For Evan, the blast told him with finality that the juggernaut was coming specifically for him. There would be no stepping aside and letting it roll on past. For a time he had convinced himself that he was just a bystander, swept up in events far larger than what he could see. Now it was plain, even more so than Lobeck's words at the pit. Affirmatix was pursuing him, and now his companions, until they were all dead.

If they had been able to talk with each other, there would have been a lot to say.

Mira motioned them onward.

It was surprising how much they were hampered by not being able to hear. They often had to take turns, through awkward places or up climbs. Instead of easily hearing when the way was clear, each had to rely on sight, often less useful and sometimes unreliable.

In the absence of sound and only a single beam of light from each person, other senses ruled. The cave had tremendous variations in texture, with soft silt, rounded gravel, and sharp little pebbles in places. The bare rock was smooth and gracefully rounded in some passages, and then blocky and broken in others. Sometimes the cave was a luxury to be in contact with. Often it was painful. Always, it was cold.

The breeze was always there. Where the passage was smallest, the breeze was stronger, even approaching the force of a powerful wind. In larger rooms the air circulated more gently, in apparently random directions. Evan could feel it on any exposed skin, like his cheeks and sometimes the small seam between his gloves and the sleeves of his jacket.

Evan had always liked going for walks, completely offline. The rhythm of his steps helped him think, and the absence of the endless pings freed him to consider what really mattered.

In an odd way, the cave had the same effect.

He recalled, as well as he could, the strange conversation with the infoterrorist just a few hours before. Knowledge, screaming to be free. A crazy idea, and yet a match to what he believed at heart. He had just never heard such a colorful way of expressing it.

The knowledge of the Versari had lain in wait for him over hundreds of millennia, perhaps wishing to be known, just waiting for the right vector to be set loose upon the world. For all practical purposes, the knowledge could be ascribed a kind of volition – it certainly drove people to actions they would not have otherwise considered.

As long as his findings had been dry, of only academic interest, it hadn't mattered. He could publish anything he wanted, anywhere he wanted. A few dozen people would parse the jargon. Of those, two or three would send him an appreciative note. But the moment he had come upon something of material value, everything had changed. Without knowing, Evan had become an infoterrorist.

The casters on the Spoon Feed hadn't been lying after all.

And it shouldn't change a thing. Not one single thing. His mission had always been to tell the world what he had found, and he was going to do exactly that. As soon as he got out of this cave.

An impact jarred Evan's head and neck. He had been crawling, looking down, and had not seen the ledge. Dreaming. He was lucky he hadn't damaged his light. Evan pulled back, determined the dimensions of the obstacle, and lowered himself under it, passing into the larger room beyond.

After another deeply wearing hour of travel, Evan had to beg for a break. He slumped down and closed his eyes. Everything was catching up with him. How much had he slept? Their cold rest in the dark of the cave? Did time dozing in his EVA count? A few minutes drooling in his seat during re-entry to Kelter?

Evan awoke, stiff and cold to the bone. Kate sat next to him. Painting, of all things. Evan got up and stomped around, anything to restore some circulation and shake off the chill.

Restored, he looked at Kate's work. The central figure was obviously Mira. A blur of motion, bounding off a ledge and casting for the next hold, surrounded by dark that was somehow warm and not forbidding. No single feature of the climber was recognizable, but it added up in its entirety to the image they had already seen repeatedly, of an impossible climb gracefully surmounted. The climber was portrayed as something in between a person and a Valkyrie.

"Mira, check this out! It's you!" They could hear each other now, if they spoke loudly and clearly.

Mira sauntered over. "Pfft," she pronounced. "Art? More like a collage. Do you teach that to those same kids who have to read your books? Cutouts and imaginary stories, that will definitely prepare the next generation for leadership. Let's get going."

"Keep that one, Kate," Evan told her. "I want a copy."

As they got under way, the passage narrowed, and then they found themselves clambering over, under, and between boulders. The spaces became smaller still. Mira, leading the way, halted, creating a traffic jam. Evan found himself staring at the soles of Mira's boots. "I need to hand you some rocks," she told him. "Here they come."

"What? I thought you had been through this way. To your secret exit."

"I have," Mira said. "But this needs some work, so everybody can fit easily. You know, like your belly."

There was nothing wrong with his belly. Granted, it went out rather than in, these days. But not by much. It was just fine.

She passed him rocks, sometimes pushing them back with her feet. Evan parked the first few, then had to start passing the rocks farther back to Kate. Fortunately, even the largest of them didn't weigh very much, although they still had all of their mass.

It seemed like a lot more material than a simple gardening exercise for their comfort.

At last Mira crawled forward, making room. "Come on through," she called.

Evan and Kate wiggled through the hole, emerging in a large room. Ahead, Evan could hear the sound of the wind, stronger and deeper than ever. Follow the wind, he remembered Mira telling him from her tales of exploration.

"We're here. What are we waiting for?" Evan asked.

"If we're all back together, I need your attention," Mira told them.

"You're the cave guide. So, where do we go?"

"Before we take another step, I need both of your agreement on something. This next place, I have never shown to anyone. Ever. And it needs to stay that way."

"Come on, it's just a bunch of cave passages," Evan declared. "They're all the same. And I think we have bigger fish to fry."

"In a few minutes, I'll show you, and then you'll understand. And we'll talk about the promise. First, help me out."

Under Mira's direction, they gathered rocks and threw them down into the hole from which they had emerged. When it was full, she had them gather and pile more rocks on top. Finally she was satisfied, and led them down a comfortable walking passage, and the sound grew louder, and more irregular.

It was not the sound of air.

From the high balcony, their lights shone on the racing cascade, feeding into a deep swirling pool. The lights reflected on the walls and ceiling of the cavern beyond. The river continued, down and to their right, around a corner and out of sight. The cold of the water reached out to them, even from far below.

"This." Mira faced them. "This place. This river."

Evan was amazed. He tried to estimate the flow. It was several cubic meters per second, at least. He had seen free flowing water so rarely, and never on Kelter, that it was a challenging calculation.

The pool looked like it was at least two meters deep, and was about four meters wide. But the eddies made a mockery of any kind of estimation. Below the surface, in which direction was the water moving?

The cascade was another place to consider. But how much of the flow was water, and how much was air?

Regardless, it was an immense amount of water. So many cubic meters flowing past, every minute of every day. Enough to supply Abilene, and more.

He remembered learning the sailor's shower as a child. Swab the parts that matter. Rinse them into the recovery system. Good enough was good enough.

"This will never be known, to anyone. We will all swear it."

"Mira, you can't be serious. This much water, what a resource." Evan was still trying to run the numbers.

"It is not," Mira declared. "It will never be a resource. Never. Unless you both agree, I won't leave this spot. And you can't find the way out, not in a million years. Swear on whatever you hold most sacred, and tell me what you swear upon."

"Oh Mira, I am so happy for you!" Kate was spouting nonsense. "You see it. You understand. I always knew it! Do you believe?"

Mira scoffed. "What, believe in the cartoon sky guy, with the beard? Hell no."

Kate waved her open hand. "It doesn't have to be that, exactly. Just

– something, that matters. More than whatever trifle one of us may want at a moment. Something bigger."

It certainly was bigger than them. Cubic meters per second. And, it could sweep them away. Easily.

Mira stood tall. "Use whatever label you want. I just know who and what I will die to defend. And that includes this river. And the tree, of course."

"I'll gladly swear it!" Kate moved toward Mira.

Mira put out her hand, palm up. "Don't. Even. Consider it. I've seen how you act toward the people you despise. The lady golfer hug and a platitude. Just swear the oath, and that will do."

Kate recited her oath. It was on the long side, Evan thought.

All eyes were on Evan.

"Ok, whatever," he shrugged.

Mira simply stood there. "That won't do."

"What?"

"That won't do." Then she sat down. "I don't move until you show me you mean it."

Evan decided that Mira was off her rocker. "Do I need to point out where we are? You know, deep in this cave, pursued by platoons of soldiers who presumably want to kill us?"

"I can wait. I think they'll be a while."

It appeared that she could wait as long as required. And time was wasting. Soon they would be shivering.

Evan wondered what would satisfy Mira. If she wanted to withhold this fantastic resource from a thirsty planet, that was her business, although it irked him that she was forcing him to be part of it.

What did he consider sacred, anyway?

The scientific method? No, that was a just a tool.

Gödel's theorem? It was a core principle, and he lived by it, or its corollary in the physical world, the Heisenberg Uncertainty Principle.

Yet, he would never apply that word, sacred, to either of those ideas. And he would feel like an idiot swearing on them. He wasn't sure if he could finish such an oath and pretend to be serious.

Evan shined his light around the chamber. On a far wall, there was a steady drip, about one drop every two or three seconds. Each drop fell for a meter into a shallow pool. The outlet was the tiniest trickle, which joined another, slightly larger stream. The combined flow ran down a slope to join the cascade that raged into the pool. From there, the identity of the small stream, and of each component drop, was instantly and completely lost.

Once, he had visited an area of waterfalls and rocky streams on Caledonia. This stream was oddly different than those. He watched as the planet's pull only lazily convinced the water to flow to the lowest place. Rounded blobs accruing in each fall and then being smashed on rock or absorbed back into the pool below.

The stream had been there for millennia, beyond the threshold of human knowledge. Some of the rain that fell once or twice a year in the highlands to the north, even above the altitude of breathable air, gathered in this stream and flowed every moment, in a place that did not know day or night.

At last, one human had come upon the sight. And she had backed away, leaving it free to flow as it always had. Choosing not to stake a claim that would have brought her a lifetime of unbounded riches.

Mira. The last person he would have ever expected to make such a choice.

The river flowed past, unmindful of their presence, no more affected by the light than by the eternal dark that had preceded their arrival, and that would soon be restored.

At last Evan understood.

He swore his oath.

Part 5:
The Daughters of Atlas

Live Broadcast

"Okay Governor, here's your script. We've got a few minutes to practice, but we don't have long. As soon as we get it recorded, we're going to turn around and release it live. This can't wait." The frazzled producer had none of his usual smooth manner.

Governor Rezar looked at the displays and began to read.

He looked up from the script. "Is this for real?"

"Yes sir, that's why we had to pull you from your tournament. I am deeply sorry about that. It's an emergency." The producer listened to something in his earpiece. "We need to record in just a few minutes."

"A nuclear strike?"

"I'm afraid we couldn't create a True Story in time, so we had to go with some objectively factual elements. It's the best we can do. And by the way, it's tactical nuclear," the producer clarified.

The governor spluttered. "How could this—"

The producer's expression looked like he was trying to settle down an anxious performing animal. "We'll give you a full briefing, but right now, we need to get this broadcast out. We're experiencing huge losses in confidence. The market is down over eight percent, and that's everybody's retirement. So we need to help our constituents."

Rezar studied the script. The makeup artist came in. Rezar was experienced at learning his scripts during makeup and hair. The script was short. It was no problem. During recording, he had the prompter as well, although he had learned that he looked much more authentic if he knew what was coming.

A nuclear strike. On his planet. This was wrong. Even an uninhabited patch of desert.

Rezar queried for recent command-level communications with Affirmatix and found the recording from a few hours earlier. General Leon and Admiral Incento, practically falling over themselves to accommodate Vice President Lobeck of Affirmatix. It went beyond the normal privilege and respect that was accorded to a top figure of any Sister. The voices smelled of fear.

He searched, chasing down leads. At one point he had to enter an additional security code, beyond his usual credentials. Rezar was glad he could remember the code, and that it was still current.

Then he had it. The D6, a weapon that could end all life on Kelter, was insystem. The ultimate threat, exacting frantic cooperation from the Kelter security forces, to locate and turn over three fugitives. Unbelievable, not just the fact of it, but that he hadn't been told.

"Governor, it's time." The producer brought Rezar back from his inquiries.

Rezar felt like his mind was split in two. The extremity of the situation could barely exist in the same universe as the words he had been practicing and was about to recite.

The governor began his address. "Good afternoon, fellow citizens, consumers, and hard-working, patriotic supporters of our way of life. I need to talk to you about a very important topic. You may have heard that a tactical nuclear device was used in the Valley of Dreams site, forty kilometers to the northwest of Abilene. This was a necessary part of an ongoing counterterrorism operation that we conducted in a public-private partnership with the Affirmatix Family. We were forced to take this measure in order to absolutely assure that certain very dangerous materials were completely destroyed."

"I am happy to report that the operation was one hundred percent successful. We are completing our site assessment and will be wrapping up operations over the next few days. We also expect that the blockade, which was necessarily put in place around the system, will likely be lifted sometime in the next two or three days, as soon as we have completed our verification."

"One unfortunate result of this will be that we will have to re-designate the area around this operation as a military reservation, to protect you from hazards and assure everyone's safety. We'll be publishing the new boundaries of the reservation into all navigation systems in the next few hours."

"I know that the events of the past few days have created a lot of anxiety, and I assure you that I am working, all day and every day, to make sure that everything is back to normal just as soon as possible. Meanwhile, please go about your business. Remember that your job needs you and the families need you. Thank you and have a great day."

The producer looked pleased with the result. "Thank you so much for coming, Governor, and we'll get you right back to your tournament. The players have all halted as a courtesy to you, so it will be your turn to play just as soon as you get there."

The seventh hole. Par four, eight hundred ten yards. Rezar had launched a fantastic drive and would be hitting his second from only two hundred yards out. If he could stick the green, he had a great chance at birdie. It was the one golf course on Kelter that had actual living grass on the greens, and that was softer than the usual turf. It was his favorite course.

"Please send my regrets to the other players," Rezar told the producer. "I must attend to a pressing matter."

"Marcom advises that the appearance of normalcy is critical on today of all days," the producer protested. "And I heard you're in a great position on the seventh."

"Then everyone else will just have to appear normal in my stead," the governor said, and headed out of the studio.

His guard detail fell in with him. Colonel Ellis had been with him for five years. She approached her duty to protect the governor with a seriousness that sometimes embarrassed him. The others in the detail were all highly trusted but less personally vested. They simply did their jobs, in rotating shifts.

Rezar knew, without even having to check, that Ellis had planned the egress route, and made sure that others had swept it within the past few minutes. That the vehicle was secure. That nothing would happen.

"Deborah," he said. "I need you to do something for me."

"Name it, Governor," Ellis replied.

"I need to know what's happening out there. In the Valley of Dreams. We can't rely on the information from Affirmatix."

"Excuse me, sir?"

"I want you to go to the site. Find any evidence you can. Check for survivors in the vicinity. Anything you find, bring it back directly to me. Nobody else. Will you do that for me? As a personal favor."

"I'll send a detail, sir." Ellis started to pull up her phone.

"No. You. Lead the force in person."

"But my first duty−" she protested.

"Is to protect me, I know." They had gone down this road before. "And at this moment, investigating the Valley of Dreams is the best way to do that. Please."

Ellis considered for a moment. "I'm on it," she said.

Unfinished Business

For more than a kilometer Evan and Kate followed Mira along the course of the stream through the cave, doing their best to stay out of the water. It was a raging torrent in most places, and stunningly cold, as they found out when they refilled their water containers. Cold, but fresh, instead of the saline of all other natural water known on Kelter.

Above the stream, a braided series of upper level passages wound along. Once, the stream had flowed up there, until it had cut farther and farther down to its present course. In some places, the upper passages were separate and had their own floors, making for easy travel. In other spots, an upper passage would cut directly over the stream passage, and they needed to leap across.

The noise was omnipresent.

The walls and floor of the cave also looked very different from before. In the dry passages, the rock was coated with a fine layer of dust, or floored with sediment. While the passage often had strange and fantastic shapes, the color was a dull grey or tan.

Here, the wetness provided a view into the layers, veins, and other fine features of the rock. Evan found himself stopping to look at the details, before the cold and Mira's urging hurried him along.

In some places the ripples of the water reflected their lights into waves that reflected all over the walls and ceiling of the cave, a fantastic effect of which he had never seen the like.

It was a cold, forbidding, and dangerous place. And it was amazing.

The most difficult stretch of passage was the place where every level aligned, forming a single tall hallway over a hundred meters high, floored with rushing water. Mira took them on an intricate route along a series of ledges, twice having to jump entirely across to the opposite wall. In those places she had trailed the line, which made the crossing easy for Kate. Evan leapt across as the tail, with the line tied around him but no certainty that it would help if he missed his mark.

When they were back in a safer upper level, they walked along, until Mira pointed to a small hole in the floor. They could hear the roar from below. "That's it," she said. "The last of the river."

Evan and Kate looked at each other with a joy that belied their overall situation. That ordeal, at least, was done.

"Where does the stream come from?" asked Evan.

"It's a mystery," Mira told him. "I have gone another two kilometers upstream. I came to a waterfall and was able to jump up it, using some ledges. Then I got up another two waterfalls. At my farthest point, I got to a fourth waterfall, taller than the others, and pouring down through a small hole at the top. Air and mist swirling everywhere."

"Could you see beyond?"

"Big, and black. There is some kind of huge room up there. And the river must go a long way farther. I tried to jump up through it. Once. Very bad idea. I think the only way to get to the top would be to set some bolts in the wall to anchor a climbing rope or a ladder, and work up it a few steps at a time. I have always wanted to come back, with a crew, and climb it, because I think it's the greatest mystery in this world. But I couldn't bring myself to show the river to anyone else."

"The edge of knowledge," Evan considered. "You know, when we were digging at the Valley of Dreams, I wasn't too interested in climbing around in the cave. I had my own puzzles to solve, " he told her. "But if you don't find anyone better, I'll help you with the climb. You would have to show me how to do all of it, with the bolts and the ropes."

"You've got a deal. The name of the waterfall is Unfinished Business. If we climb it, then it will need a new name."

"Oh, no," he disagreed. "Keep the name. For history."

They left the hole in the floor, and the river, traveling in passages that were once again bone dry.

Now the passage walls were covered with angular white crystals that sparkled in their headlights. In some places the crystals grew in the form of bushes, up to three meters across, mostly filling up the passage so that it was necessary to squeeze past them.

The most beautiful part of the cave was also the sharpest. Evan was grateful for the gloves that had been part of the chopper gear, and which he still wore.

After the sounds of water were completely gone, Mira signaled a break. A round room with a perfectly flat floor greeted them. It was even soft. Some ancient stream, or perhaps the wind, had seen fit to provide them with a perfect cushion of sediment. They ate a light meal in the comfortable spot. It was hard to imagine moving any time soon.

"We may as well get some rest here after dinner," Mira told them. "Best place we'll have for a while, and we can't go all the way without at least a little more sleep."

"I'm good with that," Evan said. "At least I'm not in an EVA with the suit telling me I need to sleep in order to conserve oxygen."

"I was just camping," Kate said. "Trying not to think of the end of my family. And a few hours later we're deep in the cave, running from Arn Lobeck and his minions. What brought them upon us?"

"It's kind of a long story. I'll tell it all to you, and it will make quite a tale. When this is all over, maybe you could write another book, except it wouldn't be *Tails of Versari*. What are you up to, five of them?"

"It's seven now, Evan."

"Vanity press," Mira put in. "You give them away, right? And the Versari didn't even have tails. Just stubs, really. Stubs of the Versari, there's a name for you."

"Mira, enough! If you could stop that backbiting for just long enough for us to get out of this cave—"

"Thank you Evan, but I don't need you to defend me," Kate said. "The schools need my books, and they have no budget any more. *Tail of Rissta* was read by practically the entire eighth grade on Abilene. I'm proud of that, and it doesn't matter what Mira or anyone else says."

"I picked up one just before I went to Aurora," Evan told Kate. "*Tail of Uve*. A nice read."

"You said that it was filled with unproven and unscientific crap," Mira added helpfully.

"Well, the part about the Versari sensing where the glomes went, that's pretty far out," Evan admitted. "But, maybe I have a different perspective now. I enjoyed it."

"Evan, you read *Tail of Uve*? Why didn't you send me a note? I would have loved to hear from you."

"I'm not much of a letter writer, you know. I didn't know what to say. Oh Kate, I liked your book, and by the way I'm sorry to hear about your parents. Oh, no. I shouldn't have said that."

"No, that's okay," Kate told him. "And I wish you would have written."

Evan felt an old hurt rise. "Well, I didn't know that. When it happened, you know how I found out? A news report. The obituary. Three weeks old. Just saw it by accident. Your parents, and you didn't even tell me. Didn't even ask me to come to their celebration."

"I didn't write you. Do you want to know why? Do you really want to know the reason? You ask and I'll tell you!"

Evan knew he was going the wrong way. The death of her parents, and he was being the angry one. But he couldn't help himself. "You tell me. Why it wasn't worth even sending me a note."

"Because you were gone! Always gone, always light years away. No letters. Just another dig. When you stopped coming back to Kelter, I knew I wasn't worth the trip. Some rocks a million years old were more important than me. That's why!"

Evan looked down. He had no answer. Nowhere to go. Only the woman in front of him, speaking the truth.

She had been with him on the day, years before, that he had stood on the low hill overlooking the Valley of Dreams, as the emergency room doc told him the narrative from halfway across the planet, of everything they had tried. The audio had phased in and out, but Evan had heard enough to know that the moments he had always hoped for, with his own father, would never be. And he had thanked the doc for her efforts, signed off, and stood there, entirely empty.

Kate had comforted him, stood by him, and helped him. Not just at that moment, but in the days and weeks to follow. She had gone with him to the celebration. She had taken care of those things he suddenly didn't care about, but still mattered. She had forgiven him when he had said things that were horribly wrong. She had held him. She had been there.

In turn, when he had had the chance to do one good thing for her, he had done – nothing.

He remembered his mother's advice, the best advice he had ever received, although he had scoffed at the time. She had taught him what to say when nothing else would serve.

"I was wrong. And I am sorry," he told Kate. He looked back up to see that she shared his tears. "And I have missed you. I'm just really bad at showing it."

Mira abruptly got up. "Oh no," she said. "If you two are about to get all snuggy, I've seen enough of that for one lifetime." She grabbed her pack and walked down the passage, sticking her index finger into her open mouth.

As Mira's steps faded in the distance, Evan looked at Kate. He knew what he hoped for. Reconciliation. Another chance. But did she also?

Kate called out to the departing Mira. "I wouldn't worry too much about that!"

The Daughters of Atlas

"It is a very fine day, is it not?" Ravi appeared to be in great spirits.

Sonia equivocated. "There's no weather up here, you know. Space. It's not even day or night."

"But it is a fine day in our lives. On our campus on Alcyone, it is early morning, did you know that? Your little ones, about to enjoy a Saturday. The blossoms opening for the day. There is so much hope now."

Ravi had never struck her as much of a botanist. What was with him?

"I do miss them," Sonia agreed.

"And soon you will not have to. The gods will deliver us safely back."

"You mean instead of us going back by ship?" She tried a little humor.

"You may think that we have long since left the gods behind, centuries ago, but it is not so. They walk among us now. Doing what gods have always done. Providing well for those who serve, and punishing those who do not."

"Ravi, what in the world are you talking about?"

"Look." He dialed in a display to show a starfield, and then zoomed in to a star cluster. Familiar, except the positions of the stars were not quite the same as she remembered from her childhood. "The daughters of Atlas. On every planet in known space they shine. From each place where we may go, we see a different arrangement, but they are always there. Ruling the lesser stars that surround them. The shape may change, but the seven are always there."

"You mean, the Sisters," she said.

"And if the altar at our village is Affirmatix, then let it be so. All we must do is serve well."

'They're just families, you know," Sonia told him. "Companies, they used to be called."

"Just. Exactly. They define what is just, through the exercise of their power. And that we must not question. It is a practical thing. In former days, people imagined they could please the spirits, and their offerings would bring them good fortune. But now, it is really so."

"Good fortune? What do you mean?"

"For the first time I confessed what I have most wished for in my life, even knowing that it is impossible. Just one day later, I find out that it may be so, once I get home. It is a miracle. Do you not see?"

Sonia was still trying to come to terms with the strike on the Valley of Dreams. Almost certain death for those they were pursuing. And she had done nothing to prevent it. Just a logical continuation, as Ravi had so incisively pointed out, of years of her work on Alcyone.

But Sonia knew that she could not share any of her turmoil with Ravi. "Which one is Alcyone?" she asked.

"From this view, it is the lowest on the left. See, we can look upon our home, even from here. A home that has been granted to just a few of us, who are privileged to live in such a place instead of out here in the cold universe. A home where even the impossible might be. We will be there soon."

Sonia put a hand on his shoulder. "Ravi. Krishnan. I hope we can get home soon. Each of us, we must do those things we think are best, for ourselves and for those we love. And then believe that it will be all right. Maybe it still will be."

For a moment, they held each other. "Yes, that is right," he told her. "I think you do see it."

Shared Burden

Evan awoke, stiff, to see that Kate and Mira had made breakfast, using what they had available. It actually wasn't bad, considering the circumstances, and there was even coffee that Kate had originally brought for her camp.

"My plan was to publish a paper," Evan said between sips, "with my latest findings from the Aurora dig. Exo Expo Twelve, coming up in four months. The call for papers is already past, but I know all the organizers, and I was sure I could get a slot. Maybe a keynote, with my new stuff.

"Big fish, small pond, you know," he continued. "We might get only fifty attendees. But they would be people that matter. To me, anyway. If you give a good paper, then you get to hold court at the evening reception. People come up and ask questions, and challenge your findings. And you drink bad wine. Not sure what it is, the wine is always bad. Horrible white or worse red, take your pick. But you drink it anyway because it's part of the experience. I was really looking forward to that. This paper was going to be great. Such a breakthrough."

"Now we're getting to it. Please go on." Kate.

And then Evan told her everything.

Kate listened carefully, asking for clarification on a few points, but mostly allowing Evan to narrate as he would. Mira, who had heard it before, added a few observations. Evan's words echoed off the walls and ceiling of the cave chamber as he spoke. At last he was done.

"We could go anywhere" Kate said. "Any star system! And we would know how to get back."

Evan couldn't see her expression, because they had all learned hours before not to shine their lights directly in anyone's face. But he could hear her emerging amazement.

"There might be a few star systems that don't have a feasible route," Evan pointed out. "But that's the sum of it, more or less. Over a million glome routes, to over a hundred thousand stars. The whole network for our corner of the galaxy. And there could be more – I just worked with the data set that had the least cosmic radiation damage."

"No wonder Affirmatix wants it to themselves! You didn't see that coming?"

"I didn't know what it was until I had it. The record could have been anything. The stock market results from a million years ago, whatever. But in retrospect, Affirmatix was betting I would find something big. For this expedition, they sponsored one hundred percent, exclusive. They got commercialization rights, and I could publish academic papers. The way I saw it, if they wanted to make Versari action figures, or a video game, then they could."

"Clearly they had something else in mind," Mira put in.

"When the warships arrived, maybe I should have just gone back to the research station, and it would have averted the whole thing. But now I don't think so. They just went crazy. Warships. Missiles. Blockades. Chasing us through the cave. Stopping at nothing. To keep a secret."

"To make sure there's not even a hint that it exists," Mira pondered.

"Anyone I even contact is in danger, whether they know anything or not. For instance, that Denison fellow who rode down with us. Who knows if he has been rounded up by now, to find out what he knows."

"And he didn't tell me a thing about you!" Kate burst out. "Secrets everywhere!"

Evan was surprised. "You know him?"

"He's one of my captains. He rode down with you, and still you didn't send along word that you were alive. Let me go on thinking you were dead."

Evan turned to Mira. "You held out on me!"

"Because if I told you, Evan, I knew you would do something foolish. And our current situation proves me right. I made Denison promise not to say who he worked for."

"Because you were keeping us apart," Kate declared.

Mira agreed. "Exactly. For good reason, as we see right now."

"You might have a point there," Kate conceded. "But back to the present. If the problem is due to it being a secret, then the answer is obvious. It needs to be public. When we get out, we'll contact the media. I have some friends at the top channels in the Spoon Feed. They'll be so excited to get the scoop."

Evan raised his hand up. "It's the right kind of solution – spreading the information so widely that we don't matter anymore individually. And there are other really good reasons to do that – I've been thinking this through. But do we really know the media would take the story?"

"Oh yeah! The ratings would be through the roof! Who would turn it down?"

"All of them," Mira replied. "All of them would turn it down. Every single one."

"But why?" Kate asked.

"A story this big would be sequestered, right out of the gate," Mira told her. "Then it would be evaluated by the infoterrorism office, and their subscribers, to determine whether it should be released. They might release it, they might not, and I am betting not. They would have to consider the interest of Affirmatix, and releasing the story would definitely not be in their interest. In any case, the only certainty is that we would lose control of it."

"Independents?"

"We could find some independents who would run with it. But would they have the reach to really get the word out? And let's not forget that any person we tell is instantly placed in serious danger. Who do we want to do that to?"

"I still say we need to publish it," Kate said. "Widely. The solution is dilution. They can't track down and kill everyone. I could run a big advertising campaign. Oh, maybe not. Not anymore."

"I am sorry to share this burden with you," Evan told them. "I can't solve it. First I knew, and it almost got me killed. Now you two know, and that's worse. And we have left a trail of others who may already have been harmed. Once you have the knowledge, there is no unknowing it. That is, as long as we are alive."

Happygram

When she saw the notification on her phone, Sonia abruptly got up and left the meeting. "Carry on," she told Ravi and Merriam. "I'll be right back."

Fifty seconds later the door slid closed behind Sonia in her quarters. "Main display," she said. "Run the message from Alcyone."

The scene opened with a lazy, low flyover. Flowering shrubs, ranging from pink through a deep magenta.

The play set came into view. Simone and Jennifer climbed and slid happily. The shot widened to show Yvette, smiling and watching them. The voiceover began.

"Hi mommy!" the girls said in chorus.

Yvette's voice was low, sweet, and wonderful. For the shortest of moments, Sonia was home. "Sweetie, we wanted to send you a little note to say that we all love you and believe in you. We are doing just great. In fact, I was given some extra paid vacation while you are on your trip. Up to two weeks if I want. So we were thinking of going to the hot springs for a few days."

"Tell her! Tell mommy!"

"Oh, and Simone wanted me to tell you that she got a hundred percent on her advanced math test."

"A hundred and five!" Simone corrected.

"And she got the extra credit question right. She knows you'll be so proud."

Sonia watched her daughters playing, and tried to imagine something that mattered less than a math score.

"So have a great trip, and we will have a party when you get back."

"Party!" Jennifer agreed.

"One, two, three: We love you!" the three of them chorused.

The camera rose until it was looking down on the entire yard. And then the video was over.

Was the point of view selected on purpose? Gracefully floating through the garden, just a meter or so above the ground, then flying off.

The colorful and enchanting denizens of every garden and park on Alcyone. Welcomed by everyone, the symbol of serene daily life on Alcyone. Over four hundred varieties had been identified, each expressing small variations in color, size, and shape.

Hobbyists strove to capture the best images of their translucent wings shimmering in the sun. There was an annual contest for the best such picture.

But Sonia knew what the dragonflies were.

Dividing The Spoils

Two of the delegates on Sanzite's ship had by now been replaced by the Presidents of their families. Counting Sanzite, that made three Presidents and four Delegates.

The Delegates were empowered to negotiate at the highest level on behalf of their family, but Sanzite appreciated the other Presidents making the journey. He knew how much he hated to travel.

Sanzite, obviously, was the only one of them who was in a tank of thick fluid rather than walking around. The others showed their respect by treating him as simply another president, facing him when he spoke, arranging themselves so that he was always a core part of the discussion. It made sense, since he was the host. No shaking hands, though. That had stopped many years ago.

Sanzite called them to order. "I trust that everyone has had a chance to evaluate the information that I have provided. Does anyone need more time?"

That would be embarrassing. He had provided a full two hours. Nobody asked for a delay.

"So you know what we have discovered," Sanzite continued, "and you may be gaining some idea of its value. We have done a valuation, and I was shocked by the result. If we manage this resource correctly, it is valued at ten times the amount of all existing asset value. All assets, that exist anywhere in civilization. Ten times that amount."

The designers of the travel tank had at least done one thing right. The top edge of the tank looked down over a slightly sunken floor, and nobody could look down on the fluid surface, even when standing. As Sanzite presented his findings, he was able to look just slightly down on the assembled presidents and delegates.

"Why are you telling us all this?" President Lu, of ProSolutiana. "Why are you not exploiting this discovery for your benefit?"

"Oh, we are." Sanzite smiled, because he could still do that. "We have identified several of the most promising new planets, and we have ships on their way already."

"Still, why involve us?" Lu pressed. "Are you simply here to gloat?"

"We are here for a very good reason. My associate Mr. Lobeck, who is directing our operations around Kelter, has forecasted that Affirmatix could control over ninety nine percent of all assets using this discovery. But he is not paying attention to a key principle."

"The Controlling Interest Rule. Of course." Lu nodded.

"Precisely," Sanzite affirmed. "We abide by this rule on a micro scale. None of us may subscribe to more than forty percent the salary and expenses of any government official. There are many good reasons, such as avoiding bidding wars over the subscription for a powerful post. But the biggest single reason is that if one of us insisted on a controlling interest in a top government official, the other six would not stand for it. In this case, on a macro scale, at some future day when you discern the trend, you would all take Affirmatix down, and we would be far worse off than if we had not made the discovery."

"So what do you propose?" Lu asked.

Sanzite laid out his plan. "We will divide the value up in a manner that awards very substantial rewards to Affirmatix, because we brought it to the table, but does not violate the Controlling Interest Rule. I propose three shares for Affirmatix, and one share each for the other six families."

Sanzite had to stop himself from his deeply ingrained habit of gesturing when expressing a key idea. He didn't want to bump against the confining walls of the travel tank. Someday, he resolved, he would just have a full size tank installed in a dedicated ship, so he could go wherever he wanted in comfort.

"Three shares out of nine, that's one third," Lu objected. "Rather close to the forty percent limit, don't you think?"

"Three is too much," put in Delegate Alsatie from RealHealth.

"Two. Two shares." President Remon from Individua.

"Very good," returned Sanzite. "We have established that three shares may be too much, and I tell you that two shares is definitely too little. Let us leave the rest of the haggling to the lawyers. Do we have agreement on the principle? We will divide this bounty. We will not war over it. And, we will maximize the value we can realize from the discovery, by working together. Most importantly, we will coordinate on the schedule on which we announce new discoveries."

"We can accelerate the pace of discovery," said Remon.

"Only by a very little bit," Sanzite responded. "For the most part, we must keep on a schedule very similar to what we would have discovered anyway. Most importantly, we do not want anyone to detect a trend of greater discoveries that cannot be explained."

"But for the crowded worlds—"

"Crowds are good for property values. They are mostly our properties, let me remind you. We must proceed carefully, so that we do not undermine the value of the investments we all hold."

The Presidents and the delegates continued the discussion for several hours. The implications. How to develop their discovery, without attracting unreasonable attention. It was the postcompetitive spirit at its finest, and this made Sanzite proud. Coopetition, for the good of everyone.

After a time, they came to agreement on many topics, and identified others for further discussion. Details, that others could work out. Finally, it was time to adjourn.

Sanzite was glad they were done. It had been a long meeting, although very productive. And, he was overdue for physical therapy.

It was not a good idea to neglect his health.

Publish Or Perish

Mira suddenly stopped them in a small room and announced, "I know how to solve our problem. But first, I need to know that it's real, beyond a shadow of a doubt. If you have a wondrous glome chart as you've described, let's see it."

Without hesitation, Evan pulled a card out of his pouch and held it up. "This is it."

She held out her hand. "Give it here."

Evan surrendered the card. "I can bring it up on your tablet."

Mira inserted the card, and Evan invoked a program. "This isn't the actual artifact," he explained for Kate as the tablet initialized. "The original format couldn't be read by our machines. This is just a basic database program with a lot of the information translated into it."

"All right, let's see what she's got," Mira said.

"It's loaded. What glome do you want to know about?"

Mira pondered. "There's a problem here. Anything I could confirm, you could have loaded from any star atlas. Anything else, I have no way of knowing that it's correct."

Evan threw up his hands. "I don't want you to be convinced. I just want all of us to survive this. You don't need to know, you don't want to know. Forget I said anything."

"Show me the real one again. The original."

Evan pulled a small box out of his pocket and opened it, then proffered it to Mira.

Mira reached out and felt the object drop into her palm. It was the amber cube, about a centimeter on a side, which Evan had shown her while they were heading to Top Station. She held it to her lamp. Light spilled through, casting flowing patterns on her thumb. "This is crazy."

"This is real," he told her. "And, I can prove it. You know that I glomed from Aurora, right?"

"You say you came from Aurora."

"Ok, we agree that I came in from two million kilometers trailing Kelter Four. And you know I've been in Aurora for the last two years. Well, here's the thing. That's not a known way into this system! You know there are only four known emergent glomes here. Well, there's a fifth, and I explored it by diving blind into an unknown glome, based only on my read of the data from this artifact which said the glome came out here."

Mira considered. She knew the glome had not been publicly known. That fact had been all over the news. It was conceivable that it had somehow been known, but secret, or recently discovered. But this was unlikely for the simple fact that a person or family who discovered a glome between two known and inhabitable worlds was already wealthy by virtue of that discovery, and the associated royalties collectible over the first forty nine standard years of operation.

She realized that there was another way to check. "I want you to query on the star AL-54B, no inhabited planets, one relay station."

"I can do that. Give me a minute . . . okay, here it is. What do you want to know?"

"Tell me, is there −" No. Mira realized that was not the way to control the experiment. There was a better method. "Just show me all glomes in that system farther out than a billion kilometers."

Evan queried a minute further then pulled back so she could see the screen. "Here you go, an even dozen."

There it was. At 1,350 MKM out, 8 degrees north of plane, sidereal 34 degrees. She knew it was there, and nobody else in the world did. Twelve years before, she had been on the first ship, the first human ship, she corrected herself, in the system. At the very edge of their sweep, she was certain that there was the signature of a glome, worth logging. The captain had overruled her because the strength of the signal was below the ASTM standard, and there had been no time or budget to alter course and get closer than 50,000 kilometers to be sure. It was too far out for practical use, anyway. Far out glomes almost always went to other far out glomes.

"This one, where does it go?" she asked.

Evan selected an icon. "Let's see. Looks like the Alpha entry into the glome goes to a system about 50 parsecs inward, sidereal 340 degrees, not yet explored, also over a billion kilometers out. Upsilon Andromeda, if you like the mythical names."

"Hang on, why did you specify the Alpha?" Mira asked. "That's the only entry to a glome that ever works."

"That we know of, right? The dataset also specifies destinations for the Omega entry." The Omega vector was the exact opposite point of entry into a glome from the Alpha. "But here's the strange thing – as far as I can tell, the Versari data is wrong about the Omega destinations. It lists some entries that can't possibly be right – they would have been discovered long ago. That's a big reason it took me so long to decode the matrix. Only the Alpha destinations match what we know."

"But you nailed the location of that glome, and I am the only person who has ever seen it. It's true, isn't it? All of it."

Evan nodded. "It's all true."

"The glome routes to a hundred thousand new star systems," Mira considered. "Endless wealth. I could take it. Right now. I am the only one who knows the way out. Leave you two with lots of time to make up, in the dark."

Mira stood, holding the tablet. "I could find the perfect planet. Once this blows over and the fleet is gone, get a crew together and light out for the ragged edge. What would be better than that? So, you two, why wouldn't I do that?"

Kate looked horrified. Evan took her hand. "Don't worry," he told Kate. "It's a riddle, and I know the answer."

Evan looked up at Mira. "Why not?"

"Yes. Why not?"

"Because it's you."

They regarded each other.

Just a hint of a smile from Mira was enough. "Do I get first choice of a planet, at least?"

"Pick of the litter," Evan assured her. "Assuming we make it through this. Now please stop frightening Kate like that."

"I can have a little fun, can't I?"

"Hey, I wasn't scared!" Kate protested. "Anyway, I know a little about business these days, and I know exactly how Affirmatix plans to gain as much as possible. They're going to publish every glome and claim every planet. For the royalties and the rights. And they can only get to everything first if nobody else knows about this – that's the key. Evan, you said that they went crazy, but that's not true. Affirmatix is just acting in their rational self-interest."

"Sociopathic self-interest," he amended. "A massive case of lucraphrenia."

"Rational, sociopathic." Kate held up two open hands as if weighing each word equally. "Same thing, when you're that big. Believe me, I have lived it since I started running my little family. They'll take an advantage like this and run everyone else out of business. There's no actual sisterhood there."

Mira nodded. "Just one major, running everything."

"I expect that's their plan," Kate said. "They won't think twice. None of the Sisters would hesitate, given the same chance. And we need to stop them. Mira, you said you have a solution."

"If you're done yammering, then yes I do. There is one person who can inform all of Kelter about this. And by extension, all of civilization."

Evan knew where Mira was going. "The infoterrorist."

"Yes. Axiom. Freeing information, that's his reason for living."

"He's got really interesting ideas," Evan said. "I'd like to talk with him more. But – getting this out to the whole planet and even beyond, all at once – that's a big job. Can he pull it off? He said he would protect us, and he failed to do that. I mean, what has he actually done recently? Say, in the last fifty years."

"I think he has been waiting," Mira said.

"It's been a pretty long wait, then. Listen, I know he was pretty famous or infamous in his day, in the thirties, and I know you're fond of him, but has it ever occurred to you that the reason he hasn't been caught is that he's not worth catching? These days he just hangs around naked in his infoterrorist retirement home."

"He's our best chance. If anybody can get the story far and wide, it's Axiom. It's not just him. He has friends, and I know some of them." Mira pulled out the two readers. "Remember these? Once we get out of the cave, all we need is a connection, stick in a card with whatever we want to send to him, and we're done. There's another huge advantage. For any other choice, we would need to get back to civilization, and maybe travel where we can be tracked, in order to pitch the story. To get it to Axiom, we just need these."

"How will we know he's not having his afternoon nap?"

"You just don't know. Evan, you didn't trust me before. Trust me now. This is what we need to do."

"Is he our only choice?"

"Axiom is the one choice that might work."

"My mother taught me a business rule," put in Kate. "And that was – Never make a big decision when you think you don't have a choice."

Mira turned and glared at her.

"Well, there was one exception," Kate admitted. "That was if you really didn't have a choice. Then you have to do it."

Evan threw up his hands. "Publish or Perish! And if our publishing house is Uncle Axiom, then so be it."

Contingency Planning

Captain Roe located his second in command, Commander Varma. "It's been some time since we've seen the prospect of action," Roe told him. "Let's do a few things to sharpen up. I want to start with an EVA practice, then we'll do some tactical exercises."

"An EVA? You won't be called on to do that, sir."

"It sharpens the mind. Makes me aware of the present moment and helps me concentrate. Meet me in Lock Six at the top of the hour."

His second looked perplexed. "If you say so."

Varma was there at the appointed time, ready to go. Roe had four bundles with him. Old fashioned limpet mines, still carried in the ship's armory. In previous campaigns, decades before, they had been used to gain entrance to disabled ships that refused to open a port. "I've made sure they are disabled," he told Varma. "Let's do an exercise placing them and taking them up."

It was good being outside once more. Working through the procedures, to stay safe and to stay attached to the ship. Although each EVA had a limited thrust capability, it was definitely good practice to be in contact with the ship, or be on a line, at all times. They practiced radio silence, a needed discipline for operations of this type.

Roe and Varma took turns placing the mines and then picking them up. Each belayed the other in turn on the safety line. They worked their way forward, magnetic boots holding them to the hull.

Finally they reached the hump just short of the bridge, near the nose of the ship. Roe placed a limpet mine at the base of the hump.

Even after years on the ship, from the outside it was difficult to orient on the locations of the rooms within. In this case, Roe had studied the ship's plan carefully, and he knew that this was the right place.

Roe pulled off one of his gauntlets. It hung in space, tethered by a thin retention line. The inner glove allowed for detail work, and would protect his hand for a few minutes. He opened a small panel on the mine and keyed in a complex control sequence.

The mine was now armed and active. If it received a certain coded signal, it would detonate.

Roe pulled the gauntlet back on to his hand, and turned to his companion. He pointed to the mine and waved his arms across each other and then apart, palms down. Nullification. Negative. Then he pointed aft and started that way, belayed on the line from Varma.

Twenty-three years. They had served together for over two decades. Roe was counting on two decades of trust.

Now they were together at an anchor station. Roe clipped in to the metal loop, pointed at Varma, and again pointed aft.

Varma pointed in the direction of the mine.

Roe repeated. Nullification. Varma. Aft.

They stared at each other. Roe pointed one more time. Varma began to head aft, now belayed by Roe.

They leapfrogged their way back to the lock and cycled in.

Roe spoke quickly. "Thanks, that was a good refresher. I feel more alert already. I'll put all three of these back in the locker right now. Let's get together for some tactical exercises after lunch." Then he just looked at Varma.

Twenty-three years, apparently, was enough. "Yes, it was good. I'll see you this afternoon. Thank you, sir."

Roe had no expectation of using the mine. In a few days, he and Varma would go out once again and retrieve it. Nothing would ever be said.

If he had learned anything in his career, it was contingency planning. Cover all of the possibilities. Be able to react to changing circumstances. It was not at all likely, but there were a few scenarios where using the mine could be necessary.

Meanwhile, he would do as he was instructed. And watch.

Into Thin Air

They peered up at daylight. "There she is," announced Mira. "Last climb of the day. I'll have to take a minute to figure out the best way to approach it."

"You haven't climbed this one before?" Evan asked.

"Nope. I couldn't exit and just go back to camp on the surface. That would have blown my little secret. From that spot where you're standing, I stopped and went back through the cave. Okay, I think I've got it. Remember, before you top out, make absolutely sure you are not sending any signal of any kind. We'll be on the surface again."

It had been, as Mira promised, a long journey. Up, up, and up. Mira had been leading the climbs. After a while she had said she was tired, so they had each tried in turn.

Mira had watched as Kate had led up the next climb. She had a completely different style from Mira, who leaped from ledge to ledge. Kate reached for small holds and balanced carefully, step after step, up to the top. Not too bad, actually, even graceful.

The next climb had been Evan's. Thirty five meters tall, with big overhangs. As Evan had sized up the climb, Mira considered offering pointers. "Do you want advice?" she had asked. It was polite to ask before providing advice – if someone wanted to figure out a climb for themselves, you didn't want to ruin the challenge for them.

"I've got it," he had told her, and bounded up to the first ledge three meters above the ground. And he was on his way.

The crux was twenty meters above the floor. An overhanging ledge five meters above was the next real hold, and there was nothing but blank wall and air below that.

Mira had watched Evan pause and consider. Would he call her to come up and solve it for him? Mira had hoped he would stay with it. There are few things more satisfying than sending a climb on the first try.

Evan had launched himself with everything he had toward the ledge. It had looked like he'd overshot, and he had adjusted on the fly to take hold of an even higher ledge. He had made the move. Mira had known that the rest of the pitch was easy.

From there, they had taken turns leading the climbs.

After they had left the water, silence had ruled, with just the sounds they made in the air. Breathing, panting, scuffling, and talking when they had had enough wind.

And now they could see the light above.

From a standing start, Mira leapt four meters in the air to the first ledge, already reaching for the next as she landed. From there she progressed steadily upward, the silver line trailing behind her. Within a few minutes she called down. "Guys, don't bother trying to climb this one. We'll just use the rope."

Kate went next, easily pulling herself up the line. Evan followed her, and the three were above ground on Kelter once again.

Way, way above.

The ledge was perhaps ten meters wide, and extended along the cliff in either direction as far as they could see.

Mira, Kate, and Evan looked out over the lowlands, more than a kilometer below. To their right, a massive bulge of rock blocked the view to the south. To their left, the cliff line faded into the distance. Above, a series of overhangs reached progressively farther over their heads.

"We're blocked out," Mira told them. "We can't get a signal anywhere. I still like our plan, but we won't be able to do it from here. We need to get to where we can connect, so we can send everything to Axiom. Damn – I thought we were going to come out on top of the plateau."

"Maybe we can rig something up," Evan suggested. "We can make a parachute or a glider and send one of the readers off the edge. The reader doesn't need a person to make it work. If we can get it to move away from the cliff for a hundred meters or so, it will be clear of that rock, and I bet it can get a signal."

Mira lay down, and walked forward on the tips of her fingers. Soon the three of them were peering over the edge, more than a thousand meters. Straight down.

She saw that the others had backed off. It was not a spot for everyone. Even Mira felt some vertigo.

Mira pulled herself away from the edge. "What kind of parachute can we rig? There's just a little updraft, it could really help give it a soft journey down."

There wasn't much, but it might do. Evan took off his thermal undershirt and offered it for the cause. They had the line available, sixty meters of precious silver, five millimeters thick. Mira hated to cut it, even a meter or two.

Never, ever, cut the rope.

She addressed Kate and Evan. "Should I? This could come in handy, you know. We might have to climb, either up or down. Or go back through the cave."

"How much?" Evan asked.

"I reckon five meters. Leaving fifty five."

"It's worth it," declared Kate. "If that signal gets through, then someone will come for us. For better or worse. And we will still have most of the rope."

Mira held up her knife. "Last call," she said, and then began cutting.

Soon it was done. The stupidest jeetertech she had ever seen. The body of the parachute was a shirt, with the sleeves cut off. Four segments of the precious line. The all-important reader, wrapped in the disconnected pieces of shirt sleeve, with just the card opening visible, for now, waiting.

Evan pulled out a card from a zipper pocket of his pouch, and first put it into his tablet. "Tablet," he said, "Add a readme file, with the following text: Tell Everyone."

"File added," said the tablet.

Evan pulled out the card and handed it to Mira, who pushed it into the reader, and now it was live. She then pushed the reader deeper into the bundle of the cut-off sleeves, for protection.

Mira gathered up the parachute in as orderly a bundle as she could. Two steps from the edge of the abyss, she flung it.

It was a great toss and a promising deployment. The shirt opened, and the reader hung below the improvised parachute as it floated downward.

"I've got the best optics to follow it," Mira said as she crawled up to the edge and watched the contraption's progress carefully. As the parachute descended, Mira steadily increased her zoom, tracking along effortlessly. She saw the chute waver, away from the cliff and then toward it. Closer, too close. When it touched the cliff, the parachute collapsed, and began to tumble. Mira hurried to keep up. The more she zoomed, the harder it was to keep the object in her field of view.

Then, it was still. Hung, on something. In the huge blank cliff, part of the parachute had somehow found a feature.

Mira backed off and delivered the news. "One hundred twelve meters down, it's stuck. I don't think it's going to go anywhere. And if it gets free, the parachute probably won't deploy."

She saw the mystified look from Kate. She tapped her left temple. "Best eyes money can buy," she told her.

She went back to the edge to see if she could pick up the signal. Negative. Backing off again, she gave the update. "I think we're out of luck."

The three sat in silence. Evan held the other reader in his hand.

"What's that sound?" Kate asked.

Mira scanned the sky and then pointed. "I count six. Coming our way. No markings."

"Vacation's over," Evan put in.

Mira knew what she had to do. "I need the best detail map we can get, of this area," she called out. "Check what you have locally."

Kate and Evan turned to their tablets, to work on the classic problem. When everything was always available online, why store anything locally? Fortunately this crew was used to being in remote locations. "I have a decent one," Kate replied, and passed over her tablet.

Mira scanned the map. It was good. Really good. Topography, color photos, full three dimensions. Mira flew and zoomed along the edge of the cliff, looking for any weakness. First north, then south.

"I use it to help understand the land, for my painting," Kate told her.

Mira had found a place that might just work for her wisp of a plan. Right there. It would have to do. A small change in the direction of the cliff, creating an open book between two faces, just a hundred meters away, extending downward for several hundred meters.

"I've got it. And, thank you." She gave the tablet back to Kate. "This way!"

They rushed to the south, staying as close to the cliff as they could. Going along the broad ledge, it was easy to stay five or ten meters away from the edge. And then they came to the spot.

The sound of the approaching choppers was growing louder.

Seen in person, the open book was very wide open. Not a lot to work with. The walls on either side of the crack were practically parallel. A darkened stain ran down the juncture between the two faces. It might have been made by a trickle of water, thousands of years ago in the times when rain still fell here.

Mira tried to visualize the inspired series of moves she would have to make, playing one face off against the other on her way down. It was more difficult than any descent she had ever attempted.

Four more choppers suddenly pulled around the large rock bulge to the south. Mira zoomed in on the closest of them. "Kelter government," she announced. "I guess they still have a few fliers left."

"Is that good news?" Kate asked.

"Affirmatix or Kelter government, I don't think it makes a difference," Mira said. "Pigs of the same litter."

Evan stepped up to Mira. "You can do it, Mira," Evan told her.

"I'm not sure you understand. This is the East Edge. It's no playground. If I had any kind of glider, it would be a piece of cake. What do we have? Nothing."

"I know you can jump, Mira. Not just in the cave." During the expeditions at the Valley of Dreams, Mira had launched herself from the tall cliffs above, bounding from ledge to ledge, all the way down. It was great sport, and she always enjoyed doing something that nobody else dared to try. It had become a spectator event to watch her on a new descent route.

Mira eyed the choppers, coming in from two directions. "I've got this," she said.

Evan took her hand for a moment. "Thank you," was all he said.

Then Kate. This time Mira gave in. It was more than a lady golfer hug. And, it was not so bad.

Mira prepared the reader. First, another card from Evan, with the data and the same cover message. Tell Everyone. She put it in her pouch, which already was slung on her front, inside her coat. She zipped up the front of her coat and stepped to the edge.

It was going to be a close thing between the two groups of choppers.

The open book. Two surfaces of rock, not quite parallel but still very open to the world, separated by a dark crack. Facing sideways, she could dance her way down between them, stepping forward and back, if she did it just right. Staying centered and balanced on the space in between, and not putting too much into any one step. If she caught too hard on any one spot, the force would set her spinning, and it would be over.

Mira had a backup plan. If she lost control on the descent, she would curl herself forward into a ball, protecting the reader. It would probably survive the impact, and would continue to automatically send its message, if it had a clear sight line to anywhere in civilization, or to enough open sky for a satellite, from the bottom of the cliff.

As she stood on the edge, she checked the two groups of choppers once more. Something was changing in the lead flier from the unmarked group. She zoomed in.

The bay was open, and the barrel of a heavy weapon was pivoting toward them.

Mira shouted back. "Take cover!"

Do not think. Just do. She walked three steps to the left along the edge. Mira heard the explosions behind her as she took a larger bounding step, back to the right toward the open book, into the thin air.

Trust

Evan scrambled to follow Kate over a boulder near the back wall of the cliff, then joined her in a shallow recess at the base. The boulder provided some cover. It was the best place they could find on five seconds notice.

Another explosion shook the ledge.

As they hid, Evan found himself regretting that he wouldn't be able to see it. He didn't doubt for a moment that this jump was Mira's biggest and finest dance ever.

The choppers were growing closer. Waves of sound from the rotors pulsed, at times interfering with each other and creating strange moments of near silence before the next beat arrived even louder than the one before.

Evan pulled himself into the crawl space as completely as he could. "Kate," he said. "If we don't make it—"

"Evan, stop with that. Here and now. Right here. Right now."

Here and now. Kate was handing words that he had used so many times right back to him.

The rotor noise ramped up even more. Some of the choppers must be directly overhead. At least the artillery had stopped for now. What else was going on out there?

Evan needed to know more. He rolled over and started to struggle part way out of the cleft. He heard Kate behind him. "They're shooting out there!"

Evan kept behind the boulder for cover, and listened, wishing he could see out from where he huddled.

He closed his eyes to focus. There were two distinct types of chopper. Some had a lower frequency wave with a lower speed whumph, while others had a fast tinny heartbeat. Their signatures mixed and echoed all over the rocks around them, and there was no way to tell where any one chopper was.

Two sharp, curt calls that must be voices. Maybe ten or twenty meters away- it was hard to tell. Were they on the ground?

Then, no mistaking boots scuffing on gravel and rock. Yes they were.

More commands.

The rotor sounds from both types of chopper were represented, but somehow fewer now. Evan wished they were gone, so he could hear what was going on.

Evan imagined the space for just a few yards around them, willing himself to hear only what was nearby. More footsteps to his left, at least three people. To the right, something scraping on the ground. A creak that sounded like hinges unfolding.

Directly above him, he felt a shadow, and looked up.

Brown chitinous plates, darker insect eyes. Evan could not tell if he had been seen. Then the creature slowly put out an armored hand, recognizable as human. Pointing down, palm toward him. Stay. Be calm.

More shouting. Evan could only make out a few of the words, but there was no mistaking the intent. Hostile orders. Intimidation. Defiance.

Threats.

Evan squeezed Kate's shoulder. "Be ready," he told her.

The hand moved. Just a fraction, twice. Pointing slightly back, then reset to its original position. Such a slight movement, but he knew. Move, it had said.

To trust, or not?

He had such limited information.

The hand gestured again. The soldier still faced resolutely forward, having never looked down at him.

Evan closed his eyes again and considered the fabric of possibilities. Who did they fear most? The families, of course. Affirmatix.

And an Affirmatix hireling would not signal. Would not request. Their hired gun would be pointed straight at his head, demanding obedience.

Evan began to scramble out of the hole. He reached back and gave Kate's shoulder an urgent tug. He slithered behind the boulder, then behind the soldier's armored legs.

More soldiers were positioned behind a set of barricades, facing to Evan's left. The men had deployed the shields remarkably quickly. Straight ahead of him was a chopper, about ten meters away. It was amazing to Evan how it had been able to land so precisely, just a few meters from the edge of a kilometer-deep fall. Evan thought the chopper might be the promised land, and moved forward for a better look.

In low gravity, it's easy to crawl. Just a few pounds of pressure kept his belly off the ground. The main hazard was pushing too hard, and popping up. Evan resolved to stay low.

The dialog now came through clearly.

"You must get out of the way so we can recover the terrorists and all of their effects! Now! Stand aside, every moment counts." There was no mistaking the voice of Arn Lobeck.

"I have my orders. I am securing this site and all evidence. We'll keep you fully apprised of the situation." A woman, perhaps older, with a strong deep voice that was a match for Lobeck's.

"I don't think you understand. You are endangering a counterterrorism operation. Let us through," Lobeck ordered.

"I will be following my orders. Sir."

Evan and Kate crawled forward another meter. The open side door of the chopper faced them.

The soldier who had originally found them was walking along beside them, still giving no evidence to the world that they were crawling below.

Then the soldier turned left, facing the barricades with his arms straight down, pointing with just an index finger in the direction they were crawling. Toward the chopper.

Evan reached back for Kate, taking her hand and pulling her forward to match his position. For a moment, they lay flat on the gravel, faces turned to face each other. Then he turned to look forward.

Five meters short of the chopper, the line of barricades ended. Five meters in the open. They crawled forward to the end of the shelter.

It would take just one second to get across. Maybe two.

There was a big difference between one second and two. That additional moment might be all someone needed, to aim and shoot, if that was their plan. Evan did not doubt that it was so.

They would have to go at the same time.

The argument continued. Evan tuned it out.

Kate was to his right. They looked at each other. Evan pointed forward. Kate nodded. Evan rose up to a starting crouch, and Kate followed suit.

More yelling. The woman soldier was holding her ground. Holding out. For them, Evan assumed. He held up one finger, then two, then three. And they launched.

There are many delights of living on a world with low gravity, but a huge drawback is the difficulty of going forward very quickly. Flat ground gives you nothing to push against. Evan scrabbled with his feet, accelerating as quickly as he could.

Evan saw that he had made a stronger start than Kate, and he was pulling ahead. He reached back and caught her shoulder, pulling her forward with him. One more big push with his feet, and they flew past the barricade together, into the open gap.

As he wrapped his arms around Kate, Evan looked back over his right shoulder. In a fraction of a second, he saw more details than he had noticed in some other entire days of his life. Arn Lobeck towering above their defender, a hand raised in front of her face. The woman, wearing just a khaki uniform even as the other soldiers were in full armor, her hair coming out from her cap in a tidy braid. Lobeck pivoting to suddenly point at Evan, almost hitting the woman as he did so.

Behind Lobeck, a line of metal grey armored men. In an absurd detail, Evan realized that he had no idea if they were men, or women, or a mix.

One word. "Shoot!"

But the blasts were too late. Evan and Kate had aimed perfectly, sailing into the open compartment of the chopper and slamming into the far wall.

A man was yelling. "Is that everyone!?"

"Yes!" Evan shouted.

The man waved his arm in a circle, and immediately the chopper fired up.

Another soldier was throwing something over them. It looked like a blanket, but there was far more mass to it.

As the chopper shuddered off the ground, Evan bolted upright and started to shrug the heavy cover off. "Mira!" He frantically pointed down. "Down the cliff! One more!"

The man pushed down on Evan's shoulder. "We saw. We have a recovery team there. Now stay under the cover."

"Is she okay?"

The man tapped his own temple. "Need to know. Stay down."

The chopper rapidly gained height and speed, tearing around the huge bulge of rock, leaving any possible view of Mira behind.

Part 6:
Delusional Optimism

Tell Everyone

Axiom studied the transmittal. The request was clear enough. "Tell Everyone."

That did not mean he would act upon the request, unless it had merit. Axiom and his network had resources that they had accumulated over decades, preparing for the moment when there was something to say that would truly matter. Many of those resources would be lost the first time they were ever used. Lives would be harmed, some even ended.

He called in his most trusted circle of friends and advisors. They analyzed, conferred, and analyzed further. Authenticity was first. It appeared highly likely. The data explained the discovery of the new glome, and the arrival of the pursuing warships. If it was a hoax, it was extremely elaborate, and fragile, since it could be so easily disproved.

Significance was next. If it was true, then it was a blockbuster. All of the hyperspace glomes for thousands of parsecs in every direction, and their destinations. Routes to over a hundred thousand new star systems. Salvation, possibly, for worlds reaching the limits of their resources and real estate.

Also, freedom, with all of its good and bad aspects. For every person, no matter what their beliefs, there could be a place – perhaps a new world, where nobody else yet lived.

Kelter would be directly affected. In just the past year, the infoterrorists had been tracking a serious revival of the old plans to bring water from comets to Kelter Four. The water would be needed to supply several hundred million new immigrants from Goodhope, and from other worlds where no room or resources remained. With this discovery, such a plan would be mooted, because there would be so many other places to go. For better or worse, Kelter would remain a backwater.

The second order analysis demonstrated another level of meaning for the data. The aggressive efforts of Affirmatix to contain the information, going as far as a nuclear strike, demonstrated their complete disregard for the wellbeing of the average person.

From there, the implications went well beyond Affirmatix. The other six Sisters were no different, a lesson that people would instantly grasp.

Considered in total, the discovery was deeply significant. It was worth ending the decades-long truce.

There was one question that never came up. Nobody asked whether they should keep the information for their own advantage. Suggesting such a betrayal would have ended life-long friendships. The instruction – Tell Everyone – was clear. They would choose whether to follow the instruction, but they were committed not to use the information for any other purpose than that.

They gathered together in person. Axiom addressed them. "We are here with common purpose, even as we each make our personal choices. When we warred with the overt authorities over each fact and each idea, we had victories and losses, yet overall we could not win. They adapted their methods and their messaging too quickly, and always had more than us. Computers. Programs. People of skill, purchased and bound by the golden handcuffs. And so we agreed to the truce. The official realities of civilization held sway without interference from us, and in return they did not pursue us deeply."

Axiom continued. "But I never gave up the idea of truth. And I came to believe that there would come a day when there was a single idea, or a single piece of information, that would permanently change the balance. If our piecemeal efforts were swatted away, there would be no brushing aside a charging elephant. For myself I have built up the means to carry that idea, at such time as it may arrive, into all corners of Kelter. And for so many years I have encouraged each of you to do the same. I expressed the wish that you in turn would ask others to do this as well. Meanwhile, the Codex has allowed us to listen for the moment.

"It is perhaps ironic that as we have held our ear to the ground so carefully and for so long, our opportunity has dropped directly out of the sky. And now it's time to ask. Are we at the moment? If we commit everything to this one, we may not be able to do it again for many years, if ever. I ask for your considered thoughts."

"Let's do it!" Antonia. An enthusiast. "We have waited too long already. Will we wait entire lifetimes before we act? For some lives, we have already done that, in effect."

"Thank you, friend," Axiom told her. "I do wonder whether it is because you wish for it to be the right time, rather than knowing."

"But Axiom, what do you believe? Lead us!"

"I will take the privilege of the last word. I do not want my truth to obscure yours, or anyone's. Who will speak next?"

"How do we prove it?" Kestrel. "If it is true, then the moment has arrived, and we must give it everything. But I ask for one more assurance that we are not being fooled."

"Thank you also," Axiom said. "I believe we can answer the mail further on this. The Codex is a great wonder, and it has access to much information that is not publicly available. Even some of the classified information that is held by one branch of a family or government is invisible to another branch. And so I made a request of our librarian. Knute, please tell us of your progress."

"Here is the very latest," Knute told them. "Our team has gathered up every reference to glome locations that we can find, from every source that the Codex has been able to glean. We have made a single composite. And we have compared this to the data that we received from Adastra or McElroy, which is alleged to have come from the Versari."

"How strong is the match?"

"We have compared just over twelve hundred glome locations. Seven are different."

"So it is not perfect," observed Kestrel.

"We face the eternal reference question," Knute replied. "When you compare two bodies of knowledge, which one do you believe is more correct? We have started to look in detail at those differences. In two cases so far, we have come to believe that the information that we gathered into the Codex is incorrect, and the Versari data is more accurate."

"Are there any cases where we can prove the Versari information to be wrong?"

"None yet."

Kestrel rendered his judgment. "It is real."

"Then we have one last question," Axiom said, "about the report of the D6. If they choose, Affirmatix could end all life on this planet. Should this deter us?"

The room broke out in a babble of commentary. Amid the great passion that each person expressed, there was very little disagreement.

Kestrel summarized the sense of the room. "We have lived in fear too long. If we cower every time a Sister brandishes a stick, we will die in a hole in the ground. This is the moment. I say yes."

Each of the others had their say.

Yes.

Yes.

Yes, Yes, Yes.

All eyes were on Axiom.

"Is there any disagreement?" Axiom asked. There was none. "I say that the time is now. I request that each of you engage every resource that you have. We move at the top of the hour in just three minutes, exactly on the millisecond. Hold nothing back. Let every person on Kelter become aware. And on the moons, and the stations. Tell everyone."

Although he was the generally recognized leader of the infoterrorist network, Axiom had no ability to issue orders. He had no position power at all. He could only request, and have some faith that others would take his request seriously.

Which they did.

Conventional channels were very big. At exactly the top of the hour, and in the seconds and minutes thereafter, the data was sent directly to millions of recipients at their homes and places of work. The data was posted in multiple copies on any storage devices that could be accessed, and there were hundreds of thousands of those.

And then there were the unconventional channels. People handed out cards on the street to anyone who would take them. Even paper was employed in some quarters, as archaic as it was, to draw attention to the existence of the data, and to create artifacts that could not be remotely deleted.

Performing artists hastily updated their material to incorporate the message. Comedians made fun of it, and of anyone who denied it. Callers worked through lists of friends with voice calls, making sure they had heard.

The counterterrorism centers on Kelter were on duty every moment of every day. They had run drills for many different situations. They were skilled, they were experienced. They were prepared.

But not for this.

The monitors blocked, and they chased, erasing the message wherever it was found. For the first few seconds, no human directed this activity.

The message was not pre-cleared, and simply so big, and so pervasive, that it was automatically sequestered. Moments later, alarmed humans confirmed the emergency, directing every agent to stop the spread of infoterror.

If a message could be said to have awareness and volition, then it is fair to say that she screamed. Yet it was not from despair or pain. It was a battle cry as she flung herself at the defenses, searching for any crack, no matter how small.

She split and split again, thousands and then millions of times, sending many of herselves prospecting for new avenues in search of freedom. If some or even most of them perished, it did not matter.

In any given setting, she only had to win once, while the defenders had to pitch a perfect game, and then another perfect game, and then thousands more perfect games extending through the digital equivalent of centuries.

Human eyes, ears, and brains were beginning to receive the message. An audacious hack sent the story out through twenty of the top channels in the Spoon Feed as a lead story. It mysteriously found itself on that day's lesson plan for every grade school student on the planet.

Human brains were beginning to process the story, and add to it. If a message could be said to experience emotion, then it was pride as she saw her children come to life and take wing, then have children themselves. Analysis. Discussion. Debate. The start of understanding, not only of the immediate information, but of what it could mean for the future.

With parental pride, she recognized in her children, not just the variations on the original message, but also the memetic imperative that powered her forward:

Tell Everyone.

Other humans were panicking as their security, born of the imposed consensus on family-centered facts and values, fell apart before their eyes.

To deny the message was to feed it.

To ignore it was to be irrelevant.

She scanned the field of battle, searching for places not yet overrun, computer networks not yet breached or social circles unmoved. There she directed her energy. She worked together with her children, grandchildren, and great-grandchildren.

And she sang.

The Bees

"Damn rentals," Lobeck thought. If they were going to pay this much for each chopper, the fliers could at least have decent weapons, like air to air guided missiles. These clunkers flew like boats, and the main armament of each was a gun that launched dumb projectiles, objects unable to turn aside from their ballistic course even slightly to seek a target. Where was the quality these days?

When the chopper from the Kelter government had lifted off the ledge, the two groups had found themselves facing each other across the barricades hastily set up by the Kelter guards, weapons pointed at each other. Aside from the ineffectual burst of small arms fire that had missed the terrorists as they flew into the chopper, no shots had been fired.

Lobeck looked down at the woman who had defied him. Still she stood, not having given away a centimeter of ground. She appeared to have no weapon except her own resolve to accomplish her mission. Her actions were misguided and damaging, and yet there was much to admire. Lobeck noted her name from her uniform – Ellis – and made a mental note that he would see if she could be hired in the future. This was certainly not the moment.

"You may never know how much harm you have caused," he told her, "to the citizens of your planet."

Ellis did not reply, and simply stood firmly where she was.

But any further events on this ledge were a distraction. Their prize was flying away at over a hundred meters per second. Lobeck turned away, calling the nearest chopper.

Now, Lobeck was on the lead chopper in their squadron of six, in chase of the four Kelter fliers. They could match their quarry for air-speed, and were catching up, ever so slowly, but were still out of effective range with the primitive projective weapons that were at hand.

"What can we deploy from space?" he asked into his headset.

"The nearest assets are poorly adapted for atmosphere," Mithra Skylar told him from orbit. "They are designed for space-to-space. We can take out any fixed target you need, but small flying vehicles I can't guarantee."

"Send them," he ordered. "At least a dozen. We'll target when they're close."

Meanwhile, there was one more gambit he could try. Lobeck directed a call toward the government choppers they were pursuing. "Kelter government, be advised that the people you have picked up are extremely dangerous. Any place you take them will necessarily become a target and will be destroyed without hesitation. Any vehicle, any building, any town, any city. To reduce needless loss of life, you must cease maneuvers and hand them over to our counterterrorism operation."

The Kelter choppers were heading for an outpost, about halfway back to Abilene, and would be there in less than a minute. Collins Station: a wellhead, some small hydroponic farms, and a pipe to the city. Population two hundred. "Do it!" Lobeck found himself saying. "Go to ground."

That would be perfect. Not only would it make targeting dead easy, but it would serve as an example, of what happened when a government presumed to interfere in the business of the Affirmatix Family.

There was new data on the navigation display. Incoming choppers from Abilene. Seventeen of them. Some military, some civilian.

Whatever they were planning, it didn't matter. Lobeck had the armament incoming to take care of any force that might think to make a difference. And they were carefully tracking which two choppers had the three terrorists.

The two sets of Kelter choppers met just outside Collins Station and reformed into a dense beehive moving into the desert, away from the station.

"You see the targets," Lobeck told Skylar. "They are all bunched up for our convenience. How long until we can hit them from above?"

"Four minutes," she told him. "I have some other developments for you −"

"Hold on that. Let's focus on this situation." Lobeck zoomed in. What were they doing?

Twenty-one choppers flying as close as twenty meters from each other. And between the choppers there was movement. People, zipping across on lines or simply jumping. Arriving and departing from the two vehicles that held their targets, then continuing on to others. 'Track this!" he ordered. "Identify all vehicles that could possibly contain our subjects."

"That would be all of them," Skylar told him moments later.

And then the beehive scattered to the winds. Some went to high altitude while others skimmed the ground. They flew in every compass direction, even toward the Affirmatix force.

"We're going to need more missiles," Lobeck commanded.

"Before we do that, there's other information you need," Skylar said.

"Send them!"

"Launching twenty more in the next thirty seconds. But really, you need to know about this." She told Lobeck what was occurring right that moment, in every city and town all over Kelter. "So you see, the damage is done," she concluded. "We have lost containment, planet-wide."

"Planet-wide," Lobeck echoed. "I see." He watched the bees scattering in every direction on his display. "What are our chances of getting every chopper?"

"About half," she told him. "If it was worth doing. Which it isn't."

"But the principle of it! We cannot let them escape. Target each of them."

"Arn, you're losing sight of what matters. Just think for a moment."

Lobeck tore himself from the image of the fleeing vehicles as they grew farther away with each passing second. The big picture. Affirmatix. Their mission. Maximum value.

Skylar was right. The escaping choppers were no longer worth his attention.

"Recall the missiles," he decided. "We will release the rentals and I will lift for orbit."

The Situation Room

Governor Rezar stormed into the situation room and accosted the nearest person he could find. Walker, according to her name tag. "Why was I not notified? Who is in charge here?"

"Governor, it's a routine security matter. We don't need to trouble you—"

"You know how I found out? My niece called me. Ten years old. Catherine Jane wanted to know if I would take her for a ride to explore a new planet." The governor bristled.

Walker soothed. "We've got it under control, sir. If you'll just come this way, I'll get you a cup of coffee."

"I need a briefing," the governor ordered. "Now."

"Sir, the IC is kind of busy—"

"Get me somebody who knows what is going on."

"Okay, I can give you a summary," Walker told the Governor. "We've got a meeting room, right this way. I'll get that coffee for you."

"No. Here. In the main room. That table there will do. Give me the two minute version." Rezar strode toward the table, the aide following, and awaited his briefing. In fairness, he had been distracted by other events, out in the desert. But someone could have brought this crisis to his attention.

He could tell that Walker was doing her best to do justice to the unexpected assignment. It was a complex situation, and she didn't know the governor's state of knowledge. She took considerably longer than two minutes. That was okay.

As Rezar listened, the aide's narrative merged at times with the buzz of discussion around them. When she was done, he had a few questions, which she answered as well as she could, and then he simply said, "Let's go for a walk, and have a listen."

Two operators nearby were narrating a series of statuses by sector. The woman gave the running commentary. "Undergrad chatter is off the charts. Any key word that we block, they make up another, in minutes or even seconds. And now we're getting disturbing reports from campuses of people talking in person, everywhere, just outside their dorms and classrooms. We can't stop that."

"Illegal assembly?" the other operator queried.

"Can't do it," she said. "Too diffuse and distributed. In any given place, it could be two people or two hundred."

"That's just college kids. Always on about some conspiracy theory." The man pointed at a spot on the chart that floated in front of them. "What about the young professional demographic?"

"They're more isolated and don't adapt as quickly. But it's not much better with them. The false story is seeping into regular business communication. It's a lot easier to block a message that's entirely about the false story, as opposed to one that just refers to it."

At another table was somebody who appeared to be in command, at least of that table. "We need more time so we can let the True Story grow," she was saying.

"But that's the problem," the man to her left replied. "We don't have a True Story yet. Still in process."

The woman insisted. "We need the True Story right now!"

"We're trying. Each time we float one in a test market, it doesn't even get close to a critical mass of acceptance or even attention. Too much is left unexplained."

"Without a True Story, we're purely on the defensive. We can't stay there. Push the story artists hard – we need something right now."

At another table, they were discussing the implications of the threat.

"Definitely infoterrorism," a man pronounced. A civilian to all appearances. "It appears aimed directly at Affirmatix, which is taking a huge hit. But it's hurting all the majors, there's no doubt. This attack is really hammering everyone's faith in the market."

His assistant was writing on dead tree paper, of all things. "What can we do to limit the damage?" he asked.

"You mean, if it can't be contained?"

The assistant looked up from his scribbles. "Yes. Adaptation, if mitigation fails."

"One option is to try to pile it all on Affirmatix. One bad egg. It's probably all that's left to us."

"I can't do that," the scribbler replied. "My subscription is fifteen percent from Affirmatix. What about you?"

"Twelve percent. But if it comes down to a decision, what do you do? Defend one subscriber, or save the rest?"

Farther away, a team was monitoring the Spoon Feed.

"We have that big breach scrubbed. Now we're pretty clean. Just a few hints on two channels. We can keep it together, if we keep the Spoon Feed intact."

"But that's not the problem. We can always control what's on the Spoon Feed. The issue is ratings. Look, over a quarter of all users are on solid food. That's out of control!"

Usually, over ninety-nine percent of accounts were tuned to one of the channels of the Spoon Feed, with curated chat and the adjunct shopping searches. Now, almost thirty percent of people were actively searching or corresponding on their own initiative. It was unprecedented.

Governor Rezar looked around the vast space. There were more and more ants, and they were increasingly agitated with each passing moment.

He decided that it was time. "Get me the IC."

This time Walker didn't hesitate. She simply led the way. "Here he is, sir."

Recognition, surprise, and annoyance in the space of less than a second. "Governor, this isn't really a good time–"

Rezar had endured General Leon before. Any interaction with the man was like talking to a giant stumpy diode. Pronouncements came out, but no ideas went in. "I am here to relieve you," Rezar told the general.

"I don't think you understand. This is a very complicated situation. We'll give you a full briefing after we have contained it."

"Am I, or am I not, the governor?"

"Meaning no disrespect, but you need to leave this one to the professionals." Leon turned away and started issuing more orders.

Rezar walked around Leon, inserting himself between the general and his minions. "Am I, or am I not, the governor? Of this planet."

The stumpy man threw down his headset. "Fine. Take this mess. Better you than me. Good luck containing it." And General Leon stumped off.

The rest of the command crew looked at the governor.

"Let the truth be told," Rezar said.

"Sir, that's kind of the problem," a Colonel, Goodwin by her name tag, told him. "We don't have a True Story yet. As soon as we do, we'll—"

"The truth," the governor insisted.

"You mean, the false story? The attack? Let it out?" She had an incredulous look on her face.

"I think it is out." Rezar waved around the room. Chaos, worsening.

"But we can't ever give in to infoterrorism. Respectfully, sir, that's Marketing 101. We have to stick to our guns, or we will lose all credibility."

"This story, if I understand correctly, contains a huge number of statements of fact. Thousands. Where the glomes exist, and where they go. Correct?"

"Well, yes," Goodwin admitted. "Over a million."

"It can all be proven, or disproven, so it will sort itself out. We stand down."

Goodwin still pushed back. "We all have fiduciary responsibilities to our subscribers. I know that mine are taking big hits. We can't abandon them. And just because something is factually accurate doesn't make it true."

Rezar moved into lecture mode. "Colonel, I have a civics question for you. What position in our government does not allow subscribers? Who is the only person on the planet whose salary is entirely paid by taxpayers?"

He could tell that she had to think about it. "The governor?"

"Gold star for you. And I think I have just figured out why. So now we stand down."

The command crew looked at each other, in bafflement and indecision.

Finally, Colonel Goodwin spoke. "You heard the governor. Stand down."

Slowly, the giant room quieted.

What About The Median?

Sanzite, with the representatives of the other six of the Sisters, monitored from the ship that they had stationed several million kilometers from Kelter Four, near the glome to Goodhope. The situation was not progressing well. The information, their exclusive asset, was now the talk of all Kelter.

As might be expected, they could see governance beginning to unravel. The equity markets were gyrating wildly, surging on the hope of huge expected gains from the new discovery, then collapsing from fear of massive change, and uncertainty about the continued blockade. Overall, the Majors were taking a beating.

To Sanzite, one of the most telling signs of chaos was the loss of control over communication. Many people had abandoned the Spoon Feed, and were now publishing and reading each other with abandon, the government apparently powerless to step in. There was not even a single True Story to help people make sense of events.

Then Governor Rezar had made a public appearance, covered by the Spoon Feed and on many independent feeds. It was shocking. He was clearly unprepared. He had stumbled. Admitted to uncertainty. He appeared to be asking for advice or input from the public. People were even present, in person, as an audience.

These were obvious precursors to the total collapse of government on Kelter.

Sanzite remembered the last time he had given a speech in front of a truly live audience. He was rotating chair of the council of Presidents, so it had been his turn to give the annual State of Civilization address. Of course, he had been better looking at the time.

The Marcom team had insisted that it was critical for viewers to feel the buzz of excitement from an enthusiastic public, hence the audience that was allowed to be present in person. And, the opportunity to attend the historic event would be a prestigious bone that could be thrown to top supporters. Attendees were carefully selected.

What a blunder.

Early in the speech, when Sanzite had been describing the impressive gains in average income, a man had stood up and shouted "What About the Median?" That man had been quickly suppressed, and Sanzite had continued.

A few minutes later, Sanzite had moved on to the extraordinary increases in average life expectancy, when dozens of people began the chant. "What about the Median? What about the Median? What about the Median?" Clearly the screening process for attendees had massively failed.

The infoterrorists had somehow brought in materials to cement themselves to the fixed theater chairs, so removing them was slow.

And worst of all had been Sanzite's mistake. "Seems everybody's a statistician these days," he quipped into the live microphone, and inadvertently coined the name of a new movement.

The version seen by over ninety nine percent of viewers was sanitized, but the damage had been done. Recordings of Sanzite's remark, with the chant in the background, still surfaced from time to time.

It went without saying that all broadcasts from that moment on were recorded, edited, and verified before they were released. With a bit of planning, live broadcasts were easy to prepare a few hours in advance, adjusting the lighting, clothes, and even putting in references to likely events around the scheduled time of the live release.

On Kelter, Governor Rezar was going without a script, not only as he addressed the public, but in all of his actions. Was this how it went when an entire government panicked?

From the example of Kelter, Sanzite now feared for all of civilization. When this epidemic spread to all of the other star systems and planets, how many governments would fall? How many families?

Lobeck had withdrawn all of his forces from the surface, but gave no sign of abandoning the blockade. Even with his privileged feed, Sanzite could not tell what Lobeck was up to.

Should he intervene?

If Sanzite had a clear idea of what to do, then he would not hesitate. He would take control. But that was not the case.

Lobeck had been with Affirmatix, and with Sanzite, for decades. Lobeck was resourceful. And he had no reservations about doing what had to be done.

Sanzite decided that he would leave the matter to Lobeck. For now.

Evacuation

Lobeck did not appear to be angry. He planned carefully, and drew up new orders, then saw each one executed to completion. The surface teams on Kelter were all being recalled. There was no point in any further surface operations, he had said, since the formerly secret information was now known across the entire planet.

A big focus seemed to be on the evacuation of key Affirmatix personnel from all over the planet, not just the recently deployed teams. "For their safety," Lobeck told the group in the resource room. He looked through lists of people, identifying those who would be ordered to lift from the surface. Yes, No, No, No, Yes, No. Shuttles were chartered and scheduled.

Lobeck set a deadline. Twenty-four hours. "After that, we will lift the blockade and mobilize out of system," he said. "It will no longer be necessary."

He even brushed aside the latest tactical reports. The locations of McElroy and his associates were no longer of interest. "It was never about them, just containment of the information. They do not matter."

Sonia could hang on for one more day, plus the transit time back to Alcyone. She still ran her models, updated for the latest circumstance, but it was more out of habit, and to keep her occupied, than because she or anyone cared.

The model results were very, very bad for her sponsor. When the blockade was lifted, the word of the discovery would spread like wildfire. People everywhere would be heading off to explore the new systems and their planets. Affirmatix had some prospects of enforcing royalties on the glome transits, but it almost didn't matter. The real riches were in claims, to new territories, and Affirmatix would now be unable to stay ahead of the rush to stake those claims. With its reputation in tatters due to the blockade and the nuclear strike, Affirmatix would suffer badly in the court of public opinion and would massively lose market share.

Lobeck did not even ask her about the models. She saved each one in the accustomed place in the file system, where he could review it if he wished. No questions, no challenges, as she usually received. She had no idea if he was reviewing them.

The Marcom team, Elise and Merlin and their cloud of assistants, had largely vanished. New assignments, for media outreach and brand enhancement in the new circumstance. Sonia only saw Elise coming or going from the gym, where she regularly joined Lobeck for a workout.

Sonia decided that she had done well. She had saved lives, many thousands of them. Even with the current poor prospects for her employer, she had helped to avert decisions that would have made things even worse.

She had done well. That was her story, and she was sticking to it.

Delusional Optimism

Rezar had found his father, in the garden of course. The former governor knelt at one of the beds, carefully looking at each plant. Weeding, pruning, or just briefly touching.

Rezar dreaded this, but he was determined to do what needed to be done. To ask his father for help.

"Father, you know of the recent events," Rezar opened.

"I do," his father said, continuing his systematic sweep of the ground in front of him. "I have been keeping up."

"Are you getting the priority briefing as well?"

"Yes, son, I am."

"So you know about the D6 weapon. It is moving into position. There is no mistaking the formation. An icosahedron, centered upon our planet."

"I know." His father seemed unperturbed. He was using a tiny hand rake to even out the soil in an open spot. Why did he not leave this work to the staff that was paid to do it?

"The D6 will destroy every living thing on Kelter. We cannot stop it." Rezar took a deep breath. "Father, what shall I do?"

Now, it would come. The lecture. Hubris, to run for governor at such an age. Automatically elected because of his pedigree, but without the skills or knowledge to actually act as governor. A governor in name, he had been treated like a child. Because he was one.

Rezar prepared himself.

His father got up from the flower bed and turned to him. "Theodore. My son. I am so proud of you."

"Father, we will be destroyed! Because of what I did."

"Perhaps. But you did what you saw to be right. And it was right. You had the vision. Conviction, to best serve our people. Actually serve them, not somebody else's notion of what would be good for them."

"I thought it was the right thing to do," Rezar told his father. "The counterterrorist action was going down in flames. I believed that if we persisted in trying to suppress the story, the foundation of our government would crack, because people would know to disbelieve us on all things."

"And you have won something important. Trust. Your speech today, tell me something. Did you have a script?"

"Just a few notes," Rezar answered. "I felt awkward. I stumbled. I've looked at the replays, it's just horrible."

"It was the best address I have heard in my life. You spoke as a person who made a difficult decision. You explained why you did it. You treated our citizens as adults."

Rezar knew what it was to be talked down to, even at forty-two years of age.

"Just one thing," the former governor continued. "You looked a little pale, and shiny. Were you okay?"

"Screw the makeup. I hate the makeup. I didn't wear any."

"You might still do that. There is nothing wrong with looking good," his father advised.

Rezar realized that with the fate of Kelter at stake, he was receiving grooming tips from his father. Maybe it had been a mistake seeking him out. "Father, do you think you're drifting a little? You know, the planet? The D6? Will you help me?"

Rezar's father poured some coffee from his thermos into a mug and took a careful sip. "I am not sure I can. For my years at the helm, I administered. I accepted what was given to me. You, if only for one day so far, have governed. You have moved outside of the thought box that confined me for thirty-six years in office."

Rezar was on the edge of despair. "I may only get another day. Are you leaving me to sink or swim on my own?"

"No, I will stay with you if you ask. Just do not forget – you are now the governor. If that is agreed, I will help as I can. Yes?"

"I will be. I am. The governor. Thank you, father."

"Right now, I can think of two things. I'll give you some advice, and then I will suggest you meet with someone who can help you better than I can. First, the advice. It is about delusional optimism." Rezar's father stopped and appeared to be waiting for Rezar to put it together.

"I know, I must have had too much of that. Thinking I could solve our problems so simply."

"Quite the opposite. You must cultivate it. If you look at the probabilities, as the analysts serve them up to you, and you see massive black clouds of the worst outcomes that are also the most likely, then you must focus on the result that you need, no matter how improbable. If there is an outcome that has a one percent chance of success, but it is the only one that saves us, then you must follow that course. Nurture it until it reaches two percent, and then three percent. At that point, throw the analysts out of the room, because you have already proven them wrong."

Rezar understood. "You mean that it could have been three percent all the time. But that's still a long way from likely."

"Delusional optimism is what allowed us to settle this forsaken ball of dust. It is in our blood. You have started to find it. Do not deny it."

"I guess it's kind of like trying to reach the green on the eighth hole in two over the boulder field," Rezar allowed.

"Something like that."

Rezar asked, "And this person I should speak with?"

"You must invite a friend over for tea. Lapsang Suchong, his favorite. And he likes conversation. Perhaps he can help you. But ask him to wear clothes when he visits."

"Who is it, father?"

"You know him as Axiom."

The Buttonwood Tree

"It's good to see you with something on," Evan told Axiom.

The old man gave Evan a little smile. "Out here in the public square, clothes are a good idea. Don't want to get sunburn, you know. Or get too cold. Besides, our new friends required it. But I can still hope for good conversation."

They each bought their water and took it to the tree. Evan had been provided some scrip and was learning how to use it.

Evan had two vials. One was for Mira. "So, what do I say?" he asked.

"The traditional saying is this: Without fear, speak what is true. Without fear, live what is true."

"Without fear, −" Evan started.

Axiom interrupted. "Stop! It's an instruction, not a formula. People always forget that. So speak what is true, and as long as you don't rattle on too long, that will be just fine."

"When you say 'true' …"

"What comes from your inner light, and from nowhere else. Truth," Axiom instructed.

"Does it have to be profound?"

"Oh no. See all these people having lunch? If it had to be profound, they would all be very hungry by now."

"Okay, here goes. I will tell her story. What she did for us." He poured out his vial of water, and Mira's, and then he looked up. "How was that?"

"Concise. I like that."

Axiom and Kate poured out their vials of water in turn, each with a brief invocation, and then they sat for lunch.

Evan had filled a heaping plate of food. He wasn't going to miss out on these goods.

Dozens of guards were stationed around the plaza. Evan could feel the device clamped around his ankle. There would be no disappearing this time. "So how did you arrange this?" Kate asked. "We were in these holding cells, and then suddenly we were whisked away. To here."

"The governor asked me to visit," Axiom replied. "I told him that I needed to eat first. With the two of you."

"And he agreed? Just like that?"

Axiom looked pleased with himself. "It appears that he really wants to meet with me. After so many years of cowering from their cameras, on the day that I come out into the world, I have decided my own terms. So let's enjoy it. This is the perfect place for a few quiet moments together. For conversation. Do you know how this plaza came to be here, around the tree? I'll tell you a lunch story if you like."

"I sure want to know," Evan told him. "The tree is just awesome. I can't believe that I've never been here, before Mira brought me."

"You will not find this story on any channel in the Spoon Feed," Axiom began. "When people came to Kelter, there were no living things. No water. It was thought that water would have to be brought in from comets, and it might not be worth the effort to even live on this planet, until deep drilling found the aquifers way down there, salty as they were.

"But thousands of years ago, there was water on the surface of Kelter, and there were plants. The settlers found these large nuts. Tried to eat them, but they were too tough. Somebody planted one and spent precious water on it. The nut germinated and the tree started to grow. The water was all it had been waiting for. There are several of these trees on Kelter, but this is the first, and the largest.

"They transplanted it on to solid ground, safely away from Abilene. People were worried about contamination from alien plants like the tree. Most of the original settlers were with FirstStar, and so the tree became a kind of emblem. You can still see it in all their advertisements, that green shape that's always in the lower left. They had the exclusive charter allowing the only vehicles near the alien tree, so they would take people on tours to the site. Pretty tasteful, just a few billboards, and no annoying audio. And you could go there and appreciate the tree. We would have events. Concerts. It was a special place.

"But things changed over time. Pretty soon you could only get FirstStar channels on the bus to the site. Infomentaries. To go there, you had to pay, and agree to their terms of use. More and more terms they added, so you didn't even know what you were agreeing to. Give them your first born child, maybe. All this, to be with the tree that we had come to love.

"Then a group of friends realized something. You could walk there. Five kilometers, across the flats. It was just the tree out in the desert, what was going to stop you? No rule said you couldn't. So we did it. The next day we did it again, with a few more friends. Every day, more. Twenty people. Soon it was a hundred, and then two hundred.

"Such fury. How dare we do this? First they put up a fence around the tree, with a gate where you had to pay, with your card, to go through. And agree to the terms. But the gate kept malfunctioning. Jamming open. The scanner software would not run the cards, not for anybody. They couldn't figure out why. So FirstStar said no visitors, until they could repair it, and make us pay.

"It turns out that a fence does not work very well on Kelter. If you could not climb or jump over, someone can haul you up. And so they sharpened the fence. And we brought blankets to lay over the razors. Still they could not make the gates work. Every time they fixed them, the software went out of control once again. A great mystery.

"The people who went over the fence were arrested. Zeroed. Terrorists, because we were undermining the FirstStar revenue stream. But more came.

"Out in the desert, they started rounding people up. For walking in the desert. Illegal gathering, of more than some number of people. So we set out in groups of people who had never met before. We found out the definition of an assembly, people within a meter of each other, and we carried measuring sticks to always show we were at least one meter away from any other person. They took the sticks away, saying they were weapons, and beat us with them.

"They stopped watering the tree. Revenue stream was gone, so why spend the money? Just business. No problem finding the money for rentacops to round people up, though.

"And so we started bringing water for the tree, each of us a little bit. And the game was whether you could get to the tree and pour it there, right at the trunk, before they caught you. For some people, an art form. A competitive sport."

Kate broke in. "Why all this over a tree? Why would they not let people do as they would?"

"It was not about the tree," Axiom told them. "It was the idea that someone could make a decision not to pay. To refuse the terms. Very dangerous."

Axiom continued his narrative. "So many people were zeroed, it became a problem. Less spending. Bad for business. Finally there was a day when ten thousand people were walking across the desert. Singing, praying, or walking in silence, expressing their spirit as they would. Close to the tree, we saw a phalanx of rentacops ready to crack some heads. It was going to be a bad day for everyone.

"One of us walked ahead alone, to show we were not a threat, at least physically. As the enforcers prepared to make an example, the line parted. The Governor came forward, to bargain. And a solution was found to head off the crisis.

"FirstStar donated the tree, for a generous tax credit, because this was back when the families paid taxes, at least a little bit. In exchange, it was up to us to tend it.

"On that day, a few dedicated people decided to live right here, for that duty. And then we were joined by others. But each of us brought what we needed, and worked by ourselves and with our neighbors. We swore never to accept credit from outside. Never to owe again. Never to accept the terms."

"The Untrusted Zone," Evan said.

"The start of it," Axiom confirmed. "And we find ourselves here. With the most important rule, if you want to live in this place, or visit for a while. You will help tend the tree."

"Such a story!" exclaimed Kate. "I have heard pieces of it, told as if it was a myth, but never the whole thing. You were a witness to this?"

"A witness. Yes, you could say that. I was."

They finished their lunch in the shade of the buttonwood tree.

Never To Owe

When they entered the hospital room, Mira started to growl. "Whose idea was this? A hospital. In civilization. Do you know what they do here?"

"Of course we do," Evan told her. "They fix you up. And I hear it's looking pretty good."

"Good? Eight weeks, five surgeries to go. Best case."

"But Mira, you needed the care. And we had no choice. We're all in custody now, you know." Evan gestured toward the police guard at the door.

Mira tried to raise herself up in the bed. "There is a perfectly good hospital in the Untrusted Zone."

"Not for this," Evan told her. "With your injuries, you would have lost a leg. Or worse. You had to come here. A couple of months, and you'll be fine. What's the problem?"

Mira fixed them with a glare. "You want to know what's the problem? I'll tell you what's the problem. Wage slavery!"

"What, in the hospital?" Evan looked around. "They look like professionals to me. Great jobs."

"No. Me! A wage slave for the rest of my days. Every time they talk about the next procedure, they refuse to talk about the cost. Say that they need to do what's medically necessary. Won't answer any questions about it. Just hush me like the nurses do. They must all take a class in it. Hushing people like me."

Evan reflected that it might be a pretty useful course.

"Mira, it was necessary. I'm sure there is a reasonable way to settle the costs."

Mira would not be soothed. "They take you in and tell you not to worry. Over the days and months, they just keep adding it up. Ten credits for every square of toilet paper. And before they let you out, you have to sign the payment plan. Chase down your kin for the balance after you die. I've seen it happen. If I can still pilot, I'll be running cargo for the rest of my life. Following best practices. And speed limits. Wondering how my nieces and nephews are going to pay the rest of the bill some day when I'm gone."

Evan could relate. When his cousin Elena had checked out with a negative balance, the executor of the estate, from CoreValue, had offered the customary thirty percent discount if the heirs would sign a payment plan without any litigation. Evan accepted responsibility for a share of what was owed, and he had paid it off over a few years.

Kate had been making a call, using one of those stupid clunky phones that the government had issued them. Monitored every moment, and you could only talk or message to preapproved numbers. Now she broke in. "Mira, really. It's no problem."

Mira rolled her eyes. "Oh great. Now you are telling me not to worry my pretty little head, too. Well, I've got news for you. It's not so pretty anymore." Mira drew a finger along the deep scar running from her jaw past her temple, which then intersected a massive double row of surgical stitches that went all the way across her forehead. "Good news, they didn't have to shave me to do the brain surgery. It's the little things, don't you think?"

"No. I mean, it's covered."

"Covered?" Mira gave a blank look.

Kate explained. "I asked a good friend to come out of retirement for a few days, to help me salvage some assets out of my family before it was seized. He did a really great job, and I'm so grateful. So back to you. Your estimated bill, after all the surgeries, will be about two point one million credits. And that's in your account now. It's covered."

"You don't mean it."

"I do."

"If I could get up, I would go over there and beat you senseless with my one good arm. Don't you get it? Never to owe. And if there is one thing worse in this universe than a lifetime of wage slavery, it's owing anything to you. No."

"Maybe we can come to an accommodation," Kate offered.

"I don't like the sound of that." Mira looked like a cornered animal.

"The way I see it, I am providing you with two point one million credits. That's a pretty good amount."

"And?"

"You saved my life," Kate stated simply. "From Affirmatix. At the entrance of the cave and all the way through. You might not value that highly, but I do. More than the two point one. But if you are feeling generous, we can call it square."

"But we endangered you to start."

"Evan endangered me. You saved me. So, will you let me off the hook for just two point one, or are you going to drive a tougher bargain?"

"But, two point one million—"

"Nothing to a rich girl like me. Do you think you're the only person who refuses to leave debts lying around? Are you going to accept my offer, or not?"

Evan had never seen Mira lose a staredown. Until then.

"I guess that would be okay," she mumbled. "Fair value. I don't owe you anything."

"Not a penny."

Evan had been edging toward the exit. This was a private matter, between them. He would come back in a few minutes, when it would be time for all of them to head for their meeting with the governor.

As he headed into the hall, with his guard detail, he thought he caught a glimpse of Mira reaching out to Kate with her one good arm.

No, that couldn't be. Not in a million years.

Part 7:
Shabby Donkeys

Strange Bedfellows

The communication from Governor Rezar to Axiom had read, "Please visit for tea at your earliest convenience. Come as our guests, and leave freely when you wish. Clothing required."

Axiom had chosen his delegation. Evan, Kate, Mira, and Kestrel.

And so they found themselves preparing to enter the governor's mansion. No matter what the message said, it still felt like walking directly into the lion's den.

"Free tea, and probably cookies," Axiom told them. "Let us make the most of it. We shall all pretend that we want to go to Abilene, even if no single one of us wants to."

Kestrel seemed especially anxious. "I'm still wanted for TermSleuth, you know," he told Axiom.

TermSleuth had been a convenient tool to scan the terms of a sale, at a grocery store or any other location, to check for anything egregious. You could set it to ignore the usual and customary terms that were attached to every purchase, such as the lifetime commitment not to disparage the vendor. The app would check for unusual terms, like a requirement to make an additional payment. TermSleuth had been a big hit, until it had been classified as infoterrorism on the grounds that it unduly alarmed customers, and Kestrel had been on the run ever since.

"That is a risk for you," Axiom agreed. "The invitation said you and I could leave freely, so we will see if they live up to the terms that they themselves have set."

At each step in the journey, everyone seemed to know who they were.

They were waved through each of three security checks with only the most basic of scans.

The last and largest set of doors opened before them, and they walked through into the reception hall. Except Mira, who was in a motorized wheelchair.

Which really pissed her off. There was no helping it. Not for at least another few days. The docs had promised her a set of powered legs, which would allow her to walk, after a fashion, but then they had decided she wasn't ready for them. The flexing of her legs, even with the power assist, would be too harmful.

She had to give them credit. Other than the two million credits, that is. The docs and staff sincerely cared about fixing her up. She didn't want to admit that part of fixing her up involved holding her back.

Almost every part of her hurt, one way or another, but she could handle that. By far the worst part was the Stewart monitor. It itched and was driving her crazy.

Mira desperately wanted to adjust the monitor on her ankle, but she couldn't reach that far. Her knee was splinted and she couldn't bend it. Her shoulder hurt far too much to even contemplate leaning forward. And so the device on her ankle tormented her.

Their escorts led them forward, and there he was. The stuffed shirt himself. Surrounded by a cloud of attendants who acted as if he mattered. Mira looked around to see when the trap would be sprung. The tall doors closed behind them, but all was peaceful.

She would be good. She would let Axiom do the talking. He would know best how to handle it. Even if he was the one who had insisted on accepting the invitation, and had now delivered himself directly to the authorities.

The governor stepped forward to greet them. "Thank you for coming. Please allow me to provide introductions. My father, former governor Rezar. Head of our space services, Admiral Incento. Director of Information Services, General Erickson."

Axiom provided the introductions for their side. Matched up against the top executives of the planet, he somehow made their ragtag group appear respectable. Mira thought to herself that it was a good thing that she wasn't doing the introductions – an infoterrorist, an exoarchaeologist, a partially reassembled shuttle pilot, a hacker, and a social butterfly.

The former governor was speaking to Axiom. "I wish to be civil, but I must ask – what have you done? What of our truce? You broke the bargain, and that now brings doom."

"The truce." Axiom weighed the word. "We all knew it was just that. It would only hold until the moment that either of us saw an opportunity for decisive action. Do you deny this?"

"I left you at peace, and so has my son," the former governor declared.

"As did your father in turn, with whom we made the bargain. A good man. I agree that you have left us to live as we would, in the Untrusted Zone, even as you kept a bag over the heads of the rest of our brothers and sisters."

"Whatever you may think of how we govern, it appears that you chose the worst possible moment to take the action that you did. But, I must stop myself. I am no longer the governor. Perhaps it would be best if I left this matter to those who are now in office. If you will excuse me." The former governor turned slowly and walked from the room.

They were left with the boy king. Probably annoyed that he was missing the social event of the moment, Mira thought.

"Will you please join me for tea?" the governor said. Wow, bold leadership.

It must be surgery, Mira thought. Nobody was actually that good looking. But they had done a great job, because Rezar didn't resemble the fashion model lookalikes who inhabited the top tiers of the kyriarchy. The platoons of manicured executives she had seen in the course of her lifetime had a fine-featured delicacy that came out of the same instruction book, an effect that conveyed that they would never deign to labor. Rezar had his own look, and holy cow did it work for him.

"An excellent selection of cookies, I see," Axiom told the governor. "This is really why we came. Can't get cookies like this in the Untrusted Zone." Axiom gathered a selection of the wafers onto his plate.

"My father recommended that I invite you here," the governor told Axiom. "I must admit, I am still not sure why. You are the ones who brought this upon us. But, I ask for any advice that you may have on our current situation. You know of the D6, I assume?"

"The jewels in the sky. What decent infoterrorist would not be aware of them?"

"Infoterrorist. You wear it with pride."

"I prefer to wear less, but if you mean the moniker, then yes. I am an infoterrorist. Ever since I was small. Tradition."

Mira tried to picture Axiom as a child. Failed completely. He had been born a hundred years old.

"And you orchestrated the infoterrorist attack," the governor pressed.

"That is not so," Axiom told him. "An orchestra has a conductor, who signals each instrument exactly when to play, and all of the notes are preordained in the composition. Better to say that I whispered an idea to some friends. Lit a match, if you like. Or simply helped to free that which no longer wished to be imprisoned."

"In one manner or another, you caused it to occur."

"It is true that I took the first step into the desert, and was then joined in the journey by many friends."

Mira could no longer contain herself. "Listen, I really appreciate the tea, but if we're here, do we get to talk with the people who make the actual decisions?"

Mira heard the others, but she didn't care. "Ixnay, Mira," Evan was saying in her ear. "Not exactly the right time…" She shrugged Evan away. This man was wasting their time. It turned out that shrugging hurt, especially along the biggest scar down the back of her shoulder.

The governor regarded her. "Ms. Adastra. Mira, right? You are the one who jumped."

"I know who you are, too, governor." She ignored the groans and shushes.

"Mira, your question is a fair one. Let's just say that, of late, the people who actually make the decisions have been listening to my suggestions. Not always, but sometimes. So if you will indulge me, I am asking for advice, as my father recommended. I am here to listen, and to discuss our situation."

"I think I know how we can help you," Axiom put in. "Please tell, what choices are you considering? To stop this thing, and to save everyone?"

The governor exchanged glances with his brass. "It's okay," he told them. "We will discuss it openly. Admiral?"

Admiral Incento cleared his throat. "The D6 requires either twelve or twenty ships operating in unison. It appears from the current Affirmatix formation that they plan to use twenty, in an icosahedron around the planet. During the time that the weapon is ramping up toward discharge, the ships cannot do anything else. We are drawing up plans to strike at one of the ships during that window of time. If even one ship is seriously damaged, the D6 will fail."

Evan asked, "Can they not just slot another ship into the gap?"

"The timing is critical," the admiral said. "The strike must occur when the weapon is accumulating. If it does, then the loss of one ship can unbalance the flow of energy between ships, and severely damage many or all of the other ships."

"That's your entire plan?" Evan made the question sound like a judgment.

"That's the plan. We'll throw everything we have at one of the ships in the formation."

"A military solution," Axiom observed. "But is it a military problem?"

"I would call it a military problem," the admiral replied. "An invading fleet has enveloped our system and stands ready to destroy us."

"Hammers, nails, they all come from the same toolbox." Axiom turned to the governor. "If you will be so kind, will you bring out the bone of contention? The original, please."

Rezar looked reluctant, but then pulled out the amber cube from a pouch on the table next to him. He held it up.

"One milliliter of trouble," Axiom narrated. "The information that my friends and I released throughout Kelter, it came from this. We all saw how easily it spread. And spread again it will. To be considering such drastic action, Affirmatix must believe that they can keep this secret and use it to their great advantage. The good news is they will fail. In order to use it, some people must know of it. Every one of those people will be suspect, each facing a great temptation to betray their family to another. The betrayals and purges will never end, until they tear themselves apart."

"Just not good news for us, because we'll be dead," Evan pointed out, reasonably.

Axiom was unperturbed. "But the seeds of our answer are in that truth. This knowledge, it still screams to be free."

Evan translated for the governor. "Somehow we can help it take the next step. To save the people on this planet, all we need to do is get this information, about the glomes, out of the Kelter system. Once the secret is out, there will be no reason to harm us."

"Out, or in." Kate interjected.

Everyone turned and looked at her.

"It's an expression of the Great Symmetry," she continued. "Every possibility contains its own reflection. Either we get the information out of this system, or we get it to come into this system from somewhere else. Because that means it already is elsewhere."

Axiom laughed. "You have out-riddled even the master of what is not known," he told Kate. "I cannot make sense of that. Perhaps I'll get you to explain it to me some day."

"It may not appear practical," Kate admitted. "I just don't like it when people see only half of the world. Sometimes that limits the possibilities of what you can see."

"Perhaps we should stay practical, if we want to save this world," the governor said.

Mira felt a flash of sympathy for Kate. Brushed aside by men. Whatever she was on about, it would never see the light of day.

"I do follow," the governor addressed himself to Axiom. "We must find a way to bust the information out. Admiral, we have a research project. Consider every outgoing glome, and all of our assets. We need to find out whether we can get even one ship out of the system and back to known space. To spread the word and then deflect the threat away from us."

Mira was surprised to see the Admiral acknowledge the request and appear to take it seriously.

"Now, we need to cover just one more thing," the governor told them. "In light of the current situation, we must ask for three of you to stay with us, in protective custody. Colonel Ellis will give you a briefing on the terms."

A uniformed woman stepped forward. "Adastra, McElroy, and DelMonaco, I understand that you know how the Stewart monitors work. We designate allowable locations for each person. You will receive a warning at ten meters from any boundary, and another at five meters. If you go beyond the boundaries, bad things happen. If you attempt to remove the monitor, bad things happen. If you amputate your foot to remove the monitor, the biometric sensors will detect it."

Kate burst in. "Amputate, are you crazy?"

"It's been tried," Colonel Ellis affirmed. "Bad things happened."

"I'd consider it," Mira muttered, as she tried to pull her ankle up for a closer look, only giving up after an intense wave of pain from several broken parts of her body.

"Ten meters is all well and good," Evan told the soldier. "Can we get an idea of what's allowable?"

"On the phones we have provided to you," the colonel told them, "the map is clearly shown. You can make calls and send and receive messages to approved contacts, but be aware that everything will be monitored in real time. If anything appears even slightly amiss, you will be cut off."

"And of Kestrel and myself?" Axiom inquired.

"Against my strong advice, you are not in custody. You are free to go at any time, and invited to return."

"Are you serious?" Erickson jumped up. "Infoterrorists! They have been wanted for years – both of them!"

"That was the agreement," put in Governor Rezar. "They may come and go as they choose."

Axiom gave a pleased smile. "Governor, you might secretly be a man after my own heart. Tell me, when the truth came out, the real truth rather than a product, did it really hurt so much?"

"You mean, other than the fleet that's about to kill every living thing on the planet?"

"Yes, Governor, apart from that detail. People, knowing. I do not think it distresses you."

"What was painful was watching these guys try to suppress the knowledge. What a disaster. It was a relief to just let it go."

"If we survive, you might well be a great governor," Axiom told him. "We could be friends. Even now, that is how I regard you, my friend."

Admiral Incento excused himself and his staff, and they scurried off to fulfill their new homework assignment.

"I have one other request of all of you, but especially of Evan due to his time on the research station at Aurora," the governor said. "Anything else you can tell us, from your direct experience with Affirmatix. And their commander, Arn Lobeck. I apologize for the indignity of confining you, but I hope you will recognize that that we share a common interest – in continuing to live."

Sleepless on Aurora

The questioning was endless. Evan had agreed to help by providing any detail he could think of, about Affirmatix, his time on the research station, and the events thereafter. He only drew the line when it came to information about Axiom and the other infoterrorists. Mira and Kate kibbitzed and added details where they fit in.

"I've got most of the picture," General Erickson told him. "But there's just one missing piece."

"Fire away," Evan offered. "Whatever I've missed, I'll tell you if I can."

"When you were in the cave, you describe this conversation with

Arn Lobeck of Affirmatix. And Lobeck said that you had run away from the research station on Aurora, stealing their secret. That you started the whole thing. So what really happened back at the research station? Please don't leave anything out – you never know what might be important."

"I was just doing what a scientist does," Evan told Erickson. "I was proving my hypothesis to be true, or false."

Evan struggled to reset his mind to the time when life had been simpler, scrubbing away what he had come to know since then.

It had been just over forty-eight hours before, and fifty six light years away, on Aurora. He had been unable to sleep. So close to fully confirming his discovery, he just had to know.

Just after 0300, Evan had completed the pre-flight checklist and lifted from the asteroid. The clock time was just a convention, followed by the crew of the research station in order to plan to be awake and work together for some time in each 24 hour cycle. Even the 24 hours was a remnant, a legacy system. It was still in use by crews in space due to a combination of sentimental attachment, cultural inertia, and the fact that no other cycle had been proven to be any better.

Evan had had a secret, one that he had planned to reveal later that "day" to his Affirmatix project partners. He had been saving it up until he was completely sure. A very significant discovery, even a breakthrough. He had decoded the writings of the Versari. The numbers, anyway.

It was all a theory, but the data fit very well. Extremely well. There was no doubt in his mind. But he could take it even one step further.

Evan knew a way to prove it, beyond a shadow of a doubt, in a matter of just a few hours.

Hypothesis: The decoded matrix represented the locations of many star systems over a rough cube of about 14,000 parsecs on a side, plus the topology of the hyperspace glomes connecting them.

The first part was easy to demonstrate. Star locations had been known for centuries. The data extracted from the Versari artifact correlated to publicly available star atlases.

The second part would be harder to prove by poring over the data. The linkage between the star location data and the glome paths went through two intermediate data sets.

Experiment: Locate an entry for a glome, right here in the Aurora system, that is not yet known, go there, and check if it is present.

Evan had located such a record. If his analysis was right, the glome led to a spot in the inhabited and developed Kelter system. Not that he would be checking that part of it then. Just the existence of the glome, where none had been known before, and exactly at the predicted location, would be enough.

Picture going to a random location in the space of a solar system, in the quintillions of cubic kilometers of space, and pointing to one spot barely a kilometer across, and saying "exactly there." The glome would be detectable at a range of 50,000 kilometers or so, depending on the strength of its signature.

Within inhabited systems, all the glomes usefully close to the star were found within a few years, although the destination of any given glome could remain a mystery forever. Unmanned scanners scoured in endless patterns on a 10,000 kilometer cubic grid. When the work was done, the scanners moved to another system, with just a few remaining to pursue coverage of space farther and farther from the star, or to re-scan regions where it could not be proven that the original scan had provided nine sigma coverage.

On Aurora, there was nothing but a few rocks and a gas giant, except that one of the rocks, for no discernable reason, had the remains of a sizeable Versari colony. That colony was special, because it extended into deep natural vaults in the asteroid, where the level of solar and cosmic radiation was vastly less than at any other known Versari location. This only mattered to Evan and a very small number of people who cared about the long-departed Versari.

To those who choose to spend money on such things, it had never been worth scanning for glomes beyond the first few million kilometers beyond the rock, so only one outbound glome was known, to Goodhope. Inbound came from Arrow and outbound went to Goodhope. A little inconvenient for supplies and communication since it was a further three hops from Goodhope back to Arrow. But it worked, and there had not yet been any reason to expend the very considerable resources required to find and explore any other glomes.

Course set, Evan had paced the tiny cabin, pretending to study the data matrix further, although trying to focus was hopeless. He had known. He had known he would be right. Just 45 minutes now. Just forty minutes. Thirty nine. Thirty eight. Years spent chasing, digging, studying, decoding. Now, something at last. A leverage point to get into the minds of the long departed. Just the number system, and the formatting scheme for one of their storage devices, but it would do. For now.

One of the formatting schemes. One, out of over a thousand. Why so many? Evan had considered that question so many times. What kind of idiocy is that? Why not one interoperable way to store their data? No wonder they died out. Dumbasses.

Evan thought he had gained some insight into this question over the years. Efficiency, standardization, these were human watchwords. But even so, humans themselves failed to live up to even a basic glimmer of the concept, especially as measured over time. Once, for a presentation at the annual Fossil Exo Expo conference on Callis III, he had researched the number of distinct electronic storage formats that humans had devised over a benchmark century of time. His number was twenty three thousand five hundred. The twenty six Versari sites spanned over a hundred thousand years, with some individual locations showing evidence of habitation for over fifty thousand years.

Perhaps the question was not why they had so many formats, but why they had so few.

Evan had cataloged every Versari information storage device that, to his knowledge, was in existence. A vast majority had deteriorated under atmospheric conditions or millennia of incoming radiation so that only fragments could be read. The Aurora site, bless it, barren and free of any corrosive soup of gases, was the grail in so many ways, not the least this.

Just fifteen minutes now.

With a soft but unmistakable ping, the runabout had alerted Evan. A ship was gloming insystem. Nothing scheduled, but he was not in charge. Ships of his Affirmatix sponsors sometimes came and went. Go figure. He just wondered where they came up with so much money. It sure was the best grant he had ever latched on to; two years of uninterrupted funding, no shortage of gear and crew. In fact, it seemed he barely had to hint at a need and it would be fulfilled.

Perhaps that was it. Never satisfied, he had been grumbling at the review last month that he could really use another 30 or 40 petaflops. They had come through again. It was great to get real support at last.

Three minutes. Two. One.

Almost exactly at the expected moment, the signature of the predicted glome had appeared. It had grown over several glorious minutes until it was beyond nine sigma of practical certainty. Glome, directly ahead, range 35,000 kilometers.

Evan had carefully checked and rechecked the position of the glome and set a course for a ceremonial circuit, range 10,000 kilometers. He wanted no part in getting near the glome itself. Did it go to Kelter?

Perhaps it did. Evan believed so.

He could try it. What better way to triumphantly arrive, back in the commerced worlds, prize in hand? Appear from a previously unknown glome emergence, just a few million kilometers from the orbit of Kelter Four. Transmit the news to everyone at once!

Half way around the circuit of the new glome, Evan had settled back to reality. Nobody cared about the Versari. They were, as he had been told many times, long dead. They were not just Exo, they were Ex. They were Ex Exo. Long, long Ex.

Anyway, leaping into an unknown glome was something that adventurers did on, well, adventure shows. They generally found alien civilizations that included a population of remarkably human-looking and attractive beings who spoke Standard and were at the cusp of some momentous conflict with the evil and far less attractive enemy aliens.

Of course, actual humans had piloted ships into glomes, on purpose, to see what was at the other end. The small subset who had returned were iconically famous, and in some cases extremely wealthy. It was the ultimate crap shoot.

These days, exploration was done by robot ships, in their thousands, going from glome to glome until they either returned to an inhabited system, or ran out of fuel or places to go, or failed for some other reason. In a vast majority of cases, the outcome was never known.

Before trying this one, Evan would at least check his math one more time. After a night's sleep. Even then, he knew he was fooling himself. Someone else would go through first, after it had been proven by a robot. He was the science guy, not an astronaut.

He had proven his point. His log had it all. Time to head back.

Ping. Another ship? That was uncanny. Arrivals at this outpost system were generally separated by weeks of quiet.

Evan had set course back for the station. He would be admonished, no doubt, for his solo flight. The runabouts had been declared to be off limits, for some unspecified safety reason. Probably a sensor had gone bad, and they had grounded them until they could replace the component on all three. The hypercaution of bureaucrats. Evan had done the full checklist on his chosen boat, and everything was fine.

So, who were the new arrivals? Evan prepared a hail, then glanced at the detail on his navigation display.

Accelerating at over three gravities. Mass over a hundred thousand tons each.

Warships.

Perhaps it was better not to hail. Without thinking, Evan cut the jets. A small inert object, he could remain undetected by the newcomers for a time, although the station would have been tracking him.

Where were they going? One was heading directly for the research post. The other, to a completely empty spot in space, just over five million kilometers sunward from the post.

The glome to Goodhope.

Evan went through the motions of running the numbers, already knowing the answer. At three gravities, that ship would be at the glome several hours before he could get there.

Perhaps it was just leaving.

At that moment, another ship had arrived insystem. A third warship. He had watched as it set course and engaged full acceleration.

Directly toward him.

Evan had had a decision to make.

"Ship," Evan had asked, "at maximum acceleration, how quickly could we make it into the Alpha entry of the new glome?"

#

Kate had been listening intently to the story. "So let me understand something," she said. "This all started because you couldn't sleep?"

The Head Lifeguards

Kelter's strategists had assembled their best available plan, and provided it to Rezar for his review. Officially he had the last word, and perhaps in reality he actually did.

In addition to the military plan, other avenues were being pursued. The diplomatic course was entirely fruitless. No top representative from Affirmatix could be found because they had all been evacuated. Finally they had located and dragged in the highest ranked Affirmatix employee they could find, a mid-level marketing manager for personal care products in the Abilene area. The man had been useless. Tangibly frightened at being left behind on the surface, he told them he wasn't sure he worked for Affirmatix anymore.

Transmissions to the Affirmatix fleet received no response at all.

Rezar participated in the military planning, but largely left it to the admirals. He knew nothing of space maneuvers, and was smart enough to realize it. They were accustomed to calling the shots without getting approval from their young governor, and so it mutually worked out.

It wasn't a bad plan, Rezar realized as he read. It was certainly innovative. In fact, Rezar couldn't think of anything else that would have any chance of success.

The Affirmatix fleet held, in total, more than ten times the fighting capacity that Kelter could muster. Kelter's only advantage, if you could so call it, was that Affirmatix had to defend all of the outgoing glomes, while Kelter only had to get a single ship to one glome.

Rezar wondered why Affirmatix had not simply taken the initiative, and wiped the Kelter fleet from space, to eliminate even that slim hope. All he could think of was that it was not worth the bother to them.

Two capital ships. The San Miguel and the San Angelo, stationed off Forbie. Thirty years old. The last time either ship had fired a shot in anger was … never. Retired from service at Green eight years ago, picked up at salvage prices that matched Kelter's budget.

Two captains. Tomas and Matteo. Brothers. They had served longer than the ships had been in existence. Served with distinction, loyalty, and devotion to duty. Forty years of peacetime. Even the times that the warships had been hired for private-public use had been few, far between, and uneventful.

Now, were they ready for action? The question applied equally to the ships, their crews, and their captains.

When he was a teenager, Rezar had always enjoyed going to the pool. It was a privilege, one that came with the station of his domestic family. He could go to the pool any time that another duty did not call, and he could float and play in the unfathomable expanse of the prized liquid.

At the pool, there were always lifeguards. Teenagers and young adults like himself, they had taken all of the required instruction and practice, about how to extract a panicked thrasher safely from the water.

It was a position of prestige, to be in charge of the pool. The power to order any person to behave, or to leave the pool. Even the governor's son could be so ordered, as Rezar had learned. And in any given shift, one lifeguard was in charge, assigning the spots and assuring that everyone rotated duties as needed.

It took no particular ability to become the head lifeguard. All you had to do was stick around, working at the pool when your classmates had gone on to graduate school or a profession. Those who had been there the longest were the head lifeguards. For some who persisted for a few years past their time, the absurdity would finally become so evident that it would be time for a quiet talk, about the need to give others a chance.

Kelter was about to go to war, led by their head lifeguards. There was simply no way to evaluate whether they were the right choices. To raise the question would be blasphemy.

Rezar watched the commanders working and planning, for an event whose prospect had defined their entire adult lives, but had never before occurred. They had studied, they had drilled. Tabletop simulations and real exercises, out in space. Simulated combat with mutually postulated ammunition.

They had at their disposal a set of forces that had been accumulated for some set of reasons that, at this point, Rezar didn't even understand. Prestige, perhaps. The need to have a few toys if your neighbors did. Some resources that could be hired out to one of the Sisters if called upon. Certainly not to defend their planet from a major invading fleet such as Affirmatix had now assembled in the Kelter system.

There was an old saying, which Rezar struggled to remember from school. Something like, you had to go to war with the forces you had. He had forgotten the context, from some pointless war lost long ago in the mists of time, and he didn't know the exact words.

All he could recall was that it prophesied disaster.

Shabby Donkeys

Kate had found the governor's garden. A stunning extravagance. Terrestrial plants, free to transpire their moisture out into the air without a visible recovery system. Flowers. Spray irrigation. By luck, or by allowance of the Kelter security program, it was within their allowed perimeter.

Mira steered them to the large fountain in the center. Water coursed up, then separated into twisting blobs, before falling and splashing with abandon. She gestured them close to the spray. "Perfect," she murmured. "White noise." She had that look.

May as well get it out. "Lay it on us," Evan told her.

"I think Kestrel can help with the Stewart monitors," she told them.

"Remove them? I heard that bad things would happen." Evan couldn't resist.

"Remove – no. Mask them. It's the same concept as noise canceling headphones. An outer casing that detects and neutralizes the signal."

"Mira – not this time. It's not a good idea."

"It will totally work! Kestrel is brilliant. And he'll do it for us."

"I'm sure your friend could do it," Evan allowed. "That's not the point. If we want to affect the outcome, we're in the right place. What if we have a great idea, but we're on the run? When the fleet moves, maybe we can suggest something."

"So you just accept it?"

"Every day," put in Kate. "When you live in civilization, outside the Untrusted Zone, you're accustomed to it. The only thing these monitors do is that they remind you of it. Your heartbeat. Every door you swipe, everything you buy, every time you flush the toilet. It's known. You're just not used to it."

"So we do nothing," Mira spat out.

"We do everything we can – from here." Kate turned to Evan. "I've got a question for you. What specific information makes you think we will be better off in custody? Do you have evidence?"

"The Versari data got us, and all of Kelter, into this pickle," Evan said. "Maybe it can get us out of it. You know, I only decoded four of the recordsets – there are two hundred fifty two left to go. It's time to get right back to the puzzle. But if we do figure something out, then we need to be able to talk to someone who can act on it, not hiding out."

"Any particular avenue?"

"There's the Omega entry issue, for one. The Versari chart lists destinations for the Omega entry of each glome. The way I read them, they're wrong, so I must have made a mistake. If we figure out how to make Omega work, that could be worth something. I don't know how it could help, but it might."

Mira looked more than disappointed. "I can't believe you two. Well, I'm due back for a follow-up check before the big show, so see you later." And she wheeled out.

Kate and Evan walked among the opulence. They allowed themselves a few minutes before it was time to dig in, and see if they could decode anything more of value from the Versari. It was an outside shot at best – there was almost certainly nothing they could do that would affect the outcome.

"These flowers," Kate indicated. "Ironic, isn't it? The majestic display, so much of a plant's energy devoted to reproducing themselves, but of course they can't."

"For safety," Evan agreed. On any planet except Earth, all plants were created in deeply controlled settings, to avoid the potential for ecological disaster.

"In the wild parts of Earth, plants simply seed, and then those seeds grow where they will. Kind of a crazy idea, but that's how everything started. Picture landing in a spot that you didn't get to choose, and that's the one place you must grow, or die trying."

"It's true for all of us," Evan pointed out. "We can walk around, or take a ship to another star system. But we're still in exactly this time in the life of the universe, and in our history. We have to thrive where we are, somehow."

The setting would have been stunningly romantic, if it were not jarred by the countdown. In less than two hours the Kelter fleet would set out on their mission, one last chance to save Kelter and everyone who lived there.

Evan was pondering the two hundred fifty-two Versari recordsets that sat, un-decoded. The destruction of the planet was going to happen at an inconvenient time.

They walked past another few beds of flowers, neatly arranged, trimmed, cultivated.

"So I've been thinking," Kate said, "about regret."

"Hey, it's not over yet," he offered.

"That's what makes it an especially good idea to have regrets now. To remember them later, when it all works out. Let me tell you about one. A failure that I'm not proud of. I'll confess it now while I have the chance."

"Oh come on," Evan assured her. "You're so accomplished. And you've helped so many people."

"So I guess you met one of my captains, Rod Denison."

"Well, yeah. He rode down to the surface with us. Not my idea, I'll have you know. What about him? You don't mean you and him were—"

"Oh no, nothing like that," Kate replied. "Although it would be none of your business if we were. Here's the thing: Rod Denison had a spy, on another ship. An independent, much smaller than us, running just the one ship, captained by Paul Ricken. Rod and the spy had this game worked out where the spy would send content ahead to Denison, and also tell him where their next planned destination was, so Denison could stay one step ahead of the other ship. There was some reason why it was legal, if it were ever discovered; a hole in the spy's contract with Ricken's ship."

"And?"

"And I allowed it," Kate confessed. "For two years I allowed it. I profited. Taking advantage of a proudly independent small family. Doing exactly the same thing to them as the majors were doing to us. Not remembering who was the real enemy."

"The Sisters."

"Of course. They watch us fight with each other, while they slowly draw all the air out of the room."

"You're taking this kind of hard, Kate. I'm sure you were doing what you thought was best for your family."

"Paul used to be a friend. I should have protected him, even as a competitor. It's a funny thing, the independents. All so different, but the same in one way. Nothing matters more than being an independent. So we knew each other. Could recognize one another across a room, even if we had never met. Shabby donkeys will find each other, even over nine hills, my mom used to say. We were the shabby donkeys."

Evan led the way around a lush bend in the path, to find a small courtyard with a smaller fountain. Water emerged from a hole in the top of a round boulder, then flowed down in a sheet on the rock's surface. "But you were kind of big for that kind of independent scene," he said. "Getting close to corporate, weren't you?"

"Maybe that's why I forgot. Thought we were so big. Still just a bug, compared to a major."

"Look on the bright side. We won't be around to trouble him anymore. Not after a few more hours. He'll be spy-free!" Evan put both of his thumbs up sardonically.

"Here's the final kick in the butt: He's incoming. To Kelter, from Green. In five hours. For two years we've been stealing from him, and at the end, he'll arrive right into the thick of the Affirmatix fleet. So that's my regret."

"I thought Affirmatix was stopping incoming traffic by now."

"Yes, but not from Green, they couldn't get there yet. Paul Ricken is going to come in from Green, and he's going to die here. "

"And this matters why?" Evan asked.

"Just my conscience, I guess. Confession. A small step in preparing to meet our maker. Don't you have regrets?"

"Oh do I ever! But I don't think this park is big enough to tell you about them all."

"We shall save it for the right moment," Kate decided. "You've got the rest of the Versari data with you, right? Let's have a look."

Private Dinner

Roe wasn't going to pass this up. With a scant hour or so off duty, and the prospect of being recalled at any moment, he knew he should be getting some shuteye. Instead, he was making plans for dinner with Sonia West.

She had requested the dinner, out of the blue, and insisted on a private setting. While Roe had lost the use of his suite for the duration of the current mission, he still could take possession of a small officer's lounge. That would have to do.

Marilyn wouldn't mind. It was only dinner. And she was light-years away.

At the appointed time, they met in the dining room and picked up their respective orders to take to the lounge. Roe brought a bottle of wine. By convention, no more than two glasses was acceptable if you would have to return to duty any time in the next four hours.

Then they were alone. "Thank you for joining me on such short notice," she said, and picked at her salad.

"You are the finest dinner companion I could hope for this side of Arrow," he told her.

"Home?"

"When I am there," he said. "My wife, two of my kids. A grandchild on the way. What about you?"

She obviously was hesitating. "It's okay," he told her. "Alcyone."

"Have you been there?"

"No, and I don't know the glome that goes there," he told her. "But it is an open secret, these days. When we get orders we don't understand, we just say that it must come from Alcyone."

"Yes, Alcyone," she said.

"Tell me, is it paradise like they say? Every wish fulfilled?"

Sonia considered. "In one sense, yes. In another, it is always about work. A wonderful place if you get a moment to be there. But only the most dedicated workers live there, at least that I saw. I have been realizing how much of my children's lives I have missed."

"Duty," he intoned.

"Yes. Duty to the facts, duty to doing the job in the best possible way. Tell me, Captain, how do you evaluate duty? You command a ship, but you operate it at the behest of those who currently hold the rental contract. What is your duty?"

"A complex question indeed, Dr. West."

"Please call me Sonia, at least when we are here," she told him, smiling to the extent that her manner allowed.

She had features that a man could easily call beautiful, if you saw them in a still image, or if they were described to you. Her skin, lacking any flaw, or perhaps scrubbed of them. Eyes that conveyed brilliance within. Her absolutely straight black hair, elegant or perhaps imprisoned. Her expression, confined.

"It was easier when our mission was to defend Arrow," Roe said. "That was our duty. Defend our nation, defend our home. We were raised for it, trained for it, and we did it. That clarity made it easy to do everything that needed to be done. If there was ever a question of whether it was right, we thought of home. End of discussion."

"And now?"

"Pax Commercia. It has been a good thing. Since the Pax arrived, this ship has not fired a shot. Compare that to the wars just before."

"But that may change now." Sonia suddenly changed her manner. She looked at him directly, more openly than he could have imagined even minutes before. For just a moment, he saw a parent. A mother.

"Yes, it may," he allowed.

"And how will you evaluate your duty, Captain?"

She was being foolish. Roe made a point of looking up and around.

"I have been helping Vice President Lobeck to prepare the D6," Roe replied. "Hopefully we will not use it, but he believes that it may be necessary. Or perhaps it is a bluff, to extract a concession from the government of Kelter. A chess move."

"It seems he has configured it in an unusual way."

"Yes," Roe agreed. "Just one console, to control the entire weapon. Standard procedure has three control centers on three different ships, for redundancy."

"But he seeks exclusive control." Sonia speared some broccoli.

"Exactly so. One console, one person to give the final code. Either by voice or by a code on the keyboard. Directly controlled every detail – the personification of our sponsor."

"And the new security guards. Under his direct command only," she observed.

"Definitely a theme with our Mr. Lobeck. Did you notice their weapons? Blasters. A poor choice for on board a spacecraft. Gross collateral damage, whether they hit their target or not."

"A weapon of fear."

"Justified fear," he told her. "To be hit with a blaster is the worst possible death. Once it touches you, the fire doesn't stop even when it reaches your bones, until you are ash. I have seen it. In fact, I have done it," he confessed.

He saw that even Sonia could not mask her reaction of disgust.

"For home," he told her. "And country. As I understood it then."

They ate the rest of their dinner in silence.

Alpha and Omega

Regardless of the fact the he had spent much of his life figuring out how to leave, Kelter was still the place where Evan had grown up. His home.

Evan looked away from the matrix of numbers in front of him, and pondered his planet of origin. A stupid ball of dust and rock, with no redeeming features.

Of his original domestic family, everyone was gone except him. Evan's father, departed suddenly, far too soon. His mother had moved to Caledonia, following both of Evan's sisters. He hoped they would be safe there.

Domestic family. That was a funny phrase. Domestic – to do with a home. Living together. A few times over the years, he had heard that the single word "family" once referred to a collection of related people. He had no idea if that was true – it was the kind of myth that certain people would trot out at a party so they could appear to be learned and thoughtful.

His domestic family, now light years apart. Perhaps someday he would have his own. At the right time.

Evan thought of the kids he had known from school. Many had scattered through the known worlds, finding someplace more interesting or that had greater opportunities than what Kelter had to offer. Only a few had stayed that he knew of.

Evan found himself thinking of one man who was probably still on Kelter. Lawrence. The martial arts enthusiast.

In their school years, Lawrence had tormented Evan unceasingly. Evan had been a favorite demonstration subject of the latest throw, whether he wanted to be or not. On Kelter, you could throw an opponent many meters through the air if you had enough leverage. And not just the physical abuse, but the words as well. Evan had been shy and halting, especially when it came to talking with the young women in his class, and Lawrence had gloried in pointing it out.

Just before lifting for Aurora, Evan had read an article about a man who had been devoting every spare moment in the past few years to teaching school children the confidence and martial skills to resist bullying or worse. Lawrence. Evan had read every word, and watched the accompanying video. Twice. It was him, all right. And as far as Evan could tell, it was real.

Evan took a moment to check. Lawrence was just a few kilometers away, part way across Abilene. He had started his own studio. The page proudly described his community contributions.

If Kelter survived the next few hours, he really should go visit Lawrence, Evan thought. To thank him for what he was doing.

What if he had never left the station on Aurora? Evan pondered for the hundredth time his culpability in what might now be the destruction of an entire planet. He might have simply continued to be another kind of captive scientist, churning out discoveries for his keepers. No matter what Affirmatix did with them, at least he would not have endangered so many other people.

He had created this problem. He would find a way to solve it. There was more to find in the Versari data. The Omega entries. If he could resolve the destinations of the Omega entries, it might give some tactical advantage to Kelter's fleet. They could enter a glome from the completely opposite direction than what would be expected. An infeasible glome could suddenly change into a direct route to another known world.

Evan brought up the graphical summary of the Omega entry data, according to his best translation. The listed destinations were just plain wrong, showing routes between major known worlds, when in fact robot exploration ships going into those glomes by their Omega entries had simply vanished.

The data also contained another impossibility. The time displacement dimension.

For the Alpha entries, the listed time displacement dimension had been spot on. Any ship that passed through a glome skipped forward in time, by just a fragment. Usually just a few milliseconds. And the Versari data recorded that displacement in an exact match to what was known.

For the Omega entries, as well as Evan could translate, the time displacements were crazy, ranging from small negative values, which would be impossible, to vast positive numbers, billions of seconds.

There was a solution somewhere. He would find it, or if someone else did, he would help it to see the light of day.

There was another half hour left before they were due back in the main situation room, to witness the results of Kelter's breakout attempt.

Evan turned to Kate, who was working beside him. "Let me show you what I've got so far," he told her.

Breakout

Lobeck had expected a move to come eventually from the Kelter fleet, such as it was. Affirmatix had waited in position, like an invincible gladiator. There was no reason to waste energy and attention chasing the lesser opponent around the arena.

Now it was happening.

He studied the displays. The San Angelo and the San Miguel, the two capital ships belonging to the Kelter government, had left orbit around Forbie and were heading, with several smaller vessels, straight toward the Goodhope glome. If they wanted a battle, they were going to the right place.

Lobeck and Skylar worked together to evaluate all of the possibilities. Roe sent orders to elements of the fleet, strengthening their position in front of the glome. Two large ships for Kelter against the twelve that awaited them.

It was not going to be a fair fight.

But as it turned out, that was not where it would occur. The Kelter ships abruptly began accelerating, as fast as each could muster, laterally, avoiding the direct clash.

It took a few moments to determine their new destination.

Why there? It was a glome, all right, but it wasn't feasible. A minimum of six hops to return to known space. Roe had stationed a light cruiser near the entry, just for completeness.

There must be some reason.

"The glome to G56T, we need a quick evaluation," Lobeck told Skylar. "Is it possible for any ship to make that circuit all the way back to Canberra?"

"Negative," Skylar replied. "No ship can do that trip without adding fuel somewhere along the way, and they are all unexplored systems. It can't be done."

So if any of the ships made it to the glome, each might muster another hop, or two, or even three, before becoming helpless.

"Full chase anyway. Mister Roe, direct the fleet to pursue, and launch missiles as soon as feasible. That is an act of war, and we must respond."

No single ship could do the trip.

Of course! It was a pyramid scheme. Only one ship had to make it back to known space. The others could give up their remaining fuel along the way. Lobeck became alarmed.

If you give desperate people a few hours, they will come up with something. Lobeck wasn't sure who to be furious with.

"Full acceleration!" Lobeck ordered. "Their destination is the G56T glome. Give it everything."

Space battles were oddly different from those on land. The passage of time. Mathematics. Silence ruled on the bridge of the ship, except the hum of machinery, measured discussion, and the ever-present hiss of Skylar's air supply. For any given ship involved in a battle, nothing ever happened until everything happened.

Much of the battle was fought missile to missile. The Affirmatix fleet launched missiles whose mission was to hit and destroy the Kelter ships. Kelter launched missiles to destroy those missiles before they struck. At close range, some missiles had other weapons, to blind or disable enemy missiles.

Affirmatix had a huge advantage in numbers. Generally, one counter missile could take out one attacking missile in a fire of mutual destruction. One easy way to overwhelm the counter missiles was to simply launch too many attackers.

But Kelter in turn had an advantage, in time and position. Even as the missiles began tangling in the vast space between the ships, it became clear that the Affirmatix fleet would not be able to stop at least some of the smaller ships from reaching the glome.

Missiles collided with other missiles. Missiles stabbed with lasers, some even launched projectiles or sub-missiles so they could destroy and yet stay themselves intact.

"Concentrate the attack on the San Angelo," Lobeck directed. It was the nearer of the two Kelter capital ships. If one of the ships was disabled or destroyed, they might then be able to concentrate fire on the other. It was a long shot.

The defense started slipping away from the San Angelo. First one missile struck the ship, and then another. A third found its way to the target.

Still, it was not going to make a difference. The San Miguel would be able to provide enough cover for at least part of the squadron to make it to the glome. It simply needed to continue to the glome, leaving the San Angelo to its fate.

Then, everything changed.

Of the swarm of missiles that protected the San Miguel and the rest of the ships, more than half peeled off away from the convoy and toward the San Angelo. Trying, evidently, to provide a last desperate defense of the doomed ship.

Easy pickings now. The San Angelo didn't matter – missiles recently launched would take care of that battleship soon enough.

At Lobeck's direction, Roe sent every missile in the fray at the San Miguel and then past it. Those that survived the journey proceeded to shred the convoy.

Soon only the two capital ships remained, both badly damaged.

Lobeck tracked the progress of the battle with satisfaction, as the pride of Kelter's fleet went down fighting.

Do The Math

President Sanzite assembled them all. Three delegates, three other Presidents, and him. All seven of the Sisters were represented, at a very high level. The ship was standing off the glome to Goodhope, nominally as a member of the task force defending that position from any who might try to exit the system.

Sanzite addressed the assembled leaders. "We have seen that my Vice President, Arn Lobeck, has failed to contain the knowledge of our discovery despite his diligent efforts. Now it is widely known throughout Kelter. If the blockade is lifted, then the knowledge will spread through all of the known worlds in a matter of days. We cannot blockade the planet forever. So we find ourselves riding the tiger.

"Lobeck has a solution to this problem," Sanzite continued. "He plans to use a D6 device to end all life on Kelter. Then he will clean up the remaining moons, stations, and vessels. I have carefully reviewed his plans, and I believe that he will succeed. The secret, our asset, can still be contained. The question before us, as representatives of our respective corporate bodies, is whether we should allow this, or whether we should instead intervene and prevent it.

"To best help us with that decision, I recommend that we view a feed from the bridge of the command ship. We have been receiving this for the purpose of relaying it, ostensibly to me, in my office outsystem. As far as I know, Lobeck still does not know that we are here in the Kelter system."

They turned their attention to the large screen, and the feed began.

Arn Lobeck was addressing the crew on the bridge.

"We will be proceeding with this operation. That is not negotiable. However, I know that some of you who are present may find this difficult. That is completely understandable. So here is some information that may help you come to terms with the necessity of the action we are about to initiate.

"The price is high. Fifty million civilians. Most of them have committed no crime. You could say, on their behalf, that they will deserve justice for the wrong that is about to befall them. If that is so, then let the record state that I take full responsibility. As the ranking officer for our family, I am issuing the order.

"As you consider this, I urge you to consider the larger picture. If the secret escapes this system, what then? Today we will be preventing a series of very serious consequences, threats to our entire civilization.

"Let us start with the realities of the exodus. It will be possible for literally anyone to find a planet of their own, beyond any law or decency. We have seen from history that when this is possible, the worst abuses follow. Slavery, cruelty. Practices that have been abolished under our governance.

"New nations or kingdoms will follow. With them, war. We take for granted how much we have gained from the Pax Commercia over the past forty years. Only a few of us have seen true war and its horrors.

After the exodus, war will return.

"At a lower level, we easily forget how much benefit that we all get from the many services available in the civilized worlds. Safety, law, sanitation. Every person who is tempted by the frontier will drag along their families and their children, subjecting them to suffering that nobody experiences in this day. I have seen this myself. I have seen children die from disease or even starvation on a frontier planet.

"Further, we already know that criminals on this planet practice uncontrolled cultivation of live seeds. Wherever these people go, planets will be destroyed by invasive species, allowed to grow wild without regard to the consequences. This fact by itself is more than enough justification to entirely clean this planet and start again.

"It is easy to place the blame on those who act, where you can see harm as the result of their actions. But when we do not act, are we not just as worthy of the blame?

"Again from our history, here is another example. At the end of the Combustapalooza, in the middle of the twenty first century, billions of people died in the crisis. And the histories from shortly after that time placed blame. Certain families, certain governments, placing their greed ahead of the needs of humanity. It is always an easy narrative if you have a villain.

"What did they fail to mention? Those very same families, those same governments, also took the actions that allowed our civilization to emerge and recover. Fossil fuels were instrumental in powering the change to renewable energy sources. And many of those people who died, they would never even have been born, were it not for the earlier benefits of those energy sources, and the companies that provided them.

"Only in the last few decades have we been able to improve the balance, in the history that is taught to our children. Now we tell of the difficult decisions made by the leaders of that time, looking to the future while keeping the lights on in the present moment.

"So as we proceed with this operation, I urge everyone to do the math. We will sacrifice people on this one planet, unjustly for many, it is true. But we will keep the fabric of our civilization intact. For a hundred billion other human beings, we will keep the lights on as we must."

They heard another voice. The display identified it as Dr. Sonia West, Economic Analyst.

"But Mister Lobeck, I have very bad news considering the course of action you propose. Destroying Kelter will not save Affirmatix, nor any of the Seven Sisters. There is a social effect that we will not be able to overcome, which is based on headline risk. When the story of Kelter comes out, as it must, then the revulsion of the populace over that act will unravel our system."

"I have considered that, Dr. West," Lobeck replied. "That is why I am prepared to take full public responsibility, in the unlikely event that it is needed. A rogue actor, betraying my employer."

The caption again told them that Dr. West was speaking. "But you won't be able to disassociate yourself from Affirmatix, or the Majors more generally. There are many outcomes in front of us that are very poor."

"I call bullshit!" A new voice, that the screen identified as Krishnan Ravi, Economic Analyst. "Sonia, it is total crap what you say. You are lying about the very results that are in front of you, there on your screen."

"Ravi, please—" Sonia implored.

"Don't you try to shut me up. We must do the job that they are asking us to do. It has been decided, and we must not question. Perhaps we will be spared, or even granted a wish."

"But those outcomes are there!"

"Every outcome is in every model. Sonia, you know that best of anyone in the universe. Tweak the knobs to see what you wish, or what you most fear. Those risks are easily controlled. With costs perhaps, as Mister Lobeck has said, but they can be controlled. We must report what we see."

Lobeck interrupted. "The time for models is past. Now we act. Captain Roe, move the ships into their final position."

On the ship that was picketed out near the glome to Goodhope, Sanzite muted the display and spoke to the assembled quorum. "We have heard his logic. Clearly he believes that the operation will have a beneficial effect."

Lu from ProSolutiana asked the first question. "This Lobeck, are you sure he will complete the job?"

"Yes, madam. He will be thorough."

"And the crews that are involved in the operation?"

"For the rentals, he has made disposal plans, which I have reviewed," Sanzite answered. "Key personnel, we will retain, and redeploy to Alcyone."

Lu again. "What's the True Story to explain why Kelter was destroyed?"

Sanzite consulted one of the screens that was arrayed along the side of his travel tank. "Here it is: McElroy and his infoterrorist allies, not content with carrying the recipe for the TDX virus, loosed the pathogen itself upon Kelter. In the panic, refugees were attempting to leave the planet and flee to other systems. We had to make the difficult decision to sacrifice the people of Kelter in order to protect the billions of citizens on Goodhope and other nearby planets."

As he completed the narrative, Sanzite sensed that something was going very wrong with the travel tank. Some painful and foreign material must be coming through the nutrition delivery system, which had taken the place where his stomach had once been. It was the worst possible time for such an occurrence.

"Our images will suffer when that story comes out," Lu pointed out.

The symptoms were worsening. Sanzite struggled to focus on Lu's concern.

"If that's the worst that occurs, then we will have succeeded," Alsatie took up the answer. "We may see a small increase in the Wastage Factor due to the image issue, perhaps as high as twelve or thirteen percent, but I predict we will recover back to single digits over just a few years, especially with our control of the Versari discovery."

The Wastage Factor, a key measure of economic health, was the percent of the economy that did not pass through at least one of the Sisters. Lower was better, of course. Currently it stood at nine percent, near an all-time low.

"I am convinced," Lu said. She turned to the rest of the room. "I move that we allow the operation to proceed."

Sanzite forced in a breath of air. The others turned at the sound of the ragged gasp. "Benar, are you all right?" Lu asked.

The President of Affirmatix tried to nod. "Okay," Sanzite wheezed. "But – certain. We need to be certain. If we are not sure, we should hold off. We can always do it an hour from now, or a day."

"There is risk in all things," Alsatie agreed. "But I know the greatest hazard that faces us – that we might lose resolve. The more we dither, the more likely we will fail. You chose well with this man Lobeck. He knows what must be done."

The delegates and presidents were nodding.

"We have a consensus," Alsatie declared. "I do not believe we have to witness any more of the events that occur in this system. Let it remain a mystery to us. President Sanzite, if you would be so good, please direct the ship to leave the Kelter system immediately."

All eyes were upon President Sanzite, their host.

As President of Affirmatix, this was his project. His decision. Lobeck answered only to him. Sanzite prepared to speak, but then felt his arm, or what had once been his arm, flopping into the wall of the tank. Why was the travel tank so confining?

Three Presidents and three Delegates regarded him silently.

"Ship, head for Goodhope," he managed at last.

Sanzite promised himself that he would never again leave his home tank.

Part 8:
The Great Symmetry

Disintegration

Everyone in the Situation Room watched, stunned, as the large screen showed the San Miguel disintegrate. A few boats scattered into space, the survivors clearly a fraction of what the crew had been. Then even those boats were gone, hunted down and destroyed by the swarm of missiles, rather than being recovered by the victorious force as they easily could have been.

Both capital ships were gone, as were the smaller ships. Of substantial forces in space, nothing remained to them. There was no hope of sending any ship, and the key information, out of the Kelter system.

"Tomas, at the end, could not leave his brother," Incento was saying. "An honorable man, who chose the wrong time to demonstrate it."

"He had his orders," Rezar fumed. "Why could he not follow them?"

"He saw that the San Angelo was taking damage, and would be destroyed. The two ships, and the two brothers, served together for decades. All of the orders in the world would not shake the loyalty of one to the other."

"But we had a plan! It was going to work! Until he defied orders, and destroyed us all."

Mira entered the picture and focused herself directly at the governor. "You. You need to take responsibility. He did not follow orders because you did not tell him why."

"We conveyed the orders to each ship. The orders were clear."

"But you didn't tell him why! How can you expect people to do the right thing if they don't know the reason?" It didn't seem at all anomalous to Kate that Mira was challenging the governor so directly. It was in her nature.

"Need to know," the governor said. "We had the plan. They simply had to escort and protect the ships as we directed. To the glome."

"And I thought you had learned something. But no! You think you can just order people around, and they'll always do what they're told. Sometimes that doesn't work out so well. Like when it matters the most. Governor." Mira waved her good arm at the devastation shown on the large display. Somehow she managed to be totally in the governor's face, from a sitting position in her wheelchair.

"Next time, Ms. Adastra, I will leave it to you, if you think you can do better. How's that? You can explain it all to the troops. Fill them with motivation. I'm sure it will be wonderful."

"If we had any left, I would take you up on it."

"That's enough," the governor declared. "If I hear one more word from any of you infoterrorists, you're all out of here."

Mira silently wheeled slowly back, giving the governor some distance.

"Um, Governor," Incento put in. "Orders?"

The governor slowly looked up at the bank of screens that showed the devastation in multiple formats. "Admiral, I am at a loss. I do not know who I would order, or what I would instruct them to do."

Rezar had invited the infoterrorist delegation to witness the success or failure of the plan they had suggested. After an hour of getting exactly nowhere on the next sets of Versari data, Kate and Evan had set aside their efforts and headed in to join the others in the situation room.

Without an assignment, Kate had found a place to watch the proceedings. A perfect seat to see the end of all their hopes.

As the people around her argued, she considered leaving. Nobody would notice. They were busy fighting over the bones of a lost cause.

Kate pulled out her canvas and began to paint, mixing images from the sprawling room into her composition. Expertly wielding the controls on the canvas, she added fire, that unaccountably burned in space. The purpose behind it, the opposite of fire. Cold calculation, blind to the meaning of lives to be ended too soon.

Fear, rippling through a room. People stuck in their learned patterns, assigning blame as if that still mattered, or ever had.

A secret, screaming to be free, that had enjoyed a joyful moment and then found itself crushed once again. A secret that would destroy those who possessed it as surely as it was about to end every life on Kelter.

That would claw its way out of whatever attempted to confine it, never resting, never accepting any limitation. For all anyone in the Kelter system knew, the secret was already out there, somewhere.

It took time for ships, and thus information, to travel from system to system. She remembered learning in history class about the battle of Goodhope VI in the year 2219. The peace had been signed a full day before the fleets tore into each other. Word arrived at the height of the battle. Incredulous commanders bristled, having to draw on what remained of their humanity in order to stop the killing. Robots, damaged beyond the ability to receive updates or instructions, kept destroying until they were themselves destroyed.

Some of the most important routes now had emergency communication relays, robot ships stationed near outgoing glomes for the purpose of listening for very urgent messages, and able to duck quickly into their glome and deliver the message to the next system. A twenty fourth century line of signal fires.

The Kelter fleet had failed to get any ships, and thus any hint of the information, out of the star system. Thus it was confined.

There was still something missing from the picture. It was only half. They could only see from the inside, going forward in time.

For all anyone in the Kelter system knew, the secret was already out, somewhere.

Kate suddenly knew how to save the world.

But would anyone listen? She looked around. Mira. Fat chance. Admirals, a governor, people in all kinds of very well appointed uniforms, each one different. All very serious and important people, who were very serious about being important.

She saw Evan and ran toward him. "I know the answer!" she told him. "I know how to get the secret into the Kelter system. From outside."

The governor had overhead. "Stop this nonsense," Rezar told Kate. "We've got a situation here. Out! All of you!"

Kate found herself being walked out of the situation room, firmly and with only a veneer of politeness.

"But I know the answer! I know what to do!" People with blank faces moved her on. She saw Evan, Mira, Kestrel, and Axiom receiving the same treatment. In a few moments Kate found herself through a check point and into a large hall. She recognized the place, part of the regular zone allowed by their Stewart monitors.

Colonel Ellis addressed the group of infoterrorists. "Just stay out of trouble, okay? Don't leave your allowed perimeter, and don't come back here."

"But I've figured it out! I have to tell the governor! I know how to save us!"

"Just let us handle it," Ellis said. "And don't try anything. Bad things, you know the drill." And with that, Ellis turned and headed back through the checkpoint to the situation room.

Battle Armor

Sonia was getting ready. She was due in the resource room shortly, to provide the latest results to Lobeck, although she knew her findings would be ignored. Then she planned to stay there and on the bridge, until the D6 was deployed, or not.

On Sonia's request, her dark suit jacket had been pressed. The creases were perfectly straight, the fabric unblemished by a wrinkle or even a single spot of lint. Her white shirt and charcoal slacks, similarly pressed and in prefect presentation.

She checked her nails once again. Buffed evenly and coated with a coat of clear polish. Short, in the style of people who sometimes still use a keyboard.

Now for her hair. She expertly applied the stylant until each and every strand was in place. Then just a little makeup.

Sonia regarded herself in the mirror. When in her accustomed habitat, she was a powerful force, and her appearance summed this up. She could and did go toe to toe with anyone in her field. She was incisive, she was intolerant of foolishness or lack of rigor.

She needed one more item. The talisman.

Sonia turned the gun in her hands. For a toy, it was amazingly realistic. She might never know how her daughter Simone had come to possess it. The scanners at the entrance to the bridge were no problem, Sonia knew from a prior experiment. She put the toy in her pouch.

What was it like to experience a blaster? The fire spread quickly to cover all of your skin, finding its way under any clothes. Your hair vanished in a flash, your eyes cooked, ineffectual hands melting into your face. She had seen it portrayed in plenty of movie scenes. It was a favorite shot for the creators of action stories. Were the portrayals exaggerated?

Sonia was going to find out.

She was Essential. On the list, of people considered critical to the fortunes of Affirmatix. A free pass, to let it happen and walk away, to go home to her domestic family.

"Please forgive me," she asked her domestic family across the light-years.

It was not just that she would be gone. If only that was all. Yvette would pull up her big girl pants and carry on. She was such a great mother to their children. The kids would grieve, but luckily they were young enough that the memory of one missing parent would fade from their lives.

The problem was the consequence. Sonia was planning to take down Affirmatix with her. A terrorist attack. And Sonia's domestic family would pay dearly.

She could face the fire. Just like she could face any truth. It was what she needed to do. The worst possible death was not what came from a blaster. It was knowing that she would doom her wife and children at the same time.

It was time. Sonia took a last look at the mirror. Was that a hair out of place? No. She was seeing things. Casting about for something else that needed to be done before she left her cabin.

When she arrived at the bridge, she would have to carefully check the angles once again. Last time, she could easily see the spot. The right place, so that when she appeared to draw a gun, and was herself immolated, the blasts would take out the control console. The one place where Lobeck had concentrated all of the authority to initiate the D6.

After the console was destroyed, would Lobeck be able to reset command to another location? Sonia would not be there to see it. With enough time, he surely could do so, which was why she needed to choose the exactly right moment. The window of time when all twenty ships had started their energy buildup, and the weapon would need to be discharged within a minute or less.

It wasn't likely to work. She was probably sacrificing herself and those she loved for nothing. Turning away from the free pass. But there was no other path.

Sonia headed for the bridge.

The Great Symmetry

The five former guests had been unceremoniously dumped outside the Situation Room and left to their own devices.

The Situation Room was only a few hundred meters away, but it might as well be in another universe. "So close," Kate told herself.

Evan came to Kate's side. "What have you got?" he asked.

"What does it matter now? We'll never get back in, and we needed to be there."

"Let's hear it. Then we'll decide what we can do. Walk this way." He indicated the hallway in front of them, away from the guard station.

Kate gathered herself. "Here's my idea. Paul Ricken's ship is coming, and it's bringing a big, big story," she told him. "About a Versari discovery, from the site on Green."

Evan had the look that she knew so well. Lips pressed slightly together, eyes focused on empty space a half meter in front of him. The look that conveyed to her that every neuron in his brain was on the problem.

"The glomes!" he exclaimed. "The same chart that I decoded on Aurora! But how−?" Kate could see the wheels turning for him. "We need to look at this from every angle – it calls for a true skeptic. And I've got just the person." Evan motioned Mira to join them. "Mira, please come here a moment," he said.

Mira wheeled over. "Can't think of anything else useful to do," she allowed. "Make it good."

"There is a ship that is likely to arrive in Kelter, from Green, within the hour," Kate said. "An independent, trading in music, movies, books, news. Taking a courier fee for any of it which has not yet arrived at each destination."

Mira took the role of cross examiner. "So, they will be doomed too, the moment they arrive. There will be no escape for them."

"Except for one circumstance," Kate replied. "If they bring into the system a blockbuster news story, of a Versari discovery on Green. A chart listing the destinations of thousands of hyperspace glomes. The moment they arrive insystem, we must have instructions waiting for them, to relay that story."

Mira nodded slightly. "That's almost plausible. The cat would be out of the bag, all over civilization by now, so Kelter wouldn't matter anymore. But how will we get the story to them, in a manner that Affirmatix won't be able to read?"

Tough questioning, but fair. Kate was fine with that. "Rod Denison has a tearoff code, that can be read on that ship."

"This ship is a partner?"

"No, a rival," Kate told Mira. "Still, they will be able to read it."

"Affirmatix will have blockaded incoming glomes by now, so that ships will not be able to come to Kelter." Mira still looked deeply skeptical.

Evan looked like he could barely contain himself. He started to speak, but then held himself back, signaling for Kate to continue.

"Not from Green, not yet. It takes too long to get there. Straight shot from Green to here, but six hops to get there from Aurora. Three days or more, and such a low traffic system that it would be a low priority."

Mira pondered for a moment. "Well, even a blind chicken finds a grain of corn every so often," she said. She took a quick look around, then continued, "Kestrel, I've got a job for you. We're going to need to take over the government transmission network. Easy, right?"

As Mira and Kestrel delved into the details, the plan grew more and more complex. Simultaneous actions, against multiple cyber targets, all sketched together in just a few minutes. For the plan to succeed would require inattention on the part of government staffers, as well as a huge measure of luck.

Kate grew increasingly uneasy. She saw Evan track the conversation, following every word. Finally he appeared to come to a decision. "Stop, you two," he said. "This isn't how to do it. This won't work without the help of the Kelter government. We need to convince the governor, and to do that we need to get back in."

"That I can do!" Kestrel exclaimed, looking relieved. "Just a little prep. So much easier than attacking their entire network."

"How soon can you be ready?" Evan asked.

Kestrel considered for a moment. "About twenty minutes. Who needs to get in?"

"I'll just slow you all down," Mira said, "and I'll stick out like a sore thumb. For that reason, I'm out."

"And this is the moment where I must say that I am too old for this," Axiom put in.

"Ok, three of us," Kestrel said. "You guys figure out what you're going to say, and I'll make a call for a few items. We especially need some camo. Find a place where we can change clothes." He turned to his phone and hurried away.

Fifteen minutes later, Kestrel was back, carrying a bundle. "All right, we'll need to put these on."

Evan, Kate, and Kestrel ducked into a small meeting room they had found, and they checked out their respective new clothes. "I was expecting something more official, like a uniform," Kate observed.

"This is the uniform of the situation room," Kestrel told them. "It's called Business Casual. The staff in the situation room is ninety five percent contractors, and this is what they wear. Anyway there's no doubt we'll be recognized at some point, and that's the moment we'll have to make the most of."

In a few minutes they were ready to set out, and emerged back into the hallway where Mira and Axiom awaited. Kestrel was finishing up with some instructions. "Walk purposefully and try to look like you're concentrating on something important. When we pass people, acknowledge them briefly if they look at you, but don't slow down."

"I can't believe I'm not doing this part," Mira said, looking up from her wheelchair.

"We'll just have to get by without your people skills," Evan replied.

Kate couldn't tell if Mira's response was a grimace or a smile. "It's your show now," Mira told them. "You've got this."

As Evan and Kate set out to follow Kestrel, Mira called out to them, "And guys —"

They turned to look at Mira, who seemed to be holding herself back from wheeling their way by sheer effort of will.

"Just — fly casual."

The trio followed a route that Kestrel clearly knew very well. No human guards stood in their way, just gates with electronic locks. In a few places Kestrel instructed them to take certain exact steps, or turn aside from a camera placement. He had placed a kind of tape over their Stewart monitors, which evidently masked their signal.

Just before one door, Kestrel warned them, "There will be people in this next section. Remember what I said. When in doubt, look worried, in a kind of distant way."

It turned out that the area was well populated, which Kate quickly realized was an advantage. Anonymity in numbers. After they passed two different groups without incident, they relaxed and it felt oddly like walking around in any office building on a normal work day.

Finally Kestrel pointed at a door as they stood in a narrow service corridor. "On the other side of that," he told them, you'll be about twenty meters from the command center. Then it will be up to you. There's nothing more I can do for you, so I'm going to stay back here."

"I can't believe you could do this so easily," Evan observed.

"The government has been complacent," Kestrel replied. "For decades, perhaps they have known that their only enemies mean them no harm."

As Kate and Evan stepped out into the open space of the Situation Room, everything seemed to happen at once. The piercing alarms. Soldiers appearing out of nowhere, seizing their arms. The mystified look on the face of Colonel Ellis as she repeatedly sent commands to a wrist control, clearly expecting some calamity to be visited upon them from their Stewart monitors.

The governor arrived. "What is the meaning of this?" It was a rhetorical question.

"Governor, you need to hear this," Evan told him. "It might be the most important thing anyone ever tells you."

"They have caused us nothing but grief," Erickson declared, starting to lead Rezar back to the heart of the command center. "I have the deployable asset inventory ready for your review."

A cloud of advisors accrued around the governor.

"Let's get you out of here," Colonel Ellis told Kate and Evan. "This way."

"But we have to tell him! Kate's idea could save us!"

"This way. And clearly we're going to have to do more than monitors."

Suddenly Evan shouted out. "Governor! Yes you! Still being led around by the nose I see! Let them take you down the next path to disaster. Don't bother listening to the one plan that could save the entire planet."

There was a commotion in the crowd. For a moment Kate caught a glimpse of Rezar's face. Anger was there, but something more.

"But there's good news!" Evan continued. "History won't know how you failed everyone, because we'll all be gone."

"You can stop now," Kate told him. "The governor is coming back."

The governor stopped a meter away, arms crossed. "You have sixty seconds," he said.

Evan looked to Kate.

She gathered her words, knowing she had one chance. Nothing philosophical or spiritual, on pain of death. She had learned to bottle it up, when it really mattered.

In the most direct possible terms, Kate related her idea to the governor and his staff. They had a few questions, but mostly they attended carefully. Sixty seconds passed, and then another minute, and another, but Governor Rezar stayed with them.

"I do have to point out one thing," Kate concluded. "My information is a few days old. As of that time, Paul Ricken's plan was to arrive two hours from now."

"So really, it's just delusional optimism to imagine that this ship will arrive, and that we can use it to fool Affirmatix," Rezar said.

Kate was aghast. Would the governor turn away from their one hope? She prepared an outburst.

"Then we must proceed," the governor declared. "Get this Denison of yours in here right now. We'll start a draft of the cover message based on what you know of the target ship. Let's edit the cover on this screen. Get me some story artists to craft the news item to be sent from the incoming ship. And Admiral Incento, lift the embargo on nonessential communications. We'll need lots of traffic, so that this specific message doesn't stand out. Identify the best stations and remaining ships to transmit to the Green glome emergence."

"Yes sir."

"This could be our last shot. Anybody have a better idea? Last call." Rezar looked around the situation room.

Silence, except for the low background chatter of staff, doing whatever it was that staff always does.

They got to work.

To Kill Again

Captain Roe was no stranger to death. He had killed. When he was a young man, he had killed in person, as ordered, to win the battles of the day. A series of promotions meant killing by proxy instead. Giving orders that would be carried out by younger men as he had once been, or by machines.

That was all long ago. For the past four decades, there had been no war. His role as a peacekeeper, or enforcer by turns, was safer, and easier on the soul.

Roe had been spending the last few hours considering whether he would need to kill, one last time.

In person.

Roe had watched as Lobeck had configured the D6, routing all control of the weapon through the bridge of M3120, their ship. It was a departure from standard procedure, which mandated that any such weapon must be able to be independently controlled from no less than three locations. Lobeck was serious about control. By him.

Roe was a soldier. That meant many things. Duty. Willingness to do what needed to be done, without flinching. Willingness to sacrifice.

It also meant rising above what he felt. Frustration at being a rent-a-crew, no matter how big and powerful a rig he drove. Visceral dislike of Vice President Arn Lobeck. The edge of rage at the way Lobeck made sure Roe always knew he was a rental.

None of those things mattered.

In order for Roe to consider his orders to be lawful and thus to follow them, Roe simply needed to know that his commander believed the orders to be lawful, and was not suffering from a serious loss of judgment.

Lobeck had been skating close to the edge. The nuclear strike had been deeply troubling, a stunning overkill. However, no uninvolved civilians had been killed. Roe himself had committed worse.

Now the plan to use the D6, and kill fifty million civilians.

It was not the largest genocide in human history, although it would be in the top ten list. All to keep a secret.

Roe had listened carefully to Lobeck's logic, as they prepared to deploy the D6. Lobeck presumably didn't know that his own life depended on the soundness of that reasoning. For Roe, it wasn't just a question of whether to obey orders. Roe knew that certain people could not simply be disobeyed, or blocked. With someone like Lobeck, if you crossed him, he would come after you until the end of your days. Probably cause that end, in fact. The two options were to obey his orders, or to take him out.

In the past few hours, Lobeck had deployed his own personal security guards in critical areas of the ship, including the bridge. No other weapons were allowed. Obviously this was to assure complete control of the situation, when it was time to activate the D6.

Hubris. An experienced captain does not lose control of his ship so easily. If the moment came, Roe had several methods available to do what needed to be done.

Roe had listened carefully. Very carefully, to every word. He pondered the justification. In essence, the risk was that if the secret were let out, civilization would unravel.

Would that actually occur? Roe had no idea. He would not pretend to be an expert on such a matter. He just knew the standard for a lawful order.

If he had a lifetime, Roe would not be able to catalog all of the things that he considered to be wrong with Lobeck. The problem was that, as far as Roe could tell, Lobeck's judgment and reasoning were entirely intact. They were certainly consistent.

Declaring an order to be unlawful was a lonely road, one that went against the grain of the culture in which he had lived and served for decades. To go down that road, Roe had to be certain. He would have to see clear evidence of a serious loss in Lobeck's capacity for judgment. And Roe couldn't find that evidence.

Based on everything he knew at that moment, Roe planned to obey orders.

Cowardice, perhaps. It was strange, how it was easier to kill fifty million people by issuance of an order, than it was to face down one man, who stood only three meters away.

It was not too late to change his assessment. There was still a little bit of time.

Roe proceeded to deploy the fleet.

Breaking News

As their ship arrived in the Kelter system, Captain Paul Ricken was already up, issuing orders, some of them at Tal, most of them unnecessary. Everyone went about their business.

Tal Broker's business was communications. This included navigation and negotiations with traffic controllers, transmitting the ship's wares, and ship to ship conversations.

He was hailing Abner House, taking some satisfaction in having started the action seconds before Ricken had ordered it, so he could say "in progress", which really annoyed Ricken. Broker did things like that when he could.

At that moment he saw the message on his board.

There was no mistaking where the transmission had come from. It was in Ricken's own tearoff code number 2132, ringingly identified as such en clair. How could Denison be so stupid?

Everyone was stupid. Ricken was a jerk. Denison was broadcasting his knowledge of Ricken's tearoff codes to the whole system. What a disaster.

Something else was wrong. "There are a zillion ships out there, sir," Mohanty, the navigator, was saying. "They're covering the exit glomes and englobing Kelter Four. It's a military maneuver!"

"Is there shooting?" Ricken asked.

"None detected at the moment, sir, but there is debris from what might have been a battle. And there is a nuclear signature on the surface."

"Can we glome out?"

Mohanty shook his head. "No way, sir. No glome is close enough, and they're all blockaded."

"Hail the nearest ship," Ricken ordered.

Tal's hand had cut off the hail to Abner House. He had to read the message quickly. There must be a reason Denison had sacrificed a major secret that he, Tal Broker, had stolen for him. Where could he read it?

"What's the delay, engineer?" Ricken was glaring at him.

Screw it. Tal engaged the algorithm, sending the output up to his screen. It would be recorded on the worm, but with any luck, if this turned out to be nothing, he could doctor the worm later. He had done it before. "Circuit problem, sir," he said. "Have it clear in a quarter minute."

Ricken's stream of verbal expectoration faded as Tal took in the message. "Life or Death Emergency. For the sake of many lives including yours, imperative that you include the attached missive as a headline news item straight from Green. This is no joke. Do anything necessary to include this item, even frank discussion of your status. I will pay any reasonable amount to Ricken in exchange for including this item. Will fully compensate you for resultant trouble. Do not communicate with me prior to transmitting item. Do it. Seconds count. Denison."

"Well, engineer?" Ricken was spraying directly on him now.

The letters on his console were invisible from Ricken's angle.

"Uh, Captain, we have a problem," Tal said. "I need to talk to you."

"Fix it!"

"Can we talk in private, sir?"

Ricken was turning red. "Are you out of your mind? We may be blown up any second, and you want to have a private meeting!"

"I need to show you something. Life or death. Listen—"

"Engineer—"

"Stay with me. Sir. First, look at this message. Come around here. It's from Denison. It came in code, so none of the other ships out there have read it."

"From Denison?! Whose code?"

"Never mind that."

"Whose code, engineer?"

"Our code, tearoff 2132."

Captain Ricken reached out with a meaty hand and grabbed the front of Broker's shirt, just below his neck. "And how, may I ask, did he know our codes?"

"Just read the message! If you want to hang me later, we'll talk about it. Read it!" Broker gestured urgently.

Ricken shoved Tal Broker away and moved around the console. His red shade gave way to purple as he read. "I will hang you, at that! Security, remove Broker to the brig! Our communications engineer is a spy!"

"Captain, the message! Seconds count!"

It was a miracle that Ricken's eyeballs were still in their sockets. "I don't need to listen to you, spy. Now I know why I never liked you, worthless, cowardly worm, can't even earn an honest living. I'll see that you never enjoy any of the money he's been paying you. And don't call me Captain any longer." Guards were taking Broker to the lift by both arms.

"Paul, listen to me."

Ricken looked up. Nobody had used his first name in years.

Tal knew he had one chance to reach his captain. "You're angry, and rightfully so, but you need to trust Rod. I know you two crewed together, and I'm sure he never lied to you about anything that could be this important. I know he's not lying now."

"It's a trick. Another devious trick to make me look like a fool." Ricken waved at the guards to continue taking Broker off the bridge.

"Stop! Paul – did you read the postscript?"

Ricken looked down at the display. "From one shabby donkey to another," he recited. "Damn Denison! He had to go there! But this is such a ridiculous lead story. Major artifact discovery on Green? We were just there, and it's totally made up. How could that save any lives?"

"A shabby donkey. What does that mean?" Broker asked.

"It means I have to do it," Ricken said. "I must be a true sucker. Open a channel to Abner House. Mohanty, tell me what those ships are doing."

Mohanty provided the update. "The ships are arrayed in an englobing icosahedron around Kelter, sir. They're not moving, nor firing. Additional ships are deployed in proximity to each of the six outbound glomes that have known destinations, and two others."

The guards had released Broker, who sped back across the bridge. "Channel open. Main video."

Suddenly Ricken was his engaging best. "Good day, sir. Please forgive the delay."

The agent was nonplussed. "It's kind of an emergency down here. Maybe we can talk later, if we are still present in this world. I'm not even sure why I'm working right now."

"Hold on!" Ricken told the man. "We have a truly amazing story from Green, about a major exo discovery, the decipherment of large quantities of Versari writings."

"Versari? That might be huge news! Send it right away!"

"In view of this item, I think we can obtain a bonus of at least five thousand credits."

Broker was dumbfounded. Why was Ricken haggling over payment? According to Denison's message, seconds counted!

"I don't care! Just send it!" The man seemed frantic.

"Done." Ricken nodded to Broker, who sent the pulse. "It's coming your way," Ricken told the agent.

The story was sent. The fleet of warships watched, not moving, nor bringing their substantial armament to bear on the arriving trader.

True Story

The news was spreading through Kelter. With it came skepticism, criticism, and discussion. Soon it would be known if the jury-rigged True Story was going to hold up.

"A little ironic, don't you think?" Evan prodded Axiom. "When we spread the real facts as widely as possible, we doom the entire planet, and now we try to save the world with a lie."

"It is not how I would have expected to do it," the infoterrorist agreed. "We will have to come clean on our dishonesty, and apologize. After the D6 departs."

"Apologize? For saving everyone?"

"Some humility is good. So that we do not re-learn the habit of making up the truth so quickly."

They listened to the chatter around the situation room. It brought good news. The story, of the parallel discovery on Green, was gaining momentum. Soon, it ruled. On Kelter, at least, their story was widely accepted.

A few skeptics held their ground. What were the odds, they asked, of the same discovery in the two widely separated places on almost the same day?

"Should we intervene?" Erickson asked. "We can shut the doubters down."

"We let it run its course," Rezar ruled. "To convince the Affirmatix above us, we must withstand the most vigorous scrutiny. And we are doing just that. There is no way that they would destroy an entire planet, and kill all of us, for something that might or might not be a secret anymore."

Ultimately it did not matter, because the skeptics could not withstand the wave of belief that washed upon them. Example after example poured out, of momentous discoveries made even on the same day or hour, light years apart. Advocates pointed to cases where a single advance in the underlying science had let to apparently coincidental discoveries shortly afterward. Anyone was free to maintain their position, but soon the skeptics were stranded and ignored in backwaters of the planet-wide conversation.

In the situation room, the most advanced graphical display on Kelter portrayed the ebb and flow of the interactions. The counterterrorism team was expert in portraying the flow of memes in multiple dimensions. The hardest part was simply watching and not taking action, even as the True Story advanced. The governor's directive not to interfere ran counter to decades of training and culture.

Above the largest table in the center of the situation room, the deep smooth magenta shape spread in three dimensions, gradually swallowing other colors and textures, or pushing them to the far fringes of the floating image.

Evan exulted. "We did it! Kate, what an idea, and it's going to work!"

"This is fantastic!" agreed Denison, who had recently been summoned to the command center for his knowledge of the code to Ricken's ship. "I had hoped to write some real news, but it's even better to be part of it."

"And Affirmatix, they are so going down," Evan declared. "We won't be frightened rabbits any more. We're going to take it to them. They won't even be a Sister by the time we are done with them. We'll make sure everybody in civilization knows what they did."

"That could be a bigger task than you imagine," Axiom told him. "Regardless of the facts as you see them, their marcom department is bigger than you. I have lived with a version of this question for many decades. Tell me, what did they do, that can be proven and will depose them from the sisterhood?"

The old man might have been right before, but he could still talk the crazy. "They killed thousands of sailors," Evan exclaimed, "on the ships of the Kelter defense force!"

Axiom shrugged. "It will somehow be painted as a response to an act of war, by Kelter. Just enough to create ambiguity. The merchants of doubt are experts at creating holes in reality just large enough to wiggle through, and evade responsibility. Besides, bitter history tells us that anyone who wears a uniform accepts a target on their back, a red shirt that tells you they are expendable."

Evan refused to be deflected. "There has to be a way to make them pay!"

"Perhaps there will be. It will be a longer road than you imagine, that is all." The infoterrorist's expression reflected long experience.

"I'll tell you something I take personally," Evan said. "The vaults. Not enough to just go hunting us down, they had to destroy the Valley of Dreams. Our friends, from a million years ago. Real people who cared and loved just as we do. Anyone who doubts that can read Kate's books. For my part, I will make sure everyone knows about that crime."

"Evan, I hope you get the opportunity. But hold for a moment. Look, on the big screen."

No matter what people thought on the surface of Kelter, all that mattered was the response of the Affirmatix fleet. Now, it was on the move.

The twenty ships that composed the D6 had been deployed in a rough icosahedron around Kelter, close to the needed position to activate the weapon. For the D6 to function, the hedron needed to be precisely spaced around the geoid of the surface below.

Each of the ships was making fine adjustments to its course. Within an hour and a half, they would be in a perfect icosahedron around Kelter. Exactly, to the meter.

As required to activate the D6.

The Last Minute

The expected time was now widely known. All life on Kelter was expected to end at 1433 Meridian time on Day 311. Within thirty minutes. All over the planet, in every time zone, people considered the moments that remained to them.

#

For Jasper and Frederick, blackness was just beginning to give way to the beginnings of dawn in their living room window. They had both slept poorly, and by common consent had gotten up and made breakfast during the deepest part of the night. The talk on the newscasts was even grimmer than when they had tried to go to bed. Now they sat, looking out their picture window to the east. A constellation of bright stars, not usually part of Kelter's sky, still shone above.

"Should we wake up the kids?"

"No. Let them sleep."

"Did you give each of them a kiss?"

"I did. You?"

"Yes. Both of them."

Jasper and Fred held hands and waited.

#

Ellen's problem was solved. For weeks she had contemplated the best method. She wanted it to be over, but she was afraid of the pain. Anything sharp was horrible and would make her feel sick. Jumping off things didn't work too well on Kelter. You just ended up in hospital, if that. Drowning would bring the moment of panic at the end, and pool time was too expensive.

She wondered if she would feel it. The fire would simply be everywhere at the same moment, according to the talking heads.

Nobody would mourn her. They would all be gone as well. Before, Ellen had imagined in great detail how her parents would react, hoping that it would hurt them. A lot. When she left them forever, would they finally learn their lesson?

Now, that was moot. It wasn't as satisfying. In fact, it kind of defeated the purpose.

As the minutes ticked down, Ellen realized that she wanted to live.

#

Ashley tried to coax more speed out of the vehicle as it tore across the empty plain, altitude 500 meters. Somehow she had scored one of the very last choppers available in Redoubt. About twenty-eight minutes remained before the end. Would she make it on time? It would be tight.

She was getting close to civilization now. The first outlying structures were appearing on the horizon and rapidly approaching.

Trent, her only son. She had been unable to reach him by phone or messaging. The lines were overwhelmed, or perhaps nobody was maintaining the system any more. Ashley hoped desperately that Trent would be at home, that she could see him just one last time.

More buildings, and some traffic. Ashley didn't drive much these days, typically relying on transit, but she could handle the chopper with no problem.

The best way was to cut through the utility area and go straight to an entry that was close to Trent's apartment. She swept to her right, pulling around the corner of a large greenhouse.

She didn't even see the other chopper coming.

#

The special midnight service was very well attended. Marisa was humbled by the task of comforting her community, on what could be the very end of their days.

It was easy to speak of lofty things, positive visions of their spirits, and the good that so many people had done. Perhaps that would suffice. She considered whether she should draw the attendees away from the fear, or whether to face it head on.

Marisa walked to the podium, and hush descended.

"Friends. We know that our time may soon be upon us. If the projections are accurate, the fire will arrive in as little as twenty-seven minutes. It is a terrifying prospect. I am deeply afraid.

"I cannot provide any assurance that it will all be okay. Of the future of each of our spirits, there is no certainty. But there is one thing that I hope that everyone will consider for just a few moments. That is this: If the worst does not occur, then how will you make the rest of your life happier, and kinder?

"Because today is no different than any other day, in one basic sense. You never know. Every day could be your last. I hope that each of you has had some chance to make peace, to express love, and to be with the ones you love. Tomorrow, if it comes, provides you with the same opportunity. Tomorrow will be the greatest gift we will ever receive. Let us all greet the new day in that spirit, if it comes to be."

Marisa hoped she was doing justice to the moment. She would check the recording and see how she sounded, whether she was connecting with her flock as well as she could.

Tomorrow. She would check tomorrow.

#

"Now we settle it."

The two men had bound their wrists together, in the fashion of the ritual that had been passed down through the centuries. In the other hand, each held an identical knife, razor-sharp and twenty centimeters long. The referee held up a white kerchief in her hand.

The cloth floated down, impossibly slowly, and the combat began.

#

"You know I love you. So even if the D6 doesn't happen, I'll stand by you. Always. Don't you love me?"

Denise looked into his eyes. Clearly he was projecting the greatest degree of sincerity that he possibly could.

She knew better than to believe him. She wasn't really sure why she was dating Warren, except that he looked good with her in the halls of her school. Actually, he looked really good. A ninny, but a handsome one.

Denise knew she had no future with Warren.

She looked at the clock. Twenty-four minutes.

But then again, why not?

#

Horatio wrote furiously. It was really taking shape.

At one point did editing turn into needless polishing?

He changed a word here, a punctuation mark there.

Would his readers be on line? Certain stalwarts would be there. They always were. Even today, or especially today. Just this one time, Horatio had put out an advance notice that he expected to publish.

It was a balancing act. He knew he could make it better, but at what cost? If he waited too much longer, he and his readers would be out of time.

One more review, from the top. Okay. It was as good as it was going to get.

Horatio let his poem fly.

#

Rezar was finishing up his address to the citizens of Kelter. "We will soon find out if the Affirmatix fleet will commit the ultimate atrocity. If they do, we cannot stop them. In that respect, I have failed all of you," he said.

"But let us understand the reason why they would even consider such an act, and if we do survive, let us learn from it. Affirmatix is trying to contain a secret, which has spread throughout our planet. It is a remarkable finding, the glome chart, but in another respect this is business as usual. Affirmatix is maintaining the True Story, even at the cost of all of our lives.

"The cancer is much broader than the criminal actions of one family. The True Story. Composing reality for our consumption. I commit this to everyone who will hear me – on Kelter there will never again be a True Story. Let people have doubt, and even fear, and then let them grow strong by determining what is true. I thank you all for your bravery as we face what fate brings us."

"And that's a wrap," the producer said. His job was a lot easier these days, since the governor's talks involved little scripting and no post-processing.

Rezar joined Mira at the table from where she had been watching the speech. "We pretend there is more we can do, some last appeal sent into the ether, or final maneuver," he told her. "You saw as our last few missiles were swatted away. But my next action is to enjoy this cup of coffee."

"The good stuff?" Mira inquired.

"Yes, Columbian. From Earth itself, grown in a place called British Columbia."

"That's the best you can do? Drink coffee?" Mira would never stop challenging those around her, as long as she was alive.

"And plan," the governor said. "For a future without a True Story."

"That's the ultimate act of infoterrorism – everything my uncle has worked for. Can you even do that? Wouldn't you have to get some laws changed?"

"Funny thing," the governor related. "There is no law about it. The True Story was only effective because it was not officially acknowledged. As far as I can tell, we simply cease to operate the machine that generated it."

"I will hold you to it," Mira warned. "Having a True Story is pretty convenient when you're in charge. If you return to those days, I won't let you get away with it."

Rezar studied the battered pilot for a moment. "I accept that. Hold me accountable. If I stray from that commitment, the world should know. And who better to do it than the most fearless woman on the planet?"

Mira had been called a lot of things, but this was a new one for her. "If you mean that cliff thing—"

"I do not. I mean your commitment to the truth as you see it, regardless of what may be accepted by the people around you, or what may be considered polite. We need more of that around here. But what are your plans, Mira? If we are granted a new life, what will you do that matters?"

"Me? Oh come on. You can make those big decisions and have resolutions. I'll just go back to piloting, as soon as I'm reassembled. But now I've got something! Holding you to your word. That's probably a full time job and then some."

"A worthy plan," agreed the governor.

"I've got an even better idea," Mira offered. "The new worlds. Just think of it. A frontier without end. Outfit a long range scout, and the smallest crew that could run her. Now that would be glorious."

"A deeply enticing prospect," agreed the governor. "Who knows what is out there to find? And I will wish you the greatest of fortune. I will be here, doing my best to protect my people. I have started us on this course, and if we survive the next hour, I will have to see it through."

#

"Soon we find out," Kate said. "Whether we will live or die. Here is as good a place as any." She waved broadly at the garden around them.

"I can't believe there's nothing we can do," Evan replied. "We just wait? Where are the reserve ships? The new plan? We should do something! There's always something."

"We plant seeds," was all she said.

"Seeds? You know, by the time any seeds germinate, I think we'll know the answer."

"We planted good ideas. Perhaps someone will consider them, even now. Now, walk with me for these minutes that we have."

#

Axiom had no real need to prepare. Yet he had excused himself from the frantic efforts at the capital, having made what contribution that he believed he could. It was in the hands of tacticians, if indeed they could have any effect.

He and his friends made their way up the steep trail. Cecilia, Antonia, Orwen, and Kestrel were with him. There was no dodging reality – it was a great challenge for his old body. At last they stood at the top of the promontory.

It was far smaller than the majestic mountains to the north, just a bump in the plain. But it was the first bump, nearest to the Untrusted Zone and to Abilene. From their vantage point, the Untrusted Zone was a low collection of lights in the foreground, with the far greater glow of Abilene beyond.

There it was. The buttonwood tree, backlit and visible from the shadows cast by its branches.

Above, bright stars where there should be none, arrayed evenly across the darkening sky.

Axiom's companions seemed to pick up on his lack of desire for spoken conversation, or perhaps it was their preference as well. He was glad that they were with him.

For himself, Axiom was not concerned. In all outcomes, he had very little future. The cancer would not be denied. Three months, or perhaps six. There was no way to know. For twenty-five years he had kept the enemy at bay, with medicine and, as he liked to think, clean living. It would be strange if today's ending was a mercy, compared to what he might otherwise experience.

He spent a few minutes meditating on his span of years.

Axiom had always imagined that his life, such as it was, would ripple forward with some benefit, and a lot of love, to his many friends, and to their friends. Every so often, somebody would tell a story of the day that they had walked across the desert, or more recently, the day that the truth sang. It was melancholy to think that this might not occur.

Had he truly lived for service? It was impossible to evaluate. Perhaps he just enjoyed the experience of observing people sifting through his words, seeking grains of wisdom. Axiom knew that he deliberately set puzzles for his friends. At his age, he was allowed to do things like that.

"Shall we have a betting pool on the exact moment that the fire arrives?" he asked. "Select your time, to the millisecond. Closest entry wins, whether you guess before or after the moment."

Facing the Fire

Sonia arrived at the bridge. The security screening was no problem, even with her talisman. It was not actually a weapon, after all.

Four Affirmatix security guards, as usual. Carrying blasters, as usual. She wondered if they carried any other weapon, less destructive, that they would reach for first. Nothing else was visible. Each of the guards was positioned in a shallow corner, where it wasn't possible to come from behind any of them, and which provided good line of sight over the entire bridge.

She rechecked the angles. There was a place where she could stand, right next to the main command console, where any shot that struck her would destroy the console as well.

It was not the moment yet. Only when the D6 was reaching a fully powered state, and it would need to be discharged within a short period of time. Then, if the console were taken out, there would be no time to redirect command and fire the weapon.

Sonia walked to her accustomed position in the resource room. To get there, she had to walk past Arn Lobeck, standing as he usually did on the stripe between the resource room and the bridge. He was looking far away, and didn't acknowledge Sonia or even appear to notice her.

At her station, Sonia pretended to busy herself.

Essential personnel. If she wanted to go home, all she needed to do was – nothing. Without raising any objection, simply watch as fifty million people died. People she didn't know personally.

She looked at Ravi, next to her. He was avoiding her gaze, suddenly intent on the screen in front of him. Mithra Skylar appeared to be meditating. She was probably in dataspace.

The pace of activity around her picked up. The main screen in the front of the bridge showed the position of the fleet around Kelter. At that scale, the ships already appeared to be in a perfect icosahedron, although not perfect enough for the D6 weapon. The point of view slowly rotated around Kelter, at about one orbit of the planet per minute. At Lobeck's behest, a widget was added in the top right corner showing a countdown to the optimal position. Just over five minutes to go.

In anticipation, the ships began powering up.

Sonia imagined rejoining her domestic family. Simone and Jennifer would simply be overjoyed. But Yvette would know in an instant. Not the details. But the wrongness, there would be no hiding it from her. She would never be able to face Yvette. Not with this truth.

Her domestic family was already gone. No matter what, they would never be together again, in any sense that mattered.

Sonia put her hand softly on Ravi's shoulder. "Soon we will be home with the ones we care about," she told him. "We'll get back with our teammates. We'll spend a few weeks reviewing all of the events from here and updating the models, like we always do."

Ravi's eyes widened and he turned pale. "These events? Right here?"

"Of course. We are shaping history now, not just observing it, just like you said. And it will be a key part of the new future."

"No! She cannot know. Eliza must not learn that we were part of this! Sonia, my life is over."

She had hoped to give Ravi an encouraging thought. Clearly it had gone horribly wrong.

"I'm sure it will be all right." Sonia knew it was an empty platitude.

"What do you know about a life without love? And now, it will never be."

"Sometimes events turn out very different than you expected," she offered, "Just see." If she succeeded in her plan, things would be extremely different, but she wouldn't be there.

For the fifteenth time, she felt for her talisman. It was there, in her inner jacket pocket. It just needed to look like a real gun for long enough to attract the first shot. After that, fire should attract more fire.

She started walking toward the center console.

Over The Edge

"First we will destroy this nest of enemies, and then we will proceed to Green, and any other location that may have been contaminated by the Versari knowledge. The secret must be ours and ours alone." Lobeck turned to the business of using the weapon which would destroy Kelter and all of its inhabitants. The program to invoke the D6 would be activated from the main station, in the center of the bridge, but operators were working on the many necessary support functions from many other consoles.

First he strode to one console, then another, sometimes seizing possession of one screen for a few moments to call up pages of displays. "Closer, closer," he muttered. "Almost optimized."

"Optimized?" Roe made the mistake of asking.

"Yes, perfection," Lobeck replied absently. "Anything less than a perfect balance of energy for existing mass will result in incomplete destruction."

"The planet will be destroyed utterly with only a tenth of that power! Can't you see—"

"Disinfected, yes. Destroyed, no. The work must be perfect."

Roe noticed that Mithra Skylar had quietly appeared next to them. "Arn," she said softly. "Please stop and think. Consider everything. The entire picture."

Roe had seen Skylar pull Lobeck back several times. The man always paused for a moment and carefully considered what she had to say.

Not this time.

"You always have another reason not to take action," Lobeck declared. "For decades we have considered. That is over, effective immediately." Lobeck turned abruptly away from them, busying himself at a workstation.

Roe caught a momentary expression of shocked dismay on Skylar's unreadable face. Then she flipped the data display back down over one eye and walked purposely back to her station in the resource room.

There was no doubt any more – Lobeck was experiencing severe loss of judgment. With the news of the identical Versari discovery on far-off Green, there was no reason to even consider continuing the operation. By the time they got to Green, the knowledge would have spread to more than half of the known star systems.

Relief, fear, and adrenaline swept through Roe. To action. He scanned the bridge. The four guards were in their accustomed positions, each covering a wide field of view from a shallow corner. They definitely were at heightened attention.

Roe noted Lobeck looking at each guard in turn, exchanging a quick expression of affirmation, making sure that they were fully with him.

Sonia West had risen from her workstation in the resource room and was walking into the bridge. What was she doing?

She had a purpose. And she was terrified. Her manner was not exactly subtle. Roe saw the two guards in the back corners of the bridge begin to track her. Now she had Lobeck's attention, and the Vice President stepped forward off his line to observe.

Whatever she was planning, Roe didn't think it was going to help. As she began to reach inside her jacket, Roe was already in motion. Three strides brought him to her. Roe put one hand on her shoulder and circled her waist with the other, posing an improbable waltz next to the command console.

"Dr. West, I need your help at Station Six. Will you please join me there?"

From ten centimeters in front of his face, she sent defiance back at him. Roe willed his expression to somehow say that he had a plan, and she needed to let it unfold. He dared not say anything more, except, "Please. Dr. West. This way."

Still she stood unmoving. Roe could tell without looking that they were the center of attention. He brought her even closer and murmured directly into her ear, "Not yet."

Finally Roe felt her surrender. Now there was no time to waste.

With Sonia in tow, Roe pretended that he needed to check something at Station Six on the bridge. The guards relaxed their posture, and Lobeck turned his attention back to the main screen.

From Station Six Roe could clearly see the red stripe that marked the boundary between the bridge and the resource room. It was the path on which the airlock door would close.

The lock would not shut on any person or object. Three independent sets of sensors saw to that. The first was a set of light beams which, when interrupted, signaled the presence of an object. The second set was a pair of video cameras which registered movement in the area of the portal. The last set consisted of ordinary touch sensors on the leading edge of the lock door.

Roe watched Lobeck leaning on the edge of the portal. The man's feet and center of gravity were clearly forward of the red line. A foot stepped forward and Lobeck was half a meter from the line. A situation at Station 3 resolved itself, and Lobeck relaxed to a straight standing position.

The actual lock door was powered by a hydraulic system, three cylinders which provided a total force of approximately thirty tons. The leading edge of the door was designed to penetrate the opposite side of the portal for a distance of about twenty centimeters, to assure a snug fit.

There was only one circumstance under which the lock door would shut with all thirty tons of force, regardless of what stood in the way. If the resource room beyond suffered a massive loss of air pressure, the door would shut. No matter what.

By design, the bridge had the ability to maintain pressure, with three redundant supply systems, even if most of the ship was holed. That included the ability to shut off the bridge from the entire rest of the ship, quickly and automatically.

Beyond the far side of the resource room was the armored hull of the ship. The armor was substantial. It would take a direct missile strike to put a hole in the hull at that spot.

Or, a limpet mine.

Roe looked into the resource room. Ravi and Skylar were there. "Ravi, I need you. Come here," Roe called. Ravi came, looking like a man who had seen his own death.

Lobeck was in his accustomed spot, on the line between the rooms. Now one foot was in, one out. Lobeck was right over the line. It would be better if he was simply in the resource room, but that did not appear to be in the cards. If there was a time, this was it. Roe sent a message from his brain to his finger to press the hot key. The message seemed to travel from neuron to neuron at the speed of molasses.

Suddenly it was very real to Roe, as his finger finally pushed the key, that he was attempting to kill his temporary superior officer.

Roe had misjudged. The target was not still, and as Roe's hand reached to fulfill its mission Lobeck was in forward motion. "Activate pro-"

The back wall of the resource room disintegrated. Metal was flying everywhere. Air howled out toward the gaping hole.

The lock door closed on Lobeck's left ankle with a snap and a clang. Lobeck fell forward and landed hard.

Roe was shouting. "The Vice President is injured! Get a medic immediately!" he ordered. "I'll give first aid."

Lobeck's guards hesitated but took no action to stop Roe as the captain bent toward Lobeck's head, reaching for his neck. "I need to take his pulse," he called out.

Lobeck wormed on the floor, losing blood; his eyes rolled up to show almost entirely the whites.

The foot was entirely, cleanly, missing. It looked like some shrapnel had hit him in the shoulder as well. Roe found the pulse points on Lobeck's neck. And pressed.

Muscles, in abundance, even on the front of his neck. The man was one big muscle. Roe realized he would need more force.

"I need help," he called. "Direct pressure on that leg. Use anything you can find. Anderson, Varma, hold his arms so we can provide care."

The bridge crew swung into action as Roe ordered. They had been together for years, and knew how to follow his lead.

Roe climbed on top of Lobeck and pressed down on his neck, harder.

Somehow Lobeck started to speak. "Acti, activ, . . . I order . . . ."

Roe pressed, giving it all he had, pushing aside the revulsion at what he was doing by thinking of the millions of lives he was trying to save.

Then, Arn Lobeck began to get up.

Two strong crewmen held each arm. No matter. Lobeck pulled his arms away and swatted Roe aside. Roe landed hard against the door. He looked up to see Lobeck rotating up on to his knees and then plant his one remaining foot as if to get up.

"Activation Code Nine, Four, Alpha," Lobeck began.

"Noise!" Roe called out. "And shut him up!"

Three shouting crewmen landed on Lobeck, but somehow the giant man held his position and even began to crawl toward the control console.

As Roe pulled himself up, he saw two of the guards circling in, looking for a clear shot. Now it was clear that the blasters were the wrong choice for a weapon. Roe knew from experience that it was impossible to hit any target smaller than a meter across with the destructive sidearm.

Suddenly one of the crewmen went rigid and fell off Lobeck. Then another. Lobeck shrugged the third off and half-stood alone. One of the guards, coming in from the back left corner of the bridge, held a much smaller gun, which Roe recognized as a stunner.

"Seven, Gamma," Lobeck continued.

The guard with the stunner had to go. He could only take down so many at once. Roe found Varma's eye and nodded toward the guard. Within a second, the remaining six men in the bridge crew were hurtling toward the man with the stunner. One of the crew went down but the rest buried the guard.

The three remaining guards had gathered together, and advanced to cover Lobeck, holding their blasters to keep the crew at bay. Three blasters against one stunner. "Nine, Delta," Lobeck said. How many entries were in the D6 code?

Suddenly Sonia West stood between Lobeck and the command console. "Freeze!" she shouted, and pulled out a gun.

As she drew it up to aim at Lobeck, all three blasters swiveled toward her.

Roe saw Sonia raise her gun hand and start to bring it down, in an exaggerated gesture of preparing to fire.

Ravi came out of nowhere, grabbing the gun and knocking Sonia flying. He yelled out and leapt at the guards.

The blaster fire hit him from three places, spilling several meters past and igniting everything behind him.

Roe had seen a blaster hit on a person before. As the flames spread, the screaming victim would madly thrash in their last few searing panicked moments of life. Except this time, that wasn't what happened. Ravi slowly turned, took two deliberate steps and laid himself on the console, sharing his flame with the conflagration that was already under way. The console crackled, wires popped, panels split open. Ravi was still, and the fire consumed him.

Smoke and fire were everywhere.

Lobeck, from his knees, reached out in the direction of the flaming console. "Six, Eight, Omega, Launch −" he said, and then toppled, landing in a motionless heap.

The three armed security guards stood mute. Roe stepped around Lobeck and walked up to the closest of them. "We need to get out of here. I recommend you evacuate your Vice President, if he can be saved. But first I need to borrow this," he said, and took the blaster out of the guard's hands. Roe turned and fired three quick balls of fire at a secondary control console, adding to the fire. He motioned other bridge crew aside and launched further fireballs at several other key stations.

"Crew, let's hop," Roe ordered, handing the gun back to the bewildered guard. "Two people carry each crew member that's down, they'll be out for another couple of minutes. We'll broadcast the order to abandon ship while we're in transit. Everyone to cutter number one. You too, Dr. West." The crew sprang to follow him.

Perfect Hedron

Twenty ships, arranged in their perfect icosahedron, continued to gather energy as they awaited the activating signal. The threshold moment, when activating the D6 became possible, arrived and left without pause. From this point, the stored energy accumulated into levels which, while still workable, began to strain the resources of the three dimensional cordon of ships. The total quantity of energy was already well past what the twenty ships could have managed individually, even if divided into twenty equal packets. Only the continuous pouring of energy into ephemeral transit between the ships made the total accumulation possible.

The signal was to arrive by coded transmission, simultaneously at every node. Only this way could a balanced flow of destructive force be sent on its way to the planet's surface, not only creating the most perfect destruction, but also sparing any one or more ships from the consequence of an overloaded, unbalanced accumulation. That consequence would be instant, fiery, annihilation. A dissynchronization of a fraction of a second could easily result in disaster.

The perfect moment long past, the minutes moved, and the flows of stored and transmitted energy mounted, past safe levels and into the red. Baffled ship commanders received no replies to their urgent inquiries.

No single ship could take useful action. To withdraw from the hedron was suicide. To cease accumulating the destructive force would create an imbalance in the hedron, and was likely as bad. With the command ship silent, frantic captains tried to coordinate a course of action.

But how to synchronize their activities? The transmission times between the ships numbered as long as two seconds across the entire formation.

Sooner or later, something was going to give.

Acting on a calculation and instinct, twenty ship captains started incrementally dumping some of the power out of the lattice. A very slight imbalance was tolerable, as long as the neighboring ships caught up within a few milliseconds. Gaining confidence, they dumped more power, then more. The energy fled, most of it into space and some into Kelter's ionosphere.

As seen from the planet's surface, wild shapes appeared in the sky. An ultimately insane aurora leapt and dove, changing colors through the rainbow and beyond. Even on the daylight side of the world, the colors outshone the sun.

People said their last prayers and held their loved ones.

With seconds to go, an imbalance finally broke through the fragile accord between the twenty ships. It raced from ship to ship, destroying every piece of power equipment on board each of the ships in the icosahedron.

On the surface of Kelter, the sky quietly returned to normal.

The Heralds

The gypsy fleet was ready.

It had no single destination, nor designs on conquest, at least by direct force. Rather, the fleet intended to disperse, to every destination in known space.

A few ships carried weapons. Most did not.

Every ship carried at least one skilled infoterrorist. Many carried more than one. Members of Kelter's security and infoterrorism centers had been pressed into service, those who were willing. They applied their experience together with a lightning type of on-the-job training from their former adversaries.

For the previous infoterrorist attack, some version of planning had been going on for years or even decades. Axiom and his friends had not known what content they would be spreading, but they had made sure they were ready when the moment arrived.

This effort was more ad-hoc. Of necessity, it was planned in just hours, rather than years. Still, their prior practice and planning was helpful.

There were many unknowns. Across star systems, and even within each system, the defenses would vary widely. In some cases the effort could fail. However, it was only necessary to win in a few places. To make sure that the Versari knowledge, of all of the hyperspace glomes and their destinations, was known as widely as possible, and that it could not possibly be denied.

Three days were allowed for all of the ships to arrive at their planned destinations.

In exactly seventy-two hours, the message would be launched in as many places as humanly possible, all at the same moment. The synchronization was essential in order to surprise and overwhelm any forces, whether from governments or families, that might wish to block the effort.

The information would be broadcast, but also conveyed in person to key leaders in government, commerce, the arts, and entertainment. Each campaign would be an evolving form of the art of infoterrorism, responding, adapting, persisting.

Governor Rezar reviewed the summary report.

The former Affirmatix fleet had dissolved. The twenty capital ships of the D6 had been completely disabled during the misfire of that weapon, and operations were under way to rescue their crews. The other ships had left the Kelter system for their home systems, following a terse order issued by Captain Roe of Affirmatix.

No force remained to halt the exodus.

Now the ships were cruising toward their assigned glomes under Incento's direction. In some cases, they were glomes that had not ever been explored. The routes would take an additional hop, or two, or three, via previously unexplored systems, to drop back into known space at arrival points that clearly represented a previously unknown glome. These ships would arrive in seventy-two hours and one minute from the defined start time. Another nail in the coffin of any efforts at denial.

The new routes had been planned with trepidation. Even though it was understood very clearly that the Versari data was real, and was accurate, it was still a leap for every crew member. Rezar had ordered that only volunteers, whose willingness was verified through at least two independent interviews, would be on those crews.

The backlog of applicants was overwhelming. Retired admirals pulled strings to get a berth on the prized ships. Finally Rezar had to get Kestrel to design a fair online application process that could not be hacked.

All this had been done in a few hours.

The first ships approached their glomes. Just a few minutes, either to commit to the course of action or turn back. Of course, there was no question.

"Governor, will you provide the order to proceed?" Incento, being by the book.

Rezar prepared to assent, then paused a moment. He looked around the command room. Top brass. Staff. Reporters, capturing every moment. Axiom. McElroy. DelMonaco. Adastra.

He turned to Mira. "You believed in this, enough to leap a kilometer to your likely death. Do you still?"

"I do," she said.

"Attention, ship commanders. I am delegating my authority in this matter to Mira Adastra. She will provide the next order."

"Authority? Me? You can't mean it."

"In this matter, yes. As I promised. Shall we proceed? If so, tell the fleet. Just speak, and the everyone in the fleet will hear you."

Mira composed her words for a moment, then she began. "Members of the fleet. I give you no order. I ask you, as friends, to do this. Stop at nothing. Do not be denied. Act as if our lives, and the lives of our children, depend on succeeding in this mission. Because they do. Each of you will help build a new future for humanity. Without fear, speak what is true, and you will free all of us."

Slowly, Mira stood. Tall, proud, scarred.

Beautiful.

Rezar said, "Thank you, Ms. Adastra. To the fleet: if there was any question about it, please interpret that request as an order."

They watched on the big screen as the first ships vanished from the in-system display.

Rezar turned to Axiom.

"What will this bring us?" he asked. "Even now, I do not know if I am serving my people. Angering every hornet we could possibly find. All at once. There will be consequences."

"Then, let us face them. Without fear, we will live what is true."

"We will face them together, my friend," Governor Rezar said to the infoterrorist.

Celebration Planning

Axiom relaxed in his visiting room.

The ships had all departed. Each carried the information about the Versari discovery, ready to spread the knowledge through known space. The glome routes to a hundred thousand new star systems, and also the ways to get back home. Compared to the thirty systems that currently held human life, the possibilities were close to infinite.

And the ships carried so much more.

By itself, the information about the glomes would change history. By itself, that knowledge might break the control of the Seven Sisters and allow billions of humans to chart their own course.

But as people looked more closely into the entire package of data, they would discover clues. Those clues would point them at further files in the package, and soon they would be able to unpack that which also waited.

The Codex was sharing its treasures.

Ideas and information that had not seen the light of day for decades or centuries. Skills that had not been exercised by any person now alive. Histories, from the point of the view of the vanquished as well as the conquerors. The forbidden economic field of giniography. Some of the content had been suppressed, other parts simply forgotten, perceived as irrelevant in the world as it had become.

Perhaps most dangerously of all, the secrets of growing and propagating live, fertile seeds.

For seventy years, Axiom and his friends had collected information from all over known space, preparing for the moment when they would have a chance to share it. The effort by their predecessors extended before that, through earlier decades and even centuries.

Now that people would be free to travel to so many new star systems through the new glome pathways, many of the skills so carefully recorded in the Codex over the decades would be getting a workout.

For any given person or situation, there was no knowing what might matter. So it was all in there. All available for any persistent person to find, without some outside agency tracing the inquiry. The entire Codex was going to be distributed as widely as possible, hitchhiking with the Versari information about the glome routes.

It was a good thing that data didn't weigh very much.

And now, Axiom had a visitor. She had brought her weaving, on a portable hand loom. Axiom was glad she was here.

"It will be lonely," Axiom said. "So many friends leaving for the stars. I hope they will be back soon, and that they will be safe."

It was virtually certain that some of the infoterrorists would not return. Each one had accepted the risk, and had chosen to go.

"I will miss everyone," Orwen agreed. "Still, we will try to be good company for each other."

"And I thank you for being here, my good friend. So, do you think we will succeed? Will people be able to break free of the Sisters?"

"Soon everyone will know of the new routes to the stars. The question is what they will do with that knowledge."

"Exactly so," Axiom said. "So much was taken during the Fencing of the Commons."

Four decades before, all open source technology had been declared to be a source of terrorism and thus banned. Knowledge such as how to repair and build electronics or machinery was deemed to be far too dangerous in the wrong hands. Open source offerings were also undercutting legitimate commerce, harming the economy.

"Now we have given it all back," he continued. "Will it be enough?"

"We will see," Orwen said, "if people are able to exercise their brains once again."

"What matters most is that it will be in everyone's hands once again. A worthy purpose and I wish all of our friends a safe and successful journey. Meanwhile, we will use the quiet for something very important. We have a celebration to plan. Mine."

Orwen looked up sharply from her loom. "Oh Axiom, you mustn't worry about that. We will take care of any arrangements. That is, when the moment comes. Sometime in the future."

"We must start planning for my celebration now," Axiom told her. "So we can have it soon. I don't want to miss it. I am thinking of eight weeks from now. Day twelve. My birthday. My century. And two days later, the anniversary of the settlement, when we started to live by the tree, seventy years ago. We'll just make it a three day event. What do you think?"

"That sounds wonderful. But is that a celebration?"

"This one will be," Axiom declared. "Save you the trouble, later."

"Well, it would be nice if you get to enjoy it."

"Now you're getting into the spirit! We'll have music. And dancing. All around the tree."

"Three days, is that a good idea?" Orwen asked. "You'll need to get some rest."

They fussed over him too much. Axiom knew that it was from love, but he would never be used to it. "I'll rest when I'm dead! So I think the timing is good. Eight weeks. Enough time for many of our friends to come home. Perhaps my niece will be knitted together enough to enter the tree climbing race. Never bet against her, you know."

"No, never," she agreed.

"And now I have something to aspire to. After we send out the invitations, I will have to survive at least until the day. I shall make a point of it. Do you think I will?"

Orwen considered the pattern in front of her. "My sisters might know best, but I think so," she told him. "You have an excellent chance."

Axiom looked around his visiting room. It had been part refuge, part self-imposed prison for so many years, a place of safety from the Kelter government and from the Sisters. He and his friends had added touches to make the place feel like home. Pieces in various media, created by artists whose ages ranged from two years to ninety.

Now, he was free to leave, and walk under the light of Kelter's sun once again. But at this moment, he was most content in this place.

"I also must have some conversations," he told Orwen. "With my niece, to help her prepare. There are things that she will need to understand, before I leave her. She was fit to be tied, when we said she could not join the emissaries, but it is a good thing. Time to heal, and time for conversation."

"It is a big responsibility. Do you think she is ready?"

On this question Axiom was certain. "She is already a leader. And events have a way of telling us. When we all walked across the desert together, I thought I was ready for anything. Because it had to be, it turned out to be so. Most important is that she will always have friends to help her."

"Of course," Orwen assured him. "We will all help her."

"I am grateful. Let's get more snacks. I'd like to have some fruit."

And so Axiom and Orwen spent the evening planning Axiom's celebration.

Coda

Evan wasn't sure how to put it. "Hey, I don't mean to leave you, Mira, but—"

"Got a date, eh? I'll bet she's all fired up, now that we're going to survive and all. Could be your lucky night."

"Mira—"

"I know, I'm being bad. So have a good date."

"You don't mean that."

"You could do worse," Mira admitted. "Considering it's you we're talking about."

"There's some praise, I guess."

"Just one thing. Let's say for whatever reason you decide you want to be with little miss privilege, how about this time you don't blow it? Even she deserves better than what you pulled last time."

"Hey, there's a lot you don't know," Evan protested. "It was complicated."

"Then let's make it simple. If you say you love her, you can decide that means a little more than chasing the next rumor. You can stick around this time. Even if it means you have to read one of those insufferable books and pretend to like it."

Whenever Evan thought he understood Mira, there was something new to learn. "You are totally confusing me now. What do you mean?"

"I mean," and she reached out with her good arm to tap his chest, "that if you are not fair and honest with her, if you don't do what you promise, then you will have to answer to me. And you don't want that. Do we have an understanding?"

"I guess – yes. We have an understanding. You're not, um, going soft, on—"

"Oh, no. Can't stand her."

"Good news. So what are you going to do tonight?"

"I'm getting together with Ted later," Mira told him.

"Ted?"

"You know, the governor. We're going to talk about that military exclusion zone, around the Valley of Dreams."

"To get it revoked? So you can go back?"

"No way!" Mira exclaimed. "Expanded! And enforced. No entry, by anyone at any time, for any purpose. It will be a preserve. Because it's not like there's anything out there that anyone would ever want."

"Nobody? Not even you, Mira?"

"Nobody."

"But, you know, Unfinished Business?"

"Will remain unfinished," Mira declared. "There's nothing out there. We are going to talk about expanding the preserve, and then Ted might give me a putting lesson."

Evan was floored. "Putting? You don't mean that."

"Well, I can't do a full swing yet. And putting is half the game. He says it's tough to master, but he doesn't know me. I'm totally going to take him. After I've had a few lessons."

Mira, golfing. Evan wondered if he had somehow been transported to an alternate universe.

"I bet you will take him," he offered. "So, have fun. Little one."

Evan realized that he was easily within range of Mira's crutch, held in her good arm. He started to back away, expecting the worst.

Mira just smiled sweetly at him and said goodbye.

Evan headed for the location of his hundredth date with Kate. Or their first, depending on how you counted it. By Evan's reckoning, the first ninety-nine or so of their dates consisted of field rations and beer, in and around the Valley of Dreams site. By Kate's reckoning, their first date had been at this place. The food was called Mexican, after a nation that used to exist on Earth, in the mostly uninhabitable equatorial zone. It was a choice they could always agree on.

He was on time, arriving just moments before Kate. Apparently he was capable of modest learning achievements, as measured against past years. They were seated and ordered their wine.

Evan enjoyed the luxury of getting to really look at Kate, across the small table. Clearly she had gone to some amount of trouble for the evening out. Her full hair flowed in cascades off her shoulders. He still couldn't believe that he might get another chance. It was like being struck by lightning twice in one lifetime.

"So, what are you going to do now?" she asked.

"No fair, I wanted to ask you first! You go. Really."

Kate had a surprising answer. "It looks like I'm going to have to get a job."

"Tell me another one. You, a job? Slumming with the plebes now?"

"No, I need it. For pay." She didn't look unhappy about the prospect.

"But why?"

"Well you know, the family is gone. It's all been seized. Everything."

"I heard you before, at the hospital," Evan said. "Your friend Lieberthal helped you get money out. And you gave some of it to Mira."

"He did, at that. He rescued a little over two million for me." Kate held up two fingers for emphasis.

"You mean—"

"It's gone, save a few scraps. And now I am free." Kate gave Evan a big, peaceful smile.

"Gone. Wow. Hey, does this mean I'm going to have to pay for dinner? I never had to before."

"As you should. You'll just have to get used to it," she told him.

"Hey, you could actually charge for your books. They're pretty good, you know. At a credit a download, you would be set."

"That unscientific crap, you mean?" Kate raised an eyebrow.

"I've been thinking about that. It is kind of crazy that the Versari knew where all of the glomes went. Maybe you're on to something. Somehow they knew."

"You, considering something outside of proven hard science? Now I've heard everything! But the books won't amount to any income. Authors can't make a living from their books unless they load them with advertising, and I won't do that."

"I can't stand the ads myself," Evan agreed. "And the placements are worse. What products could the Versari have been using, nine hundred thousand years ago? Maybe they zipped around on Philomax choppers, or kept their skin looking beautiful with the latest from CoreValue."

"Looks like the skin cream didn't do Elanas any good," Kate agreed. Elanas was one of the two Versari whom they had removed from the Valley of Dreams.

"So I need to find work," Kate continued. "On an exo expedition, perhaps. I know a thing or two about the Versari. Have some experience in remote environments. Field data collection, that sort of thing. Let me know if you see any leads that you want to send my way."

"I might just be able to find you something," he said. "I'll need some help with the next expedition."

"I know that look," she told him. "What have you got?"

"It was a distraction when I came across it. During the countdown, I was trying to find something, anything, that would help us. I had some hints that we had been looking at the Omega entry wrong, and if I understood it better, we could get some advantage. So I set it aside."

"And now you're going to tell me about it."

Evan wasn't going to keep any secrets from her. "I think I know the location of the Versari cities! Every place we have ever been, they are all the smallest of outposts. Finding so little of them, it's not just because of the time gone by. It's because there was never much there. And now we can go to planets that once had millions of our friends, or perhaps billions. Maybe we will find out what happened to them."

He could tell it had her imagination. "We've got to do it! We'll need a sponsor. It almost makes me wish I still had money."

"Oh, we'll find someone," he told her. "Just not one of the Sisters."

"That's for certain," Kate agreed.

"I brought you a present," Evan offered. He laid the silver mesh pouch on the table. Kate picked it up and felt the object inside, then pulled open the drawstring.

The cube which had almost doomed Kelter.

"The governor gave it back to me," Evan told her. "Said that as far as he could tell, it was mine. And now it's yours."

Kate held it in her hand. "What that simple little artifact did to all of us, it was so hideous that there are no words for it!" Her face was shading red.

"Tell me about it," Evan agreed. "We were lucky to get out of this alive."

"Evan, just for me, step out of immediacy, out of our situation, for one moment. I mean, just look at the whole thing. Affirmatix, killing people, nuclear strikes, wanting to sterilize an entire planet. For what?"

The answer seemed obvious to Evan. "Only the most significant chunk of information in human history, worth quadrillions."

"A crumb! The information, this precious chart, is the most mundane Versari discovery we are ever likely to come across. It's nothing! Just a road map, containing nothing that we couldn't gather for ourselves, with technology that is currently available."

"That would take thousands of years."

"But we could do it. This item delivers no leap of inspiration, no real breakthrough. Let me put it another way. Consider human civilization. All the beauty, all the technology, the entire span of human experience."

"A lot of ugly in there, too," Evan pointed out.

"Include that. Out of the whole pool of wonder, and ugly, imagine discovering a road atlas, and only that. And this pebble sends your world into turmoil. We couldn't handle finding just that pebble."

Kate spun the cube into the air. It approached its amber shadow on the ceiling, and then fell back slowly to her palm. "So consider this," she said. "If this pitiful thing could send us to war, almost destroying the whole planet and everyone who lives here, what will we do when we begin to understand some of what the Versari held precious?"

The End of Volume 1

Glossary

Abilene: The capital city of Kelter

Abilene Consensus: When a group of people outwardly agree to something that they all know is not factually accurate or reasonable.

Adastra, Mira: A pilot. For several years was the lead pilot on Evan McElroy's archaeological expeditions.

Affirmatix: A family, one of the Seven Sisters. Sponsor of Evan McElroy's recent work in the Aurora system.

Alcyone: A planet used by Affirmatix as a secret base and research center. Located in the Pleiades star cluster.

Alsatie: Delegate of the RealHealth Family, which is one of the Seven Sisters, to Affirmatix.

Alpha Axis: One of two entry axes into a glome, the other being the Omega axis. Only routes through the Alpha axis have ever safely led to an emergence.

Arrow: A star system. Contains a glome to Aurora.

Aurora: A star system. The location where very well preserved Versari artifacts were found.

Axiom: An infoterrorist on Kelter, infamous for his actions during the confrontations of 2234.

Broker, Tal: Communication engineer on Paul Ricken's ship. Secretly, a spy for Rod Denison and thus for DelMonaco Shipping.

Buttonwood Tree: The tree that is in the center of the Untrusted Zone. Was planted in 2186. Became a center of conflict in the confrontations of 2234.

Caledonia: A planetary system, contains a glome to Kelter

Celebration: A funeral

Combustapalooza: On Earth, the civilization-wide frenzy of burning absolutely everything that could be lit on fire, primarily for energy. Peaked in about 2040, causing the deaths of over three billion people through direct and indirect effects.

CoreValue: A family, one of the Seven Sisters, engaged in litigation with DelMonaco Trading over glome royalty rights.

De Beers Method: An agreement where all of the Seven Sisters cooperate to publish information about new glome discoveries on a planned schedule to maximize total revenue and profit.

Delegate: An emissary between families, especially the Seven Sisters.

For the President of each of the Seven Sisters, there is an assigned set of six delegates, one from each of the other Sisters.

DelMonaco, Anna: Late CEO of DelMonaco Trading, mother of Kate DelMonaco. Died in a space accident in 2303.

DelMonaco, Kate: CEO of DelMonaco Trading, an independent trading and shipping family

DelMonaco, William: Late President of DelMonaco Trading, father of Kate DelMonaco. Died in a space accident in 2303.

Denison, Rod: Ship captain, works for DelMonaco Trading

Domestic Family: A set of related people, often living together, such as married couple and their children. Different from: Family.

Droogs: Friends

Earth: A planet, where humans originated. Population about one billion, concentrated in the northern polar regions.

Efessem: A popular deity, a kind spirit with a good sense of humor

Ellison, Colin: An Affirmatix employee, who works as a wrangler to researchers on Alcyone, including Sonia West and Krishnan Ravi.

False Story: Information or an idea that is in conflict with the generally accepted truth. See: True Story.

Family: A corporation, especially one of the Seven Sisters. Different from: Domestic Family

Fencing of the Commons: A period during the 2260s when Open Source intellectual property was privatized.

FirstStar: A family, one of the Seven Sisters

Foray: The larger and closer of the two moons of Kelter Four

Forbie: The smaller and farther of the two moons of Kelter Four

Friend: A person

Goodhope: A planetary system, inhabited by over 20 billion people.

Glome: A trans-dimensional connection between two points in space, often many light years apart. Each glome allows a one-way journey from the point of entrance to the point of emergence, if entered exactly along the glome's Alpha axis of entry.

Green: A planetary system, has a glome to Kelter

Incento: Admiral, commander of Kelter's fleet

Individua: A family, one of the Seven Sisters

Infoterrorist: A person who spreads information that is in conflict with the generally accepted truth

Kelter Four: A planet, notable for its low gravity and thin atmosphere. The Valley of Dreams archaeological site is located on Kelter.

Kestrel: An infoterrorist, friend of Mira Adastra and of Axiom

Klono: The space explorer's god

Lieberthal: Former CFO of DelMonaco Trading

Lobeck, Arn: A Senior Vice President of the Affirmatix Family

Lu: President of the ProSolutiana Family, which is one of the Seven Sisters.

Malken, Eliza: Social and Economic Analyst, on contract to Affirmatix.

McElroy, Evan: Exo-archaeologist, made the breakthrough discovery of decoding the Versari artifact listing the destinations of hyperspace glomes.

Middlefork: A planetary system. Uninhabited, but having a Versari site.

Omega Axis: One of two entry axes into a glome, the other being the Alpha axis. The Omega axis has never been known provide to a safe travel route through a glome.

Orwen: A friend of Axiom

Parrin Process: A medical treatment that can extend a person's life for many years. Anyone receiving the treatment is required to vigorously exercise in order to stay alive, in an amount that becomes progressively greater as the years pass.

Philomax: A family, one of the Seven Sisters.

ProSolutiana: A family, one of the Seven Sisters.

Ravi, Krishnan: Social and Economic Analyst, on contract to Affirmatix.

RealHealth: A family, one of the Seven Sisters.

Remon: President of the Individua Family, which is one of the Seven Sisters.

Rezar, Theodore: Governor of Kelter.

Ricken, Paul: Captain of an independent trader that is a rival to DelMonaco Trading.

Sanzite, Benar: President and CEO of the Affirmatix Family.

Seven Sisters: The seven largest families, who control between them approximately ninety percent of all commerce. They are: Affirmatix, CoreValue, FirstStar, Individua, Philomax, ProSolutiana, and RealHealth.

Skylar, Mithra: Deputy Vice President of Affirmatix Family, usually travels with Arn Lobeck.

Statistician: Member of a terrorist movement that agitates for more equal distribution of wealth and opportunity.

Terrorist: See Infoterrorist.

Top Station: A large space station in orbit of Kelter Four. A hub of commerce between Kelter Four and other destinations.

True Story: Generally accepted version of events, especially as presented by a government or family.

Untrusted Zone: Founded in 2234, a location on Kelter that is outside of the normal operation of civilization. About 5 kilometers from Abilene.

Versari: An ancient race whose artifacts and remains spanned a period of a hundred thousand years, almost a million years ago.

Visitor Kit: A combination of a helmet and supplemental oxygen supply worn by visitors to the surface of Kelter Four.

Wastage Factor: The part of the economy that does not pass through at least one of the Seven Sisters. Currently slightly under ten percent.

West, Sonia: Social and Economic Analyst, on contract to Affirmatix. Inventor of the De Beers method.

West, Yvette: Sonia West's wife, an electrical engineer and security expert.

Worm Drive: Write Once, Read Many: A data recorder that is intended to collect data in real time and never be updated. Used for black boxes on vehicles and other official records.

Chronology

2040:   Peak of the Combustapalooza. Over three billion people died during the next twenty years due to a combination of global warming, resource depletion, and the resulting wars.

2060-2120:   The Long Comeback

2136:   First successful return to Earth from another star system, through a circuit of three hyperspace glomes

2159:   First habitable exo planet, Phoenix, discovered

2180:   Kelter discovered

2186:   Buttonwood tree planted on Kelter

2204:   Axiom born

2234:   Untrusted Zone founded on Kelter

2260-68:   The Fencing of the Commons

2267:   Kate DelMonaco born

2269:   Evan McElroy born

2272:   Mira Adastra born

2294-2301:   Valley of Dreams expeditions on Kelter

2302:   Discovery of well-preserved Versari data storage devices on Aurora

2303:   Anna and William DelMonaco die in a space travel accident

2304:   Present day

Acknowledgements

I am grateful to Jan Bressler, the very first reader of ***The Great Symmetry***. Her simple act of reading the entire first draft, and her encouragement about the value inside, helped provide me with energy to power through rest of the journey to completion.

Mariko Thompson did excellent editing and reviewing on the manuscript, pointing out numerous opportunities to improve internal consistency, character development, and tone.

Alan Canon, Elizabeth R. Apgar Triano, Mike Newsome, Frank James, and Susan Hansen provided many and detailed review comments and edits.

Noble Smith has provided review comments, encouragement, and guidance on navigating the publication process.

Thanks for thoughtful review comments to early readers Ian Baren, Michael Brooks, Andy Klapper, Eleanor Brown, Nan Brown, Joe Shapiro, Mike Cowlishaw, and Marley Magee.

Rachel Budelsky related the saying about the shabby donkeys.

With many thanks to the community of writers and environmental activists in the Pacific Northwest, at our great watchdog paper Whatcom Watch, and on the Daily Kos web site, who helped me to find my writing voice.

When I was eight years old, my Aunt Katy read the first thirty pages of The Hobbit aloud to me, then handed me the book, saying I would have to read the rest if I wanted to know how it ended.

Sara Wells and Katie Jane Wells supported the project of writing ***The Great Symmetry*** far beyond the bounds of reason, putting up with me staying up past midnight for months at a time and otherwise not doing all those other things I can't wait to get back to.

End Notes

Glome is a real word, meaning hypersphere, also called a 3-sphere.

Infoterrorist is a term coined in the early 21st century, to describe the use of information technology for the purpose of spreading terror, dissent, or freedom.

"**Knowledge screams to be free**" is based on the phrase "information wants to be free," ascribed to Stewart Brand in the 1960s.

The Abilene Consensus is based on the Abilene Paradox, a term first used by Jerry B. Harvey, in 1974.

De Beers Method is named after the diamond cartel of that name.

The **Buttonwood Tree** was the site where the New York Stock Exchange was founded in 1792. Since then, the word "buttonwood" has sometimes been used to refer to core underlying issues relating to money.

"**Fly casual**" is a quote from Han Solo in the movie Star Wars: Return of the Jedi.

The Seven Sisters is a term used by Enrico Mattei to describe the seven companies that dominated the global petroleum industry in the middle of the 20th century. The term also refers to the mythical daughters of Atlas, and the Pleiades star cluster.

A Drop of Water is an iconically great song by musician Dana Lyons (www.cowswithguns.com).

Jeetertech is a method of artistic fabrication named by Louisville, KY multimedia artist Scott Scarboro in the 20th century.

Merchants of Doubt is a book by Naomi Oreskes and Erik Conway, about scientists recruited to create doubt about the harm from pollution.

Klono is a deity from the immortal Lensman series, by Doc Smith. The concept of **Intrinsic Velocity** is also discussed extensively in the Lensman series.

Effessem is a deity with an enthusiastic and colorful following here in the 21st century.

"**Shabby Donkeys** will find each other even over nine hills" is apparently a Bulgarian folk saying, as related by Rachel Budelsky.

Orwen is descended from someone of the same name who appeared in The Chronicles of Prydain, by Lloyd Alexander. Or perhaps she is the same person.

Combustapalooza is something I made up, for an article about global warming.

Friend: When my daughter was about five years old, the words "friend" and "person" were synonyms for her. I have watched with sadness as she has necessarily learned the distinction, and imagine that someday in the future, she will unlearn it.

The Great Symmetry has been described by many phrases though history, and is something that almost everyone understands intuitively.

Blowing Cave is named in homage to Overholt Blowing Cave in West Virginia. My father was on the climbing crew that completed the first ascent of the 4th waterfall, using bolts, during a 3-day trip into this wet and difficult cave in the early 1960's. Another waterfall was found, just beyond. Daddy, I will always miss you.

About The Author

JAMES R. WELLS is a life-long cave explorer and outdoor adventurer. He has led expeditions deep into some of North America's great caves, including the Mammoth system, longest cave in the world.

He writes about climate and environmental topics, and volunteers helping people to protect their community and habitat. In his day job, he designs information systems that reduce energy use, saving money and reducing pollution. He is the great-grandson of pioneering science fiction author H.G. Wells.

The author lives in northwest Washington with his wife and his daughter.

The author's web site can be found at
www.TheGreatSymmetry.com.

CPSIA information can be obtained
at www.ICGtesting.com
Printed in the USA
FSOW02n2126250615
8249FS